The Viper's Chase

By Stephen Hagelin

The Viper's Chase
Copyright © 2018 by Stephen Hagelin
Varida Publishing & Resources LLC
www.varida.com
© 2018 Cover art by Antonia Hagelin

ISBN: 978-1-937046-12-5

For my friend Jon
Who said that I could write
Something meaningful

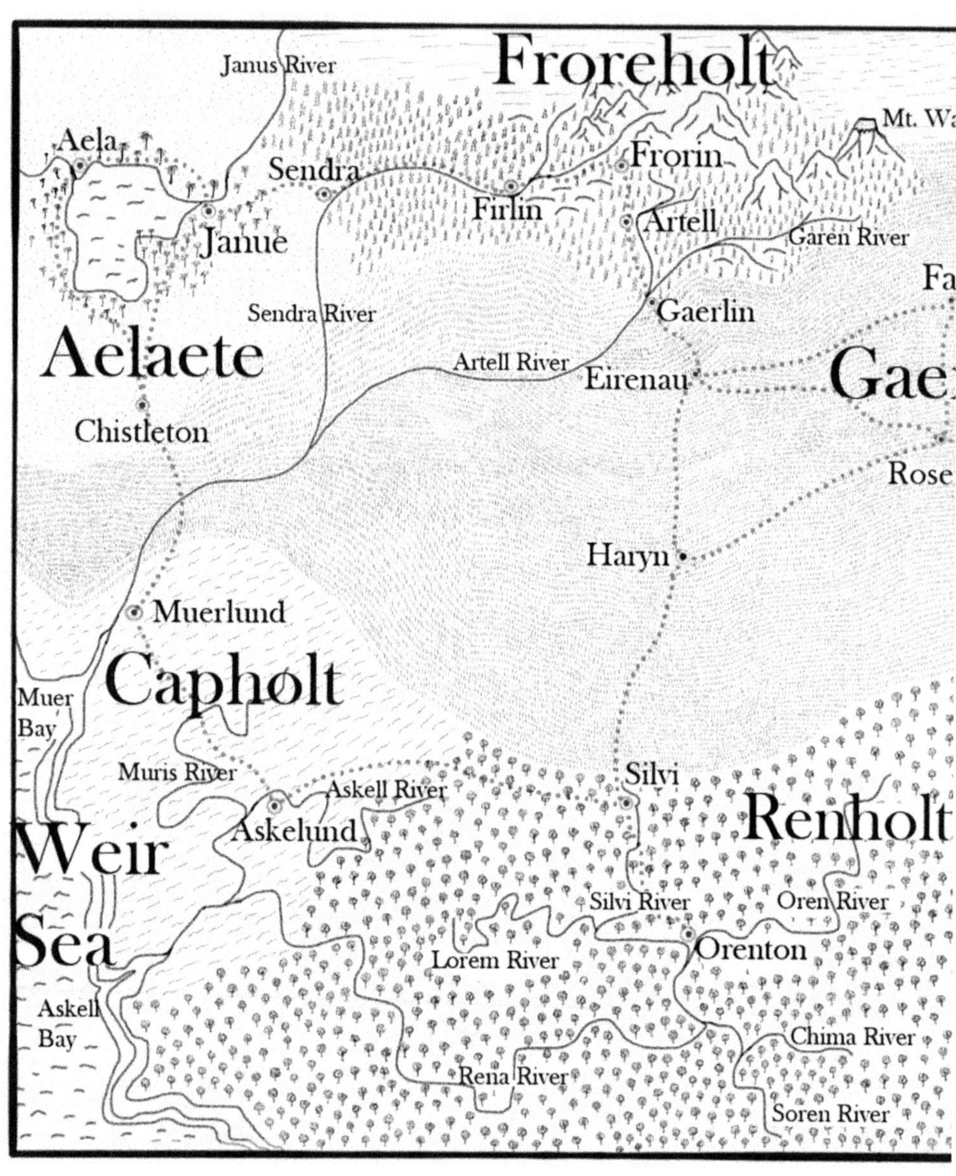

Froreholt
Janus River
Mt. Wa
Aela
Frorin
Sendra
Firlin
Artell
Janue
Garen River
Gaerlin
Fa
Sendra River
Aelaete
Artell River
Eirenau
Gae
Chistleton
Rose
Haryn
Muerlund
Capholt
Muer
Bay
Silvi
Muris River
Renholt
Askell River
Weir
Askelund
Silvi River
Oren River
Sea
Orenton
Lorem River
Askell
Bay
Chima River
Rena River
Soren River

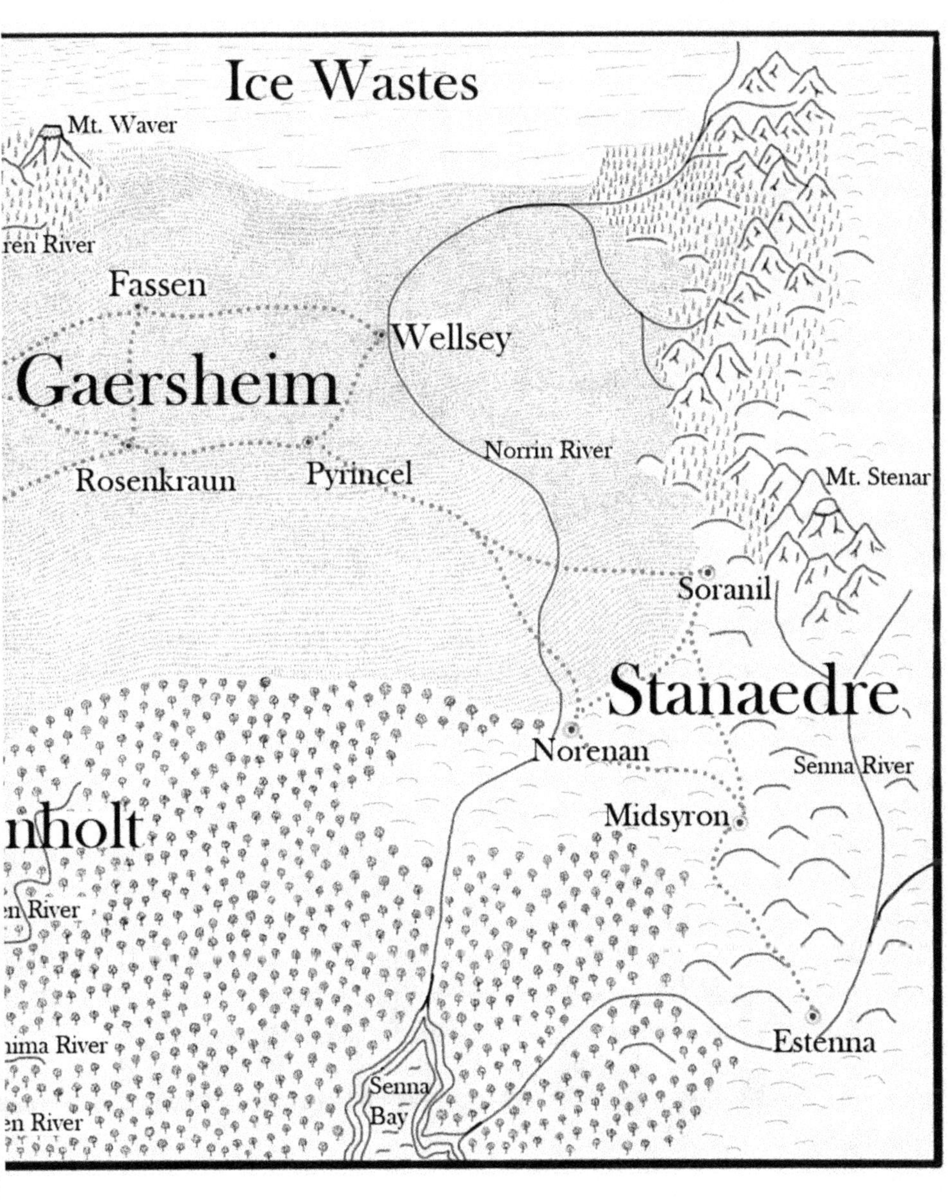

Ice Wastes
Mt. Waver
ren River
Fassen
Wellsey
Gaersheim
Norrin River
Mt. Stenar
Rosenkraun
Pyrincel
Soranil
Stanaedre
Norenan
Senna River
nholt
Midsyron
en River
nma River
Estenna
Senna
Bay
en River

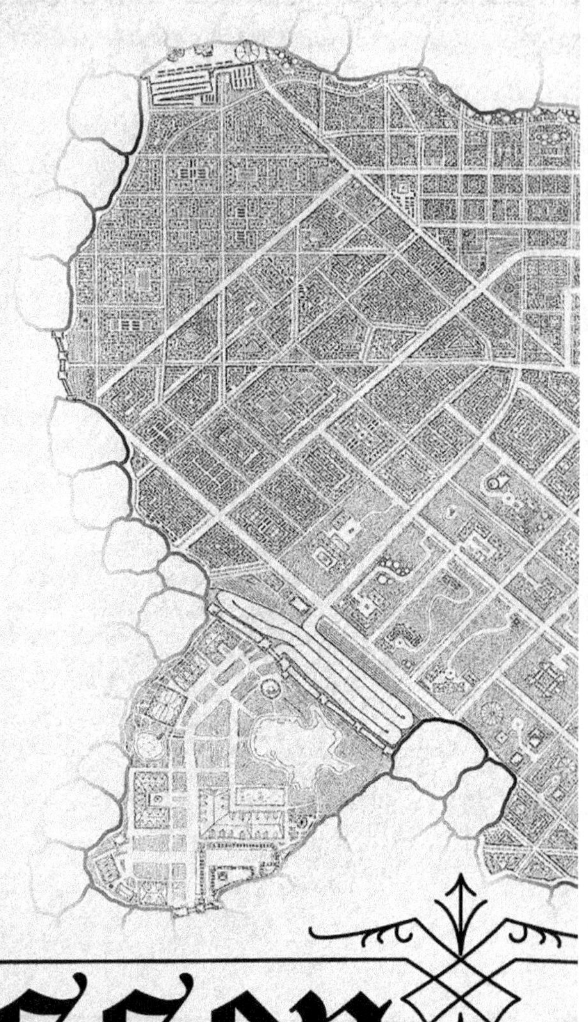

Fassen

Prologue

An astringent wind blew across the sandy horizon, dry, and stale, seeming to tug at his hair, as it raked the black-red sky. Turning on his heel, Aldyr Havrshyk felt the grains of sand grind and crunch beneath his boot, but he couldn't hear its sound in the gale that blew his hair back in front of his face. Looking up at the congealing and shifting currents in the sky, he moved his hair back out of his eyes and said, with a wry smile forming on his ice-chapped lips,

"I don't know what he was thinking locking me in here... But I suppose every 'place' has an exit of some kind."

The wind declined to answer, but in the distance over the rolling dunes of sand, barely visible in the shadowy red light, he caught sight of something at least halfway bright, like the reflection of a single ray of light off a mirror or glacier. Aldyr took a step in the direction of that glimmer, and started down the charcoal-tan sand dune on which he stood, his black coat trailing back from his waist as he stalked down, head-first into the wind.

"When I get out of here, I'll be putting you in my place," he said bitterly. "After all, I am the Lichblade, and you... You're not really anyone yet, Viper."

His footsteps vanished behind him, seconds after he left, and his face went white as he drained his blood to preserve his form. "Even in this space, I will not be consumed. I'll find your heart. I'll drain your soul."

Forest of Grass

Gaersheim:
Forest of Grass
Near Fassen
Leif

Fryn cocked her hat back on her bun, as she flitted eagerly past President Hans for the edge of the clearing. The King still raged in his throne, alternately bemoaning his loss of the Harvest Crown, and then fuming incoherently at the outrage, the ignominy of it. It took a bit more than his usual self-control to refrain from laughing at his outbursts, but Leif was also distracted by the excitement of the chase, as he followed Fryn's sleek shadow over the heads of the open-mouthed, appalled guests. Even as they darted into the forest of grass, he admired the gold sheen and the brown maple leaves that glinted on her woven-dyed hat, wondering if she even knew what trail she was following.

"Fryn... Where are we going?" he asked, tightening his sword belt, and shifting his tan scarf to cover his mouth against the wind.

She didn't turn around, but her wings twitched and pulsed with a purplish spark of irritation. "What, can't you feel it?"

"No, I can't," he replied, brushing a low blade of grass out of the way.

"Our thief left a bit of a trail in the air, it must bear her element, because I can still sense the lingering traces of her enhanced flight," Fryn explained, ducking under a bent seed stalk, and then sweeping around a particularly thick bunch.

Leif missed the sharp turn, and hit the wall of grass face-first and rebounded back, spitting and cursing, rubbing his nose, until he caught his flight and hovered in the air. Fryn flew further and further ahead. For a moment he almost felt like he was being laughed at, and immediately he flushed, and darted forward following Fryn's lingering scent, the perfume she'd worn for the Harvest Festival; something like a blend of rose and pine, that couldn't be mistaken in the Forest of Grass.

Fryn had apparently flown quickly out of sight, because as he rounded the bends and turns, weaving through the bunches of grass that grew in thickness and height the further he flew, he felt she only grew further away. Chasing her scent, and a small tickle at the nape of his neck, his instinct, he smiled as his suspicions were confirmed. Now he was getting closer. Sure enough, he darted into a clearing, and ran straight into her from behind, and they both rolled and tumbled to the ground, landing in a tangled heap of legs, wings, and arms.

She groaned and stretched her neck as she pushed off of his chest and sat on the dirt beside him. The clearing stood before a cliff edge that towered over them, so there wasn't enough sunlight to encourage even the clover or weeds to grow; but it didn't look cultivated. If anything, it looked more like the resting place of a hare, or large animal, with the way the sides of the grasses were bent or chafed, worn by the frequent passage of something or someone. Leif sat up and scratched his head, shaking his wings of the dust that covered them. Fryn had been fortunate enough to land on top of him, so she was relatively unsoiled, which was a pleasure she didn't seem to appreciate at that moment.

"Are you that unbalanced that you had to fly right into me?" she demanded, rising to her feet, and patting off the dust that clung to her blazer and trousers, particularly her knees.

"Well, you're the one just sitting there, hovering for no reason," he protested, glancing down at the black sword that'd slid partially out of its silver scabbard by his leg. He slammed it home, and stood beside her, "What were you doing there anyway?" The latch on the sword did not seem to be very reliable, and he made certain that he locked it tight again.

She turned away as a hint of red flashed out to her wingtips and ears. "I... lost the trail."

Leif crossed his arms with a triumphant 'hmph' and pointed up gloatingly. "If you lose a scent, then either they are hiding here, or above, or below; elementary tracking really."

She turned her head slowly toward him with a smile painted on her face; but her characteristic dimples did not show themselves as she said, "Fascinating, really, how good of a hunter you are."

He swallowed, and allowed gracefully, "Well, I am sorry..."

She waited for him to uncross his arms before shaking her head, dimples showing honestly on her cheeks. "You're not wrong about which way to go, I just lost my head for a moment. I highly doubt they'd be beneath us, so let's see what's above the canopy."

Putting aside the matter of the so-called 'canopy', Leif followed as she swept up into the air with an ice-chilled wingburst and rose to the level of the clifftop. There wasn't a whole lot to see, just the endless swaying tops of the grass as the sun began to set, turning the entire Forest of Grass golden under its orange gaze. They shifted and rolled like a burnt orange sea, and Leif threw out his arms to the side, yelling indistinctly to the east.

"Ah, that feels good!" He lowered them again as he landed on the moss-covered stone on the clifftop. "You know, this is hardly a cliff," he said, looking around, "more of a giant boulder really."

Fryn frowned as she settled a few paces ahead of him, glancing back with a sigh, "It doesn't really matter that much to me what it is, so long as we catch that crown first."

He nodded pleasantly. "Certainly, the thought of President Hans lording it over us with the crown on his head wouldn't paint a pretty picture."

She tilted her head back and smelled the air, which made him chuckle, as if she took the bit about 'losing a scent' literally. She scuffed her boots on the moss in frustration. "The only thing I can smell here is just more grass." Her wings flicked back and forth, twitching in her mixture of absorption and distraction.

He laughed, and stepped up behind her, stopping beside her shoulder so her wings would accidentally brush against his if she continued their movements, and tilted his head back to smell the air. The winds shifted just a bit, and he caught something else, just a hint, from straight ahead; a mixture of wheat, and dry fur. He flicked his wings against hers, causing her to start, with a flash of red that was immediately, and consciously, drained from her face. "I think I found something," he declared, pointing at just a slight angle slightly west of north.

Her lips quirked as she put on a smile, "Very good, Leif," she allowed, and dove into the air, flying low over the ripened bunches of seeds: barley, wheat, and various kinds of grass.

He followed as best he could, what with the unbalanced weight at his side, wondering how Fryn was able to fly so easily with a knife on one side, and nothing on the other. Still, one way or another, she managed just fine; he would just have to get used to that sword.

"Why do you think he gave it to me?" he asked her, getting a look and a raised eyebrow in return. "The sword, I mean. I fight with my fists. Why did the Prince give me the sword?"

She shook her head, and focused on following the faint magical scent on the wind. "You give that fae too much credit. Do you think he really knew that you fought with your fists? Maybe he thought it was because you didn't have a decent blade. You are the one who defeated Havrshyk, so it stands to reason that you'd be the one to claim his weapon." She pointed down toward a slight clearing in the grass, bounded by impossibly positioned stones matching the one they'd stood on earlier. They shrouded the glade in an impenetrable shadow as the sun sank beneath the level of the grass, and the stars peeked out overhead.

The Lancer and the Serpent constellations fought directly overhead, one bright star marking the eye of the serpent, as the dim ones trailed out its body, and the dull figure of the Lancer thrust a rod of stars into its belly, with several bright points hinting at his wings flung out behind. Leif shivered. This time last year he'd faced his own, same as the omen overhead. He had only been allowed to leave for Frorin a scant five weeks earlier, what with the length of time it had taken to recover the strength in his arms after the muscle-shearing injuries. The sparkling branches of the Vine, the herald of the Harvest season, progressed slowly as the greater moon waxed and spread across it.

In the last light of the sun, he pulled out his map from the pocket of his jacket, and scanned the general area. The Harvest Festival had been on the outskirts of Gaersheim's northernmost city, the first city to experience the harvest, as it moved down to the rainforests on the southern coast. He squinted in the dim light, reading the letters, Fassen was marked in bold, with roads leading west toward Eirenau and the river, branching off to Gaerlin, Sendra, and Artell, before finally reaching off in the direction of Frorin. A tiny line trailed off toward the East, one arm widening and curving around a low hill where the smaller line led to an unfolded circle without a name, as if it had been a town, and then was too small or unimportant to be included.

"There are no small towns north of Fassen, just one east of here, but it's not in the right place," he announced, reaching out to stop her before she could descend. But she'd already sped off toward the dark mass below. He sighed, and folded the map carefully, shoving it into his pocket as he glided down on the descending air currents, rather than on his own power.

She hit the ground hard, almost invisible to his eyes adjusted though they were to the dark, and rolled into the deeper shade of what looked like a pebble-stone house with a thatched roof. He settled on the mossy floor of the clearing and walked over to the wall where she hid, crouching in front of her.

"Well, what have we found?" he asked, leaning uncomfortably close, almost to the point of tipping over.

She pushed him back with one hand and held a finger over her mouth with the other. "Shush! They are nearby."

"I figured *that* out myself," he stretched and looked around. There were three more buildings in his line of sight, as well as the outline of a covered well further off. Two of them looked like houses, with meticulously spaced windows and decorative eaves. The third, with its double sliding doors, was obviously a barn. "My point is, why is there a farming town that's not on the map?"

Fryn pursed her lips and rose onto her toes to peer through the woven-grass shutters of the window beside her and didn't reply. "Just a little more and I could see inside..." she complained. She stood back and placed her hands on her hips. "There's nothing for it, no lights inside. Let's check the others," she added in a whisper.

She led the way around the corner, and then darted across the distance to the next house; careful even of casting a shadow in the dark. As Fryn edged along the wall, sneaking looks through the cracks in the shutters, Leif followed nonchalantly, walking behind her, watching as her wings ticked out the rhythm of some northern tune.

"This is hardly an urgent mark," he said, "at least, compared to what we just went through in Frorin. Why don't we just go back to the inn, and open the first bottle of wine that you ordered?"

"I thought you were the one all excited about this. You said, 'It's a race'. I remember," she replied, crossing her arms. "What changed your mind?"

He yawned.

"You seemed fine with the long hours when we were chasing Mythrim," she said, smirking at him.

Leif nodded. "I was, because our lives depended on it, but it's getting late, and I think it'd be best to plan ahead, and scout more before we go diving in. I don't think any of the other hunters made it this far. They must have turned back."

She frowned, and sat down in a crouch. "I don't see why veteran Hunters like Yarrow or Trel would stop their search just because the sun set. As far as I know they don't have owls here."

He swallowed, and glanced around. "I've heard they tend to bite you in two, or sometimes just swallow you whole. But I don't really think Trel and Yarrow are that active in the Commission anymore, I mean, they just hang around Savis for the Ceren and cards."

"Yes... well... they'd probably not like to hear your estimation of them. Yarrow is a renowned duelist, and Trel holds the record for violent marks rewarded... so it's best not to underestimate them." She stood and moved over to the next house, and sighed when she saw no sign of light, and not even a glimmer from the dark shapes farther in the clearing. "We have no way of knowing where they'd be hiding."

The only other building nearby was the barn, storage shed, or whatever it was called. It had no windows, so they had to squeeze through a slim opening between the two doors, which would only open 'so far' because there was some kind of lock or bar in place. Fryn went in first, and he followed after, only able to get in because she pulled him through by his scarf.

"Why would it be locked from the inside?" he whispered.

Fryn tripped over something on the ground, and froze, as a stray bit of starlight glinted off the dipped-gold weave of the harvest crown lying discarded on the ground. She covered her mouth and then looked up, pointing to a shadow on the bundled grass rafters overhead.

Leif covered his mouth, pointing as well, nodding and holding back a question behind his hand.

She shrugged, and he nodded, so she waved between them with her hand. He held up one finger, pointing at himself with his wings twitching in question, and so she flicked hers in answer and held them back—a clear negative. She wanted to do it.

Leif picked up the crown while Fryn drew her Bloodknife, stretching up, and a tremor went through the ground. Halfway in the air, she quailed and sunk to the packed clay ground, crouching as she hugged her knees to her chest, wings drooping behind her back.

The ground shivered beneath their feet once more, followed by a softer creaking in the rafters. Leif and Fryn watched, startled as a third figure landed between them, her four wings swept back, pulsing with green light, one hand on the crown, ready to leap into the air, with the other signaling silence with a finger placed over her mouth.

Nothing moved, no one stirred, no one breathed. They waited, as the heavy footfalls outside reverberated through the clay and a light sniffing sounded on the air. Minutes passed, and with every minute that passed, the burning in his legs intensified into an urgent demand, as he too was readied to spring into the air. Finally, after a full thirty seconds of an intolerable, unadulterated silence, all three of them sprang into motion. The thief leapt up, kicking off the rafters, to make a dash for, or rather through, the door. Leif pounced into her path, with one hand still holding onto the crown, and Fryn threw her knife, slamming it and effectively locking the door bar to the wall of the storage shed.

The thief bounced off the door, unable to force her way through, and fell on top of Leif, who fumbled around the awkward weight of his sword to grab her hands as she batted at him with her abnormally sharp wings.

The door shivered as a great body threw itself against its frame, loosing a cloud of dust from the ceiling, and sending everyone back onto the ground, motionless.

"I thought it was gone..." Leif whispered.

"Shh!" Retorted the thief on top of him.

Fryn didn't add her response in the usual verbal form, but she did seem annoyed, even without saying anything.

"What is it?" Leif asked in an even lower voice.

The thief groaned, yanked the crown free of Leif's grasp, placed it on her barely visible head, and pushing herself off of him, leaned against the door, bracing it against a second attempt. "That is a weasel."

Fryn shivered, and took a step further from the door.

"Well, why don't we just kill it?" he asked.

"In the middle of the night?" the thief demanded in a rough, incredulous whisper.

"I *did* defeat a sand viper," Leif preambled, "What's a weasel to that?"

"Worse," the thief shook her head. "Much worse."

Another shudder ran through the door, parts of the Frorin pine boards cracking under the pressure.

"But together it won't be so bad, I'll hold its attention, you two support me from the sides," he pressed, "I, for one, don't want to be stuck here all night. There's an entire crate of wine from the Harvest Festival waiting for me at my hotel."

Fryn gasped, rousing from her silence. "Only you could... We should just wait for it to leave."

The thief hissed, her features still invisible in the low light, though her determination shone through clear. "On one condition."

"What's that?" Leif asked, raising one eyebrow, even if no one else could see it, hoping they could hear the irony in his voice.

Fryn and the thief shared a look, which neither of them could see, and the thief continued. "You don't turn me in, or the crown." She took off the crown and spun it around on her hand.

"*Tch*," Leif clicked his tongue, "Fryn, what do you think?"

"We don't have much of a choice, do we?"

"We could take it on ourselves," he shook his head.

The thief shook hers. "No, you can't. Even for the best Hunters, defeating a weasel is out of the question... And if you try to hold me here, I will raise my voice, and watch it break in."

"Then we can always chase you once it leaves," Leif said.

Fryn's wings twitched, visible thanks only to the slight pulse of gray light that shot out to her wingtips. "We chased you too far into the night; we're not about to go back empty-handed. Give us the crown and we'll agree to let you go."

The thief shook her head. "No, I can't."

"Just give it to us, and you can go," Leif pressed.

Fryn added, stepping closer to the thief, so that they blocked her path on either side, "there's no need to hold onto it."

"No!" The thief yelled, and then covered her mouth in horror, as the weasel outside crashed against the side of the barn, and a large crack formed in the center of the door-bar. Fryn's knife loosened its hold on the wall, and fell to the ground. In an instant, even before the hilt of her blade had touched the hard clay, a shadow formed in the space of the opening doors.

The shadow loomed, blocking out the slight amount of light cast by the stars, erasing the end of the Serpent, and the Lancer's iconic weapon. The stars were replaced by two red eyes that glowed dully in the narrow pointed face of the beast, as it stared into the warehouse, searching for them. Leif found he'd been holding his breath. He let it out slowly without a sound. His fingers itched, alive with the initial reaction, the first tingling of his Sparks, the few tiny hairs on the back of his hands standing up.

One hand drew up a crackling line, a tendril of light from the ground, as the other tightened its grip on the hilt of the black sword at his waist, wreathed in a cloud of icy fog as if anticipating a fresh influx of blood. His eyes never left those of the weasel that blocked his escape, who stared back, equally still and waiting. Leif's hand felt numb against the frozen blood handle of his sword, and he repressed the recollection of how he'd first used it against its master, severing his head, and leaving his body in the snow.

The thief edged back, further into the warehouse, just a step, and dove to the side as the weasel's head snaked forward, jaws closing on air. Leif ducked under the attack, and slammed his charged fist under its chin with a powerful twist from his legs and hips, throwing its head back against the rafters as he drew the sword in a shadowy crimson arc across its chest, A sizzling frozen gash stretched from one side of brown coat, through the soft white fur on its chest, to the other shoulder.

It lurched back, tail swept to the side, as it retreated to the doorway once more. Fryn found her blade, and held position to the left of the door, still unnoticed by the beast—still trembling before it. The thief stood somewhere behind him, fully hidden in the dark, and Leif wondered for a moment if he'd managed to scare it off. He hadn't. It lowered its head, fur standing on end, black tip of its tail puffed out, as it emitted a long low growl.

Leif looked to Fryn, only with his eyes, as he felt something from the first touch of blood. It seemed almost as if he saw the outline of some far off coast from the barren sands of the sea, with black-red storm clouds rising to the east, a chill resentful wind. He felt the first beat of new blood, and it burned in his heart, through the scar that marked the place where Ieffin had stabbed him with the sword to bind him to it. Fryn did not meet his gaze, she crouched, wavering between her urgent desire to attack, and what seemed an arguably appropriate degree of fear.

I suppose I am the only one with any experience against our more natural enemies... he mused, grinning back at the bared fangs of the weasel in the door.

The weasel lurched forward again, only this time, it drew its head back as Leif's fist and blade cut through empty air, and its six-clawed arm raked across his guard. The sword flew out of his grip, turning end over end, and as Leif flew back spinning in the opposite direction, it sunk deep into the center beam of the warehouse, and Leif crashed wings-first into a neatly stacked array of barrels filled with grain. Leif's lower wings bent at an odd angle, and a long tear formed from the tip of his upper right wing to the hardened joint at his shoulder, wheat berries spilled from the barrels he'd disturbed, and covered him to his chin.

As he tried to shake off the worst of his disorientation, and rise painfully from where he'd crashed, he heard the weasel thrashing around the door, cutting through sections of wall with its claws, with sharp gusts of wind that tossed loose debris around the barn. He heard Fryn's voice as she accentuated forceful strikes from her diaphragm, or grunt as she took another blow, sending scattering slivers of ice in every direction.

Climbing free of the wheat, he saw Fryn facing off against the beast, her skin pale and bloodless, frozen blue and hard; the weasel was covered in a new array of ice encrusted cuts and slashes, shorter than the one across the chest, but more painful and inhibiting because of their strategic placement: below the eye, under its chin, its claws, its arms, and even the end of its tail.

Leif struggled to stand, and watched grimly as Fryn was thrown back against one of the supporting pillars, cracks forming on her face, and down her hands. It was impossible to tell just how damaged or broken she was, but he could see she was running out of time. As soon as she broke, she'd be defeated, just like he'd dealt with Havrshyk. He held his hands in tight fists by his sides, drawing from his own reserves, from the potential of the ground, and tried to reach toward the far off storms of the autumn sky, and then, as the hair stood tingling on his head, he drew the full charge into himself, and pointed its path toward the gash he'd cut on the weasel's chest.

The surge of sparks leapt from his finger tip, and arced in a blinding flash of purple electric fire, burning through the thin ice, the soft fur, and the bones in its chest, leaving a glowing orange hole and the acrid stench of burned flesh. Leif fell to his knees gasping, trying to guide what remained of his sparks to keep his heart beating, as the edges of his torn wing disintegrated, trailing away in a wisp of thin smoke.

As his peripheral vision went black, he saw Fryn's chin sag to her chest, and a flash of gold, as the thief they'd chased made a break for the open door; flying past the dazed weasel. Only—she didn't leave, she carried a black shape in her hand, and buried its tip in the throat of the beast. Leif's heart beat, as if pushing its contents up a several story pipe, straining as a surge of fresh blood washed the blackness from his eyes. His pupils widened, and he felt the pain fading from his limbs, bathed in the warmth of the weasel's heart; cuts closing, bruises fading, and the torn section of his wing fusing together. He saw once more, as if by some mirage, that far off shore overlaid on the image of the barn, and Fryn's weary face, and the thief who gingerly stepped around the fallen beast, and flew off into the night. He grit his teeth against the pain as his bones and cuts fused and healed, and he nearly fainted.

Whether because her injuries had been less severe, or she'd been more accustomed to healing herself with the blood, Fryn stood first, and leaned over him with a worried expression that he could only see because she bent over him, her face only an inch or so away. Her lips moved, but it didn't occur to him that she was speaking, until halfway through her sentence.

"...have to force it where you need it most..." she was saying.

He nodded and drew what he could from the weasel's veins through the link of his sword, until it was fully saturated, unable to hold any more. It flowed where it willed, running through the myriad veins, as if eagerly exploring its new home, and only after a full cycle, was he able to grasp it, and guide it to the cracks in his shoulder blade and collar bone. The blood used to heal the wounds was consumed by the action, and he continued to drain the weasel until the sword remained full.

Fryn took his hand and helped him to his feet, and glanced over at the sword that stuck out from the ice-encrusted jugular of the weasel's neck and shook her head. "Well, at least she was kind enough to save our lives."

Leif smiled, though it was too dark for her to see, and walked stiffly to the sword. He leveraged out the sword with a quick tug and a boot braced against its jaw, and nearly fell over as the sword came free. It weighed darker and heavier in his hand, and in the late harvest humidity a light fog formed around its frozen blade. He slid it into his sheath locking the clasp purposefully, and sighed. "We should probably bring something for a souvenir, or as proof that we killed it."

Fryn crossed her arms and tapped her fingers in a syncopated rhythm on her elbow, frowning in the dim light of the Serpent, Lancer, Feather, and on the other side of the greater moon, the Forest, which were now more clearly visible outside the ruined door and walls of the warehouse. "We didn't do it alone."

"Well she doesn't deserve any credit," Leif replied, glancing up at the large red star that comprised the Serpent's eye. *He always had a sinister look*, he thought, scratching at the scars on his left arm, where the sand viper had left behind the tip of its fang.

"Why don't we take a tooth or claw?" Fryn suggested, her translucent blue-lined wings fluttering for a second as she flitted over to the body and examined one of the large brown paws.

"A claw for each of us then," Leif said, walking over since his wings were still slowly repairing, seeming to draw all of his sparks for the endeavor. Fryn set about the grisly business with her knife, and retrieved two ice-covered claws the length of her upper wings, and stuck one through her belt, passing the other to him. He couldn't help himself, he had to have a tooth, so he delayed Fryn a little longer than she'd have preferred as he messed about the weasel's mouth, and finally returned with one of its perfectly white, and insanely sharp canines. "You know, maybe someone'll pay us handsomely for these?" he wondered, and then tested the beat of his wings. Fryn hovered in the air, and he flew up, wavering and wobbling as his lower wings made up for the weakness and slight misshapenness of his upper right wing. They flew off, Leif longing for the linen sheets and cottonwood down comforter at his room in the inn outside Fassen.

Skin and Bone

Fassen:

Faerie Hunter Bounty Office

Leif

Leif studied the finch-nosed, sparrow-faced clerk behind the glass, frowning in disappointment as he remembered Caelyn's playful smiles and helpful attitude back in Frorin. This face was far from helpful, and lacked even the most placid expression, as he nodded dutifully and searched through a sheaf of papers on his polished slate desk, holding the tip of a thin silver tube pen in his mouth. Fryn waited patiently behind him, wings twitching as she scanned the south wall looking at the marks available on the bounty board; pickings were even slimmer than in Frorin—two illegal peddlers, a fae suspected of selling stolen roof tiles, and a tax-collector who'd run off with little more than two-hundred mint in taxes. (The reward for that last one was only fifty mint.)

The sharp-nosed clerk nearly dropped the pen in his mouth as he stifled a yawn, and then looked up with a bland arch to his eyebrow. "It appears that there is an outstanding bounty for the slaying of "dangerous animals" such as the northern Gaersyn weasel, but no one has submitted anything in the fifty four years since it was instituted. The Earl of Fassen is responsible for the signing of this offer, as well as the reward of the amount... Some five-hundred and forty mint."

Fryn frowned, and gestured resignedly with her wings as she stepped forward. "How do we obtain this reward?"

For such a fearsome predator, it was a remarkably small amount of money to risk one's life for; even the sand viper had earned Leif seven hundred mint, as well as advancement in the School. "If I might interject, you said that this bounty was submitted fifty-four years ago, correct?"

The clerk looked up. "I did."

"Is it not possible that the value of mint has changed in that time? Perhaps the amount should be updated to account for that?" Leif smiled winningly and was rewarded with a slight twist to the bureaucrat's mouth.

"I am not a member of the Commission Bank, so I cannot say for certain if the silver content of the Rosenkraun's mint has changed one way or another in that time," he replied evenly, "but I can summon one of my colleagues from the Bank—seeing as they are in the opposite section of the building." He found a silver bell in an alcove hidden from Leif's view, and gave it a single clear ring.

In about thirty seconds, a middle-aged fee in the green and silver patterned dress of the Commission Bank flew through the archway behind the clerk and landed soundlessly beside him. She wore her golden hair in a long braid, with her long bangs tucked behind the silver arms of her cut crystal spectacles. If not for the tiny lines at the edges of her eyes and mouth, Leif would never have guessed her to be more than thirty, so he supposed that she must be closer to forty.

The new arrival smiled pleasantly with her eyes almost closed, as she addressed the clerk in a smooth alto. "Good morning Norran, is there something I can help you with?"

He nodded, "Good morning Denise, there is some small matter I had hoped you could assist me with..." He trailed off, prompting in the usual mercantile speech for her to ask what it was.

"Is that so? I would only be too happy to help." She glanced over at Leif and Fryn, and then her eyes widened as she saw the large claws on the counter opposite the glass separating the Hunters from the staff. "What seems to be the trouble?"

Fryn placed a hand on Leif's arm to stop him from answering as she took the lead, stepping past him with a delicate smile, without her dimples. Leif covered his own smile, wondering just how she'd proceed.

"How has the value of the Rosenkraun's mint changed in the last fifty-four years?" She asked, leaning against the counter, one finger trailing the edge of the nearest claw. Her smiled remained, as she looked up and away at some blank space on the ceiling.

"That would have been during the reign of Edrick the III, his coinage compared to today's would be worth 72%, I believe, but I would have to confirm with my records," was the reply.

Fryn sighed, whispering over her shoulder to Leif, who leaned uncomfortably close to see just how close she'd allow. He got too close, and she pushed him back with a tap of her wings. "I think we shouldn't press the matter."

"And what matter would that be?" The fee in the green and silver dress asked.

The clerk replied off-handedly, "they were concerned that they might not be paid the correct bounty for the slaying of a weasel in the Forest of Grass."

"How much is the reward?"

"Five-hundred and forty, at the time it was placed, so 72% of that..." The clerk went on, waving his hand, with a vindictive smile.

"I think we'll present this to the Earl..." Leif interrupted.

"I'm afraid that without our account and receipt confirming and validating the reward, you will receive nothing. Please sign the documents here, and here," Norran replied, sliding a few papers through the gap in the glass, along with the pen he'd held in his mouth, "then we will contact the Earl on your behalf and have the funds transferred to your Commission accounts."

Fryn sighed and wiped the pen on her sleeve before signing the papers, then Leif took it and grudgingly signed his, and followed her out to the street in silence, the claws left weighing the papers down. Even in harvest the sun shone golden overhead, filling the boulder-walled clearing in the forest of grass that made up the provincial city of Fassen. The Commission had something of its own miniature quarter bordered by the intersection of the Five Mainways, and as they stood on the curb of Shadowvine Way, Leif could just make out the view of several of the vintners flitting about the far off boughs of the Fassen Vine to the southwest.

He pointed at the shady overhang of the gigantic eight-branched vine. "What is the Fassen grape like?" he asked.

Fryn shrugged with her wings. "It's probably similar to the light wines we had at the Harvest Festival."

The Shadowvine Way ran about 30 degrees south of east from the Earl's Square, meeting up with the other streets outside the Bounty Office, in an irregular star with a pub on the opposite side called 'The Vineskin' with a figure of an inebriated middle-aged fae squeezing the side of an enormous grape on its signboard.

"We could stop in there," he suggested, smiling wryly at the slight frown she gave in reply.

"Perhaps we'd do better to investigate local sources of information. We may not have access to the sort of connections I enjoyed in Frorin," she alluded, "but I imagine there are similar 'powers of influence' here." Fryn's family really only had influence in Frorin, and that centered in the outer districts. He wondered what Harissa would think of Fassen, if she'd look down her nose at their wine, or if she'd quickly brush wings with the important and powerful without effort.

Leif scuffed the toe of his boot against the smooth-worn surface of the feldspar flagstones, "I can't see us just walking around asking the common people where their Stone Market is."

Fryn chuckled, covering her mouth with her hand. "Well, they'd probably just look at you like you'd asked them to sew your belt to your pants; so far as I know, the Stone Market is a reference found only in Frorin."

"I see..." he nodded, and flitted carefully between two hare-drawn wagons loaded high with the fresh golden grains of autumn tied under thick layers of jute netting. The drivers ignored him as he zipped across the street and settled under the eaves of the questionably titled pub, and tapped soundlessly on the door. He was followed soon after by Fryn, who flew delicately and dutifully, as if to show off her resignation and hesitance. Leif pulled on the heavy vinewood door and groaned as he heaved it to, just as an elderly fae in an over-large cap bustled out gratefully.

They shouldered their way inside, Leif all too conscious of the hot-and-cold sensation of his wings against hers since the opening required that they squeeze together—as if forcing or reinforcing romantic inclinations or emotions. At first it was completely dark, not even a cracked window to let in a little light, as the peat-fired room undulated with the slow-moving currents of air, each bearing in succession the scents of grizzled travelers, moss-covered rocks, stewed mushrooms, and the citrusy tang of pale ale.

Dark as it was, Leif could see Fryn's nose wrinkle at the assault of smells, and decided that he was glad he'd decided to explore this particular location. They were assaulted once more, only this time by the obtuse call of a serving boy with messy curls in his brown hair that would have covered his eyes if it hadn't been for the comical strip of linen he'd tied over his forehead in the double looped knot made to imitate a fairy's four wings.

"Food or drink, sirs!?" he demanded, not even noticing Fryn's horror at being called 'sir'.

Leif placed his hand at the small space on her back where her wings met, or rather sprang from, and sidled up to the serving boy intimately as he whispered in as tough and mysterious a voice as he could, 'information'.

Glancing back, he saw Fryn's dimples flash in the dull light of the peat-fire in the hearth opposite the little entry that was bordered by a myriad of coat and hat pegs, that were in turn mostly occupied. She didn't seem to notice the hand, or perhaps she didn't mind.

The server looked up at Leif, and then his eyes lit on his and Fryn's matching boots and coats, and at the black and silver sword at his waist before narrowing his eyes and replying, "Who's your patron, sir?"

And in a flash of inspiration, Leif responded instantly, allowing some of that darkness that undulated within the somber depths of his sword to float over the surface of his eyes. "I come by Mythrim."

The boy blinked, and then nodded knowingly, "then the meister will be wanting to see you." He pulled them through the double swinging doors into the kitchen, and past the two-wingspan stove, into an alcove office opposite a set of stairs leading into the cellar.

The meister, a tall and slender fae with graying black hair stood behind a long walnut-shell desk with his musician's fingers tracing the graceful line of his chin, as he stared intently at his own reflection in a framed mirror set behind his desk to give a constant view of the entrance. His wings betrayed no reaction when his green eyes passed over them, and he turned and waved a thin hand toward two red upholstered chairs with matching walnut-shell wood to the wing-backed one in front of the mirror.

"Please have a seat. Germaine, you may go," he dismissed the serving boy with a tilt of his jaw, and waited till Fryn and Leif had seated themselves before settling into his own chair. "I understand that you were an associate of one 'Mythrim,' who is now, I hear, deceased. Might I ask your business regarding him?"

Fryn smiled. "Indeed, we were hoping to make use of his connections to acquire certain information."

The meister didn't use any body language, no subtle shifts of his posture, or gestures as he replied gently, "I am afraid that might not be possible. As a private investigative service, we cannot assign the same agents to one fae or another since it is our primary ambition to connect agents and employers who are most suitable. If you would detail the information that you require, I will review the appropriate parties to facilitate the investigation."

For an older gentleman, he felt oddly slippery, like oil on sand. Leif began to question the wisdom of his gambit. "What are your fees?"

He was answered with an arched eyebrow, and a form-sheet. "Your needs determine the costs. Of course, some information is more difficult to acquire or maintain its relevancy."

Fryn took the sheet and found a fossilized wing-shard pen, hard like crystal, but gray and black, like onyx or charcoal. She shivered unconsciously as she dipped it in the tiny glass bottle of black ink that the meister passed across the polished surface of the desk, and set its sharp nib against the double-weight sheet. She scrawled and scritched, writing in a firm yet delicate hand, that she required information on a thief, described as a native to the area, a fee between the ages of thirty and thirty-five, and that she was a wind-elemental.

The meister read as she wrote, looking pointedly, obviously, over her shoulder, lips twisting as they pressed together in a grim and unwilling token of respect. "I believe you may know more of your quarry than my agents may be able to discover. What manner of information do you need, contact to hire, location to rout, identity...?"

"Location." Leif decided, sharing a confident look with his partner. "After all, we can learn anything else once we meet." He turned to the meister and added, "we wouldn't want to detain your agents any more than necessary as well."

This off-handed remark was taken gratefully with a false smile. "We appreciate your consideration... Would you remind me once again who recommended you to us?"

Fryn's smile was equally cloying and false as she said, "we were referred to you by Mythrim... One of his many names of course... Though he may have been in your records as Alan Hartlin?"

"One of several names..." The meister allowed, "I will not delay you further. Indeed, it is my pleasure to be of service. I will send a runner to you when we have obtained desired information. Would twenty mint an hour, at a maximum of two hundred mint be acceptable to you?"

"That will suffice," Leif replied importantly, "One more thing before we go... What would be your personal recommendation among your choice beverages?"

Fryn rolled her eyes at his phrasing and stood from her chair with a slight flutter to shake the dust from her wings. She waited at the archway separating the 'private' office from the kitchen and cellars, as the meister mulled over the question.

"Much as I am a native of this city: avoid anything made from Fassen grapes. I prefer wines made in Estenna, or the Norenan cerens. Fassen is all brash tannins, but low alcohol. Do not trust their wine..."

The last part was added mysteriously, as if a euphemism about the local people.

"Well then, I'll go meet the bartender," Leif said, rising from his chair.

Leif followed Fryn out to the entry, where they spotted Germaine adjusting his tattered serving apron as he spoke in stilted dialogue with a white-haired fae who shouted and then leaned forward with his hand cupping his ear to the lips of the server. The hearth area had four tables, two by shuttered windows and two in-line with them further in the room, while the 'bar' was really just a long tall bench of some dark indistinct wood with several mounds of candle wax topped by tiny burning white stubs. Behind it, across three shelves, was an impressive collection of nearly-empty bottles and bare spaces where bottles had been taken down and not replaced.

At the left end, a spiral staircase led up an unlit column to the second and third floors, where the soft laughter and resigned groans of fae at cards trickled down to the nearly empty common area.

"Looks like you just played 'the Lost!'" Came one particularly loud ejaculation from upstairs, as they slid onto the bench.

The space behind the bar was empty, but not for long, as the meister reappeared with a clean white apron, tying its strings behind his back, in the small between his wings. He examined them with a placid indifference, as if it were a first meeting, and of little importance at that.

"The Viper and the Lich, have come at last to terms..." he said, tracing a scrape that marred the surface of the polished vinewood bar. "Perhaps... Ceren is in order."

Leif and Fryn shared a look, surprised at his intimation, but even more at his forwardness in mentioning such clandestine terms in public. The old man hollered in Germaine's ear once more, and they both relaxed.

The meister leaned forward placing two tumblers before them, adding to his forwardness, Leif supposed, "I am aware of the nature of your recommendation."

Fryn chuckled. "Oh? It is legitimate, if you consider our relationship with Mythrim."

He smiled in return, more honestly than before as he uncorked an unlabled, brown bottle. "Your affiliations do give me some measure of confidence, Miss Martin. However, I am afraid that the one I am more concerned about is Master Aellin. Aside from some involvement with your House, he is as clean as wax paper."

"Master?" Leif and Fryn asked together, looking between their host and each other.

"I suppose you wouldn't have heard. Sigleifr has been promoted in his standing as a member of the Strafe-Curling-Viper school, the style of Master Yarl. This is, of course, due to his performance immediately upon his registration with the Commission... Which I doubt I need to clarify, but merely do out of habit. We do not wish to become involved with..."

Leif's mouth hung open, as he searched for words, and, finding nothing, he took the plain octagonal glass that their host had set lightly on the bar, and took a healthy swallow from its dark amber contents— nearly choking in his haste. Sputtering, he asked, "Could you repeat that?"

"I would rather not," the meister replied, "it is rather a mouthful."

Leif took another sip, matched by Fryn, who seemed equally surprised... which hurt, just a little. "Shouldn't you be sharing my joy in this, partner?"

"There are several stages, the first of which is disbelief," she said, eyes glinting in the dim flicker of the peat-fire reflected off the bottles on the shelf. "Still, I find it troubling that they would wait this long."

"I don't," he said, listening as a few heavy thuds sounded through the ceiling as a fae wandered purposefully to another room.

"That's even more troubling," she added in a light, teasing tone, "after all, haven't you heard the name they gave you?"

"The name who gave me?"

"The proverbial 'they', who else?" she asked, "The Viper."

He frowned. "But why would you be 'The Lich'? They're enemies."

She shook her head. "No, you're thinking of the Lancer and the Serpent, as far as I know, or at least according to what little I know. The Lich is both noone's enemy, and is feared by all. But I think it is entirely natural to call me what I am; the only Lich."

"Still..." he swirled the ceren in his octagonal glass and looked over suspiciously as the old fae rose on unsteady feet and wobbled over in their direction on a cane as crooked and bent as his back.

"I cann' ear 'im, meister, wotever he's sayi'n I cann' tell. Jus' por me a glass o'what 'ave you and ai'll be settled," he declared in as raised a voice as could not quite be called a yell. He caught a trip over a thin jute rug that spanned the walkway between the hearth-room and the bar, and clambered indelicately onto the space beside Leif at the bar. "Don' my me lad, I jus' an old fae an' won' bother with yor business."

"I can see that," Leif said, shrinking away from him, scooting closer to Fryn.

"See wot?"

"Nothing!" Leif said leaning toward him, projecting from his diaphragm without yelling, throwing a strained look in the direction of the meister.

The old fae nodded, as if he only pretended he could hear, and then held out a hand expectantly as a glass of dark red ale slid across a layer of foam and landed squarely in his grip. He drank, throwing back his head, his throat rolling as he gulped and swallowed it in one go. Then, he set it back down with a shaking hand, and fumbled around his pockets, searching for his coin purse. "Left it in one o' these..." he mumbled.

Leif dropped a Frorin-minted 5-mint coin onto the bar, and watched it spin until the snowflake-crown emblem showed on top. "I'll cover his drink," he said, flicking the coin toward the meister.

It was snatched up quickly, and the old fae didn't even notice. The heavy footfalls of a descending party sounded on the stairs, as the ale-warped laughter of four fae in work-clothes made their way to the bottom level.

"...throwing in the double-crown was the worst thing you could have done..." the one in front declared, stumbling off the second to the last step, catching himself with a careful wingburst.

Immediately behind him came a sorry-looking fae with patches sewn unevenly on his tweed jacket. "The chances of your having a Lance and Vine under the deck were extremely low," he complained.

"Never play the odds," the leader replied ceremoniously, "the astronomers say they only apply on the long term."

"They also say there's no difference between fee and fae," the apparent loser of the game added.

They left in a tangle out the front door, calling their thanks to the bartender and host, before vanishing and returning the room to its relative silence—disturbed only by the perturbed mumbling of the white-haired fae. Their host sighed quietly and leaned over the bar.

"Your immaculate record of connections, Viper, is something of a concern for us; and just as how the previous comment on the minor moons is inaccurate—as on close inspection they differ considerably in appearance—agents are as varied as their employers. As such, I would like you to work with Jessam here, one of our most experienced informants."

The old fae turned and placed a firm hand on his shoulder. "If ye'll be needin' information on this li'l finch, I can use these ears and see wot I can find."

"Twenty mint an hour for him?" Leif asked dubiously. "He doesn't look all that capable, even if he *does* look 'experienced'."

He felt Fryn's hand tug gently on his sleeve. "Perhaps that is the reason he will be effective," she whispered, "my cousin has learned much through service, he will likely be ignored."

It was an old trick to be sure, but Leif had his doubts that it would turn up anything useful. "The venues for his eavesdropping will be limited by his legs..."

The meister chuckled. "I will also be adding what I can hear... through my various sources. We will contact you in the next few days at the latest, and find you if we discover anything... time sensitive." With that he turned and walked up the spiral staircase, narrow enough that his dull matte gray wings brushed the curved wall and center post, as he went to clean up after the last party.

They finished their drinks and left the aged informant to his thoughts, and stood on the street; Leif taking a deep gulp of fresh moist air. A quarter or so past ten, according to the Commission Bank's tower, so he stretched his arms wide and twisted his torso to loosen up. "We still have to find a place to stay." They'd left their things in the lobby of the Fassen Lodge that morning, and hadn't even settled in yet, nor even reserved rooms.

"I hope Trel isn't there waiting for us," Fryn said, eyebrows narrowing. "She'll want to play cards, or whatever game those fae from before were talking about. It's hard to believe they're still considered 'active' in the Commission, when they seem to be little more than tourists."

They went up North Forest Way, the first point of the intersection's star, to the Lodge which sat on the corner of N. Forest and Commission, the east-to-west segment that connected the two five-ways on either side of the Commission Quarter. Entering the Lodge, they saw their travel bags and the crate of wine they'd purchased the day before at the Festival sitting beside one of three low vinebark tables in the solarium to the right of the door. Each of these tables sat before a rich green love-seat arrayed in an inverse arc to the angled windows giving a cheerful view of the planters to the north. One of these was occupied, the one furthest to the right, by a young fee with a little boy playing with tiny carved wooden figures of guardsmen on the cushion beside her. He balanced and adjusted his woven-grass conical hat, and purposefully smacked two of his toys together with soft grunting sounds.

Leif knelt beside him as he picked up his bag. "What have you got there?" he asked pleasantly, showing his shining white teeth in a friendly smile.

The child regarded him with a suspicious gaze, eyes angled up at him from under the too-forward brim of his hat and his unkempt brown bangs. "Toys," he replied.

"Oh, I see..." Leif trailed off, looking up at Fryn who watched him mysteriously, as if learning by example. He returned his focus to the boy, whose wings were tinged purple with shyness, as Leif picked up one of the unused guardsmen and made him fly around and land on the low table, balancing him on his carefully painted green shoes.

The boy accepted his challenge, and flew his obvious favorite—the only toy with a different colored hat, blue—and he knocked Leif's toy over with a pronounced 'yah!' And then leaned back triumphantly.

Leif sighed. "You did it, you beat him," he said, standing with his bag slung over his shoulder. Fryn had already picked up the crate, and was moving to the desk, when the boy's mother smiled and instructed her son, "thank the nice fae for playing with you." The boy mouthed a quiet 'thank you' and watched Leif follow Fryn to the desk.

They were greeted by the receptionist with a smile and a token twitch of his wings, as he rose slightly in his seat. "Good morning," he said, brushing a stray bit of his straight black hair behind his ear, "How can I be of service?"

Leif slid his license onto the polished barkwood desk and looked to his companion as he replied, "We require lodgings for the next few days."

The receptionist sighed dramatically, "With the Harvest Festival, the Hunter's Lodge has been nearly fully booked—especially with the report of the theft of the crown..."

Fryn set the crate of wine on the counter, "should we book rooms at one of the inns in town?"

He shook his head. "I'm afraid that the inns are even more occupied, with various fae coming from around the Kingdom, or even from *abroad*. Your best option would be to lease one of the family housings on the corner of Shadowvine and Commission, just west of here."

Fryn looked away with a pale face, as Leif blushed. "But... we're not..." He added in a low whisper. "Where do the large teams stay?" he asked.

The secretary leaned forward and smiled as he looked between them. "They normally book a suite in the family housing; the first two floors are almost entirely devoted to teams."

"Just west of here then," Leif almost placed a hand on Fryn's arm, but caught himself, and instead picked up the crate of wine and pushed the door open with his back. She walked out gratefully with a shy smile, as if she secretly enjoyed *and* was uncomfortable with the proceedings. The north side of the street was occupied by a few squares and forum-blocks with shops peeking out under the pebble-stone eaves, marked by their plum, puce, or peach colored awnings. One of the more visible businesses, a grocery run by a tall, thin fee with brown hair plaited down to her lower wings, had a display of fresh grapes. They were ignored by all who passed, even though she insisted that the imported Pyrincel would be the perfect combination with a bit of nectar and cream as an after-dinner treat.

Leif turned and walked toward the Earl's Fiveway, one eye on the wedge-shaped six-story building at the corner, and the other on Fryn's nervously twitching wings. He had to admit, whatever their solution was going to be, it wouldn't be easy... But then, they had both performed better than most stage actors when Mythrim spotted them by Havrshyk's tomb. Leif swallowed.

Unlike the shops to the north, the family-lodgings for Hunters and Commission staff were constructed of solid stone blocks, aligned with precision and white-washed. The roof, unclear against the late morning sky, looked to be shingled with carved slate. Fryn rushed forward with a quick wingburst, glancing back with a smile as she beat him to the door, and pulled it open, waving him through with her free hand, and her bag braced behind her back.

"After you," she said playfully, following him into the entry as soon as he'd stepped past. Large teams often reserved such rooms, so it was quite possible that they'd be able to secure private rooms within a given wing, so he relaxed and watched Fryn run up to the counter to address the middle-aged fee behind the desk.

"We were hoping to arrange accommodations for the next few days," she began, eyes flicking back toward him in a cheerful flash.

The secretary in this building wasn't nearly so young or interested as the other, as she covered a yawn and searched her directory. She shook her head. "It appears that we are entirely booked up. If you are with a team currently situated here, then..." Her voice trailed off.

Leif wondered how he could ask who was there without making it obvious that they weren't a part of a team, and Fryn looked equally confused and displeased. The lobby to the west gave a view of the intersection, with a fireplace on the angled corner, and the soft patter of descending feet alerted them of fae entering from the stairs. A tangle appeared at the door, as a fae in his fifties embraced a fee with graying brown hair, and looked over his shoulder at what was presumably his son. His gray-tinted wings flicked as he addressed him in a serious tone. "I expect you to be careful in the city. I expect I will not hear anything more about your adventures or you will find yourself in the Eirenau Boarding College this year as well."

"Yes father," he said, glancing over in their direction as a flash of jealousy and disgust pulsed through his wings.

Leif nodded to himself and looked back at the secretary. "Our companions may have already reserved a space here," he said, knowing how displeased Fryn would be if it turned out that way.

"You are Hunters, yes? I do not have any teams here aside from the Silverblade and the Blackbow, but they are in a couple's suite."

The reply sent Fryn's wings drooping. "What rooms do you have available?"

"There are two more couple's suites available, but we can only assign two to each..."

As the doors on the other street side opened, and the fae from before went on his way, the archway to the stairs were filled once more by a tall slim fae with black hair, and a shorter, strong but not thickset, fee with a leather belt arrayed with a multitude of small tools, a compass, several pouches, and a leather-wrapped hip-flask.

"Well, look who it is!" The fee declared, pointing at them with a grin and a white-gloved hand.

"If it isn't the Blackbow," Fryn said, eyes flicking toward Yarrow's reserved smile as he met her gaze over his partner's shoulder.

"Good morning," he replied gently, nodding at Leif politely, "I trust you are well."

"Well enough," Leif answered, setting his mixed-crate of wine on the counter. "Where are you two going?"

Trel winked as she brushed the tip of her nose with her forefinger, wings matching the motion with a backwards and forwards wave. "Well, we heard that there was a dangerous criminal on the loose, and that the reward for her capture was worth two-thousand mint!"

Not quite as high as he hoped... Maybe with the prevalence of Hunters in Gaersheim, the rewards weren't as high as in the more provincial regions such as Capholt or Froreholt. Leif sighed. "Then it seems we are competitors in this race."

"Pfft," Trel countered, "I'm sure as long as we can fund our 'vacation' the four of us could break even and enjoy ourselves if we split it evenly."

Yarrow's eyes widened in shock. "We never discussed..."

"Tut," she replied, "I work with whom I like, and so do you."

Yarrow rolled his eyes with a modest amount of decorum as he walked over to them. "It appears that we have entered into a partnership."

Fryn swallowed. "But we haven't..."

Yarrow's gaze set on Trel as he cut her off gently, "she works with whom she likes." He shook hands with them and took their bags as he added, looking at the receptionist, "put them in the room beside ours."

Trel led them up the green carpeted stairs to the third story, and stopped shortly after the arch to the hallway, in front of a set of double-doors on the north side, mirrored on the south. "We are here, and you," she pointed, "across the hall."

"But Trel..." Leif started, almost simultaneously as Fryn complained.

"But we aren't..."

Her right eyebrow arched as her wings shot back mischievously. "I thought I'd do you a service, but if you are really so adamant, Yarrow, you can share the south room with Leif."

Fryn paused, biting her lower lip, eyes glued to the crate in Yarrow's hands. "But then... Leif... I'd thought in the evening."

He caught her meaning and smiled. "I was thinking of exploring the vineyard or the Tower District."

The rush of air, not footsteps, announced the arrival of the secretary as she swept up the stairs on the wing and landed beside them. She put the key in Fryn's hand, thanked them, and vanished as quickly as she'd come, leaving them pondering the intricate brass key that sparkled with a burgundy loop that hung nearly to the level of her knee.

"A moment, if you would," Fryn said, sliding the key into the lock. She turned it and pulled the lever, an ornate brass handle matching the flowery filigree of the key, and stepped inside.

Leif took the crate and the bags from Yarrow, thanking him quietly as Fryn's voice, muffled by the door, declared indistinctly her appreciation of the space. He followed her inside, and then gaped, closing the door behind him. The couple's suite was far more than it sounded, it would have made more sense to call it an apartment, or flat, since the term it was given inspired a narrow closet-like space suitable for a bed and washbasin... Not a living space intended for actual 'living-in.'

"I don't think we will need to switch rooms," Leif said, looking at the two chairs and low table in the entry, flanked by two rooms and an array of windows. "I wonder why they bothered with two rooms in a couple's suite."

The door opened as Trel pushed her way in. "I can answer that thought," she said, opening the door on the left. Inside was a large double-width bed with white and green quilts and matching curtains pulled to the sides of an array of windowpanes. "Oh, wrong room." She swept over to the other side and charged into the second room with an "aha!" as she presented a tiny room with a short sofa bed. "This is why..."

"Why?" Leif asked.

Yarrow coughed as he entered. "Some couple's using these spaces need a secondary room if they have a small child, or an argument."

"How considerate," Fryn mused, "Leif, you can have the couch."

"Thanks," he shared a look with Yarrow, who seemed grateful he hadn't asked to share the other large room, if Trel would with Fryn. He tested the firmness of the daybed, it was a couch really, with cushioned arms that could be adjusted to lay flat. Not too hard, at least, not like sleeping on molded sand at his school. "I had hoped I was past this stage," he exaggerated, "see for yourself." He patted the seat beside him, and crossed his legs, waiting for Fryn to roll her eyes and humor him. She sat down and leaned one elbow on the side, and propped her chin on her fist. "It's not that bad a bed for a Master of the Strafe-Curling-Viper School." She smirked, which he could distinguish from her smile only because she only presented a dimple on one side of her face.

Yarrow let himself out, and Trel paused at the door. "There's a bell and booklet if you need anything, but we will be going out for lunch. If there's nothing else, we'll stop in this evening and exchange what we've learned... If you wish to cooperate that is."

She left, so they sat with their bags on the ground and the crate of wine beside them, looking out the windows toward the grocer who still tried to sell her head-sized grapes. Leif wondered why she bothered, but it wasn't even noon yet, so he supposed she'd sell once everyone was more aware of the heat.

"It's a bit early for lunch," he said, wondering if Fryn's sitting beside him were an invitation to place his arm on the back of the couch.

She didn't lean back against the back of the couch, so he decided it wasn't. "They could be going to one of the restaurants in the Shadowvine District, or at the Tower."

"Or Boulderwall," Leif guessed, "I get the sense Trel likes to explore things most would consider below their station."

She chuckled, leaning against the white cushions of the couch. "Yes, I can see that."

"You know, we might as well see what some of those things are like, maybe they have grilled oats and honey," he ventured, slipping one arm across the back of the couch, not touching her or her wings, but lounging.

"Grilled oats? Probably not," she shook her head and rocked forward to stand from her heels to her toes. "But they might have something simlar."

"Perhaps, perhaps," Leif allowed, "But should we go northwest, west, south, east, or southeast?"

She counted the directions listed on her fingers. "Five. Well, it doesn't much matter to me, just so long as it's far enough away that we won't run into that withered old fae."

They locked up the room, relieved to notice that the 'main bedroom' had a lock as well, so that she could maintain a certain level of privacy and distance, and wound their way down the stairs once more to the street.

"I still don't know what to do," Leif admitted.

Fryn shrugged. "Neither do I, at least in Frorin I knew my way around, and what was interesting, but I've never even heard of anyone going out of their way to come here before."

"Shocking that they'd host the Harvest Festival, but I suppose it doesn't need to make sense to *me*." Leif shaded his eyes since the sun was at its zenith, blanketing the entire town in its tired gaze, reminding them of the last hints of summer. "Maybe we should just go away from it," he suggested.

"Hmm?" Fryn asked, following as he wandered down Shadowvine in a roughly southeastern direction. "The holders and low-lords mostly occupy that district, there's little we can do there without an invitation. From what I've heard, the Lords in this area are too occupied with their petty posturing or internal squabbles to entertain, and even if they were willing I doubt they'd consider us prestigious enough to warrant an invitation... Even the Earl faces consistent criticism I hear, with the next lords in line all wanting to remove him and claim his seat. I don't think the young King takes notice of them at any rate."

"Then we'll continue to the south wall and see if there are any nice Rosenkrauns to drink, or if there's honeyed oats further down." He continued with his hands in his pockets, glad to have the sun out of his direct line of sight, even if walking with the sword at his side still felt unnatural. Every so often, he'd find it slipping at his side, or dangling awkwardly around his leg so that he'd almost trip or stumble. How anyone could comfortably wear a sword, he had no idea. When they reached The Vineskin, they continued straight ahead, where the street changed its name to Boulder Street, toward the far corner of the city.

The buildings were shorter, made of rough segments of mortared shale or crumbled granite from the carved sides of the wall that formed a protective border around the city. He could just make out the wall and gates that rose halfway up the gap at the end of the street, a tower on one side. A few pebbles shifted loosely in their cemented joins as they got farther from the Commission Quarter, and the paint peeled away from the shutters of most of the houses set off in their blocks a bit away from the main road with soot-stained chimneys.

"A bit dreary here, hate to see it when it rains," Leif said, picking up the pace as the tower gate grew closer. "No chance at honeyed oats either."

"It's not as common as you think," Fryn started to say, but stopped as she tugged on one of his idly moving wings, "but then it just might be worth holding out for."

He followed her pointed arm to the south where a market square was filled with carts and booths set up for the afternoon, fae from the surrounding regions and local farms proclaimed their wares with woven-grass hats and green and gold clothes. "See I *knew* they'd have honeyed oats..." Leif swept over in one flight, landing before a small cart with a charcoal-grill, smoke rising from its iron grates, arrayed with the sweet-smelling combination of honey and cooked wheat grains divorced from their husks all pierced together by a hardwood stick.

Fryn leaned over his shoulder since he blocked access to the grill, and smiled. "But it's still not oats."

"At this point I'm not about to complain," he said waving to the fae with the gold linen apron who stood waiting patiently behind the grill, "two please."

The fae tipped his hare-wool cap and pulled two skewers from the heat, drizzled them with a honeycomb, and wrapped the ends in a shell of fibrous paper. "That'll be two mint," he said, holding the treats in one hand, and presenting an empty palm with the other.

Leif dropped the two desired coins into his hand and passed one of the skewers to Fryn. "Now, I know what you're thinking, 'can it really be that good?' But I stake my reputation on it..."

"I have had these before," she interrupted, taking a delicate bite from the first steaming wheat-berry, nearly the full size of her mouth. She covered her mouth with her hand, steam rising as she breathed out. "Am I allowed to use my frost to cool it down?"

"I thought you knew how to eat it," Leif shook his head, "the burn on the roof of your mouth because of your haste is a necessary part of the experience; it serves to the remind you to be more patient."

She shrugged and they left the square, hoping that a stroll would give them a better idea of what there was in town, and where and how they could find the thief before anyone else—and before Trel could get them to sign onto some sort of partnership. For only two-thousand mint, it really didn't make sense to split it four ways.

Tower and Rain

Fassen:

Tower District

Northwest Parapet

Leif

Looking down at the city shouldn't have been an exciting thing; he had flown much higher than this, and he was certain that even if he were in the canopy of the Fassen Vine he wouldn't come close to his record— but still, standing on solid, constructed ground that overlooked the city and the grasslands to the south, with a clear view of the river far off to the northwest, just felt more significant. His wings danced unconsciously to a forgotten rhyme as he reached over toward Fryn's hand, wondering if she'd welcome some kind of advance.

She stepped forward and gripped the granite battlements under her snow-white fingers, staring at the matching edge of white on the northern horizon: the only hint of the Ice Wastes that went up to the pole. His hand closed on empty air and he swallowed a sigh, adjusting the fit of his scarf. Its tan, hare-down wool warmed his chin and mouth, as a faint mist coalesced around his partner's wings, neck, and shoulders. The pendant she'd received from Ieffin glowed in the cold light of the only-just-set sun.

I want to ask her, or just try, but why, oh why can't I? Leif stepped up beside her, admiring the crimson remnants of the sun to the west, a color so like the details that pulsed through the veins and patterns on his wings. *It seemed so much easier before, to tease, to play, to joke... But who'm I kidding anymore?*

He felt a slight tickle at the nape of his neck, a tingling rush of sparks from the soles of his feet to the top of his head, aligning his parted blond hairs with the sky. The sensation faded, and the clouds grew closer from behind, the tingling falling deeper, slowly to his gut, and to the sword. A dim burst of light flashed against the stones from the unheard lightning of the end-of-summer storm.

"I wonder what Master Yarl would think of this," he mused.

Fryn's wings pricked up like the ears of a hare, "I can hardly comment when I have no idea to what you are referring."

He smiled. "Really? But your response was just what I wanted... for you to ask me about it."

She cocked her head sideways, a lingering crumb from her earlier treat sticking to her cheek. "Clever as you are, there're always unintended consequences when you speak," she yawned, "you wanted me to ask what it was about, and I did, but now I'm getting tired and disinterested."

"I meant, simply, that my sparks are divided between my liver and my sword," he replied, "and it is hardly polite to tell someone that you're bored."

She laughed, and recoiled as he picked off the crumb stuck by honey to her slightly reddened cheek. "That's not my fault," she argued, "the blame is all yours."

Yes, that is what I wanted. He chuckled and turned to face the east, and his smile faded as a young fae in a brown cloak landed silently on the stones before the stairs. Fryn hadn't seen him yet, so Leif tapped her shoulder with his wing, and waited for the fae to approach. The next tower over, a waxed tarp dome, opened as a telescope rotated in its berth to face the sky, astronomers rushing to get a reading before the storm.

Fryn nearly took his hand as she turned around, or at least, it seemed she did, but then she noticed their company, and to Leif's disappointment, she held her own hands together behind her back.

"I was told to bear a message for the Viper and the Lich," the fae explained. He presented an envelope sealed with green wax pressed with an ornate 'M' and nodded dutifully as Leif accepted it.

They shared a look, both with raised eyebrows, and when they looked back at the messenger, he was gone without even a gust of wind.

"I suppose we should visit the meister for a drink before we turn in for the night," Leif ventured, carelessly breaking the seal and slipping out the single postcard-sheet of stationary. "Information has been found," he read aloud.

Fryn nodded. "Perhaps you're right, but all the same, I had wanted to catch a glimpse through the glass." She pulled the edges of her jacket, draped over her shoulders, sleeves unused, and tightened its fit. "I'm sure we have time enough for a peek."

He trotted after her resignedly, wondering when and why she'd suddenly become interested in Gaersyn Astronomy. "I'm sure we have little to worry about, last I knew the moon blocked 'The Vine' and would continue to do so for the next month."

She returned a gratuitous single laugh. "Of course it will, since it is that month." Fryn found the door to the observatory in a cobbled arch, and pulled with all her strength, then, she tried again with her wings beating, straining to pull it open.

Leif pinched one of her lower wings in a firm, yet gentle grip, and pulled her away from the door. As she began to complain that he could have damaged her wing, he pushed on the door and it swung open easily.

"...I would have figured that out," she stammered, looking torn between the embarrassment of pulling on the door and that of him tugging on her lower wing.

He took hold of her sleeve as she'd been waving her hands about in confusion, and pulled her through the door. "I'd rather take a look before the rain comes, it'll make it much easier to get back."

She pulled her hand free and walked over to one of three fae who were gathered around the eyepiece of the telescope, which had elongated within its series of brass tubes to stretch far out over the battlements, angling up toward the darkening sky through a slit in the dome. "They'll let me look really quick."

"Miss," one of the three astronomers asked, turning to prevent Fryn from drawing closer with one arm outstretched, "is there something you need?"

Fryn frowned. "I had hoped I could take a look through the telescope."

The fee who'd blocked her pursed her lips, and fiddled with the notepad in her gray single-buttoned waistcoat. "With the storm soon to arrive, there is a limited window for us to take our readings, I am afraid the telescope is unavailable to the public."

Leif stepped up beside Fryn and absently ran a hand through his hair. "Even just a peek while you record your findings between glances?" He added a warm smile for good measure.

The fee couldn't have been much older or younger than them, and she looked away shyly. "Well... if it's that quick, perhaps."

"We'd be grateful if you would," Fryn pressed, not even noticing him.

Leif watched as an elderly fae in a green felt coat and spectacles leaned back from the eye-piece of the telescope, and Fryn flitted over, and put her eye to the glass, wondering when and why she'd suddenly become interested in the stars. "What do you see?" he asked.

Her wings fluttered and twitched for a few seconds, and she mumbled something about the lesser moons. "...more rocky than expected..."

He sighed, sharing a look with the fee in the gray coat, and shrugged. "Why do you need to take readings?"

The old fae in the green coat looked up sharply. "I wouldn't think I'd hear that question from someone native to the Aelaete," he said, "Isn't it common practice there as well?"

Leif politely stifled a yawn. "I knew they did it, but at my school I had little time to learn about the superstitions of the astronomers, just what is common knowledge."

A twinkle appeared in the old fae's eye as he blinked. "It's best to be careful what you describe as superstition; most wouldn't believe in that sword you have there." He pointed at the black edge of the blade that shone from the top of the sheath, since it's latch had somehow gotten loose in their flight up the tower.

Leif pulled out the sword a little bit further and looked at it. *The existence of one superstition doesn't prove another,* he thought. The surface currents shifted a little, as he added softly in a wry tone of voice. "The stars give bad advice."

Fryn still stared through the telescope, and the gray-coated young fee gently pulled on her arm to try to separate her from it, her wings twitching impatiently.

He almost shook his head, watching her playing with her coat-tails with her free hand.

I'm not Arta, the Lancer, that I could be her guardian, he thought, smiling outwardly as Fryn was finally pulled away from the telescope, and returned to his side as the old superstitious fae returned to his prognostications.

"I suppose we should head back into town," Fryn said, turning on her heel and opening the door. The first raindrop splashed against the stones, scattering the loose layer of dust that had accumulated over the last few days of summer. "Well, that's nice," she shook her head sarcastically.

Her behavior *was* a little odd. Maybe there was something about what the astronomer said. "We're just going to have to brave it. Do you have an umbrella?"

She bit her lip in thought as she faced him. "I don't, but I could make one." She closed her eyes and held her hands in front of her chest, forming a cloud of mist and fog into a ball of ice the size of her head. She stretched it out into an arm-length rod with an oblong sphere at one end, which she squished and pulled out into a slight-angled conical sheet. A layer of frost went up her arm, with little tendrils frozen on their way up her neck. Fryn stepped outside, and the first raindrop splashed off her white-blue crystal umbrella, and she stretched out her opposite hand toward him with a smile.

"We can't have a repeat of what happened last time," she said, "We'd better hurry before it gets any worse."

Leif linked arms, ducking his head under the cover of the umbrella, and let his wings droop like hers, both for protection and to avoid brushing against hers. It felt almost like when they'd first gone to see the Pine-Martin, or when they'd pretended to be on a date to spy on Mythrim... But now their only reason was the rain...

Walking down the stairs took a lot longer than flying up, but they were free of water because of the slight grade that channeled the run-off to the outside edge; a pleasant sound, gurgling with the spinning and white-foamed first rain of the harvest. Fog settled over the city, encased in the towering boulder walls, clinging to the base and canopy of the Fassen Vine and, Leif thought, it might actually be a better city than he'd first expected.

"I imagine by now most everyone in Sendra has moved to the southern banks of the river," he said, glad to feel her arm so tightly linked with his.

She smiled. "It seems awfully ineffective, having to move that much."

"On the contrary," he replied, stepping in a shallow puddle that had formed in one of the worn stairs, "with winter housing already prepared, it is very convenient."

Fryn nodded absently, as if remembering some of her own childhood. "Before I moved to the Rain District, I used to play with Harissa and Jaeson, always wanting to be the guard, and never the thief..." She chuckled. "They loved playing that part..."

"How old were you when you moved?" he asked as they stepped off the last stair and onto Tower Street, and looked out toward the far-off five-way, unable to see further than fifty wing-spans or so since the fog was so thick.

She looked down at the damp toes of her boots with a sad smile. "I was eight."

"I was nine, when I joined my school," he said, "Why did you decide to become a Hunter of the Commission?" He glanced at the hardened awnings along the eaves of the street, yellow ones for the florist, green for the bookstore.

She looked up at him, biting her lip in thought, almost conflicted as she considered her answer. "I didn't want to at first. No, I wanted to join the Guard; but when I became a Bloodcrafter, I realized that I would never be welcome there."

He couldn't tell how much further it was to meet with the Earl's Five-way, but they had walked a good distance, and it had grown quite dark. Warm golden light streamed from the lampposts spaced along the curb, shaped like delicate stalks with twisted stems, and glowing starlamps at the tops. There weren't very many artificers in Aelaete, but their art seemed more than prevalent in Froreholt, and Gaersheim. "I can't imagine why..." he said, eyeing a thinning section of the frozen umbrella over his head.

She laughed softly, and they walked on in silence. The street were mostly clear, except for a few mail-runners beating a hasty retreat, or a hare-drawn wagon drawing a load covered by a tarp. Everyone seemed to have been ready for a quiet night indoors, which he supposed, was exactly what they meant to do. At the Five-way they followed Shadowvine Way down toward the Vineskin. They passed the looming walls and hedges of the low-lords' estates that graced the sloping hill around the foot of the Vine, with their invisible, private estates and Leif wondered just what sort of faeries they were. Were they self-important yet harmless? Were they subtle, intelligent, and dangerous? Or were they simply faeries with slightly more money and larger houses than their neighbors? Leif shook his head, and hauled the heavy bound door to the Vineskin once more, as Fryn released his arm and tossed the umbrella into the street. It scattered into a myriad of fragments, and melted away under the patter of the rain, and she stepped inside.

It was much noisier than it had been in the morning, but it made sense, after dark, in the rain, and fog, that it should fill up with fae looking to avoid the weather. Fryn frowned as they were blocked from entering into the common hall by a velvet rope hitched between brass rings between the host's booth and the wall covered in hats and coats. The smell of burnt honey and butter drifted out from the kitchen with the slurred ramblings of too-many patrons stuffed into the insufficiently-large space.

It wasn't Germaine who greeted them, but a busty tavern fee in a white blouse and a dark green apron who appeared behind the booth with a wide smile and a loud 'hello.'

"We're looking for a private table for two," Leif explained, raising his voice as he leaned closer. Fryn's wings twitched irritably at his proximity to the fee and at the undone top button of her blouse. She took his arm again with a sweet smile bordering on cloying and protectiveness; but she needn't have worried. Not that he minded of course.

"There's a table on the third floor, overlooking the south side," the hostess said, "right this way." She unhooked the far side of the velvet rope and waited for them to cross into the common hall before securing it again and making her way carefully around a number of slightly inebriated customers to the foot of the stairs.

In the corner by the hearth, half-obscured by the cloud of poorly ventilated peat smoke, Leif noticed the three brothers they'd sat with at the Harvest Festival, but quickly avoided looking in their direction lest he be noticed and forced into a communal evening. Fryn saw them too, if her tightened grip on his arm were any indication, and they quickly mounted the spiral stair, passed the second level, busy with the sound of shuffling cards and the porcelain clack of plaques or tablets, or whatever other local games they had, and found that the top floor was arrayed with quiet booths.

Their hostess brought them around the banister of the stair to the south side, where a few dormers looked out on the street through a series of wingspan windows. Even though only a single couple was seated in the dormer to the right of them, they whispered romantically over the light of a dimmed starlamp shaped like a candle on a brass candelabra—as if concerned their conversation might be overheard.

Little of any importance, Leif figured, but faeries were inherently shy about such things, he thought.

Fryn guided him into the booth with a view toward the stairs, and slid onto the bench beside him.

The hostess covered a smirk as she tapped the amber bulb of their starlamp activating its warm glow, adding, "It's always nice to see a couple sitting together like that, doesn't happen often enough I say."

Leif blushed. "We have often thought the same... if we might start with a pitcher of water and a flagon of one of your darker barley ales, we would appreciate it." From the corner of his vision he could tell Fryn had raised one eyebrow at the suggestion, but didn't comment.

"I will bring them right up," she replied, "Make yourselves comfortable." The hostess flitted off toward the stairs, with her green-lined wings pulsing with a bit of yellow amusement.

Fryn relaxed into the burgundy upholstery of the bench and sighed. "Barley?" She prompted.

"When it gets colder like this I find the lighter ales don't suit," he said, "and I heard once that the barley in Gaersheim makes for good drink."

She snorted lightly. "Be careful who you believe."

He nodded. "Sound advice for anyone." Maybe this time she'd actually be receptive to some sort of advance, seeing as how she'd held his arm... He'd rested his hands clasped together on the table, but dropped his left hand to the bench, and finding hers he held it and gave it a light squeeze. "But I think my sister knew what she was talking about."

He thought he saw a flush of color on her cheeks, but the air went cold as if she'd purposefully drained in order to hide it. "Now now, we're partners, no need to be coy," he teased, but before she could reply, the hostess appeared at their table with two large ceramic pitchers and four stacked brown-glazed mugs.

"Now it's not a full barley beer," she explained, "but the meister recommends this one for you personally."

Leif filled two of the hand-high cups with the water in the white-glazed pitcher, which smelled slightly of lemon or mint, or both, as Fryn leaned over the table to stare into the depths of the green pitcher. She took the other two cups, and filled one as the hostess departed; but she stopped when she noticed something inside of the last cup. She pulled out a folded piece of stationary, stenciled with faded pink floral lines bordering the edges, and read it aloud in a soft husky whisper.

"I will be along shortly to provide the information you requested. The tavern area is busier than usual at the beginning of Harvest, but not altogether surprising given the happenings at the Festival. Signed, 'M." Fryn looked up, and slipped the note into one of her jacket pockets, and finished pouring the dark ale.

Leif accepted one of the mugs, and took a healthy sip. It was rich and creamy, and tasted like hazelnuts and spice. "You know, with how long we've been on the road," he said, wiping his mouth with the back of his hand, "I haven't once had a chance to wash my clothes."

She offered a subdued groan. "You *do* smell like dirt and grass, though I can hardly imagine why," she conceded ironically.

He hadn't had long to examine his clothes after their fight with the weasel, but the smear of dirt and green grass, and a little bit of blood had dirtied the back of his coat, particularly the coattails. "Well, what is your secret?" He asked.

Fryn shrugged. "What secret?"

"Well, your clothes are in much better condition, and you don't smell dirty at all," he pointed out.

She glanced away and took a sip from her beer. "I am merely more careful than you are."

"I doubt that," Leif rested his chin on his hand, the one that wasn't still occupied holding hers; and he was grateful that she'd seemed to forget about it. "You probably use your frost to remove any stain as soon as it appears."

"I..." she closed her mouth and opened it again for a few moments. "I actually do that quite often."

"Well I can't do anything truly convenient with sparks, but I can make my hair stand on end," he said, demonstrating with a slight tingle that rose from his feet to the top of his head, little arcing shocks running between his wings and individual hairs as they stood on end. He felt Fryn's hand reflexively tighten as a small shock went through her as well.

"Parlor tricks," she chuckled, "but you'd best stop that before you attract a lightning bolt and burn a hole in the restaurant." Her eyes flicked out the window, where the light from the street lamps pooled and reflected off the rising levels of standing water that scattered and splashed under the percussive force of the thickening rain. A low rumble reverberated through the ground, the wood of the bench, and the air, as a flash of lightening burned a trail in the direction of the south wall, and the thunder followed in an instant.

Leif smiled. "I haven't heard thunder like that in a long time."

Fryn's hand had gone cold, and her shoulders were bunched and tense, as her wings twitched. "I'd prefer it if it weren't so nearby."

Soft footfalls announced the arrival of their original host, and as they looked up, they saw the graying fae in his black suit settle smoothly into the bench opposite them with a platter of toasted grains and a few small plates to divide them.

"I trust you enjoyed your tour of the city?" he began, giving a half-smile as he set a small white porcelain plate before each of them and placed a steaming wheat berry on top. "I would also recommend taking small bites with the knife and fork," he added, sliding a few utensils across the table, "since it is very hot."

Fryn cut off a bite and popped it in her mouth, chewing slowly with a pleasant smile before swallowing and taking a sip of beer. "The Boulderwall District is very quaint and charming, and the view from the Tower was most impressive."

"Unfortunately we were unable to tour the Vine-Gardens, or the Earl's estate," Leif interrupted, "but altogether it was a most enjoyable day."

The meister nodded as he chewed his own bit of food. "I hope you don't mind if I join you, but we have been very busy of late, and I need to take my breaks and sustenance when and where I can." In a lower voice he added, "and it does make it more difficult to meet with my clients, even if it also grants greater privacy."

"Do you work with many in the Commission?" Fryn asked softly, tilting her head as if it were an errant thought, an absentminded question.

He shook his head. "Doubtless you ask because of my proximity to the so-called Commission's Quarter," he said, jerking a thumb to the north, "but my establishment has been here for two hundred years. In fact, when they started expanding their offices, and building the Commission's Gardens, they were a chief competitor of the previous owner. At the time, most wanted 'reputable' sources of information... but there's always a need for *other* sources. However, I usually do business with other clients, merchants and nobles and politicians, or even the common folk."

Leif hadn't even touched his water, so he poured it back in the pitcher and filled it with the nutty beer and set the mug in front of their host. "I have been hearing a lot of dissatisfaction surrounding the Commission lately," he replied, "but I thought it was because most fae didn't like having to deal with President Hans' eccentricities."

The meister smiled and took a long drink. "That, is a very good word for it, but the Commission's executives can hardly complain as long as he continues to generate more revenue than did his predecessors." He reached into the pocket of his black silk vest and retrieved another slip of folded stationary. "I think we may have uncovered the identity of the thief—one Lia Karyn—an old enemy of the crown. Six years ago she stole a series of documents from the Royal Archives in Rosenkraun, and through her machinations brought the previous king to an early grave from anxiety and constant threats... Some say there was proof of infidelity, embezzlement of his own kingdom, or worse... and finally his heart couldn't hold out." He leaned closer to the table, eyes flicking down for a moment as he noticed that Leif and Fryn were holding hands, and continued, "She was known as 'The Scissortail", a peerless thief. I wonder if perhaps she wasn't a victim of one of the king's fits of infidelity..."

Fryn frowned. "While that would give plenty of reason to set herself against the previous king, I don't understand the theft of the Harvest Crown."

"We could just ask her when we catch her," Leif said, cutting off a bite of his toasted wheat with the edge of his fork.

"This envelope," the meister added, pulling out a yellowish packet of paper from his vest, "contains the report that Jessam provided, it should include leads on her current, or most likely last known location." He set it on the table, finished his beer, and stood. "It has been a pleasure, but I must return to my duties, as I can hear the complaints from the first floor."

As he left, Leif nodded to himself, the rowdy group of fae on the first level were knocking on their tables, or doing something to call out the bartender.

"I don't like him," Fryn said.

"I like him, but I don't trust him," Leif replied, squeezing her hand once more. "We should probably finish this food before it gets too cold."

He let go of her hand and used a knife and a fork as usual to cut his wheat into bites and then took a pull on his drink.

She smiled and nodded, holding her hand absently for a second before returning to her food. Just when Leif thought he could get used to this, their hostess reappeared with a slip of paper detailing their two bottles of wine, full course meal, one pitcher of beer, and the honeyed wheat appetizer. The check came to 187-mint, but only 17 of that had actually been consumed. Leif signed a check to the Hunter Bank across the street, and waited for Fryn to stand to let him out.

Fryn lingered in the bench, drinking slowly from her water glass, so Leif placed a hand on her shoulder to get her attention again. She shook her head, looked at his hand, flushed, and then swept up the envelope and started for the stairs leaving him behind to scramble out of the bench after her. Before long they were back on the sidewalk, shielded by the overhang of the building as the rain came down on the street in a fury. Fryn's wings drooped as she fashioned another umbrella and looked shyly in his direction, biting her lip, one hand outstretched. "It isn't very far," she said. He chuckled and accepted her arm, and her protection once more.

In the thick fog, the pitch-black starless sky, and the nearly impenetrable wall of rain, they could barely make out the lampposts set at each of the corners and the dull glow of the windows to the north. Leif held her arm more tightly, and and pointed at the sheet that separated the eaves of the building from the blanket of rain. "Maybe we should just find the thief in the morning?"

She shook her head, wings brushing his for a moment with a soft laugh. "I imagine we have an opportunity, being able to move about in this weather, and we should probably use it." With that she pulled him into the torrent, and they crossed over to the edge of the Commission Quarter. "It'll be easier if we take the Gardens around the tower," she said, pointing at the dark shape that rose from the center of the triangular district, "and then we'll cut through the offices to the Lodge."

"So we are going back," he teased, noticing how the planted clover drooped sadly over the stone benches in the miniature park around the tower. Sconces of amber starlamps marked the entrances to the surrounding buildings, but they avoided them, and slipped between two large stone-brick offices to the family-lodgings they'd found before.

As soon as they'd reach the doors, protected by a firm steel awning, which rang with the thunderous pounding of the raindrops, Fryn tossed aside her umbrella, and dry except for boots and coattails, pushed through the door into the lobby. "We are only stopping here for a moment to prepare."

The same receptionist as before nodded in their direction as they passed by and climbed the stairs two or three at a time with a wingburst, until they'd returned to their suite. They sat in the armchairs in the morning nook, and Fryn cut open the envelope, careful to avoid breaking the seal as Leif had. She extracted two sheets of rough double-weight paper, and narrowed her eyes.

"Still pretty much exactly like what the meister relayed to us, the Scissortail, the rumors about her theft ten years ago, and, wait... information that she was once a member of the Commission? He didn't mention that," she said, passing the first sheet over to Leif. He didn't bother to read it as she continued, "there's a rough sketch here of an area in the South Shade Quarter, looks like a warehouse near Sir Lyma's Aviary was the last location she was seen at..."

There was a knock at the door, and Fryn gave a start, covering her mouth with one hand, signaling silence. "Maybe they'll think we're out?" She whispered.

Trel's voice echoed through the door. "I know you're here," she declared, "I paid the secretary to tell me."

Leif shrugged and walked to the door as Fryn hid the papers in her jacket. He turned the handle and opened it with a painted smile. "And what might we do for you this evening?"

Yarrow leaned against the opposite wall, and Trel held her hand in the air, ready to knock again. "We had thought you'd join us for a game," Trel grinned, "I feel like it's been too long."

Leif could tell that it was really only Trel who wanted to play, since Yarrow covered a yawn. "We're rather tired from exploring the city, perhaps tomorrow would be better?"

She made a show of sulking, shooting a mean look over Leif's shoulder toward Fryn, who leaned back in her chair lethargically. "Well, give a knock on the door if you change your mind."

Leif nodded politely and closed the door, and smiled when he saw how relaxed Fryn had affected to be. "Really, there's little point in pretending *that* much." Her wings stuck out from the gaps in the back of the chair, and her closed eyes were angled toward the ceiling with a slight tilt to her lips. She had her arms spread out to the sides, and her legs stuck out before her. "You look as though you'd run around the city five times."

Her eyes opened, and she turned her head to look at him. "Close enough to that..."

"Come now, don't be like that," he walked over and leaned over her with a mischievous smile and a pulse of red to his wingtips. "We still have to go back out in the rain."

She leaned forward, closer to his face, looking away. "I can't exactly get up with you in my way."

"I'm too tired," he said, "maybe we should just wait on it."

She pushed him back a little. "No, this is our chance; we catch the thief, we get our prize, and then we have a holiday."

He caught her hand and pulled her to her feet, hesitating for a second, so close, wanting to hold her, but knowing it wasn't good timing. Letting go, he paced around the low table that had separated their chairs. "We're going to need that umbrella again, and it may take some searching to find the location... and there's no promise that she'll still be there." He held up a hand. "No one will be around to ask any questions so I propose..."

She interrupted, "that we merely take a quick look and then start fresh in the morning?"

"Right!" He pointed toward the door. "Well then, let's be off." They locked the door and stepped outside again, and Fryn resignedly made another icy umbrella.

"I am going to get a lot more elemental practice than I had ever intended," she said dryly, and swung the umbrella over her shoulder. This time however, it had a much wider brim, and Leif could tell she intended to keep a little distance between them.

Linger and Lost

Fassen:

South Shade Quarter

Corner of Midwall and Avian

Leif

It was still raining, though much slackened off, as they stood underneath the warm-colored unwarming light of the amber-stone lamppost. Fryn had maintained the overlarge umbrella for the entirety of their walk, which had somehow seemed all the colder after the former closeness. She hadn't taken his arm, or looked at his face, but had instead focused on the map and the note that they'd received from the meister earlier. He craned back his head, looking up at the frozen ribbed underside of her umbrella, and sighed, breathing out a column of fog that clung to the icy undersurface.

"This will be the location," Fryn said, obviously ignoring his melancholic display, "as for why the Scissortail would choose such a hiding place is beyond me... maybe this is the location of her fence?"

Tightening the fit of his black, oiled leather gloves, he took the umbrella from her hand, and held it up higher at an angle to let in more light from the lamp. "She is a disavowed Hunter, so it'd be best to thoroughly scout out the terrain—no telling what kind of surprises we might run into."

She glanced up at him, even though she was only slightly shorter than he was, with a mixture of a smirk and a thoughtful pout. "I was hardly imagining that we would just burst in through the door demanding to see her."

"Is that so? I thought that was exactly what you were intending," he replied in a mock imitation of Ieffin's tenor-like voice.

Fryn shook her head and examined the toes of her boots, wings flicking in pace with her thoughts. "We should take a quiet walk around this block, and get a sense of the layout. If we have to pursue and corner her, then we'll need to leave no easy way out."

"I still don't get why she'd steal this king's crown... what'd he ever do to her? It's like she got away free, and then risked everything for what amounts to an elaborate prank," Leif said brushing his chin with his free hand. "Still, if we are going to be lingering in the area for a bit, it would be... um... wise... to find some sort of pretext." He angled the elbow of the arm that held the umbrella toward her expectantly. "It is a trade district, so far as I can gather, and we just passed a Muersyn restaurant, most would think that we were merely walking off our dessert."

She replied with a playful frown, "your problem is that anytime you mean to do something nice, you have to make up an excuse for it, which negates the niceness of the thing you want to do."

He chuckled. "Surely you'd know by now that sarcasm is meant only to make things easier."

Sliding her arm through his, they affected an awkward gait, as if they'd eaten far too much mousse, and were trying to ease their discomfort. To the southern side of the block the Boulderwall loomed in the dark, telling only because it turned even the fog into a black mist. Below the wall, the irregular streets led to the offices and loading docks of an array of warehouses for some trading company whose sign on the far side of the street was illegible in the dim light.

They crossed over to the east side of the intersection, slightly toward the moss and flowerless beds of a nearby park, turning toward the north to examine the buildings more carefully. A three story structure with dormers on the north and south sides dominated the block that their quarry had supposedly hidden herself within. It was paneled in some kind of deep-brown flaky bark, cedar, Leif guessed, though he'd never been to Renholt, and the roof was shingled with finely cut slate. He tipped back the umbrella to look up, and caught a large raindrop on its edge, splashing water over his face and hand. He sputtered for a second and retreated under the eaves of one of the dormers and sighed.

"I thought it was bad in Frorin..." He said, shaking his head.

Fryn chuckled. "I'll have you know that aside from the occasional winter storm, it is quite temperate... if a bit cold."

Leif nodded graciously, as if pretending to believe her, and lifted the umbrella to guard their exit from their moment of cover. "If she is in this building, I just can't imagine why." He pointed across the street. "There're offices and marketplaces everywhere, it's far too busy for a wanted person."

Fryn lifted her eyebrows at him. "Maybe it's because you're from a small town, but it is far easier to hide in a crowd—change a hat, wear a scarf, or a new jacket, and you can vanish in an instant. It's probably why Mythrim was able to elude us for as long as he wanted before springing his trap."

"She's not Mythrim, it's hardly that difficult to catch her once we find her," he countered.

"She can hide better than he can at least," Fryn bit her thumbnail in thought. "Which makes me wonder, how did we get this information?"

They walked up the east side of the building, seeing that there were doors centered on each face, polished cedar planking that glistened from the water that'd splashed up from the sidewalks. The windows were shuttered, and the only light around came from the street lamps, which only lit the areas directly around them, as the fog thickened, and the night deepened, and they wondered why they even bothered to 'scout' the area.

"Four doors, but plenty of windows for her to use in a pinch, and she's most likely hiding in one of those dormers, easy to fly out," Fryn summarized. "What say we head back, and take a better look in the morning?"

"That sounds good to me," Leif said, tugging her along as he followed Miren Way north toward Boulder Street, on the way back to the Commission's Quarter. It was an easy stroll in spite of the rain, which fell heavier, but there were plenty of awnings and overhangs along the sidewalks. It seemed that no one was about, still hiding out inside, and when they had finally returned to the Family Housing Lodge, and come in through its heavy vinebark doors, the secretary looked up in surprise from a newspaper that he'd opened across the counter.

"My goodness, I hope you weren't caught out in the storm," he said, rising from his chair with a concerned smile.

Fryn released her reluctant hold on Leif's arm and crossed her arms. "Well, someone insisted on taking a nice evening walk…"

Leif chuckled and gave a shrug, "Not the best idea I've ever had…" He started up the stairs wondering why it had to be his fault, but let the matter rest. It was after ten when he opened the door to their suite, and he hung up his tan red-detailed coat and scarf on the pegs just inside the door.

Fryn followed him in and dropped her gloves on the low table opposite the wall pegs beside an unlit starlamp. She went to her door and stood there, looking uncertain whether she should go in, one hand on the handle. "I predict we will be accosted by Trel in the morning, should we try to make an early exit?"

Leif nodded with a smile as he adjusted his hair. "I'll be out here waiting by six, then maybe we can visit the meister again for an early bite."

She frowned as she turned the brass handle and let the door swing open. "You'll be waiting for me? I doubt that," she replied, and went in with a flick and a wave of her wings and hand.

He watched the door close, and heard the delicate soft 'click' of the lock, and went into his room with a satisfied smile. It wouldn't be proper otherwise. Though, growing up in Sendra, he'd gotten used to the thin walls and partitions of the tented estates. Some drapes were so thick and heavy that he couldn't crawl under them, and they were often tied together from one side, functioning just as well as any locked door. Then again, he'd gone off to the permanent housing of his school at ten, so he never had any opportunity to do anything foolish.

The bed was still unmade, so he left off his reminiscing, and went into his small room. The arms of his couch folded down, and the thin cushion on top of the frame turned out to be firm enough to soften the hard wooden frame. He opened the closet to the right of the couch and pulled out a finely woven gray sheet, tucked it around the cushion, and laying down a matching sheet on top of it, he layered a quilt and a felt throw, and stood back to admire the arrangement. The closet contained one of those old-fashioned Gaersyn night robes, a white sheer piece that served a useful function, but when he'd put it on, made him feel three times his age. He dropped into bed and fell asleep instantly and deeply, till awoken by a dream he could only partially remember.

Back on the Vineroad, with snow blowing past him, he saw Havrshyk standing before him, pointing the tip of his blackened Bloodsword at his face. His mouth moved, but he couldn't hear the sound, just the impression that he was gloating, threatening, or even laughing at him. Leif couldn't feel the cold in his dream, or the wind, or even hear it. The only thing he remembered was stealing Havrshyk's sword again, and cutting off his head, almost like the first time, but it took much longer, as Havrshyk countered all his strikes, and was ready for his every move. Even cutting through his neck took a great deal of effort; but when he did, he sat up in his bed with a victorious cry, and then leaned back covered in cold sweat. The sword rested in a slant against the wall behind his head, radiating chill, and it took a long time for him to return to sleep.

In the morning, he dressed quickly and waited in the lobby on the first floor for Fryn, glad to have beaten her even at something so simple as getting ready for the day. It seemed as though they were in a competition, or were playing a game without knowing the rules, and from her confidence, he'd been convinced that she was winning... but if neither of them knew the rules, she was just bluffing, and whatever it was they were doing, it was reasonable to assume they were at least on an equal footing.

He rested his feet on the low table in front of the bay window, looking at the morning paper unfolded across his lap, and his eyes glancing over the top of it at the fog that still filled the streets. No one else sat in the lobby, and the secretary, this time a young fee in a utilitarian white canvas uniform with grass-green detailing, had been kind enough to supply a tray with two tea-cups and a pot that smelled slightly of barley or wheat.

Leif poured a cup through the steel strainer balanced on the grass-blade patterned finch-bone china, and savored the rich earthy aroma that the cloud of steam dispersed throughout the air. He fanned it toward his face with one hand, wings settling behind his back so he could sit back against them comfortably, as he took the first sip. It was a simple thing, the morning cup of tea, but he hadn't had much opportunity to enjoy it as frequently as he used to when he trained under Master Yarl. The tea was definitely a mix of barley, and Haryn-leaf, and was robust enough that he was more than satisfied. Most of the teas he'd tried in Frorin had been too light, or thin, but here, the flavors of most of the food and drink weren't all that different from his native desert—perhaps a bit softer, with less pepper, or clove. He had finished reading the first page of the newspaper, and only just refilled his cup of tea, when Fryn descended the stairs in the company of Trel.

He was alerted to their descent thanks to the snippets of conversation that wafted down the air, since they had apparently flit down and around in a hover to create less noise for the other residents; ironically, their speech was louder than their footsteps would have been.

"...with the rain it was difficult to discern much..." Fryn's light alto demurred softly.

"...certain it was around there?" Trel asked.

"...o reason to suspect the information..." Fryn replied. They appeared at the top of the platform three steps higher than the lobby from around the rectangular spiral, and approached the secretary without seeming to have noticed him. Leif didn't move, wondering how long it would take.

"Still, to think you've managed to narrow down a lead in so short a time," Trel praised in a teasing tone, "almost makes one wonder if you weren't in on the whole affair."

Fryn's laugh was forced, but he doubted anyone else could tell; they didn't know her like he did—no, they didn't know her at all. He smiled as she responded with an icy undertone. "If that were the case, would I be so willing to cooperate?" He frowned, since when had she wanted to cooperate? Had the bounty on the thief and crown gone up?

As he mused over that thought, his eyes scanned one of the local headlines on the right page, printed clumsily in over-large movable type. "President Hans promises to equal crown bounty." He ran a hand through his hair and leaned his head back against the vinewood frame of the couch and stared at the ceiling in thought. *That would mean that he would be effectively doubling the reward, out of his own personal expense, or that of the Commission. Would the Commission really lose so much from the ongoing disgrace to the local crown?*

Fryn's face appeared above him, smiling with her dimples etched deep into her cheeks, and her silver hair falling forward—most was pulled back in a braided bun, but her short bangs dangled above her eyes. "So here you *are*..." she said softly, accentuating the 'are' a bit more than required.

"Last one down gets the dregs," he said, not moving his head, not wanting to lose that unusual perspective of her face, as he pointed with his left hand at the pot of tea on the table beside his perfectly clean and polished boots, crossed at the ankles in relaxation.

Trel snickered in the background. "I'll warn you not to deprive a lady of the better tea."

Fryn tilted her head, and flit over the couch, through the air in a flip, as she landed soundlessly on her toes and bent over to pick up the cup and pour herself some tea. It sloshed indelicately in the cup, and she settled into the seat beside him on the loveseat, purposefully leaning back on his wings.

He covered a grimace at the discomfort, and how the pressure of her elbow poked into the translucent weave of both his upper and lower wings. But it wasn't so bad, he realized, as she leaned over his arm and noticed the headline. "Well, it seems you know about it too," she said, so close, as she turned her head to make eye-contact. Then, as if she suddenly noticed their proximity, she flushed before she could drain her blood, and pulled away.

Leif laughed, coughing into a fist to hide the color of his own face. "I take it working in a larger team will result in the more expedited capture of this criminal, and serve to assuage the wounded pride and dignity of the King?"

Trel found a seat on the couch to his right, angled slightly toward the table to facilitate a feeling of inclusion. "When I woke up this morning, I found a note on my door," she said, alluding to a scrap of paper which she waved in her hand so they couldn't actually read it, "it appears Yarrow discovered the increase around 6, or so, and rushed out to file the appropriate papers for our collaboration."

Leif blinked and shared a look with Fryn, who lifted an eyebrow at him. "Do teams need to notify the Commission of their partnerships? Fryn and I never…"

Fryn looked away. "While you were still recovering from the Guardhouse Ball, I had to sign a great many forms, one of which was a certificate of our partnership, valid for the next year. You signed it as well, but you were still in the early stages of recovery."

Trel nodded distractedly. "If we wish to divide the bounty equally, we have to be registered as a team. If the Commission is certain of how many Hunters are pursuing a bounty, and with whom, then it is easier for them to coordinate the groups in case of a threat against the Commission."

"Threat against the Commission? This is just one thief," Leif complained, "and what could the Commission have to prepare against?"

Fryn frowned, placing a hand on his arm. "Three years ago, in Frorin there was an unexpected change in the owls' migration, and the city had to defend itself against their attacks for nearly a month. The Crown organized the Hunters in the city to assist with the defense. There are plenty of reasons to manage the movements of the Hunters in case of an emergency. If there had been more than that one weasel we fought, then… we could have been decimated in a matter of seconds. What if they had invaded the city here?"

He sighed. "Well, how long till Yarrow gets back? We should divide our forces to inspect the warehouses from separate angles to cut off her retreat."

The door opened on the north-east side, almost as if Yarrow had heard him, and waited till that moment to appear. He walked toward them without missing a beat, and passed a couple sheets of paper to Trel. He nodded to each of them, and sat beside his partner without a word. Trel mumbled about the division of funds for a second, and then, pulling a tiny glass stoppered bottle and a clean pen from one of the many loops on her leather belt, she signed the pages, apparently four of them, and then waved them over to do the same.

Fryn scanned the pages as Leif absently signed each one, and when she was satisfied, she nodded and dipped the nib of Trel's walnut-wood pen into the bottle of iron-black ink, and scrawled her name in one go, one line of cursive, with a flourishing line through the 'F" and "T" and no dot for the "I." Fryn Martin, a fine enough name, Leif considered.

He wondered about that for only a second, as she rose from her seat, placing a hand on his shoulder. "At least it isn't raining," she said with a smile.

"Yes, I suppose you're right," he answered, placing his hand on hers for a second with a wink. "But I am also rather famished."

Trel groaned in agreement. "I *cannot* express how much I feel the same way," she expressed rather effectively.

Fryn shook her head at this and held up an arm toward the door. "If you have some place reasonably priced in mind for a light breakfast, we will follow you, so long as we do not allow the other teams to get the Scissortail before us." Her wings twitched, ready to fly, but Trel seemed unable to make up her mind. "It isn't my first time in Fassen, yet, I can only think of places in Haryn or Rosenkraun: like The Thistleberry, or Mullinhaus."

Yarrow pinched his temples between his thumb and forefinger. "If memory serves there is a tavern near the Bounty Office, but their food is substandard and unsuitable for a morning meal."

Leif wondered just how expensive their tastes were. "I've found the easiest and most effective way to find a good meal is to simply stop in at the first place that piques your interest," he suggested, but Fryn shook her head quickly, three or four times.

"That would only add to the delays," she whispered, "do you really think they know what they want?"

"Serpents! No," he chuckled, "but neither do I."

The secretary caught their attention with a polite—and if he hadn't been in Fryn's company, what he might have thought, cute—wave of her white-gloved hand. "I couldn't help but overhear your conversation," she began, pursing her pink-glossed lips, and shifting her light brown forelocks out of her face, "but since it seems you are going toward the South Shade Quarter I thought I might mention that there are a number of cafés near the Southeast Gate along Boulder Street. They are quite popular among the merchants from the eastern cities, and even among the artisans of the local merchant guilds."

Trel's eyes skipped past them and landed squarely on the thin figure on the young uniformed fee. "Would you name one of them? I would be sorry to miss a fine location while looking for something non-specific."

She glanced down under the friendly, but piercing gaze, which reminded Leif once more of Trel's reputation as an archer. If the old stories were true, she'd once had a staring contest with an eagle in the wilds north of Stanaedre, and forced him from the sky—it was said that it crashed into a tree and died instantly. The secretary looked up proudly with redoubled determination burning in her eager green eyes and in the tense splaying of her wings. "The Lanjaeger is a fine restaurant with morning rolls and pastries to rival anything in Norenan or Pyrincel, and I am sure their quail-quiche is the rival of all you might find outside of the capitol."

Yarrow nodded slowly, slipping one hand into the pocket of his gray jacket, and fishing out a silver watch. "That sounds acceptable, come Trel, if we delay any longer, I fear our new partners will cancel the cooperation altogether." He looked over at them with a wry glint in his steel-gray eyes, black hair combed and shimmering from the aromatic oil that ran through it, only slightly grayed by age.

Trel winked at the secretary and dove out the door, turning a sharp corner into the alley that accessed the angled Shadowvine Way that bordered the Commission Quarter. A block further was the Five-Way where Shadowvine changed names and continued to the southeast as Boulder street, and from there it was roughly three blocks until they saw the wonderfully painted sign and the fenced balcony seating of The Lanjaeger, which occupied a triangular section all by itself, as if Boulder Street had cut a block in two.

Fryn whistled as she landed on the paved sidewalk, admiring the three-story café, and its dark-stained vinewood plank fence. Several steps up from the sidewalk, the balcony was occupied with six round tables. The morning sun burned warm, for the beginning of the Harvest, or The Vine as the locals preferred to call the month. For Leif, being from the desert, he simply referred to it as the beginning of autumn, since viticulture did not do well in Aelaete, and the constellation used to measure the month looked more like an outpouring saucière than anything else. So in their calendar, it was often referred to as the Feast.

A fae with wavy brown hair that hung partly over his eyes ascended a series of concealed steps from the cellars around the corner of the balcony, and stopped as he noticed them with a bag of rich-smelling flour in his arms, his dark brown eyes mentally darkening as he noticed their swords and travel clothes, but he warmed instantly. "The balcony is currently open, and tea is complementary with any meal for Hunters so long as the chase is ongoing," he informed pleasantly.

"Do we need to be seated or may we have any table?" Yarrow asked considerately, noticing that none of the tables were currently occupied.

"By all means, you may be seated wherever you would prefer," the café employee replied, "I will send word to our staff that you have arrived, and one of our servers will be with you shortly." He flitted up the steps and waited for them to settle in the dark-stained chairs under the southernmost awning and eaves of the café roof. The sun hadn't burned off even a fraction of the morning fog, but the streets were busy with the fleet-footed and quick-winged traffic of the first deliveries and commutes. A messenger flashed by overhead on the back of a dew-covered sparrow with dark brown spots, wearing a brilliant bright green scarf that set off her exuberant eyes, and the streaming black hair that was tucked under her Commission's Post cap.

Leif wished the Commission messenger's disguise they'd worn in Frorin had involved such free-flight, and such a finely tailored uniform, even though he'd only had a glimpse. Fryn watched him carefully for a few seconds, but finally looked away when the glass-paneled door to the indoor area of the café swished open and a twenty-something fee swept out with a bright green porcelain teapot in one hand, and a tray of matching cups and saucers balanced in the other.

"Almost like her scarf," Leif thought aloud under his breath as the teapot was placed in the center of their circular table, and cups were distributed with gentle ease.

"Helay," their server interjected with a cheery voice and matching smile, "welcome to the Lanjaeger Café and Waverly Cuisine Restaurant." She certainly didn't look like most of the other locals of Gaersheim that he had met before. She had an almost yellow or rose-gold tint to her hair, and amber eyes—both traits unusual to the region.

"Waverly?" Leif asked Fryn softly.

"In a minute," she held up a hand just slightly to stall him, and looked over at the server who stood across from her, between Yarrow and Trel. "Helay," she replied, "I've heard your quail-quiche is well-regarded around here, what else would you recommend?"

The server maintained her amiable smile as she nodded several times, wings flicking up and down in the same motion. "I am not surprised to hear that word of our quiche has spread throughout the Commission," she commented, "but there are a few other favorites for which we are known. My name is Elinya, and I will be your server today."

"Good morning," Leif said with a smile, but Elinya, though she accepted the token greeting with a slight blink and bow of her head, almost looked a little disappointed.

"Is there a special this morning?" Trel asked, unable to hide her eagerness.

"The Gysrahn rolls this morning are stuffed with finch-breast, smoked Waverly cheese, and dressed wheat-sprouts," Elinya replied.

Trel mulled over that for a few seconds before looking up sharply. "Two of those," she said, pointing meaningfully between Yarrow and herself.

Leif chuckled, and curious as he was what this 'Gysrahn' was, caught her attention and ordered the quiche.

"Anything for you, Lyr?" The server asked Fryn, the ties at the back of her apron falling and shifting as her wings twitched and disturbed the tied bits of string.

Fryn frowned. "Quail-egg Gysrahn, if you have it."

She nodded. "Should be ready in about ten minutes," she added, and swept back through the door.

By the time their food had arrived, the small clock inside the café chimed 8 and the incessant traffic on the street slackened off to a trickle of shoppers and errand-runners, and adolescents stealing off from their lessons to have some fun.

Leif's quiche was a steamy, fluffy bit of egg, cheese, and chives in a flaky pastry in a bit of green crockery. He was supplied with an enameled knife and fork, as were the others, with their flaky rolls stuffed with egg, or meat and cheese spilling out onto their plates; but before he could cut into his food, Trel held up a hand and pronounced in a strange accented utterance: "Linella søran helay" and closed her eyes in respectful silence for an instant before cutting off a bite of her food.

"What was that?" he asked Fryn quietly.

"I didn't study Waverly," she said, "but I believe their customs included showing respect before the Wing-Giver in all aspects of life."

He glanced away and then back again as a little color flushed through his wings. "I'd never even heard the word 'Waverly' before today… who are they?"

"Before Gaersheim was established as a cohesive realm, the Forest of Grass was ruled by three or four different clans or kingdoms. One of them was Waverly in the north. They were decimated by disease, famine, and disaster shortly before being annexed by the clan of Rosenkraun," she partially explained. "What Trel said, I think, was an old Waverly blessing or greeting."

Elinya had returned with a fresh pot of tea and paused beside the two of them with a conspiratorial smirk. "It is both. It means, 'By grace we greet the day' and is one of several similar expressions used in the language." She turned her gaze to Leif. "Helay means 'to face' in the old tongue and has often been used as a friendly greeting."

When Elinya had departed once more, Trel added, "what Fryn failed to recall was that many of Waverly descent think that the Rosenkrauns were responsible for the plague that followed the eruption of Mt. Waver, and used that to steal their heritage."

Something made a bit more sense. He drank from his fresh cup and appreciated the hints of mint and chamomile. "The village to the north, arranged in the same bouldered way… where we first found the Scissortail: that wasn't on any map. Were they outlaws?"

Yarrow shrugged slightly. "I have heard of nomadic or independent settlements scattered through the northern reaches of the forest. It wouldn't be too surprising if some of them were predominantly Waverly."

Fryn nodded, clearly more aware of this than he'd expected—whether because of her cosmopolitan education or the proximity to the area they discussed, he had no idea. "I'm not surprised you haven't heard of them," she added, "after all, they are a small minority of the population, and their history has never had much connection to the Aelaete."

He took a long sip in thought and finished his quiche before replying, "I suppose it didn't occur to me that there would be remnants of fallen civilizations since my clan's heritage goes back to the first ancestors... or so they claim."

Fryn shook her head with a laugh. "Everyone tries to trace back their ancestry to the first ancestors, the gods, the stars, or what have you: just to legitimize their rule or traditions."

Leif reviewed what he'd learned of the legends of Froreholt. "Such as claiming that the Martell royal line is directly descended from Arta?"

"Precisely... though I have no idea who your family is supposedly related to," she confided with a snide smile.

Trel held up one hand as if she had wanted to join the conversation, but closed her mouth when their server returned and left their bill on the table, clipped to a pressed-bark board and written in a flowing script on a piece of green-bordered stationary. Gaersheim it seemed, was a land fixated on paper.

Yarrow took the bill and examined it, narrowing his eyes as he deciphered the overly-decorative hand, and set it down again. Then, reaching into the pocket of his day-jacket, he retrieved a small leather coin purse with silver clasps, and dropped three 10-mint Gaersyn coins on top of the bill. "Now, we'd best be on our way to investigate those warehouses before our quarry steals a ride on one of the couriers' finches."

They rose from their seats, tucked their chairs under the lip of the table, and walked back down the steps on the west side of the patio. Fryn and Trel made certain to leave their knife and fork beside their plates, knife closest to the plate, with the fork beside it, tines facing the table. Elinya waved to them as she came out to retrieve their dishes, saying, "Mønsør fasay!" And Leif wondered whether he ought to learn a little more about their customs, especially if The Scissortail was descended from that clan.

Before long, they had flown back to the corner of Avian and Midwall, the same point they'd searched the night before, and stood in a small circle on the curbside south of the building that the informant had located for them. They were about to split off, Leif and Fryn to the east, and Trel and Yarrow to the north, when they noticed another conspicuous group of Hunters approaching from further north—who crossed the street in a quick bound and landed before the west-side doors to the warehouse.

"Serpents," Leif sighed, "I should've known that the other groups would get the same tip… as long as they're paying customers…"

"No exclusivity," Fryn finished for him. "Trel, it might be best if you watched from the south, Yarrow, the north. Leif and I will try to counter them from the east."

Trel winked as she closed a circle with her forefinger and thumb, and scanned the building through that little circle held up to her eye. "I knew we were alike," she said, "I'll guard this side." She reached down to a black vial fixed to her belt at the small of her back, partly hidden by her dark-green coattails and lower wings, and popped off the cork that was tied with string to the neck of the long-thin bottle. Immediately the black-red liquid swirled from the opening, and fluidly rushed through the air to swirl before her outstretched palm.

Leif watched in amazement as she pricked her opposing palm with a rose-thorn sewn into a fibrous bracelet on her left wrist, and drew out a tendril of blood from the wound. The sphere hovering above her right palm stretched out and coalesced into the stiff but recurve form of a long bow, with a black cord of fibrous blood tightening and pulling the ends together. Fryn swallowed, also impressed, as in the opposite hand, the tendril of blood from her other palm flowed into the delicate shape of a blood-red shaft with a black barbed end, and a winged notch opposing it.

"So this is the Blackbow," Leif whistled, "remind me not to upset you."

She spun the blood-arrow in her fingers, and maintained a perfect smile. "I know, it's beautiful."

As Leif looked around, remembering his and Fryn's role in the mission, he noticed that Yarrow had already disappeared, and was likely waiting in position north of the warehouse. He shook his head and followed Fryn to the east doors. Already they could hear raised voices, as the three Hunters who had preceded them into the building interrogated the workers. Fryn slipped through the door silently, glad for the commotion to distract from their entrance, as she held it open for Leif to follow.

They crouched behind an array of grain-stuffed barrels, listening to Grifton Francis question them in a severe and gruff voice. "I asked you, foreman, whether you had seen a fee matching this description…" He demanded, and the sound of his hand slapping a piece of paper followed. "Surely it cannot be hard for you to recall, with such an unusual face..."

"...really don't recall, Sir Hunter, I'm certain of it! If I had seen this fee I would tell you at once!" The foreman assured the eldest of the trio of brothers that they spied from through a crack between the barrels.

"I didn't know he was this intense," Leif whispered, "he honestly didn't seem all that impressive at the Harvest Festival."

Fryn's wings shrugged against his in silent agreement. "I can't imagine what they thought of us... that we just got lucky."

"We did though," Leif said, shaking his head, and turning back to watch the other two brothers as they walked around the edges of the room. "We should find a better spot to hide," he cautioned.

Fryn waited for the youngest brother, Germaine, to glance back toward Grifton for a second before flying up to the next level out of sight. Leif joined her at the next opportunity, listening and breathing shallowly.

"I told you, foreman, that you'd tell me the truth, and yet still you lie!" Grifton's exclamation came with a subdued *'thunk'* as if he'd slapped the fae with a brick, or struck him with the pommel of a sword. Gagging and coughing sounded from below.

"Hard to believe there're such fairies in the Commission," Leif commented, shaking his head once more. "Here they go tarnishing our reputation."

Fryn looked about to chuckle, but the pained cry of the foreman below distracted her from any humor. "I don't want to disillusion you, but there are a great many imperious Hunters; and few Hunters are especially liked up close."

"...thought I heard something up there," one of the brothers interjected, "I thought you said this was everyone, huh?" Leif peeked over the edge long enough to see the second-eldest, Gerard, trip the foreman with the handle of his lance.

"...there *is* no one else.... If there is... they're not mine..." came the scratchy-voiced reply.

"I see, a disavowal eh? That works for us. Gerard, you sweep the second level, Germaine, watch the floor, I'll go up to the top and work down." The orders issued forth in a quick series of snapped barks, and he unsheathed his sword as she leapt into the air.

"...Wingless-spawned 'tooth-of-the-mountain' my ass..." groaned the foreman in a near whisper. He exhaled forcefully as the youngest kicked him in the side.

"I heard that, you spineless fool; as smart and tough as a snail, that's what you are!"

"Germaine, cool down, no need to start a fire," Gerard admonished from the other side of the crates behind which they hid. "Nothing so far, Grifton, just one more corner to check."

His footsteps came closer, but before he even appeared, Leif and Fryn were surprised to see the thief slip around the edge of the crates and crouch behind a pillar as if making ready to descend. She looked up at them, eyes wide in shock, wings twitching as a breeze shifted through the window to her path.

Leif held a finger over his mouth, and waved her over, not quite sure why. The window overlooking the south side was open, and he knew that Trel had that side covered—and the brothers wouldn't dare to steal their prey so long as she had her bow ready. "Follow us out the window as soon as you have a clear moment," he whispered.

Fryn nodded at this, beckoning her closer, "We won't let them hurt you, and all we need is the crown... you'll be free to go... like we promised."

"Lia, we'll help you get out of here," Leif added.

She smiled softly and brushed her auburn hair out of her face, though most of it was already contained in the uncommonly thick and luxurious braid that draped around her neck, and dangled toward the ground. Then, she simply nodded, and waved, and faster than either Leif or Fryn could have matched with their eyes, she bolted through the air on a massive gust of wind, and disappeared through the window, the green tails of her long-tailed waistcoat fluttering silently as she went.

"What was that?" Demanded Gerard as he cleared the corner of the crates, the whites of his eyes expanding unbelievably as he noticed them. "Why are you here?"

Leif affected a yawn. "We were tracking someone, what brings you to this area of town?"

Fryn stood and stretched, her arms high overhead, wings splayed out to the back, looking long and thin, not unlike an ermine; dangerous, and sensuous all at once. Her hands were empty, but Leif knew that in an instant, she could be armed with that jagged-edged Bloodknife if the need arose.

Gerard narrowed his eyes, almost to slits, as he regarded them suspiciously. "I expected some competition... but not from you two."

"That hurts," Leif said, taking a deep breath as he sighed. "Surely we are equals."

Fryn looked away, and Leif suspected she already knew what the other Hunters thought of them—that they'd been lucky, and weren't really worth the attention that they had received.

"Tch," Gerard responded childishly, and took off through the window after her, Leif and Fryn just watching him go, Fryn hiding a smile. A dark red blur flashed by, as one of Trel's Blood-arrows sailed through the air, fastening its barbed head in one of the scrubwood beams supporting the next floor.

"Inbred five-winged..." Gerard cursed, "Who's that?" He'd barely dodged the arrow and hovered at the edge of the window looking down at the street. The other brothers darted over beside him, noticing Leif and Fryn for the first time.

"What're they doing here?" Germaine sneered.

"Forget about them, there's another Hunter out there taking our prey!" Grifton swept down to the door on the ground level, waving Germaine to the west. "Get back out there and draw their fire."

"Never thought we'd be in competition with our own comrades," Leif said, following the youngest with his hand on the hilt of his sword. "Keep an eye on Grifton," he suggested, "Trel can handle one lancer."

"Sadly, there are all too many mercenaries working for the Commission," Fryn added, flying to the ground, "Justice *is* rewarding... as they say."

Leif turned and followed Germaine out by a window on the west side, calling after him in a light slightly-mocking voice. "Now, I can't let you get in our way."

Germaine was already halfway to the southern corner, the air wavering around his fists like the haze above the desert sands, and Leif knew then just what an annoying elemental affinity he had. "Oh yeah? Same to you!" He snorted at this, and spat a thick globule of saliva onto the damp cobblestone street. He raised his fists, held close to his chest, by his chin, in what Leif had heard was the tradition of the Southern Gaersyn martial styles.

Landing smoothly on the sidewalk, Leif settled into a wide stance with his feet spread, and two thirds of his weight on his right side, and his fists closed and poised against his waist. Trailing webs of sparks wound down the length of his arm, tickling his fingers, and standing his hair up on end—not that he wanted an elemental challenge per se, but he figured that Germaine probably hadn't had much experience—but then, neither had he. Mythrim had used a sword to focus his heat; Leif wondered how Germaine's body could withstand it.

Germaine was light on his feet, wings up and out, as he stepped forward with a sly grin. "You wanting to rough it up a little, right?"

He found he actually did. Bringing up his hands, both loose, but ready to tighten if need be, he rose and stalked toward his opponent. The sword at his waist had collected a great deal of sparks, drawn to the iron in its blood, and Leif considered using it; only for a moment though, because he really wanted to test their styles.

He lunged forward, and was barely able to pull back and to the side just in time as the heat intensified around Germaine's fist, which screamed past his cheek like a red streak of lightning. Drawing his hand back by the wrist, Leif pulled Germaine off the ground, and slid under his hovering kick—a would-be counter—and thrust a charged palm into his stomach.

Germaine flew back, smoke rising from the front of his green felt jacket, teeth set on edge. "Elemental power is no compensation for a lack in style, or ability," he taunted.

"Funny, I was going to say the same to you. All power, no finesse." Still, if he actually evaluated the peculiar boxing style that he used, it was efficient, and its strikes looked as if they would deal a troublesome degree of damage. He circled the boxer, who balanced on the balls of his feet, turning to face him unperturbed. He circled closer, and faster, and with a wingburst he descended under the chin-high guard Germaine had been maintaining, and twisting his torso, and kicking from the ground, he struck Germaine across the stomach with his outstretched winglike forearm.

Germaine caught his arm with one elbow, and cracked him across the face with a sharp jab with his other fist scorching his cheek without flames. Rolling with the blow, Leif allowed him to hold his arm, as he 'fell' to the side, and placing his free-hand on the street, he rotated and kicked him on the side of the head. Releasing Leif's arm as he struggled to block, they staggered apart, breathing fast, and stared each other down.

"You're not as weak as you look," he grudgingly admitted, wiping away a dribble of blood from the corner of his mouth with the back of his hand.

"And you're a lot more… sturdy than I expected," Leif praised in kind. "That's a good trait for a Hunter."

Inside, he heard Fryn and Grifton's blades clashing in a clatter of ice and steel. They both looked toward the building, admiring the trading of blows, and the way that Fryn never gave an inch in her defense, and her opponent never let up in his attack.

"She's not so bad," Germaine laughed, "shame we didn't team up with you sooner… because we're not going to let this go…"

The fight inside the warehouse escalated, and Leif spied Yarrow rushing in through the northern door to Fryn's aid. Turning to the south, Leif called out to Trel, "Just take her and go, we'll meet up later!"

"Sure, as if we'll let you get away…" Germaine started to say, but Leif smiled and punched him in the face with a powerful burst of sparks— far more than he probably should have since they were technically affiliated—and watched in satisfaction as the youngest of the three brothers crumpled to the ground and skidded off to the curb. "Right now, Trel!"

The Scissortail flashed past, an expression of mixed thanks and concern as Trel trailed after her with her Bloodbow drawn. Gerard pursued from his window with his oak-wood-handled lance held back in preparation for a swing with the butt, as if he didn't want to fight the more veteran Hunter 'seriously.' Leif sped into the air and intercepted him, grabbing with both hands the other side of his lance so that they struggled for the weapon.

"Get off of me, you sand-viper!" Gerard complained, and pulling with his arms and wings, threw Leif off the lance and sent him flying into the side of the building.

Leif groaned and rubbed the back of his head, and noticed a small collection of ice-shards, as if his sword had subconsciously protected him from the worst of the impact, and sat up with a frown. "I didn't know anyone could fight with such strength in the air," he said, grinning as Gerard's face twisted in confusion and then broke into a smug smile.

"Do not underestimate the West-Haryn Spiral Lance," he replied maintaining his position in the air for a moment before shading his eyes to scan the horizon. "Well this is one corked situation…" He sighed, and descended to the street. "Best you stay there, Viper, we'll settle things with your wife soon enough, and then find where the Blackbow has our prey."

Covering his face with one hand, Leif hid his laughter with a mocking smile, in spite of the slight bit of blood that rushed to his cheeks. "We're not married."

"That's what they all say… but I can tell…" Gerard landed on the toes of his green felt boots, laced all the way to his knees, with his freshly-tailored finch-rider trousers that bloomed from his waist and then tucked tightly under the curled tops of the boots. He lowered his lance and balanced it under the crook of his arm, tucking his hands into the angled pockets of his military-cut jacket, and whistling as he passed the unconscious form of his younger brother. "Well I'll be corked… looks like he couldn't size up his competition." Then, he walked through the door.

Leif stood on wobbly legs, and bracing his hand against the side of the building, he looked inside. Fryn and Yarrow had boxed Grifton into the far corner, and forced him to stand down for the moment, but as the lancer stalked in through the door, Leif saw Grifton's eyes brighten and look pointedly at Fryn.

Gerard's lance snaked forward in a crooked path, passing through an impossible torqueing movement toward her heart. All pretense of camaraderie fading as Leif took in that silver arc, and opened his mouth, and almost before he could get out the words: "Fryn! Behind you!" She began to turn, and kicked away the point of the lance with her boot rebounding off the middle of the shaft, as its uncommonly long blade slid across her thigh and cracked her frozen skin—damaging her expensiv e trousers in the process.

A groan from behind him alerted Leif to the reawakening of the boxer, but it seemed that he stood with unnatural quickness, flexibility, and lucidity.

"I'll need you to stay back a bit, *Master* Aellin," Germaine struggled through sore teeth, but his fist was faster than anything he had thrown before, as it pierced through Leif's clumsily rising guard, and found purchase under his chin, and sent him spinning into the air.

Stars flashed before his eyes, and he felt very foolish before he blacked out, and landed on the street—thinking that he might have mistaken the starlamps for the stars themselves.

Stars and Scars

Fassen:

South Shade Quarter

Fryn

She felt the warning and concern through the quickening of Leif's pulse, before he'd even opened his mouth—and she spun on an instantly fashioned spot of ice beneath her boot, as she kicked and fended off the would-be lethal blow of Gerard's lance. Fryn smiled, one eyebrow arching up ironically, as Yarrow stepped forward so that each of them could duel one opponent... or at least she supposed that might have been his reason since he was an experienced duelist. It was with some regret that she noticed the five inch gash across her leg, and she pulsed in just enough blood to heal the shallow cut. It was suffused with light pink under the skin, and then faded in a matter of seconds, the blood used in the process dissolving and flaking away like rust. The trouser leg would not be so easily fixed, and the lower belt and buckle of her knife's sheath was visible through the hole.

Though Leif's body was something of a secondary reservoir for blood, she could not access the segment that comprised the Bloodsword Ieffin had forcibly bonded to him, however, she found, Leif's sparks-filled blood was ready and willing to be used by her. One eye glancing back to the door, she knew she was blushing at the thought, as Leif's heart quickened, and caused her own to accelerate its mad-dashing beat. Then, almost without reason, Leif fell back and away, and his heart slowed to an unconscious rate.

She couldn't keep an eye on him any longer, Gerard slashed across her chest, nearly damaging her new coat; but she was protected with a thick layer of ice, which cracked but otherwise caught and held his blade. Bursting forward with the momentum of her wings, aided by gravity as she went down, she copied something from Leif's style and twisted from her center as she outstretched her palm and launched her assailant back with a growing impact of crystal ice.

Fryn maintained her mask-like, expressionless face as she considered that such an attack would be fatal if she had made the ice shards sharp like blades, and even more dangerous, if she had imbued them with her blood. Backing away a step, she considered how the lancer fought like the ideal of his favored constellation.

"You're rather skilled, but you're nothing like the stories of Arta," she said, concentrating her blood in her legs and lungs and brain.

Gerard swept his lance in a dual-orbit arc and regarded her with a cold frown. "The students of my order live by association with that ideal, and with the motto that "Arta never lived." Stalking toward the south with the tip of his lance angled up toward her throat, his eyes burned, and the wind shifted to the north. "You're no Yndril, though you're 'fair.'"

"If for you, 'Arta never lived,' then 'Yndril never died,'" Fryn revealed her teeth in what she thought would normally be a pleasing smile, but which wouldn't show her dimples. It would therefore seem threatening without reason since no one but her friends would know that she had dimples. Strangers couldn't know what it was that bothered them.

"Known only as the *victim*, the First Bloodcrafter in the world—The Maggotless—and what? And that's supposed to be you?" Gerard smirked and lunged, his lance angled away from her, but slid into a parabolic pathway toward her face. "She is pathetic... and so are you!"

Gerard, she decided, was an offensive blight on the Commission, who in spite of his talents as a lancer, was wholly inferior in his identity and integrity. Anyone who'd blame Yndril for her fate deserved less pity than they got... and anyone who hated her because of what she'd accidentally become... couldn't expect her sympathy.

"Well, you and Fhorae can go enjoy the Wingless Cult together," she retorted with the blood draining from the rest of her body. "Because, you are an Ermine if ever I saw one... and oh how I have..."

"I don't care," Gerard replied simply, his blade glancing off an ice-enhanced shield put up with the flat of her blade. "You're just some five-winged orphan who cut off the sign of your own degeneracy."

"Haha! Think what you like," she spat, but it flew from her mouth like a tiny cluster of crystals. "I'll cut you a new set of eyebrows to mock me with!"

He laughed, and held back a second. "Now, now... that... hahaha, that was a pretty good one... hold on... hahahahaha, no, Grifton, you have to hear this!"

Fryn blushed. She'd meant that to be both threatening and offensive... but it appeared to have quite the opposite effect.

Grifton sighed, his sword never leaving off its defensive slaps and cuts against Yarrow's epee. "I heard it, Gerard, but I don't understand."

Yarrow coughed lightly in his gloved hand. "Do you wish to continue, or shall we pause to consider this conversation?"

Grifton ran a hand over his face. "Just stand down a moment, Yarrow… it's not as if I wanted to duel you just this second. Fryn… may I call you Fryn?"

"…yes…"

"What kind of threat is that? Here we are in competition, and fighting for our prey and for our pay, and you threaten to cut someone a new set of eyebrows? It'd be effective if it weren't so funny! Why, I almost feel like it's something your husband would come up with."

Fryn's face coursed furiously with an involuntary rush of blood, and she forced the rest of her blood into her knife, and what wouldn't fit, she stored in Leif's veins—which could hold a lot more than she expected. "We *aren't* married!"

Yarrow looked away, and Gerard crossed his arms, as Grifton greeted Germaine, the youngest brother, on his way back in. "What do you think, brother… shall we 'cut you a new set of eyebrows'?"

"What? It's not my fault, he surprised me with those sparks! And what kind of punishment is that anyway?" he demanded. "I don't deserve this!"

"See, the counsel is out, and that is not much of a threat at all." Grifton sheathed his sword. "Where's the thief?"

"Honestly?" Fryn shrugged. "I didn't even know she'd gotten away."

Germaine dragged in Leif's unconscious form by the collar, and dropped him unceremoniously on the floorboards in the middle of the room, standing between Fryn and Gerard, and Yarrow and Grifton. "I don't think he knows either, all he said was, "Trel, get her out of here!"

"If we're lucky, then maybe the thief was able to get away and both groups will be at a loss," Grifton added. "Gerard, either subdue her or secure an agreement to stand aside."

She shook her head. "I'm not going to agree to anything while Germaine holds onto my partner."

"Germaine…"

"Aye sir," he added, and scooted Leif in her direction with a shove from his boot.

She crouched and closed her eyes, wondering whether she could trigger his return to consciousness from the inside. Her ability to affect his internal flows of blood was not as free as she'd have liked, and try as she might, it flowed sluggishly as if it couldn't sense her haste. He could not be wakened. "Yarrow, I have something of a burden to mind here," she alluded.

"Fear not, miss Martin," he replied, "I could distract even three opponents for long enough..."

"You overestimate your talents, Yarrow," Germaine interrupted, "against the three of us, brothers, mind you, you'd last less than twenty seconds—because we know how to work together."

Grifton scratched his chin. "Whether that is accurate or not, I have no basis to say, however," he regarded Fryn and Leif, who two out of three had joked was her husband, obviously but irritatingly baiting her sensibilities, "we are somewhat related through our mutual connections to the Commission... and seeing as we have both arrived at the same location... doubtless thanks to the meister and his non-exclusive information... it seems it would be better to go our separate ways."

"You really think that's wise?" Germaine asked incredulously.

"No," Grifton said, lifting one eyebrow, "I don't."

"What?"

"Idiot." Gerard stowed his lance in a set of leather loops across his back and sighed with an aggrieved air. "Still, we're all exactly where we started at the Festival." He walked over to the doors on the north side. "I'm going back to The Vineskin. It's not as if I'm willing to kill them and then get kicked out of the Commission"

Yarrow let him pass and moved over to Fryn and Leif. "I think it would be most effective if we retired to the Lodge. Trel will likely contact us sooner rather than later."

She grudgingly agreed, wishing she'd had the chance to humble Gerard a little. "If you wouldn't mind lending me your wings." She picked up Leif, supported him with one shoulder, and waited for Yarrow to move to the other side. Together, they pulled him through the west door and flew back to the Lodge.

Making sure they weren't followed, they took a longer circuit to the south, to approach the Commission quarter from Earl's Street, watching the flights of the finch-post and the Commission's messengers pass by overhead. Leif's head rested on her shoulder, and she was almost sorry that she'd be putting him down as they got close to the family and team lodgings.

"I predict we'll find more competition the longer this chase drags on," Yarrow said, looking up at the eight outstretched limbs of the iconic Fassen vine—which still sported great clusters of grapes, and cast a wide shadow over the entire southern section of the city. "If Trel has the Scissortail in hand, then we should try to leave the city."

"There is the unmapped hamlet where we first encountered her," Fryn ventured, somewhat reassured that at least they didn't have to compete with Trel and Yarrow; it was trying enough racing and fighting with the Francis brothers.

"Unsurprising that she'd have hidden away up there... the descendants of old Waverly are private and secretive, and if she'd proved useful, they would be loyal in their defense of her." The graying black-haired duelist scratched his chin with his free hand, pausing at the Earl's Fiveway.

Leif knew little of the historical kingdoms of the region, and she was glad that her family had insisted on a thorough study of history. Ostensibly, she'd gathered, it was to protect her, and to enable her to protect their own posterity. "You're from the Capitol, Yarrow?" she asked.

"From the Rose District," he replied, "why do you ask?"

"I'm just surprised you know so much about the northern reaches of Gaersheim." She adjusted Leif's slumped body so that the bulky items in his jacket pocket, and the hilt of his sword, wouldn't stick into her side. "I thought that most would have considered such topics inconsequential."

"That may be the case, however, I have found it is often the overlooked and obscure who 'cast the greatest wind' as they say." He signaled her to rise to a hover, and they crossed the street, and entered the Lodge through the south-west doors.

There was a different secretary behind the desk, this time a middle-aged fee with worry lines around her blue eyes, and unevenly grayed streaks in her long braid. She barely even glanced in their direction as she slid an envelope across the desk, and returned to her busywork. Yarrow was gracious enough to hold Leif erect, allowing Fryn to step over and accept the parcel—which she turned over in her hands several times. It didn't tell her much, simply that the plain white paper envelope, sealed by a quickly pressed blob of green wax, contained a single sheet of double-weight card-stock. Even holding it up against the light showed no indication of decorative lines. If anything, it showed either extreme haste or hinted at a perfunctory nature.

She helped Yarrow fly Leif up the stairs to the hall, opened the door to her suite with one hand, making sure that Leif didn't crack his limp head against the frame, and dropped him indelicately into one of the two chairs in the entry by the windows.

The veteran Hunter watched her, taking a stand beside Leif, as she cut a precise slit through the envelope and dumped its single sheet into her hand. The envelope she discarded on Leif's chest, and the note, she angled toward one of the starlamps and scanned it.

"It's from Trel," she explained, wings ticking out the timing of her thoughts, "apparently she had time enough to catch one of the finch-post messengers and leave a note with them..." she continued reading it aloud.

F, Y, L,

I am still in the company of a certain feathered acquaintance, and we have decided that it is possible to come to an agreement; however not within the definite region of the vine, as it were. As such, we will be departing immediately from a certain gate in a certain direction. I have reason to believe that there is one suitable meeting place not too distant from yourselves, notably quiet and undisturbed. Your departure is not necessary altogether at once, but if Y would not object to bringing my things sooner rather than later, F and L would be able to move about less encumbered.

~ Until then,

~T

"That is quite mysterious," Yarrow looked up and away, "however there are some things that I can gather at first pass." He moved to the door, and placing one hand on the handle, looked back. "It would appear that your knowledge of the location will be required, but in the mean time, I will see about packing up what she will require."

Fryn held up a hand, the one holding the letter falling to her waist. "I will mark your map, but I think it would be best to continue to lease the rooms, so that if we manage to slip out of the city, our competition will not know outright."

He nodded. "Agreed. Though, I wouldn't have been able to carry all of our baggage by wing." Then, he stepped out, and closed the door behind him.

She absently watched Leif's unconscious face, smiling as she saw how crookedly he had been dumped into the chair. Their own map had only been slightly marked by Leif's angular hand, but their estimates would at least give Yarrow a good heading to find the hamlet even if she couldn't recall the exact distance they had flown. She frowned. Had they given the precise location of their fight with the weasel? Or had they just dropped off the claws and waited for payment?

Leif's eyes flickered for a moment, but he didn't wake—or rather, it seemed that he was lost in a dream. Fryn wondered if it were a pleasant one, or if she were in it. Shaking her head, she took a seat across from her partner and waited for Yarrow to return. She counted the beats of Leif's heart. It seemed the link she had accidentally created when she'd used her blood to heal him, after Mythrim had pinned him to the wall, had caused her heart to beat in time with his... at least when it was at rest.

The door opened a crack, and then more fully, without a sound, as Yarrow entered with a yellowed stack of papers. "I have the map," he said, passing it over with an arched eyebrow. "Though I find myself wondering whether this Scissortail will actually lead Trel to the same place that you are thinking of."

"We can only hope so, after all, Trel has no way of telling; she could lead her just about anywhere." Fryn stood abruptly, and fiddled with one hand in her pocket, and the map in the other.

He gave her a gentle shrug. "Then we will find them."

This time it was her turn to nod, so she did, and she spread out Yarrow's well-worn map on the side table next to her chair. The blooms of the flowers of the starlamp cast their mellow light on it, allowing her to read clearly the roads and cities of the entire region of Gaersheim. It was a much larger map than the one she and Leif had bought before the Festival, and even had a number of small villages penned in with a slightly lighter shade of ink. None of those were to the north of Fassen.

She found a small bottle of black iron-gall ink in the drawer of the side stable, as well as an elegant aluminum pen with a clean steel nib, and drew a dot roughly twelve leagues northeast of the city. It seemed that whoever had made his map had been knowledgeable enough to include the scattered boulders that littered the region—likely relics that had tumbled down from the mountains from some of the worst winter storms.

"I don't know the name of the place," she said, looking up as she cleaned the pen. "But if our thief takes Trel somewhere, it'll be around there." She stepped back and lifted the map closer to her face, blowing on the drying ink. Then, dabbing it with the note that Trel had sent, she folded it again and passed it back to Yarrow.

Leif still slept, and she wondered why she felt such a mixture of annoyance and amusement because of it. As if, she reflected, it was a relief having him nearby but inactive, though it was also an inconvenience. When she'd watched over him the night Mythrim died, fearing for his life, it had been a much different experience. Yarrow departed, and she locked the door before moving into her room to pack what little she had brought in her canvas duffle bag.

A few toiletries, two changes of day-clothes, and several pairs of socks filled most of the bag, and the crate of wine, now only five bottles, that they had purchased at the Festival comprised the whole of their baggage. Leif still had his drawstring bag, and she didn't know what all he had brought.

In a flash of intense curiosity, she remembered the small sandalwood box that Leif always carried, and she returned to the entry. Most often, when he wasn't busy, he'd have one hand in his left pocket. Hoping he wouldn't wake, she searched the pocket of his jacket, and found the thin box with the silver serpent on the lid, and pulled it out into the light of the starlamp beside him. The wood was dark, polished, or stained, or both, and the metal plate cut into the shape of a coiled serpent was smoothed by Leif's frequent polishing.

It needed no latch, the tightness of the joins of the wood was such that it held itself shut almost to a perfect seal. Cracking it open took a bit of effort, but she eased open the lid and her eyes widened in surprise. Lying in a diagonal, barely forced to fit, was the immaculate white narrowing curve of a section of bone—a chipped fang. It almost glowed in contrast with the darkness of the fragrant wood, and she remembered the trial Leif had alluded to before his being sent to join the Commission.

"Only by proving yourself in the Commission could you attain the title of Master?" She recalled. "But wasn't this enough?" She picked it up and examined the fatter end, sawn with a delicate hand by a fine-toothed instrument. The tip had broken off, and she could see the tracks through which its venomous liquid had flown. Fryn closed her eyes and felt her way through the coursing of his veins. There was something there, kept alive, foreign, assimilated, fused into the bones of his arm, constantly leaking and building a minute amount of poison; the missing tip of the fang She closed the box, and put it back in his pocket. If he'd woken right then, it would've been one of the more inopportunely timed things in her experience.

"The meister bears more careful examination," she said, standing back from Leif's chair. "If you would just wake up, we might continue..." She frowned, there might be a way, somewhat kinder than pouring water over his head. Closing her eyes once more, she willed the blood in his heart to pulse out more quickly, to beat faster, and bring him back to a state of wakefulness. It surged through his arteries a bit more intensely than she'd intended, and he gave a start and a gasp, as he staggered up from the chair—eyes wide and unfocused—as Trel's note drifted to the ground between his feet.

"Ah! You're up?" She asked, covering what she could of her own sense of responsibility for his uncomfortable waking. "That's good."

"Good?" He demanded in a strained tone, head spinning to examine each corner of the room. "Where? Why? What happened?"

Fryn folded her wings and sat back in her chair nonchalantly. "It's probably best to answer the last question first; you were knocked unconscious by the southern boxer, because you were foolish, and distracted, and so we were forced to drag you back here." She presented the room with one hand, her palm up like a merchant trying to sell drapes.

He blinked a few times and rolled his head, slowing his breathing, as he placed his hands on his hips. "Where's Trel?"

She glanced away with a smile, lowering her hand, and turning her head toward the window, she flicked her eyes back at him in what she hoped was a good blend of the mysterious and coquettish. "Trel escaped with the Scissortail, so far as we can tell. She even left us a note." She pointed at the slip of paper between his boots.

He bent down and scooped it up in his hand, wings stretching behind his back. "Oh, I'm so stiff," he said, scanning the single paragraph.

"What does she mean? *A notably quiet and undisturbed location?* Have you been there before?"

"Haha, yes, I have... with you," she replied with a light laugh escaping her attempt at seriousness. "You see, notably quiet can only mean that it is isolated, not far, but far enough... like where we just encountered her."

Leif looked at her with a thin smile, which widened as understanding spread down from his eyes. "Of course! But... won't the Commission move to collect the weasel there?"

"I honestly can't say," she said, standing again and spreading her arms wide, and twisting her torso side to side to loosen her back. "But there is only one thing we can do."

"Indeed," Leif stepped through the door to her room for a moment, and returned with the Norenan wine from the crate they'd bought at the Festival. "We need to enjoy the evening, and pretend we don't know where she is. In the mean time, we can plan our rendezvous with Trel and Yarrow."

There were only three bottles remaining in their crate, a Norenan, a Pyrincel, and a Rosenkraun; she wondered what criterion he'd used when he chose that one, if any, but with his only just having been unconscious there was a chance he had confused his sense of time.

"Not yet," she said, shaking herself from her reverie, wanting almost as much as he did to open a bottle and relax, "we should wait until the evening. It is still barely past noon. I had thought it best to go question the meister again, see when and how he set those brothers after us."

Leif affected a forlorn expression as he set the bottle on the table by his chair and adjusted the placement of the cuffs of his coat. After he'd been trained by Jason in the gentlemanly art of service, she noticed, he'd been much more attentive in his grooming and presentation... and even if that had been the only thing they'd gained from their training, she admitted, that wouldn't have been a wasted effort.

She watched him in his semi-trance, brushing off imaginary pieces of lint from the front of his coat. Yes, in the past he'd had a rugged sense of desert-charm, but now he almost seemed refined, and genuinely interesting, as if some of Mythrim lived on in him.

"Are you going to get ready?" he asked, flashing her a smile with his incredibly white teeth.

"I was already ready," she answered, rising from her chair and flitting to the door in a single fluid movement. "Because I did not waste my time when you were wasting yours," she added, lifting one eyebrow with the final syllable.

"Really," he said, shaking his head, "you are impossible."

"Don't forget it," she said, opening the door and stepping out. "We have much to do."

"And much more to be seeming to be doing." Leif followed her out and locked the door with a brass key as she led the way to the stairs.

When they were back on the street, Fryn pursed her lips and looked over at him. "Do you still have that note?"

"This one?" Leif presented the notecard, folded into a quarter of its size, which he held between two fingers.

"No I meant the other one," she teased.

He shook his head sadly. "I'm afraid I can't let you read those letters yet."

Playful as the conversation was, she paused as she considered the slight seriousness of his tone, which intimated that he actually had some other letters. Was there a hidden compartment in that box? Or some custom that required him to write mysterious letters to an unknown, and possibly significant, fee? "Well," she said, looking at the piece of paper, "I recommend we find a match and burn it."

He nodded distractedly, his eyes tracking the outline of the various buildings across the street. Then, a spark of bluish light flickered and flashed from his wrist to his fingertips, igniting the corner of the little note. He unfolded it and let the flames lick their way almost to his fingers before dropping the burned scrap of paper and ash to the sidewalk, and twisting the toe of his boot on it to put it out.

"It seems there's no end to the applications of your element," she said, smiling playfully, "I wonder what you'll surprise me with next."

"I can't tell you, it's a surprise." He took to a low hover and led the way back toward the Vineskin. "At any rate, I'd rather get this business of talking with the meister over with."

She agreed, but said nothing as he swung to the corner entrance and held back its overweighted door, with a sweat drop forming on his forehead. "I'm really starting to dislike this place," she whispered to Leif when the door closed.

He placed a hand on her shoulder, just beside the more sensitive wing-joint, and it was warm—stirring a forgotten feeling, a nostalgia that seemed like it didn't belong to her. It was vague and… pleasant.

"I admit, I wish we could just go back to that Waverly café." He hung back, allowing, or more likely, prompting her to lead the way.

Once more, the disheveled server greeted them with a scrap of linen tied around his head to keep his unfashionably long hair out of his eyes. "Hello again," he offered, winking at her with a cheeky smile. "Come to taste our fine foods and drink again?"

"In good time," she provided, wrinkling her nose at a stray scent of anise or fennel from the kitchens, "we'd hoped to speak with your *manager* if it wouldn't be too much of an inconvenience."

"Of course, m'lady, it's nothing of the sort," he replied good-naturedly, though it seemed he hesitated, ever-so-slightly, to meet her gaze. "I will seat you upstairs then, and let him know that you are here." Fryn recalled unhappily that the serving boy shared his first name with the unpleasant Hunter who'd incapacitated Leif not too long before.

Germaine led them past the fire—even though most of the tables were empty, save one, which was seated by a single young fae who occupied himself with a well-worn book—and led them up to the third level. They were placed in one of the further dormers from the stairs with a southerly view of the city, where if she angled herself just so, she could see the Fassen Vine.

"You know Fryn," Leif said sitting down beside her with a sigh, "I'm serpents-tired of this game already."

She chuckled. "You and me both. Hopefully the meister will be gracious enough to pay for our drinks since he sold information to the competition."

"Greetings, Viper, Lich," the meister said, appearing as if from nowhere. He probably flew up to surprise them. "I think, even though it is my business to whom I divulge information, it would also be bad business to leave a Hunter unhappy with my service—so Miss Martin, I would be only too happy to offer you a glass of today's Fassen Wine."

"You are obliging as always," Leif replied sarcastically in an exaggeratedly deferent tone.

The meister laughed gently and sat across from them, parting his coattails to prevent wrinkles as he folded his wings. "I must say, I am surprised that you were successful in preventing your competition from securing the prize… though at equal price…" He looked over to the stairs as the coming footsteps announced Germaine's entrance. "A bottle of the '784 Fassen red blend, if you would, Germaine."

Germaine had only just become visible, but he stopped and nodded, which looked rather odd, Fryn reflected, as they could only see his head. "I will return shortly, meister."

Apparently, shortly meant only a few seconds, because he returned as if he had only gone down the stairs, with three glasses balanced between the fingers of his left hand and a nondescript bottle in his right. He set them down with practiced ease and produced a walnut-shell-handled corkscrew and opened the bottle with a loud satisfying 'pop,' and left the bottle on the table with a folded green napkin wrapped around its neck.

"Fassen red blend," Leif asked, "isn't that a contradiction in terms?"

The meister leveled his gaze at Leif with a barely-restrained sense of ironic irritation, as if he was tempted to laugh, and hit him in the face at the same time. "It is *primarily* Fassen grapes, and so, it is named after that fact."

"Oh indeed?" Fryn found that she couldn't resist the temptation to tease him, and she blamed Leif. "What percentage?"

Leif flashed her a wide, knowing smile, his wings brushing against hers, like a nudge of the elbow. "Yes, I would like to know to what degree this is counted as a Fassen wine... after all, you said that we should drink Norenan."

He poured the first glass with a slightly jerky movement at Leif's words. "It is ninety-five percent Fassen... two percent Rosenkraun... and three percent other varieties—whatever they had on hand." He finished pouring with an embarrassed smile and set the now-empty bottle on the side by the window. Then, sliding two of the glasses forwards, he glanced out at the view for a second, and then picked up his own glass. "To amiable business relationships," he half-heartedly cheered.

They clinked glasses, but Fryn could feel Leif's mischievously quick-beating heart as he took a drought and then grinned. "You couldn't think of anything else?"

The meister bristled, but relaxed with an awkward chuckle. "No... I could not. What would it take to appease you slippery Hunters?"

Fryn sighed dramatically and looked out the window. "I'm afraid... either a partial reimbursement, or..." She let the thought drag out, and wondered if Leif would continue with the right phrase.

"With new and relative information!" He *had* caught on. That was good. She met the meister's eyes and smiled sweetly without her dimples.

His tension seemed to melt from his shoulders and neck as he gave a single laugh. "You are far too easy, and yet frustrating, to work with. Yes, I can offer you something as long as you help me polish off this moldy, rot-berry wine."

Her eyes widened at his vulgar phrase, but she shook it off; to the best of her knowledge the free use of expletives was a sign of membership in a more private tier of 'closeness' and signified a better relationship. At least, that was what Harissa had said of Gaersheim the day before she left Frorin.

"I do have something you'd appreciate to know, my bloodless friend, and it really has a lot to do with you. You see, our Earl is rather young, and has a reputation for being… exuberant and busy. Many will attribute his flighty personality to his birth-moons. He was what? Vine, Forest, Star? That is correct if I recall." He shook his head sadly. "It is fae like him that encourage the poor and the stupid to believe in such silly superstitions." His use of the epithet 'bloodless' was wry and teasing.

"Well?" Fryn prompted, leaning forward over the table toward her glass. Then, thinking better of the motion, she glanced over at Leif and took a long drink of her wine. The meister watched her face as the blandness of its flavor washed over her, with its tart, cloying jammy-ness clinging to her throat. She coughed, and frowned at their host. "We may…" she coughed again, "deserve something better than this after you give us the news."

His eyes reflected a quick twinkle of the starlamp's light as he switched his gaze to Leif. "I'm afraid that when I tell you, you will not want to wait for it—so, I will require you to drink that glass, because cheap or not, it would be a shame to waste."

Leif drank deeply from his glass without any difficulty, as if even after all his experience tasting fine wines in Frorin and at the Harvest Festival, he still retained his bucolic ignorance of flavor.

"Lord Loren has decided to go and visit the body of the weasel the two of you had slain in order to confirm your story before releasing the funds. I hear that Vinellin, his butler, was distraught, having to venture into the unsafe expanse of the Forest of Grass." He regarded them with an intimate and sly grin as he continued. "I almost think his discomfort is worth telling you for free."

"Then… it is?" Leif confirmed.

"Hardly, I am losing more than I'd care to admit. Still, I imagine that this information is relevant to you today at least, since he has only just left for that unmapped town," the meister said, waving a hand leisurely toward the window.

Leif and Fryn shared a look.

"My sources of information are limited, but even I suspect that you have some reason for concern. Even so, I will require you to finish your wine before you go." He added the last part with an evil grin.

Fryn suspected he had set this up. *So much for our bluff to keep the Brothers guessing…* she thought. "Then I hope you get caught in the rain without an umbrella." She raised her glass, expecting them to cheer.

Leif, of course, raised his glass to hers, and they both waited for the meister to join in.

"I'm not superstitious, I'm just suspicious…" He lifted his half-full wineglass and clinked it against theirs. "Now drink your swill… I have a hard enough time giving it to the drunkards on the workday mornings."

Some thanks. They made a show of drinking what they could to be polite, and Fryn thought all the while about what they would inevitably have to do, and how far they'd have to go, if the other Hunters caught up with them.

The meister set his glass down as they finished, and watched them with level, calculating eyes. "You now know why they call this city 'Fassen,'" he said with a smirk playing at the edge of his mouth, "it used to be called 'Fas-set,' but it changed."

Fryn stood by the edge of the table, and Leif waited by the stairs.

"Fassen means 'thrown away,' and Fasset means 'flown away.'" He finished his wine and frowned. "The last survivors of Waverly counted themselves as discarded, and even their grapes, were 'thrown away' and you can see that it is the same of their Earl. He is overripe. Fryn Martin, be wary if the grapes smell sweet. Even those in power have those that they might fear, and the Earl has his own competition. Careful that you don't catch the attention of the wrong faeries; Wellsey is self-important and Pyrincel is arrogant, but Vassidel and Hasryth have even won in the Grassblade Tourneys…"

She glanced over at Leif, and then moved slowly in his direction. "I am always careful," she finally replied, and suppressed a shiver as she descended the stairs.

"He's the one who smells too sweet," Leif commented under his breath, "my people say, 'beware the one who tells you to beware.'"

Fryn shook her head to keep herself from laughing outwardly at his comment; she'd been thinking something along the same lines herself.

Forest and Vine

North of Fassen:

Forest of Grass

Leif

Leif dodged another bunch of wild grass, veering too close to the next so that his path would be impossible for any followers to track. It was more than likely that the Francis brothers had either heard about the Earl's movements, or that someone had told them what was on Trel's note, or that the meister had betrayed them for a pittance as soon as they'd gone... but no matter the meister had done, there was only one thing they could do—and that was to fly as quick and as straight as they could, to find Trel.

Fryn thought that they should tell her to take Lia out into the Forest until things quieted down, but Leif figured that the brothers, if they managed to follow, would watch and wait until they met up again. That would give them little time, but it would be enough, or at least he hoped it would be. The sun glowed low on the horizon, slashing dark shadows from the grain-stalks across their flight-path, but they could see the tops of the boulders up ahead, and would be safe before night fell.

"I don't want a repeat of the last time we visited this town," Fryn informed him, speeding ahead in a gray flash. The four panels of her travel long-coat fluttered around her legs, spinning as she turned to fly backwards with a cheeky smile on her face. "But then, I doubt there're any more weasels brazen enough to jump the boulder wall. Besides you, of course."

Leif gave a snort. "I am hardly a weasel. I doubt they'd bother anyone when there's a *real* monster around."

Fryn laughed, as if she'd forgotten the pressing matter of the Earl, Trel, and the brothers. She settled on the boulder overlooking the unnamed town, the same rock they'd landed on previously, Leif suspected. Her boots sunk almost to ankle depth in the coating of lush green moss, and well past his when he landed beside her. She wasn't smiling. Under the last orange light of the setting sun, the town was clearly visible below—built of several rings of houses and barns in concentric half-circles from the center to the eastern side of the clearing, which were framed by a carefully maintained row of strawberries, clover, and an aviary on the west. At the center of the city, bordering the first barns and houses, was a large well set in the middle of a circular plaza. Congested by a large gathering of liveried finches or sparrows, as well as an extensive entourage who surrounded the brightly-dressed figure of a fae who stood making a proclamation from the well.

The townsfaeries gathered loosely around him, but from a distance it was hard to tell if they were pleased with what they were hearing; only the presentation of the weasel's skinned pelt brought a ragged obligatory cheer.

Leif led the way down to the pebble-stone plaza in a quick glide, and waited for the Earl to notice them; and he did, immediately. He stopped mid-speech and gaped at them, amber-lined wings twitching.

"A'a'and here they *are*!" He articulated, pointing with one thin-fingered hand. "The great weasel-slayers!"

"We're hardly 'great' my lord," Leif said coolly, suddenly recalling the meister's unenthusiastic appraisal of him.

"NONsense," he countered, "this has been, well still is, a standing bounty for decades. I understand that the bounty was too little to encourage Hunters to pursue it, and so I wished to thank you personally for protecting my people!"

"Definitely a Vine," Fryn commented idly, as if she were testing the local superstition.

"I want to hear all about it," the Earl continued.

"What, really?" She stared at him for a moment, and then scanned the interested eyes of the miniature crowd. "Are you sure?"

One of the nearer strawberry farmers nodded seriously. "*Someone* left that body for us to clean up, we'd like to at least know who to thank for the trouble."

"You can thank these two Hunters," Earl Loren Fassen interjected with a gleeful smile on his too-pale face. "They also rid the world of one of the most notorious assassins this side of Elin."

"We don't care about Elin," one of the townsfae replied. "What are you going to *do* about the work we had to put in to get rid of the stench?"

He glanced away awkwardly, eyes darting to meet those of his valet, a tall gray-haired fae in a form-fitting black uniform and a bowler hat. "I have an idea about that exact problem, you see, I wanted to hear the story, and you would most likely enjoy some recreation... so, I initiated a plan to host a local festival in honor of the weasel slaying."

"Some weasel slaying, it took three faeries," one of them complained.

"How'd they know that?" Leif asked, looking to Fryn for the guidance she had no way to supply.

"I don't know!" She replied under her breath.

"Well," the Earl interrupted, "I'm sure we'll all find out when we hear the story around the fire with several bottles of my proprietary wine."

"Fassen wine?" More than a few of the faeries whined.

Leif smirked.

"It's *my* wine, so you can take for granted it is drinkable and well aged. The bottles I brought are at least '765 vintage." He paused for effect, and frowned as no one reacted. "That's a very good year!"

They relaxed a little bit, and waited for him to continue, though Leif just kept searching for Trel and Lia, the Scissortail. He wondered why he hadn't studied the more notorious or famous figures before becoming a Hunter, but at the time, it had seemed more important to focus on building the skills he'd need to face any occasion, rather than tailor his talents to specific challenges. No, he wouldn't have done it any differently if he'd known he would face Mythrim, perhaps he would have trained more with a sword... but aside from that, he'd taken a long-term approach.

Earl Loren hopped down from the well and waved his footfae forward, tossing an arched eyebrow at his disgruntled butler. "Bring a '759 for myself and the Hunters to share, Vinellin, or you'll find yourself earmarked for the next flight back to Zella."

Fryn leaned close and supplied the answer to the question Leif had forming on his lips. "That's the nearest region of Elin."

"But how'd he get here, and why?" Leif asked, scratching his chin.

Vinellin shifted his gaze to meet Leif's eyes. "By the Norenan Air Express ship. To train up the Earl in the proper niceties of his station, and to improve the status of the Gaersyn landholders."

"Ah, yes, I see..." Leif didn't, but he let it pass. "Is this going to be another folksy dance?"

"I hope not," Vinellin sighed, adjusting the tilt of his bowler hat, and then tracing his unusually long and angular jawline with his fingers. "From what little I understand of the area, the Waverly are not very festive, something about it being unbecoming." The butler guided them to a clear space beside the well and snapped his fingers, summoning a group of attendants who assembled a long table in moments, and brought over two equal-length benches that they somehow had harnessed to a carrier-sparrow.

The Earl seated himself and waved for Leif and Fryn to sit across from him at the end of the table facing the town, grinning, as Vinellin placed three crystal glasses on the table. They were cut with a stylized variation of the standard Vine constellation, so that the stars were overlaid on a view of the Fassen Vine from the side. The stars didn't fit very well.

Leif poked Fryn's leg to get her attention, so no one else could see, and pointed out the glasses. "Very fine crystal, Earl Loren," he lifted one eyebrow toward Fryn.

Loren caught the motion and frowned. "Yes, I have heard it before, but I like them."

Vinellin coughed as if he agreed with Leif's opinion, and poured a rich blood-red wine from a dusty green glass bottle in one movement, without spilling a drop, as he filled all three glasses evenly.

The wine actually smelled good, in fact, they could smell it over the scents of the farm, or the boulder-moss, and the grass-roofed houses. It was almost like the strawberries, but less sweet, or cloying, and not heavy like the musk of the decaying greens or tilled ground. Leif wondered how they manage to till so much earth, but was quickly distracted, as the Earl interrupted.

"My congratulations and thanks, for making my lands one weasel safer," he toasted, slinging an almost petulant eye toward his butler. "For though some of us do not understand the dangers, my people have always been wary."

He didn't respond to the obvious jab, and merely walked over to instruct a few of the servants to prepare the meal. Leif half expected the townsfae to ignore the proceedings, since they'd been so annoyed by their Earl's arrival, but they dutifully began setting up more tables, and even stretching lanterned ropes between the eaves of the nearby houses and a few posts spaced around the circle to the covered well. A farmer brought out a scuffed, worn case, and produced a working fiddle, and set up a stool on the well's step.

Then, Trel appeared at their table.

"Why if it isn't little Loren!" She declared, setting herself directly beside him with a smile.

He nearly jumped at her surprise entry, and his mouth moved a few times before the words came out. "The Blackbow, here? What are, why...?"

"I wanted to see the prize of course!" Trel waved a hand toward Leif and Fryn. "I also wanted to see them again."

"Helay," Fryn said, greeting her in the traditional Waverly way. "You see, my Earl, Trel has only just recently agreed to cooperate with us to catch the thief who stole the Harvest Crown."

"Oh I see," he said, turning to Fryn. "Well I'm glad we won't have to wait long for justice in that department."

Leif spotted Lia Karyn, their server from the Harvest Festival, turned thief, wearing farming clothes and blending in with the others decorating for the impromptu celebration. She was instructing a little girl on how to braid a garland of clover sprouts into a crown. *"How appropriate,"* he thought. A shiver ran up his spine, and he shook his head. Ever since he'd gotten Havrshyk's sword, or been healed by Fryn, he'd felt slightly more cold than he was comfortable with, and equally unable to warm up completely.

"Trel, my dear, is your impeccable partner going to be joining us tonight?" Loren asked.

She glanced away, surreptitiously keeping an eye on the theif. "I am not sure. If he is, then it will not be right away." Then, she smiled, as the little girl trotted over and presented the crown she'd woven to the Earl.

"This one is for you fyr," she said, staring innocently up at him.

He paused, and took it gratefully. "Thank you, I will wear this with pride." He put it on and nodded seriously, and the girl ran back to the thief to begin working on the next one. It was a little small for his head, but he looked around the table beaming. "It is a very good sign in these parts to receive such a gift."

In Aelaete, Leif had been able to attend most of the local functions, even while training with Master Yarl; but he hadn't noticed any sort of significance to the gifts they had exchanged. Usually he'd had to perform duels for the locals to admire and place bets on—without the use of sparks or any elements of course. "It does look very fitting," he admitted.

They sipped their wine quietly, enjoying the darkening sky as it faded from orange, to red, and the shadows from the boulders blanketed the clearing in a pleasant shadow. The tiny glass oil lamps hanging from the ropes cast pools of warm light around the circle, and the farmer with the fiddle began to play. There was no announcement for the beginning of the party, just the fading of the last light of the sun, no speeches, no orders, just fee and fae sitting, or talking, or sipping from their cups.

"They really aren't ostentatious," Fryn mused, "this is a nice party though, no pressure, just a relaxing gathering."

Lia, the Scissortail, surprised them with another unexpected skill. She stood beside the fiddler, and began to play on a strange flute, all wood, with a reed mouthpiece, and a low humming sound. The little girl danced with a few other children before the well, spinning in slow circles, and trading places with each other through the center, and Leif watched, wondering when the adults would join the dance.

A few stars of the Vine shone almost directly overhead, the most of its branches obscured by the ominously large and full greater moon, and Leif stood. He winked at Fryn, and took her hand before she could object, and led the way to the foot of the well's step, and when he saw an opening, he pulled her into the circle, and spun her out to the opposite side, where they took the hands of the nearest children and spun and twirled with their shocked laughter.

"You're not supposed to join yet," one of the older boys said, shaking his head as he traded spots with a girl who looked almost exactly like him, with matching shoulder-length curly brown hair, and a thin pointy nose.

"But we don't know that," Leif countered, spinning through the center to switch with the boy who'd spoken.

Fryn was pulled around by the girl who'd been making garlands, and then ejected back toward the tables. "Not yet, miss!" She pronounced, and then smiled at Leif, and the other boy caught him by the shoulder of his jacket, and spiraled him back toward Fryn.

They sat back down, Fryn looking relieved, Leif frustrated, and the townsfae just hiding smiles at their expense. The Earl laughed openly. "Really, you should know better than that. In the north here, it is the children who begin opening ceremonies, because they are the ones who are the future—and it is the future we should always be building towards."

Cryptic as the explanation was, Leif supposed it made a sort of cultural sense. After all, in Aelaete, he and the other children were basically entertaining the adults. "What do you think Fryn?"

"I think you're lucky to look so obviously like a foreigner," she sighed, "if I were to do that on my own, some might think I were Wingless sympathizer."

"A bit dramatic," he countered, drinking lightly from his wine. "Still, we've never had to deal much with the cultists in my lands."

Loren frowned, and stared into his wineglass. "My people know only too well, that some things are best forgotten, or destroyed." He looked over the top of the boulders to the northwest. "The kingdom of my ancestors was destroyed in a night, when the wrath of the mountain fell, but we survived, in exile. Many blame the former kings for converting to the Wingless, for what they did to their neighbors and themselves... but who can say it wasn't just a natural phenomenon that wouldn't have happened anyway?"

Vinellin hovered nearby, seeming intensely interested in the conversation.

"Jakaren, the Wingless Prophet, was said to come from the Ice Wastes east of Stanaedre, after he was cast out by his people. This was around a thousand years ago I'd guess, but he had an unnatural elemental strength, which he attributed to his sacrificing his wings— saying that you didn't need to become a Lich in order to have power." Loren looked toward the children and smiled. "Of course, the practice has been forbidden since Rosenkraun... but there is always someone who tries to promote it."

"Doesn't sound natural," Leif said, shaking his head. "Still, we are here now, and if it's any comfort, I hear that the Renholt clans do far worse."

He actually seemed to brighten at that. Leif suspected that being descended from a group associated with evil, or taboo, or an incredible sense of guilt, could be difficult; and it was always comforting to have that alleviated.

"Indeed, in my homeland, we fight wars over much smaller doctrinal differences, rather than some of the more serious moral crimes. The Prescians are especially dogmatic... Guardians of the Sacred Vale..." Vinellin commented, adding a chiding 'tut' at the end.

Leif grinned. "Still, I'm sure the children's' tales from Aelaete are far more frightening than any of yours."

Fryn chuckled. "I doubt that."

Leif spied the three brothers entering the lamplight, and gently nudged Trel's boot under the table. "In the east, they are constantly in fear of the stars, but in my homeland, the mountainous sands are home to true dangers. In the dawn of time, there were three serpents, one with fierce blue eyes and iridescent golden scales, another with blood-red eyes and light brown bands, and a third, that was tan, and looked around through gold-slitted eyes."

"Why do we need to know their eye-color?" Loren interjected.

"Um… well in Aelaete, I admit, we are a bit superstitious about eyes… anyway, there was a little boy who'd seen something shining in the desert, and flown away when his parents weren't looking. He landed before the first serpent, and thinking that its eye was a sapphire, he tried to grab it. It was frighteningly cold, and the serpent's eyelids closed on his hand, freezing it, and breaking it off at the wrist," Leif continued.

Fryn lifted an eyebrow. "Are you making this up now?"

He ignored her. "Then, clutching the frozen stump, he back away, but he could not move very fast because even the air was thickening. The serpent, accidentally blinded in one eye, demanded why the boy had done this, so he answered, that he wanted to take the stone. 'But my eye is not a stone,' the serpent replied, 'you must pay the price for your greed, by giving me one of your eyes.' The boy, numb from the cold, could not feel the pain of his injury. 'But I've already given you my hand,' he complained. 'Isn't that enough?' The serpent was angry, and snapped forward, thinking to eat him in one bite, but the boy flew into his blind spot, and took off for home."

Lia vanished into the crowd, and left her flute in the hands of the little girl, who started playing modestly well. Grifton sat down with a graceful nod toward their host, and waited for Leif to continue his story, joined by Gerard and Germaine—who seemed so obviously disinterested, Leif bristled in irritation.

"So, as it grew dark, he looked for the light of the town's lamps, and seeing the starlight reflecting off the second serpent's ruby-red eyes, he flew down and landed in a valley before him. This serpent radiated waves of heat, and looked longingly at the ice that had formed on the boy's arm, and asked for what price the boy would give him the ice. The boy, understanding that the serpent wanted to *eat* him, after what he had just gone through with the blue-eyed serpent, he said that he would give him the ice for one of his ruby eyes."

"What kind of story is this?" Germaine groaned.

"The serpent did not like this deal, and threatened to eat the boy, who offered more ice than the serpent could eat, in exchange for his life and the eye. The serpent didn't believe him, so he flew toward where the first serpent was, or where he thought he was, and landed in a barren space. The ground shifted under his feet, and he realized that he was standing on a sleeping serpent, and from the north came the red-eyed one, and the south, the blue-one-eyed one. The serpent beneath his feet woke, and stared through slit eyes at the boy.

"'If you help me, I will let you feast.' The boy said. The serpent waited, hearing the approach of the other two, and watched. The blue-eyed serpent leapt forward to bite the boy, and the red one, seeing the frozen hand, closed his jaw on the blind side of the blue serpent. The blue serpent's teeth caught in the side of the slit-eyed tan serpent, who in anger, lunged, opening his mouth, and threw the boy into the air, as it bit the red serpent. All three died, and the ice, and fire, and sparks were so intense, that the boy's hand was completely disintegrated, and six perfect gems landed in the sand.

"He tied the frozen blue eyes to his wounded arm, and stuck the yellow ones in his pockets, and used the red ones to light his way home. In the end, he showed that any danger can be turned against itself, and some sacrifice is required to obtain anything truly valuable." Leif leaned back proudly, crossing his arms.

"But that doesn't teach children to not go out at night!" Loren complained.

"It also isn't a scary story," Fryn added.

"Sure, but it shows that with cleverness, and a willingness to lose, even a boy can become powerful. It is harrowing and exciting!" he replied.

"Still," the Earl went on, "your partner is correct of course. It was not as frightening as you'd promised."

The little girl who'd given the braided clover crown to the Earl appeared beside them, the flute-like instrument in one hand, and her eyes wide in wonder or interest. "I thought it was a good story," she said, nodding twice.

Leif decided, one day, he wouldn't mind having children.

"Are all your stories about serpents?" she asked, "Why are you called the..."

"Certainly not, that'd be ridiculous," he answered, leaning closer. "There're greater beasts that even the masters fear to face, much less defend themselves against. Near Chistleton there's a great lizard that's as big as an oasis, and has been living in one for over a thousand years. To face him would be like trying to kill a mountain... which come to think of it, has already been done in a way." He smiled sheepishly at Fryn, thinking of the volcano that had destroyed Waverly in the past, but she frowned.

"Not appropriate humor, Leif, too close a shave, as they say."

Loren chuckled. "We don't truly blame ourselves for that, though some are of course a bit more strict adherents to the Exile's Doctrine."

He decided that there were far too many new terms to come to understand in one evening, and simply nodded. Even the most devout in his homeland were pretty lax, or rather casual, in their devotion to the Wing-giver.

The girl tried again, tugging on his sleeve to get his attention. "But why do they call you the Viper?" She asked softly.

"Well, I imagine it's because I defeated a sand viper, using sparks, which everyone said was impossible—since we share the same element. That, and, I still have a bit of its fang stuck in my arm, feels almost like a part of me now," he replied, absently scratching his arm where it still itched.

Grifton smiled and accepted a glass of slightly younger wine than the bottle split between Leif, Fryn, and the Earl, and took a grateful sip. "I had thought you were out chasing your tail, but here you are tapping wings with the local nobility. I had heard that you two were fond of ingratiating yourselves to important hosts... what with your stay at the Crown District in Frorin, and all."

Loren narrowed his eyes at the uninvited guest. "I choose my associations, Fyr Francis, and if you had been the one to slay the weasel over there," he pointed toward the nearest house, where the pelt was stretched out to cure on display, "then you may be rest assured that I would be celebrating you right now."

"Fyr?" Leif asked, whispering in Fryn's ear.

"Means 'mister' or 'sir' in Waverly." She refocused on the exchange with a grimly mischievous smile. "They used to write their 's's like 'f's and so they ended up pronouncing many 's's as such."

"Ah, I fee," he joked.

She shook her head with a smirk, and pinched his arm. "That's a bit much."

Germaine sneered. "All the same, you can't buy a reputation with favors except for one of being a crony."

"Said the crony," Leif retorted with a laugh. "Back to our original conversation, let us see if Lord Loren here has a better children's story."

Loren grinned and downed the contents of his glass. "It was the darkest night of Star, and the moon had blocked out all its light, when the wind began to blow. The snow was light, and swirled in spirals through the town, encasing the Vine in an icy coat. But in all this change, there was a little girl, who wandered out beyond the wall. At first, beyond the Eastern Gate, the road was paved and cleared by the trader's wagons, or the wings of the last Finch-Post, and she walked farther and farther from home.

"Her parents always told her not to go outside after dark, but she didn't think of that, she followed a snowflake as far as it flew in the wind, barely keeping up with it on her wings, until she saw it land on a bare spot of ground. Then, looking around, she realized that she had quite lost her way, and seeing a mound, she began to climb up it to see if she could spot the town over the top of the grass. As she started up the slope, she tripped over something hard and cold in the snow, something long and thin, and white.

"It was the slender rib bone of a hare, and she wrapped her shawl around her shoulders in fear, but she needed to get home, so up and on she went. Bones poked through the patches of snow, building a hill out of the discarded carcasses of the lesser beasts, and fee, and fae, and she trembled as she finally stood at the peak."

Grifton nodded as if he'd heard this before, and Trel just watched Leif's face. Fryn looked much more interested than she had during *his* story, and once more he felt a sense of mixed contempt and gloating from his sword—as if it retained the animosity its creator had felt toward him as well.

Loren continued with a sinister smile. "But when she looked out across the tops of the grass, she saw just how far off the city was, and knew that she might get hopelessly lost unless she flew straight there—but in the winter, she might well freeze, or be killed by the flurries of snow. She memorized the stars that lay in the direction of the city, and started back down the hill... when something went 'snap' behind her back. She froze, and slowly turned to look over her shoulder, and beheld two enormous yellow eyes, glowing white fur, and snow-white teeth bared. She dashed away, forgetting the stars, and felt something close on her leg, and flying up, she felt much lighter on one side. Glancing down, she realized, that one of her legs was gone, well above the knee, and in her horror, she couldn't move, as its teeth bit off her head.

"And that is why, we don't leave the safety of the bouldered walls at night."

Fryn shuddered, and turned to Leif. "That was a much more frightening story."

"Well, what was it?" he asked.

"An ermine, what else? Though, I didn't know they turned white down here," she replied.

"Well, that wasn't a true story though," he said, drawing another frown from Fryn.

"Close enough," Loren added, "The Weasel Cairn is a real place, a valley strewn with the collected bones of several ages, and some travelers have seen children's bones."

Germaine nodded sadly. "In Haryn, where we're from, we don't have weasels so much to worry about, but there are large scavengers that will raid our storehouses; big white and gray banded creatures, that are quite vicious if bothered."

"What are they called?" Trel asked, suddenly interested in the conversation, rather than the others' reactions to it.

"Black-eyed Bandits," he answered simply, "we've had to join teams of Hunter's down there fighting them off before. Not easy. No one's killed one of them for decades."

They let the conversation lapse, and Vinellin opened another bottle of wine—this one much lighter in terms of alcohol content. Leif suspected he was not about to let them get intoxicated, and he was glad he didn't have to make some excuse to stop drinking. Though Fryn seemed able to store her affected blood in her knife, he hadn't her skill, and didn't even know if he could use his sword in that way. He saved that topic for a later conversation.

More musicians started playing, a folksy tune with a plucked fiddle, and the reed-based flute, with the accompaniment of a light timbred drum. Several local couples started to dance. They held one hand, lifting their coats or skirts slightly so they wouldn't get dirty, as they stepped and twirled in a gentle pace. This time, Fryn took the lead, grabbing him by the sleeve, and drawing him away from their competitors, whispering as she held his hand, "We need to do something about them... Or somehow get *her* out of here; if we don't, they might take her from us."

It seemed that Yarrow had arrived, as pretty soon, they saw Trel and her partner fluidly joining the dance, while they were struggling to match the 5/4 tempo step. The accentuated movements were with the first beat stepping forward, the third away, and the fifth joining back together with a twirl. It was simple-seeming, but difficult at first. They quickly adjusted to the flow of it, with its syncopated stepping rhythms and unexpected turns, and after a few minutes, they were able to keep up with the villagers.

Still, Leif did not really want to join the next dance, so when the music stopped, they relaxed and returned to their seats, unhappily noticing that the three brothers hadn't moved. "Earl Loren, my Lord, you wished to hear our tale?" Leif prompted; maybe the brothers would think that that was all they were planning on doing—wining and dining.

Loren turned with a flash of realization, and rose to an awkward stand at the table with his hands pressed resolutely on its surface. "Of course! What are we doing? Oh, but there should be three dances... first the children, then the couples, and then everyone... Vinellin, what's next?"

"The proceedings, I believe, my Lord, but I am not an expert in your culture, especially on your mother's side." The valet's response was not especially helpful or sympathetic, and the Earl merely frowned. After a few seconds he looked around at the others, and when the music slowed, he hovered and held out his hands to draw attention to himself.

"Now, in accordance with our traditions, this festival has officially begun. I would like to invite everyone to join us before the well, with your lanterns, and candles, and chairs, to hear just what exactly transpired." He dropped down gracefully and stood on top of his table, clapping his hands together twice to summon his attendants. "Bring out the wine for the tables, please."

In seconds, the townsfae had gathered around the foot of the well, looking up from their seats at the four columns of tables, young and old, at the 'Great Hunters' who returned their gaze with barely contained embarrassment.

"What are we supposed to say?" Fryn asked softly, her lips almost brushing his ear. Her breath tickled.

Leif cleared his throat, and coughed again for good measure. "We simply, give a good show of it." He confirmed the procedure with a good-natured wing-tap and nodded seriously, and began:

"Thousands of years ago, The Ermine slew Yndril, and brought death, and the taste of blood to Fae. I hope you will forgive my use of the old-fashioned "Fae" instead of "faekind" or "faerie-kind"... ahem..."

Fryn interrupted with a well-timed save. "Ever since, we have been at war with the beasts of the world. Whether it was because they were jealous of our wings, or because as some legends have it, they were recruited by another faerie to destroy the object of their jealousy, we'll never know, but we have always lived in fear of them, and as far from them as is practicable."

"Indeed," Leif added, "the cities in the grasslands are known for their walls, erected in forgotten times, but there were always some beasts who would not be dissuaded by them—or some towns that had no walls."

Fryn nodded beside him, as if she had been checking his facts. "Those towns had no alternative but to fight the beasts, and learn the martial styles. My own tradition stretches back to the early Martell Kings, who fought with their guard against the birds of prey and ermines of the north."

"And mine," Leif interjected, pulling back his sleeve on his left arm to reveal the hideous scars left by the venom-filled fangs of the sand viper, "has protected my clan from the serpents of the sands for hundreds of years. When we heard that your people were plagued by similar dangers, ignored by the guard and Commission, we were stirred by compassion." He was, perhaps, exaggerating the facts a little, but the farmers were nodding, and the eyes of the seven or eight children glowed bright with interest and the reflected light of the candle-lanterns.

"What nobility, what honor!" Loren shouted, losing himself in his emotion, clapping his gloved hands softly.

"Hear, hear!" yelled a young fae, trying just a little too hard to grow a mustache.

Leif stepped to the side to allow Fryn to continue their narrative. She grinned, seeming to get into the show of it. "And so, even with the grand chase for the thief who stole the Harvest Crown, we thought to leave that to the myriad other Hunters and pursue a more worthy goal—to make safe the people of the plains." She held up her hands against the sudden burst of applause, and continued. "And so we came into this town at night, and thought to continue our search the next day by waiting in the warehouse overnight. But the irony—what chance? We were followed from the Forest of Grass!" Fryn laughed with a touch of color on her cheeks, affected, Leif supposed, since she was quite skilled at controlling her own blood.

Several of the villagers laughed with her, especially the Earl, who wiped his eyes with a handkerchief embroidered with an elaborate vine. The little girl with the flute had seated herself beside the Earl and was clapping cheerfully, though the Francis brothers frowned and muttered to each other as if they didn't believe the story.

Leif waved his hands to calm them and went on. "And so, when the weasel sniffed us out, and turned our ambush on our heads we were at a complete loss!" The little girl gasped. "I gave it that long gash across its chest," he said, pointing toward the long stitched area of the hanging pelt, "but that did not stop it from tossing me through the boards and beams of the warehouse like a cottonwood boll. It broke my ribs, and split my wing, and Fryn just barely saved my life—she distracted it long enough with various cuts and slashes, blocking and dodging its hairy, long arms, and dagger-sharp claws, so I could summon a lightning bolt and pierce through the hole I'd made before."

"Why didn't you use your sword?" Grifton asked, narrowing his eyes.

"An excellent question, you see, at that point I'd been thrown back, and I lost my grip."

The Earl tapped his fingers on the table and shared a look with the little girl. "Was the lightning bolt enough?"

"Hahaha, no," Fryn sighed, "it only grew angrier. I was barely able to dodge another swipe of its tail, and Leif was wounded and exhausted... when..."

The little girl stood and shouted, "my mother saved you!"

The circle of tables around the well, glowing under the strung-out lights, was silent, and everyone's eyes turned to her. The Earl blinked and then gave a surprised bark, "one of my citizens came to your aid? How marvelous!"

"Can we convince them that she's making it up?" Leif whispered in Fryn's ear.

"I'm afraid not, the Waverly are very strict with their children, and raise them to speak the truth, and immediately take to heart whatever a child declares."

"Ah..." He turned to the little girl. "What is your name, child?"

"Nora!" She curtsied and sat on the edge of the table.

"Well, Nora, I'm afraid that we were unable to see who it was who saved us. Is she well?"

Nora narrowed her eyes and frowned... "But I thought for sure... she's well, I think."

As if worrying what the child would say next, the thief they'd been chasing since the Festival came out with a festive dress of green and red, and a bright red ribbon in her hair. Compared to her 'work attire' Leif figured no one would recognize her except those who really knew her. The brothers examined her carefully, but it appeared, at least for the time being, they were fooled by her disguise.

"I did not wish to draw attention away from the Hunters who came to help us," she said meekly, in a slightly higher pitch than usual.

"Your modesty is commendable," Gerard complimented gratuitously, almost monotone, barely putting on a smile.

"Commendable, yes, and she shall be commended!" Loren rose from his seat and held out his hand toward her with a grin. "Please, come and stay at my estate with your family to dine with mine as a gesture of my thanks." Turning to Leif and Fryn, he chuckled. "Of course, you two are invited as well. I feel I may grow fond of you—such compassion, and capability combined; a rare occurrence in your organization."

Leif was about to decline the offer, but Fryn stopped him with a hand on his elbow. "We would be only too pleased to accept your hospitality, my lord." She smiled and then glanced in the direction of the other Hunters, adding under her breath. "They cannot be seen to infiltrate the Earl's Estate, we will have some measure of security to plan our next steps."

"Then it is decided! Vinellin, as soon as this festival here has ended, begin preparations for a night flight to the Vine." Loren reseated himself and waved for the servants to pour everyone's glasses. "Before we toast this occasion, we must hear the end of the tale."

Nora skipped up the steps, and pronounced in slightly over-accented tones, "She picked up the black blade of the Viper, and flew under the weasel's head, and stabbed it in the neck!"

"How did you know that?" Lia asked, growing pale.

"I heard the noise and wanted to see what it was; I wondered if you'd come home yet, and thought I could surprise you." She answered without guile, and a little guilt, or embarrassment, as she looked up into her mother's frustrated gaze.

"A fine end, the strength of three regions, and the fruit of one kill, celebrated with the sharing of one glass." Loren raised his crystal in salute and said, "from one vine, and one glass, the flowing from one vein, your victory is mine, and ours, and all. Linella søranim helay."

Following the lead of the crowd, Leif and Fryn raised their glasses and joined the others saying, "Linella søranim helay."

Even though he couldn't tell what the expression meant, Leif pondered the tradition of oneness and shared misery and joy, musing that it was not all that dissimilar to the clan-structure of his own society; even if it included non-family.

Fryn smiled, likely understanding it, and held his hand, looking out over the faces of the gathered members of the town. "I didn't think much of slaying the weasel at first, but now I wonder if it wasn't even better than what we did before."

He squeezed her hand gently. "I'm glad we came to this city, even if we didn't get to enjoy our dessert at the Festival."

She nudged him with her elbow, and gave a light snort. "Of course, that was your concern..." She looked away, and Leif couldn't wait to go see the Earl's Estate. Maybe then, free from the constant pursuit of the thief, and constantly being pursued by the Francis brothers, and who knew who else, he and Fryn could enjoy some peace and quiet, just to themselves.

Turn and Ties

Fassen:

Earl's Estate

Leif

The base of the vine occupied the majority of the northeastern corner of the Earl's Estate, with a twisted ancient trunk that rose like a monolith of living stone into an eight-pointed star of trained branches. They were heavy with the thick clusters of dark blue and purple grapes, that the workers of the Fassen Vine Guild had still not finished harvesting. Their entrance to the hill that comprised the district, because of the root structure of the vine, went up a series of stone-worked switchbacks to battlemented walls which separated the ruler of the city from the common folk. Through its massive gates was revealed a causeway, with mansions and garden plots along the west, leading to a lake.

The Estate ended to the south at the mouth of the Boulder Wall, which was guarded by an impressive barracks and a veritable castle built into and against the boulder so that the gate provided the only access to the Forest of Grass. But they weren't walking in.

The Earl had insisted that someone make room for the guests to ride on one of the supply finches, which wasn't too much trouble, since they had exhausted most of the food and drink they had brought to the anonymous town. He and Fryn had joined Vinellin on his bird, much to the Elin-born fae's displeasure, which he graciously refrained from showing. Still, Leif knew how annoyed he was, mostly because of the sharpness of the air around him, and because of the clipped aspect of his words.

Fryn was seated behind him, holding onto his jacket, since it wasn't that easy to embrace someone through their wings, and Leif felt a measure of warmth and security that he hadn't experienced since before he'd left the desert. The wind blew through his messily-combed blond hair, and Fryn kept her head low, shielding her own hair behind his shoulder.

"Why do you think he's going to such lengths?" he asked her.

Vinellin heard him, and replied dryly, "because it is a fault of his character."

"I think he is a fae of some great integrity," Leif countered, even if he mostly just wanted to explore... just with Fryn.

"Why did you come to this land, really?" Leif asked.

"For the reason I told you before," the valet answered, shading his eyes against the glare of the Greater Moon, "to bring culture, and the fear of the Wing-Giver to this land's wandering fae."

Their finch swooped low over the barracks and landed before an aviary reaching all the way to the top of the boulders, built into the sides of the rock. Their guide flew down gracefully to the granite flagstone courtyard, and bowed with an outstretched hand. "Welcome, to the Estate Fassen, home of my Lord Loren, the Earl of the Vine."

Leif lit on the stones beside him, and took Fryn's hand, to help her down; she flew on her own wings however, so it was mostly a formality. She smiled sweetly at his gesture, and then covered it, when she noticed Vinellin's eyes on them. He seemed really disapproving, as if they had some sort of an indecent relationship—which couldn't be farther from the truth. He had only ever treated her in the most respectable fashion, as a fellow Hunter, and professional, and as a fee.

Vinellin coughed and released the finch to an attendant who rushed over with a starlamp in one hand. "Stable the beast, if you would, with fresh water and seeds. She has born more than her fair share of burdens."

So had they, Leif supposed, tapping his sheath absently, and felt a slight tremor through its frozen-blood blade. "I understand that your master has invited us to dinner tomorrow, but what shall we do for the night?"

"I will lead you to suitable accommodations, where guests of the Earl are situated with a view of the swimming pond. Before you ask, no, it is not warm enough to swim in at this time of year. However, members of the Earl's family and staff have often enjoyed feeding the goldfish, sometimes too much." He started along the road to the west, toward one of three large houses built in an arc opposite the barracks, bordered by miniature trees trained to grow only tall enough to cover the walkways with shade. The first house was busy with servingfae in black jackets moving about its many doors and terraces, manually switching on the first-generation starlamps with long opal-tipped rods, and carrying in crates of sliced vegetables to the storage rooms inside.

The second was quiet, with curtains drawn, and shutters closed, an unoccupied Spring dwelling, Leif imagined, as it had a view of the northeast. Better sunlight that way.

Vinellin paused before the eastward-facing house, three stories, with dormers on the angled eaves, and raising one hand, snapped his fingers. A young maid and butler immediately opened the double doors of the entry, and bowed slightly to usher them in, and they walked up the granite steps wondering if they were the only ones staying. "I must attend to my master, but Fyr Lodt and Lyr Mila will ensure that you are prepared for the evening tea." Looking at a pocket watch he added quickly, "which will be sharply at eleven." Then he flew off to the northeast, where the main house rose like an oblong block, some five stories just by the foot of the Vine.

Inside, the butler, Lodt, escorted Leif down a corridor to the right, up a flight of stairs, and into a small, but comfortable room looking out on the courtyard, and Fryn went off to the left. Setting his jacket on the iron coat hook on the back of his door, Leif examined the fae with a smile. "He said eleven, but I'm not sure exactly how much time I have to get ready, much less what I need to do."

Lodt nodded politely, and scratched his chin with his white-gloved fingers. "Two hours, or somewhere near there, I'd recommend that you allow us to wash your clothing for tomorrow, and after a bath, we will supply you with a suit of the House Colors."

"I'd be grateful if you did, I didn't exactly have time to bring my bags." Setting aside his long scarf, and unhooking his sword belt, he bent down to undo the laces of his boots. "Where are the baths?"

"If you go down the hall to the right, the corner room leads into the north baths, Fyr Aellin, I will set out a clean change of clothes when you're ready. The towels should be hanging from the radiators," he replied, and then stepped out pulling the door closed behind him.

Not long after he'd left, Leif folded his outerwear and padded down the hall in his travel linens and socks, with his sword and sheath held loosely in one hand. He wasn't comfortable with the idea of leaving it behind, not sure whether the serving staff would be curious about it. Of course he also wasn't happy with the idea of someone else washing his clothes, but to decline their service when he was a guest didn't seem wise.

The 'corner room' turned out to be built into the actual corner, with an angled wall rounding the turn of the house, and an extension jutting out from the 'curve' through a vinewood door with a brass handle. Opening the door, he found that it was a small space with a triangular tub built into the far wall, with the radiator supplying hot water to the bath which was already full, and blooming with a sea of white bubbles smelling of honey-clover and oats. He undressed and folded his clothes by the door, and leaned his sword against the wall by the towels, to obscure it if Lodt popped in to retrieve his clothes, and stepped into the steaming water.

Steam washed over his face, and his wings shivered from the instant wash of warmth, and the pores opened in response, as he sunk into the foam.

He savored its heat, and after what felt like only moments, the door opened slightly, and the butler took his clothes, leaving almost before Leif had realized he'd appeared. *Didn't expect him to be so discrete, I imagined servants to be a bit more… forceful or resigned in their duties? I suppose Ieffin's servants were energetic, but the others seemed constantly nervous.* Lifting one hand into the air, he noticed just how dirty and grimy his skin had gotten in the course of the last day, and he stretched his upper wings over the side of the tub, wondering just what they looked like covered in bubbles. *Fighting with Hunters, racing through the grass, it's a dirty business.*

The air was completely filled with the steam, but around the sword, it turned to mist, or fog, as ice clawed its way around the handle and sheath, and Leif felt a cold tugging at his mind.

"You expected something else? Going to the Commission? Why'd you bring me in here? I can't stand the heat…" Demanded Havrshyk's voice from the fog-shrouded sword.

Leif swallowed, and sunk lower into the bath. "Am I hearing things?"

An ironic laugh echoed in his head. "Yes, but that doesn't make it less real now, does it?"

"But you're dead, I killed you, cut off your head!" Leif insisted.

"Whose blood do you think it is that keeps this sword's shape, hm? Mine, and since I despise this heat I guess I shifted things around inside it and separated enough from your blood that we could talk. I admit, it's been a bit dull…"

"So you're still dead then." Leif sighed. "Just talking to your ghost."

"Ghost, dead, I don't care, as long as you're holding me, I have a few demands—or I won't heal you next time." His voice trailed off in a dry warning, as if he were about to laugh. *"Did you think that you were the one who could use it? You're not a Bloodcrafter, Leif, just a borrower, or did you think that it was that fickle partner of yours? I survived the tomb, Leif, I did. Do you know how? By barely sustaining myself with what blood I had left."*

"You're pretty skilled at staying alive for someone who seems to lose all his battles. Some successor to the Swordhand Fist or whatever."

"Swordhand Palm you imbecile, but it doesn't surprise me if you've forgotten. Finish your bath and get me out of here already, or I'll give you something to worry about."

Leif yawned. "You're trapped, I can tell," he said, closing one eye and regarding the frozen sword with the other. "Your threats are as useless as your style. Still I should've known that you'd be alive in some respect, you'd completely drained yourself into the sword, so when that was all that was left, that was where you'd be. The Lich in concentrated form, distilled, undiluted, the cure for any ailment... I doubt you can withhold that from me."

"Can't I indeed? When that Germaine fool smacked you in the head, who prevented a concussion? How quickly does an internal bruise heal? Not very, I can assure you, even for a Lich—which you are not. Mind your manners Leif, because your concussion is about to come back."

Immediately, the heat from the bath sent shooting pain up to his temples, and the cool protective ice that had soothed his head injury melted in the steam. Leif gasped, and slipped under the water, which only made the pounding in his head worse, and he drew water into his throat. In blind panic, he floundered, and rose coughing and sputtering over the lip of the tub with his red-lined wings drooping and twitching behind his back, and he stumbled over the side to the cream-tiled floor.

The coolness washed over him, and he struggled to his feet, grabbing hold of the towel and radiator for support, and slipped back to his knees with the towel in one hand. He wrapped it around his waist, and took the sword, and fumbled with the handle of the door. Steam flooded the hallway, and the light of the amber starlamps in the wall sconces stabbed at his eyes. Holding his temples in one hand, he barely managed to retreat to his room, where, leaving a trail of water, he found the piled garments that Lodt had promised.

He dried off as best he could, and dressed in the white and brown suit, and left the bow tie unfastened, and his sword loosely belted, as he tugged on his boots, and collapsed on the bed.

He didn't wake to Havrshyk's mocking voice, which taunted him incessantly, but Fryn's cold hand on his forehead.

"What's wrong Leif?" She asked, bright blue eyes glowing with concern. "I had thought that you might be alright after earlier, what happened?"

Sitting up with a groan, he shook his head, and immediately regretted it. "I'm afraid I don't know if I healed properly."

"*You know for a fact you did not*," Havrshyk added in a snide undertone.

Fryn did not seem to hear him though. Leif smiled gratefully as she helped him to his feet, and placed a thin layer of ice at the back of his head to numb and protect it. "We're running late, they're waiting for us."

"Everyone? Lia, the girl?" Leif wobbled for a second and recovered his balance. "Now?"

She nodded. "It's eleven fifteen, they've been waiting, we all were, finally sent me up to get you. Loren was not pleased."

"Course he wasn't." He made it to the door and straightened the fit of his suit.

Fryn caught him by the sleeve. "You can't mean to go down like *that?* Your tie's not tied, your hair's a mess, you're not ready."

"My tie?" He looked down, it was loose around the collar, and threatening to fall. "I'm not good with bow ties."

She waved him back, and sighed. "Allow me." Fryn tugged on both ends of the bow tie and evened them out, crossing them in an arcane fashion, tucking here, turning there, until all of a sudden, she pronounced, "finished."

He made once more for the door.

"Stop," she commanded, holding up a tired hand. "Come back."

He obeyed, drifting back half on the wing, and allowed her to point at his hair. She breathed on her fingers a light cloud of fog, and ice, and found his part, and ran the delicate coating of frost through his hair.

"That will hold the styling until the end of the night, but don't mess with it." She waved him off, and caught up with him at the door. "One last thing," she added, almost as an afterthought, slipping an arm through his, "tighten your belt."

Leif blushed, whether from the embarrassment, or her proximity, which by rights he *should* be used to by now, and tightened his belt. "I'm ready, are you?"

"Yes," she chimed in response, smiling prettily.

He caught his breath, and looked away. "It's not right for a fearsome Hunter to be so pretty," he declared.

She stiffened but did not withdraw her hand. "It only sharpens an already perfect blade, does it not?" she chided. "Don't you think?"

"Of course you do, stupid fools, both of you," Havrshyk commented in his head. *"It's not fair to make me live like this, as if I'm accidentally overhearing the reading of some cheap romance novel. Forced, really."*

Leif agreed with her, putting the overbearing presence of the undead sword out of his mind. "Perfect, yes. Now, I heard there's a fancy pot of tea or something."

"He said 'tea' but I'm fairly sure that there's already an opened bottle of Ceren on the table, warming over a hot bath of the excess from the kettle." She led him back down the stairs and through the double-doors, which were once more held open by the two servants from before, and out onto the flagstone courtyard. "The Francis brothers insisted that they be invited to share in the celebration, but Loren did not like them, and told them as much, saying that they were as 'bloodless as a wingless worm' and would not be suited for the table. Vinellin was shocked by his language, his lips were pressed together so hard they were white, and his wings quivered once."

He listened as she regaled him with the encounter, eyes drifting off toward the tiny lamps hung from the myriad branches of the vine overhead, which did little to light their path, but made for a wonderful atmosphere for an evening walk.

"Why didn't he simply call them caterpillars?" Leif interrupted, quirking his mouth to the side, looking away.

She coughed to cover a laugh. "That's about as bad as such insults get, too vulgar you know. Loren had to allude to what he really meant. It's the same in Frorin, though I guess you didn't get to see that. Do they insult each other more openly in Sendra?"

They ascended the rose-colored granite steps of the main house, and entered through a set of doors held open by hooks in the stone, into an ornate foyer with gilded wood paneling, marble floors, and rich green and red carpeting that extended under the arms of the curving double staircase, down the hall, to the dining room that, with its echoing whispers, portended their destination. Leif shook his head, ignoring the pain, and tried to clear his thoughts. It did him little good to think in the esoteric way his master had spoken. After all, who used such expressions as 'portend' anymore?

"I'm afraid that our insults, at least in my clan, have more to do with the characters of our folk traditions than with derogatory terms," he explained, "but it's clear enough to those who know the stories. And for me, it might not be so flattering to be called 'The Viper', hmm…"

They walked down the shadowed hall, unlit for effect, arm in arm, like they had when they were trying to blend in, searching for information in Frorin, like when they'd first met Harissa, and her father—the now deceased Pine Martin. The glow of the peat fire, and the soft whispers of conversation greeted them as they entered the dining hall, a long rectangular room with a hearth at the far end, and a long vinewood table with a deep blue runner. The walls glistened matching the paneling in the foyer, and oversized portraits detailed the stern faces, and blunt noses, of the previous Earls posing with their wives, or visa versa, since from what Leif could tell, in more than one painting, the House had been ruled by a single daughter.

"At long last!" Loren declared when he caught sight of them, rising from his chair with both arms in the air. "I told Vinellin that he was a fool, and indeed he is," he said, eyes darting over to his grieved valet.

"I never said I didn't wish them to attend, my lord," the valet confided softly.

The Earl did not look convinced, and waved them to their seats with one eyebrow raised. "Hasetta yndra helan, Vinellin, see if you know what *that* means."

"It means you doubt my understanding, a loose translation, but semantically appropriate, my lord Earl." Vinellin sighed and pulled out the chairs where Fryn and Leif were meant to sit, side-by-side, with Lia and Nora across from them. Quietly, to them, he added, "the Waverly assume that theirs was the original tongue of all our peoples, which the Wing-Giver Himself spoke, but, we hardly trust *their* exile traditions."

"You'd do well to revise your opinion, Fyr," Leif retorted, "I've often found that it is the humbled who are most genuine, not those presuming to have knowledge."

Fryn choked on her own air, and coughed for a few seconds. "Leif, that is exactly the sort of comment that is not welcome in high society."

Loren, however, beamed. "Indeed, very rude of you to correct another fae's servant, very improper… but nonetheless correct. Vinellin, you are very knowledgeable, but I regret to inform you, that education does not ensure that one is wise. Neither does it establish one as an authority."

Vinellin's eyes narrowed, but he bore the insults well. "My lord, I apologize for any discourtesy, I meant no offense. In my tradition, authenticity is the most important of virtues, since without it there can be no truth, or cooperation."

"Commendable certainly," the Earl allowed, waving a hand toward the thief who stole the crown, and the girl who was, apparently, her daughter. "We in Waverly, without fail, know this for a fact: that true knowledge comes from loss, and that the price we pay, will be in turn repaid, with interest, by those who know, who remember, and our family. To deal generously, to lend kindly, and to protect, all these things breed congeniality—which is not the state of your empire Vinellin."

"I would remind you that my homeland is not actually an empire, but at this point, there is no, as it were, point." The butler grinned, a first, at least as far as Leif had seen.

Nora looked up from her china cup of peppermint tea. "Mama, what… where's Vin from?"

Lia blinked, and looked at her daughter, pursing her lips. "I don't know, child."

"The City-States Council of Zella, child," he provided, "along the northwestern peninsula of Elin. We are a mercantile people, but cognizant of the necessity of in-depth study, and most particular over the matters of history—contrary to the Earl's 'hasetta' pronouncement."

Wrinkling her nose at the response, Nora laughed. "Zella is an odd name."

He frowned. "It is named after Sir Harran Zella, the founder of the First City. He was an exile from Prescia, since he disagreed with some of the doctrines of their theocracy."

The girl shook her head. "I don't know much about those things, Lord Butler," she said with a coy smile, "but here we have only the words of Darsin the Prophet."

"Quite right, child," Loren added, "for it was Darsin who predicted the explosion of Mount Waver, and the epidemic. He raised his voice from the Boulder Sheath, now buried beneath the lava flows, and told of the coming storm, but few listened. That is why we now remember, because even though he fell under the fires, his words lived on."

Leif marveled at the complexity of their history, and found his hand tightening his hold on his teaspoon. "Why is it, that your people have such a rich past?"

Fryn shook her head slightly.

"We all have something in our histories, Master Aellin," the Earl reminded him carefully, "but your own people, aside from a few clan struggles, has remained as their ancestor was—swimming in the oasis, drinking the water, and basking in the sun. I do not expect everyone to have experienced our follies, but, by the leisure of your ancestors, I suppose you would not understand.

"When Fharys* set the Ermine on Yndril, your forefather was lounging in the tide, they say, and since then, your people have known nothing but the sand."

"I see," Leif said, lifting his porcelain vine-patterned teacup toward the valet, "that would be one explanation." The clans of Aelaete had of course been through many tumultuous times, but he decided, now was not the time to correct someone when they were discussing their own past. "When the mountain erupted, how did anyone survive?"

The Earl rose from his seat with a triumphant raising of his hands and wings. "By the last word of the great Darsin! Those who listened took their families and fled—immediately, and as the ground shook below, they flew, all the way to Fassen, to Gaerlin, wherever might be safe. My own family too, not that we were descended from the then line of royalty, they stayed behind, but through a cousin house, we still remain."

Lia nodded. "That is true, according to the traditions, at least. Hundreds of years old, as the tale goes, but still, unchanging with each telling."

"But, it's not like that in the other lands?" Nora confirmed.

"No," Leif agreed, "at least in some respects, my own country has been free of such troubles."

Fryn relaxed at his response, and took a sip of her freshly filled cup of tea.

**Fharys is known elsewhere as Fhorae*

Leif copied her, and breathed a sigh of relief. It was a fairly decent tea, just enough barley, just enough green, just the right hint of pine. He understood why the girl had been given mint though, it was mild enough that she might like the taste, and would not keep her awake—which he suspected the Earl would not have liked, if she had remained alert for the whole of the evening.

Nora finished her cup, and leaned back in her chair, little wings sticking through the holes in the back of it, twitching idly. "I'm… I'm tired mama," she said quietly.

"Run along then, I'm sure Vinellin will have you tucked in," Lia admonished lightly.

The girl frowned, little mouth angling downward awkwardly, unused to the expression. "But I want you to tuck me in, mama."

Loren gave a single nod, and watched the pair leave with his tiresome valet. Then, smiling toward them, he covered his own yawn. "But indeed, it is growing late for all of us. Fyr Leif, I blame you for making us wait so long, tell me, were you consumed with interest in my paintings, or just taking a nap?"

"If anything, you could say I was taking a nap. I have not fully recovered from my injuries from when we fought the weasel, and then again when we fought against other Hunters, and so I was quite helplessly tired. I apologize," he said, confirming his wording with Fryn through a surreptitious nudge of his elbow.

She nodded sadly. "I am afraid that we are both still weary from our exploits, and we are no closer to the greatly contested prize of the Harvest Crown."

Their host politely waved away her comments, and picked up the crystal carafe of Ceren which had been basking over a steaming bowl of water for the entire conversation. "But that is precisely why you are here, tonight," he explained, "I am aware of certain things, that you perhaps are not. One of which, though it will come as little surprise I am sure, is that this liqueur is invigorating, and restorative. Another, would be that I am fully aware of who our lately departed guest is, and have no incentive to turn her over, to you or anyone else." He poured three full snifters of Ceren and waited. A few seconds later, Lia and Vinellin returned, and the Earl poured out two more glasses, and Vinellin distributed them—his glass notably less full than the others.

Leif swallowed. "Literally no incentive? Or no inclination?"

Lia's eyebrow twitched, and she watched them alternatively, obviously dying to know what the conversation was about.

Loren held up his glass, prompting them to do the same. "To our valiant guests, and their service to my people, in ridding the Forest of Grass of one more predator, and for embarrassing the Imperials who have taken and shamed our land." He drank, and they followed suit, and set their glasses down. Leif's hand shook a little nervously, so he drained the sparks flooding into his fingers, and let the limb rest limp in his pocket. "Do you mean to say… you approve?"

Lia turned to him, worrying at her lip with her teeth.

"Why, that Hasetta is not only an incompetent ruler, he is an unlawful one."

"What is that word?" Leif whispered to Fryn.

"Little bird, I think…" she answered, and they looked up again as their host went on.

He took a long draught of his Ceren and smiled. "I am a loyal servant of the people, but I am most loyal to *my* people, you see. The Rosenkraun's understand nothing of our ways, and assume that we don't have them! They stole Haryn from the Cherim, and they stole Gaerlin and Fassen from us, and they bought out the corrupt prince of Wellsey, you see; they are an illegitimate empire. Well, I have no reason to support them, or to mollify them when they are shamed."

"But you didn't… hire… the thief, did you?" Fryn interjected.

"Sørasan, no!" he replied, "but that doesn't mean I can't share in their joy. If they were here at my table, I'd pour them another drink." He raised his glass once more. "May those in Exile, be restored, and our bad-hosts be reviled." They finished their glasses, and Loren waved enthusiastically for them to set their glasses forward again so he could refill them. He paused, holding the carafe over the glasses, and filled Lia's glass, and set the carafe back on the table.

Lia turned, about to run, or fly, or something, but the Earl barked quickly.

"Helayalan!"

And she stopped, and turned back, and wings twitching, she accepted the cup.

"Don't turn away, little bird," he added, "not anymore."

She took a sip and looked down, but not away.

"I will not turn you over to the Rosenkrauns, nor to the Commission. Neither Leif nor Fryn may have you. Didn't I say that looking out for one's family bred congeniality? We are not their people, we look after each other. Tell me, why did you do it?"

She sat, staring at the table top, and the light brown runner and its gold-thread embroidery. "I did what I had to," she replied simply.

"Not your plan then," Loren pressed, and Vinellin leaned closer, suddenly intensely interested in their 'quaint' happenings. "Why did you do it?" he repeated.

She set her glass down on the table cloth, its amber contents not quite gone, swirling around the bowl. "I was threatened. My daughter, she's not very strong, she couldn't survive in the wild—but they knew that. I was a Hunter once, a surveyor, really, scouting and mapping the Forest; until I was forced out of the Commission, a patsy for a crime I didn't want to commit."

"Why the crown?" Leif asked, and then shut his mouth as everyone but Lia glared at him.

"I don't know, maybe they didn't like the King, maybe it was you, Loren, though now I see it wasn't."

Loren leaned back into his chair, and finished refilling everyone else's glasses. "I see, this will also put me at risk. Little wonder, I've never been very popular with the other lords."

"So, I still don't understand, what were you supposed to do with the crown?" Leif pressed.

She looked over at him with a shrug. "I was supposed to hand it off to an intermediary in the Warehouse District, then I would be left alone… no added payment. But when I got there, those Hunter thugs were waiting for me."

"They got the same information we did, maybe whoever hired you let it slip to be rid of you," Fryn proposed, accepting her glass from the Earl, and passing Leif his. "That would make sense… then perhaps the meister at The Vineskin was involved, or one of his informants. I wish… well, never mind."

"The meister you say? I doubt it, he's a loyalist—just like his Gaersyn name. He'd have to have been misled." Loren yawned again. "But there's little more we can discover tonight. We may need to move you in case I receive unexpected visitors tomorrow. Mahaps I'll have to deal with the lower lords… Vassidel's been too vocal lately… and the King needs mollifying."

"We could blend in with your serving staff if need be," Leif offered, "we have some experience."

"Not necessary," Vinellin said with a frown, "it would only add to my work."

Loren looked up sharply, "then it is a perfect time for a Vine Inspection!"

Leif and Fryn shared looks, and then exchanged them with Lia, who also apparently didn't know what it was.

"Then, at seven sharp we will have a light tea, and at seven thirty, we will gather at the foot of the Vine." Loren stood, finished his Ceren, and stepped out with a graceful wave of his hand. Vinellin sighed, and gave a polite bow before following his master out.

They were left alone with Lia, awkwardly pondering the discussion.

"So, you're not exactly a career criminal then," Leif guessed.

Fryn chuckled.

"Not exactly, no, I was just pressed into it." Lia glanced toward the door, and then smiled at them. "I would like to see how my daughter is doing. I don't suppose we could talk more about all this later?"

"Before you go, I have one question," Fryn replied, "what if we were to turn you over to the Commission for the reward?"

She stiffened, and then relaxed. "Then you'd learn why I was able to save you from that weasel, and you wouldn't get a mint. I'd take my daughter, and we'd fly as far as we'd have to."

"You don't think we will?" Leif asked, standing with one hand edging toward his sword.

"*I certainly don't,*" Havrshyk commented idly in his head, "*you're too idealistic to be truly successful mercenaries...*"

"*You almost sound jealous, Havrshyk,*" Leif thought back.

"*You would be too, Viper, you would too.*"

Lia smiled. "I can tell whether you are actually threatening me, or just acting, Leif; gift of being a wind elemental. No, I don't think you will. Say what you want, but you aren't Hunters, Leif, Fryn, and pretty soon, you'll know what that means."

She turned and flew out the door, and Leif and Fryn were left alone beside the fire. They scooted their chairs up before the low red-glowing flames, and toasted their glasses of Ceren etched with the symbol of the

Fassen Vine. Fryn crossed her legs, and looked over at him with raised eyebrows. "You're not yourself Leif, how hard did you hit your head?"

He could see the slight creases of worry around her mouth and eyes, and felt his pulse quickening with warmth, and he smiled sadly. "I hit it pretty hard, think that ice patch is going to need replacing soon."

She rose and scooted her chair immediately next to his and placed her pale hand on his forehead. "You're feverish, Leif. Here," she pulled his head down to her lap, with one frozen hand supporting the cracked and bruised area of his skull, and the other over his forehead. "Just relax for a bit. I'm not sure just what I can do to help, but we'll see."

"*She can't heal you, you're not her, you're not her blade,*" Havrshyk mocked, laughing, though his voice grew fainter as her ice numbed his thoughts.

Sun and Sky

Fassen:

Earl's Estate

Fryn

Fryn tied off the ribbon to her woven-grass hat, looped under her chin, and turned to watch Lia tying a bow in her daughter's curly hair. She was mostly obedient, except she fidgeted as her mother lost a bit of the springy hair, and tried to pull it back out of her face again, and giggled when the end of the ribbon tickled her ear—but that could hardly be her fault.

Leif was late again. The day before, Vinellin had helped her carry him to his assigned room, and she looked down sharply as she remembered how tired and peaceful he looked with his head in her hands. She shook her head, and frowned as one of her longer bangs, which hadn't been trimmed in over a month, fell over her eye. She brushed it back, and resolved to cut it herself that very evening, if she could remember.

Loren stood on the steps outside their guest house, with the thief, her daughter, and the butler arranged on the courtyard behind him, with two saddled pigeons that cooed absently in the background. The Earl was bright and cheerful, though she supposed that bright meant cheerful, so it wasn't necessary to use both. He looked around whistling loudly, in a mysterious allegro melody, that sounded like it came from a significant piece of music.

It was odd that in Frorin they had worked so hard to assist and avenge the royalty, when all of a sudden, in Gaersheim, they were effectively working against them. But one monarch is not often like another; at least as for how they are regarded by their people. Monarchs probably at least pretended to respect each other, no matter how they felt for diplomacy's sake.

The doors swung open, and Leif marched down the steps with his hair sticking up on one side, still tugging his arms through his sleeves to adjust the fit through the shoulder and around the wing-joints. She noticed that one of the buttons on the back of his jacket wasn't even fastened, and she suppressed a laugh.

She sighed, and flit up beside him. "You can't expect to be seen in public, in the company of the Earl of Fassen, looking like this."

"It's not *so* bad," he countered, giving her an unconvincing smile.

"It's bad enough," she parried, and reposted, shooting out a frosted hand, and running it through his unruly hair. Then, she turned him around, and buttoned the jacket flaps around his wing-joints, and then stood back to examine her handiwork.

Leif was thin. He was much thinner than when she'd met him, and then, he'd had the toned physic of a hand-to-hand fighter. Aside from his slightly unhealthy or underfed aspect, he looked quite handsome with the long coat, and the black sheath sticking out between the coattails, and his wavy hair slicked and combed with frost. He looked almost like Mythrim, but more real and honest in his expression.

Fryn linked arms with him, and led him down the steps to the Earl's side, and gave a light bow. "We are all here, my lord, shall we proceed onto the Vinery?"

He nodded happily. "I was worried, Leif, when you missed tea, but there will be plenty for you to eat when we have breakfast on the east branch."

"My apologies, and I thank you for your concern, but I am quite well."

He was lying. She could tell. His heart pulsed sluggishly, as if maintaining the sword was costing much more blood than before. Almost half of the active blood in his veins was what she had given him, and a good portion of the rest had been taken from the weasel—and was degrading faster than his marrow could replace. His injuries had used up a lot of his own blood; and the blood of a weasel could only go so far. But she could spare some. Instead of funneling her excess blood into her knife, she diverted some of it to him, and felt the air grow cold around her skin. There was no substitute for faerie blood, just stop-gap solutions. Her Bloodknife felt thinner and lighter in its hidden sheath on her leg.

Better a partial draining though, than to drag a thoroughly exhausted fae around picnics all day, and Leif wasn't a true Bloodcrafter, so he wouldn't notice the help.

"Before we go however, I received a letter addressed to you," Loren said, looking up mysteriously, "I doubt I need to repeat what I said yesterday." He held out an opened envelope with an innocent smile.

She frowned but accepted it, and relaxed when she noticed that on the inside there was an untouched envelope addressed to them. The outer envelope had simply been addressed to the Earl. Cutting it open with an ice-sharpened fingernail, Fryn slid out a single sheet of paper with a single question. "*Where should we meet? –T*"

Leif shrugged. "Do they even know or agree with our change of... circumstances?"

Vinellin peeked at the letter and said, "I doubt that very much."

"I'm fairly sure that everything he does is affected by that word, 'very," Leif commented softly in her ear.

She smiled, and looked back at the paper. "Vinellin, can you get a message back to the sender?"

He considered for a few seconds, likely a lot longer than he really had to, she figured. "I imagine this is from your associate Hunters? It shouldn't be too difficult."

"We'll draft something during the picnic then," Fryn decided, and flew up to the 'pigeon-backed carriage' and sat on the bench facing Leif. "Come on then," she said, waving and then glancing away.

Lia and Nora settled opposite her, and Leif sat down on her right. There was only room enough on that bird to support four passengers and the driver, so Vinellin, Loren, and the two servants from the day before flew in the other with most of the supplies. The pigeons flapped their wings and rose in a shaky glide toward a cultivated perch on the south-facing branch of the vine. The rising and falling from the strained flapping slightly upset her stomach, so Fryn swallowed, and froze the tea she'd drunk too much of while waiting for Leif to come down. It only added to her discomfort, a solid rock bouncing in her gut.

Leif looked green as he looked at her, and placed a hand on her shoulder. "Are you alright?"

"No, are you?" Fryn forced a laugh.

"No," Leif covered his mouth and relaxed as the wind stilled, and Lia chuckled.

She twirled one finger in a tight circle in the air, bending the oncoming wind around them. "Sometimes, just a little change is enough to put us at ease."

Leif leaned over the railing, and vomited red-tinted bile, and sat back again with a frown. "I'm used to the wind... because I fly, I have wings."

Fryn found her a handkerchief in her pocket and passed it over to him without thinking, adding to Lia, "I think I'd prefer to have it back too."

The wind resumed blowing in their faces, but they reached the perch, and landed with a lurch, which sent the small orb of frozen tea partially back up her throat. She groaned and let it melt. They hopped down onto the gentle sloped branch and waited as the servants brought out the basket of goods for snacks and tea, and from the direction of the vine-trunk, a pudgy, middle-aged, balding fae trotted in their direction with barely contained worry on his almost youthful face.

"My Lord Earl! I hadn't expected your inspection until after we'd completed the harvest..." he exclaimed, panting between words.

The Lord Earl sighed, and shook his head. "It wouldn't be a surprise inspection if I had."

"Forgive me for saying so, but it is most irregular, your father never... but then I suppose, well, it makes no difference to me..." He juggled several expressions and continued breathing hard until his shoulders slumped and his wings drooped, and he relaxed more than Fryn thought was proper. "We are making good progress, just two more branches left to harvest, and then the shipments to the wineries and traders, and of course the annual tax to the crown."

She bit her lip in thought, and added softly to Leif. "I didn't think he was done talking there, odd way to end a sentence."

Leif smiled and covered his mouth. "I don't think it was a voluntary stop."

She chuckled and they continued watching their host and the overseer of the vine. The overseer's fat face made his jowls look like he was constantly frowning, and it only looked worse when he actually did, as he turned to examine them with cold disdain. "I see you have brought company, my Lord."

Loren nodded. "I did, glad you have eyes."

The overseer gave an inaudible gasp at his cutting reply, and shared a horrified look with the butler. "I've never been... but it doesn't matter... if you would all follow me, we can begin." He recovered quickly, and walked down the branch toward the center of the vine where a large interweaving of the initial growth had been coaxed into a frame for an office and overlook with a view of the city and the surrounding walls and fields. They had to step off the branch in order to enter the 'building' since it joined the confusing knot of its frame, and they crossed a suspension bridge to a roped-off balcony with a wide set of polished vinewood double doors.

The first level was a relatively narrow circular space, with eight doors, one for each direction, and was polished and mostly empty with a small musicians' dais on the south side, and room enough for a ball to allow all the surrounding nobles to attend and dance at once. Fryn wondered if the Earl rented out the space, and smiled. Harissa would probably want to host an event here.

The north side had wide steps cut into the curve of one of the branches, and led up to the main offices of the Vinery. Low desks ran down the center of the space, filled with workers tallying shipments of grapes, gross weights, and notes on quality for the various buyers, and on the east side there was a loading dock with perch-mounts for carrier pigeons, and a rope-lift to ferry supplies to the ground, or from the ground. The western end of the offices was isolated from the main 'lobby' by a wood-panel wall with doors leading off toward private offices, or archives, or other things, and the overseer waddled through the alley between his frantically-busy employees, to stand before the door to the loading dock.

"Everyone!" he began, and then choked on his own spit, and coughed four times. "I..." He coughed again. "It appears that our inspection is today. The Lord Earl has decided to grace us with his company today, so please, prepare your reports on the harvest by the end of the workday." He nodded and then looked at the Earl. "As you can see, we are quite busy finishing the inventory of the first six branches," he explained, "but we do have one of our first batches of this year's wine that you can enjoy on the Canopy Lounge."

"Canopy Lounge?" Leif wondered quietly, "that sounds nice."

The Earl nodded and flew over beside the overseer, and addressed the office workers with a loud clap of his hands. "Ahem! Good work everyone. That is all."

They watched him in stunned silence. Even Vinellin seemed surprised.

"That's all?" One of the workers, a young fee with a silver monocle asked.

"Yes. I really only wanted to have a picnic. I'm sure you are all doing your jobs well, I will read your reports at the end of the month." He laughed and then went out to the loading dock. "The Canopy is accessed from the dock."

They left the flabbergasted overseer standing by the door, and followed the Earl outside, with all their packages and attendants in tow. The loading dock was busy, crowded with corduroy-clad faeries tossing grapes through the air, bundling and netting the loads onto the pigeons, puffing on pipes and comparing smoke-rings—oblivious to the Earl's presence. The overseer had only announced him for the inside workers, and Loren didn't seem to care if he went unnoticed. A short walk to the right brought them up another carved-in set of steps to the top of the vine, where an expansive sun deck had been built over the conjoined ball of branches, ringed with rope to prevent falls, and arrayed with umbrella-covered tables and lounge chairs.

It was a rare sunny day for the fall, and passably warm, now that the sun had risen a bit more. A covered bar was set up in the middle of the deck, a circular set of shelves with a ring around it for bar seating, so that no matter where the bartender stood, they looked out.

"I'm impressed," she admitted loudly enough that the Earl would hear her.

He slowed so they could catch up with him. "It is impressive isn't it? Not my idea of course, been here for generations. It's the number one wedding-party location in the city. Oftentimes, even when there is no special occasion, one of the noble families might rent it out for a day just to enjoy the sun. I always have a few balls or parties here in the summer." He walked over to the bar and took a seat. It was unoccupied, so Vinellin flew over the counter top and started setting out glasses and moving bottles.

Leif and Fryn sat down in a couple of chairs nearby to enjoy the sun, and Leif shook his head. "This seems even fancier than Ieffin's palace."

"It is," Loren said, turning on his stool. "Took a lot longer to build, but cost a good deal less per year." He paused to enjoy the sound of the wind rustling through the leaves below and around them. "I like to spend as much time as I can here, but it really isn't all that often."

Nora flit over to the stool beside the Earl and perched, folding her legs underneath her to sit 'properly' on the padded cushion, and improperly rested her elbows on the bar and looked up at the shining glass bottles that Vinellin was still arranging. Fryn wondered once more why the butler had even come from Elin, and how long it took to travel, and just what kind of ship could cross the sea. She'd heard of little row boats being taken out on shallow ponds like the one Ieffin maintained, but to cross the ocean with its mountainous waves... they'd probably have to swim.

"What's on your mind Fryn?" Leif asked her, tilting his head to the side, looking at her and then at the bar. She could feel the slowness of his blood. He barely had any of his own left. After she'd been injured, and revived by Mythrim's blood, she'd been able to convert most of it within the last two weeks—but that was faerie blood. The weasel's blood would degrade, and likely flake off through the sword... but he'd be left without blood enough to feed his lungs and heart. Anemia would be the least of his problems. He couldn't fully drain, he couldn't freeze himself like her, preserve himself through lichform... he'd need fresh blood. She looked deep into his eyes, distracted, worried, and bit her lip as she subconsciously leaned closer.

He stiffened and looked away.

So did she.

"You look a little better than yesterday," she said at last. "You need to eat if you're to recover."

Lia sat down beside them, one eye on her quiet daughter, who watched everything the butler did with a simmering intensity that made Fryn smile. "Have you considered what you will do about your partners, and the other Hunters?"

Leif nodded, and then shook his head sadly. "I am afraid that even if we decide not to turn you in, those other three Hunters, and probably others too, will not just let you go. Seeing how they went after us at the warehouse district..." he winced and held his temple for a second, and brushed away Fryn's hand as she reached out toward him. "...I'm fine... Or, I'll be alright. We'll probably have to fight with them again."

"I think you're right about that," she said, and watched Vinellin stir a mixing cup with an overlong spoon. She'd already given Leif what she could of her own blood, perhaps she could help filter out and process the weasel's blood. They'd both be weaker for a time, but he couldn't do it. She drained him of the weasel's blood, and poured it into her knife, replacing it with even more of her own blood so that her knife cracked and rusted in her sheath; but she left enough that she could repair it with time. Though it was bound to shrink and wear away to a butterknife's shape and size.

The butler strained the contents of his cup into a tumbler and set the purple liquid before the little girl with a flourish. "Your juice, miss," he said, adding a slight bow of his head.

Her eyes widened. The crushed grape concoction glittering under the sunlight. Her hand reached out to grab it, and halted, and she looked up at her mother. "May I?"

"Yes, of course dear," Lia responded, absently adjusting her hair. She turned to Fryn with a concerned smile. "I am afraid that you are right about the Commission, and its Hunters—they do not stop chasing a mark, as long as they believe that they can catch it. Whether they must go against the local laws, or betray their friends, or hurt their comrades, they will as long as they can make a mint."

"This is based on your previous experience?" Loren asked, swiveling his stool so that it squeaked.

Leif smiled. "I'd imagine so."

"Well, you'd be right. As I said before, I used to work for the Commission, and I was betrayed, but by whom I don't know." She sighed. "Sometimes I think... no..."

Fryn shook her head. "You can't just leave us hanging," she said.

"Well she *can*,"Leif clarified, "but we'd rather you didn't."

"If you insist, then; if I could repay them my inconvenience." She gave a crooked smile and looked out toward the boulderwall. "They have quite the debt."

The Earl agreed softly, 'hmm'ing once. "But, it is not our way to charge interest on debts—even for revenge. In proportion to the crime, the indictment, and 'reward.'"

"Oddly high-minded of you Fyr Earl," Vinellin praised gently, "almost as if you would judge fairly given the opportunity."

"I would, I would," he replied, "but I cannot be sanguine without cause."

Leif gave a sharp laugh, and then pressed his fingers to his temples again. "I shouldn't have done that," he commented, waiting for it to pass, closing his eyes. "Still, we need to write a letter to Trel, either have her meet with us, or explain the situation."

"I'll figure something out," Fryn said, tempted to smile at his discomfort, but not feeling comfortable enough to do so. She got up and took the stool beside the girl and waved the butler over. "Pen and paper, if you don't mind."

He nodded and produced a thin notebook from the inside pocket of his jacket, and setting it on the counter, he brought up a corked bottle of black ink, and a goose-down quill pen. It was clean, so she held it in her mouth, flipping open the notebook with one hand, as she popped off the cork with the other.

The main problem was that they now had to go against their common goal, but, she felt her dimples showing for a moment and relaxed, Trel had only insisted on joining them and pursuing the thief together because that was what Leif and she were doing. It was possible she was only interested in the activity, rather than the objective. She dipped the pen in the bottle, and wrote.

T,

We have had something of a Viper's Chase, and turned wings, or tails. The direction we'd pursued this far seems to have been in error, and we are out of leads. We might set aside our plans for this mark after all, and return to the Lodge for a few days off. If you come by later tonight, we can share a bottle of wine, and maybe even play Serendipity again— though L might complain, since he always loses. I fear as our search has been fruitless, it will be for the other Hunters as well. It might be better to choose a new mark.

I look forward to seeing you,

~F

She finished with a swish, and left a blot beside her final character, and frowned. "That was not how I wanted that to end," she complained. Loren looked over it and shrugged.

"It looks perfectly fine to me, blots happen all the time," he said.

"Maybe with *your* penmanship, my Lord Earl," Vinellin teased in a dry monotone, "but I know many a fae who writes excellently." His eyebrows edged up slowly, and his wings twitched once, but aside from that he barely moved.

"This is the sort of behavior I choose to tolerate, it is good for me to learn patience with insufferable circumstances," the Earl alluded.

"And you also see how much forbearance I am required to show," the butler retorted, but he looked over the letter and nodded. "This will do, though I'm unfamiliar with the expression, it seems appropriate. I will have the letter hand delivered to your associate Hunter."

"But do you mean to give up the chase entirely then," Loren confirmed.

Leif sighed, leaning too-closely over her shoulder as he read the note with an expression of intense concentration. "I think it should be fairly obvious by now, that we will 'side' with you Lord Earl."

"You don't have to speak as stiffly as old Vin, you've been as useful to me as necessary to afford a certain level of informality." Loren rested his elbows on the bar and his chin in his hands, wings drooping in time with his voice.

"Whatever you prefer," Leif insisted.

He still leaned too close, and she looked back at her note, focusing on tearing out the page and handing it to the butler. She purposefully corked the ink, and cleaned the nib of the quill on a napkin. She glanced back out of the corner of her eye, and relaxed, as Leif stood and stretched his arms and wings, and breathed out as if very relieved. "What?" she asked.

"I had this tight spot in my lower back, it finally loosened up," he answered, seating himself in the empty stool to her right.

I'm pretty much all tight spots and knots, she thought, staying drained for too long.

The large overseer reappeared, sweating profusely and breathing hard, as if he'd barely made it up the stairs. He strained against the weight of two abnormally large bottles, unlabeled, and looking remarkably light-red even through the green-tinted glass, that he carried with slumped shoulders and an almost hunch-backed appearance.

"We have found the latest vintage… which… you…"

"A few more breaths, then you may continue," interjected the Earl with an exasperated wave of his arms.

Almost a minute later, the overseer set the bottles on the bar and groaned, putting two hands behind his back and then pushing it forward. It did not pop, audibly or otherwise, because he whined and then sat down. "I really hoped that it'd, but no, that's not what I meant to say. What I meant to say was, I mean to, that, I have the first test here."

Fryn's eyes narrowed. "I thought you aged wine in casks."

"We do, from the vinebark," the overseer answered, gesturing vaguely toward the bottles, "but this is just juice, not truly corked even, just squeezed. Its juice must be tasted to see how it will turn out."

Loren met her eyes. "Yes, I have tasted far too much juice in my days. But I don't regret it, having a sense of the sugars or characteristics of the juice makes me anticipate the final product. I'll already have a longstanding relationship with it. Sadly, few outside of Fassen have such a kind outlook on our wines, but then, we usually only export the wines we don't like."

The overseer's face reddened as his cheeks puffed out, and his eyes bulged. "They have no respect for the complexity of our grapes: they mix them in blends of less than ten percent, and say we have no spice, or taste like dirt... but then, I suppose they might not age well if they travel too far."

"He seems more knowledgeable than he looks," Leif whispered.

She subdued the laugh, and chuckled. "I could say the same about you."

Leif nodded soberly, accepting the fact as it was. She supposed he was often misrepresented by his first impressions. She had known what sort of fae he was when he first bumped into her in the street, and gave the wine thief dirty looks as he rushed to help her up.

"So how do you make a rich Fassen wine?" she asked, turning her stool to face the overseer with what she hoped was a humoring smile.

He looked around suspiciously, and then realizing she'd been talking to him and not someone else, he grinned. "It's simple, you crush the grapes, and let them age. You keep them in the cellars where the temperature and the moisture can stay mostly constant, and you give them as much time as they need. Tasting periodically is important," he added with an absent pat of his large stomach.

She looked over at Leif, as if to share in her eyebrow raising, but he just sort of frowned. "What's wrong?"

"I understand they need to be sure that it's progressing well, but I have no interest in tasting anything but the final product," he replied.

"But what about the wines we tasted at the Harvest Festival?" she asked, making sure no one else was listening; Loren seemed like he was trying to hear, but couldn't, Lia was busy helping her daughter drink her juice, and the overseer was still talking.

Leif shrugged with his wings. "They were meant to be drunk at those times... but I'm not sure about tasting something that's basically spoiled juice."

She smirked. "Well, you might be onto something there," she allowed.

"You finished it!" Nora complained, cutting into the overseer's monologue, her over-long wings nearly wilting behind her back.

Lia shared a wry look with the butler, who immediately placed another glass on the bar. "That was already finished," Vinellin explained, "but it was not enough."

"...and we have a saying," the overseer continued, unperturbed by the girl's interruption, "if the juice is good, then the wine is better."

Vinellin sighed gently, mumbling under his breath, that that was precisely the problem their neighbors had with Fassen wine. All the same, he opened the first bottle and poured out cordial-sized glasses for everyone, even the little girl, since it was basically juice; and Fryn suspected he wanted her to see that he made a much better juice than the overseer.

It was a pale rosy color, with mottled bits of skin not-quite strained out. She wrinkled her nose at it, and lifted the glass to her lips, waiting for Leif to taste it first. She smiled.

Leif had a way of showing exactly what he felt clearly on his face. He didn't hide his expressions quickly enough, so his attempt to hide his horror was met with disapproval by all except Vinellin—who Fryn thought secretly agreed. Leif had drunk it all at once.

"Oh, agh, what is this? If the juice is good... what kind of nonsense is that?" he demanded, and she could tell that the constriction of the blood vessels in his head had given him a migraine, which was the cause of his lack of inhibition. Still she grinned.

"Surely it's not all *that* bad," she suggested, "maybe you don't have a sense of the local palate?"

"Skin the local palate," he coughed, swallowing to get the taste out of his mouth, "and then turn it into shoes. Because that is what that tastes like: moleskin."

Loren burst out laughing, even as the overseer's face reddened and swelled, and his eyes bulged angrily from their sockets, threatening to pop out. "The tasting of the juice is vital to the making of good wine!" he insisted.

"I feel it is vital for killing one's love of wine," Fryn observed, watching how Nora, who still hadn't tasted it, held her glass suspiciously.

"Do I have to drink it?" she asked her mother quietly.

"Just humor him," she commanded, taking a sip of the new glass of juice that Vinellin had prepared for her daughter.

She obeyed, and then sputtered, and sprayed the juice over the bar. Tears sprang to her eyes, and the butler, prepared for such an eventuality, wiped the counter clean with a damp towel. "It's awful, mama... Vin's juice was so much better."

The butler grinned for an instant, and then scratched his nose, wiping away the expression. "Kind of you to say, child," he said, looking over at the Vinery's overseer with gloating eyes, "but not kind to him. I suggest you apologize for your untrained palate.

"I'm sorry," she sniffed, "what I said was unkind."

But not untrue... how Waverly. Unapologetically speaking the truth since their fall. "I have a cousin who tends to speak her mind without consideration," Fryn interjected, "and it has often seemed to me that even when one is absolutely right, they might be wrong to say so."

"Wise words," Leif said foolishly, nodding as he waved a hand toward the butler. "But I'll need something new to taste."

The overseer began stalking away, looking wholly destroyed by the girl's pronouncement, muttering about the collapse of 'everything he'd worked to accomplish over all these years.' The Earl groaned softly and looked up and over at him. "Well, for one who's accustomed to tasting something before it is perfected, I can say that the high sour notes and the amount of sugars will lead to a cherry-aspected red wine with a high alcohol content. There's nothing wrong with this juice, just the expectations of those who drink 'juice.'"

Turning quickly and rushing back on his stubby legs, the overseer beamed. "Truly? Oh marvelous! I *knew* that it would make an excellent wine: the slight drought early in the year, the unusually warm and sunny summer... yes perfect for rich grapes." He looked sharply at Leif, making him start. "And as for you, I'll have you know, that many excellent shoes have been made from cheap leather, and the same is true for wine."

Leif shrank back into his seat, and nodded. "You're the expert here... not me."

The overseer 'hmph'ed and left the way he'd come, whistling as he went.

"You shouldn't antagonize such people Leif," the Earl teased.

"And what sort of fae can I antagonize?" he asked.

"Antagonistic ones, obviously." Loren grinned. "You can usually tell, if they act like you did earlier."

"I remember you saying I should speak more informally with you earlier, but now I'm beginning to know why."

"If I recall," Fryn added, leaning over the counter a bit to draw his attention, "you once complained that even during a first meeting, you invited being teased."

"You've got a good memory..." he sighed. "Still," he said, glancing over at the butler, "how do you intend to get that letter to Trel?"

He blinked. "Personally."

"Ah yes, of course." He chuckled and turned his stool to look out at the city, what was visible anyway, since the umbrella of the vine's branches blocked a good portion of it.

They sat and enjoyed a taste of the previous year's wine, which was better than Fryn expected, and better than Leif's earlier judgement would have led someone to expect. The butler signaled to the other servants, who had apparently been waiting things out below, and they brought out the baskets of bread, and meat, and cheese. The loaves were fluffy and fat, and sliced thinly, so that when he laid out the pieces, he spread a layer of dark brown mustard, and alternating slices of roasted, thyme-dusted pigeon-breast, and some kind of mild white hare-cheese. He cut them into triangles, removing the crusts with sharp hard-to-follow flashes of his blade, and arranged them in a spiral pattern on a white ceramic platter with a small bowl of mustard in the center; for dipping, she supposed.

He slid the platter over the counter, surprisingly without disturbing the contents. Fryn picked one up, about to dip it in the bowl, when the Earl held up a hand with the first two fingers raised. "You haven't paid attention have you, Fryn."

She set it back down and waited, tapping one foot on air. The butler closed his eyes solemnly, and flicked one wing toward the girl.

"Linella hasrinhyn møn weray," she pronounced, looking up at them self-consciously.

Fryn noticed the girl's mother silently gesturing for her to continue, mouthing "go on..."

"Setfjeø me sørje." She smiled and fidgeted with the edge of her dress.

"Møn serø," the Earl commented, patting Nora's head, and ruffling her hair. "It is important to remember our own words, and customs." He faced Fryn and then Leif, with a wry turn to his lips. "Today we are well, Wing-Giver be praised, it is an old blessing, and a favorite... not least because I want always to be well." He finished by swiping up one of the triangles, dipping it deeply into the mustard, wiping it around the bowl to fully coat the most of it, and then eating half of the sandwich in one bite.

Leif followed suit, snaking one arm out before she could react; grabbing a sandwich and dipping it messily, he got a dab of mustard on his face. "You shouldn't rush," she said, though she figured it was probably best he eat more food to help his body replace his lost blood. She took one of her own, but wasn't quite as liberal with the sauce, and tasted a small bit on the corner of her sandwich.

It had a light, springy texture from the fluffy bread, but the spiciness from the horseradish and brown mustard made her nose burn and her face turn deep red. She turned away from Leif, smiling, and coughing. "There's almost too much going on in there..." she commented.

He just nodded pleasantly, with a silly grin. "It's not that spicy," he said, "makes me feel like I'm eating a cool summer sandwich at the School."

"I miss having mint in my sandwiches," she replied. The horseradish was the worst part, and she found herself trying to stifle a sneeze. No success. She sneezed—and a cloud of ice crystal clattered forcefully to the ground. Fryn was grateful she at least missed the bar, and her coat.

"Now that is a handy trick," Loren observed. "Takes away any unseemliness from an otherwise disgusting and unfortunate act, and turns it into an amusement."

"Indeed," Leif agreed, "very amusing."

Fryn sighed, and looked to Vinellin for support, but he was no use; he just averted his eyes. So she settled for distracting them. "You said that this picnic would let us taste something aside from shoe leather," she reminded the Earl, tapping her chin with her sandwich, cheeks still red from the spice; blood refusing to obey her and drain from her face.

"Bless you, yes!" he cheered, "Vin, the vine."

The butler produced proper wine glasses, with long thin stems, and wide, cut crystal bowls, decorated with the symbol of Fassen: the eight-pointed vine. She watched him soundlessly pull the cork from a dark green bottle, unlabeled, and pour a modest amount in the four glasses arranged in a semicircle on the bar. He didn't spill a drop, and the bottle remained half full when he stopped. "It is getting on in the day my Lord Earl," he admitted, "past noon at any rate."

"Then empty that thing," Loren suggested.

"I'm afraid it would be better to see now if it is to our guests' tastes…"

The Earl watched her for a few seconds, and then looked hard at Leif. "My guests will enjoy it, have no doubt."

Leif yawned and picked up his glass. "Is there a special toast or something we need to do?"

"No," he replied.

"Alright then," Lia cut in, switching seats with her daughter to be closer to the company, "this one's for you, Lord Earl." She picked up her cup, and shoved her hand toward the middle of the group, the Earl and Leif did too, and Fryn felt she had no excuse not to do the same. She shot Leif a smirk and took her cup, and was surprised when she realized that the glasses made a perfect 'A' note with their ringing. They tasted it, and it wasn't bad.

"I have an errand to attend to," Vinellin announced to his master softly, but clearly enough they could hear. "I will return within the hour." And with that, he adjusted the fit of his coat, and gloves, and flew off toward the Commission's Quarter, vanishing before long, as a dark black speck against the backdrop of the buildings below, the boulderwall beyond, and the far off reaches of the Forest of Grass.

Dust and Moss

Fassen:

Commission's Quarter

Bounty Office

Leif

His headache had not gone away since Havrshyk had decided to withhold his regenerative abilities. It had been three days, and Fryn was looking tired as well. Leif noticed that his condition was barely improving, that Havrshyk refused to talk, and that Fryn was becoming more distant—to the point that if he initiated a conversation with her, she'd jump in surprise. He stood in the Bounty Office looking for something to occupy them with but...

The bounty board did not have much of interest.

"Can I help you?" The clerk asked, staring him down over silver-rimmed glasses through the security glass separating his desk from the dangerous elements. "Are you not going after that thief from the other day like all the other Hunters?"

Leif glanced over his shoulder at him. "Oh, if it isn't Norran, the unhelpful clerk."

Norran's eyes narrowed and his mouth pressed into a thin line. "Unhelpful, you say? I could just as easily disparage you: the so-called womanizing viper, Sigliefr Aellin."

"Now, now, Norran," called the bank teller from down the hall, "don't stoop."

He groaned loudly and let his iconic pen fall from his mouth to his desk, getting ink blots on the paper he'd been about to write on for the past half hour. "If you'd had to deal with the Francis brothers, Danice," he said, over accentuating the syllables of her name, "you'd also have exhausted your daily allotment of patience."

Leif's wings twitched in response. "The Francis brothers, you say? Not fond of them, eh?"

Norran gave him another cold look. "No one says 'eh' unless they're from Stanaedre or Muerlund. But, no, I am not—surprisingly I like them even less than you."

"But you don't have any problems with my partner then?" he asked.

The clerk blinked. "Not as much as with you."

"Glad we understand each other. Now, what were the three fools up to?" Leif pressed, flitting over to the clerk's window and leaning on the counter conspiratorially.

"Not my business, not yours."

"Oh, please," Leif said, unable to keep his smile off his face. "I have a debt I'd like to pay off, to Germaine specifically."

"Debt? Perhaps you'd be better off bothering my associate at the Bank." The clerk picked up his pen and once more balanced it in his mouth.

"He gave me a concussion, just because he was going after the same target as me," Leif added.

"I'm sure you were told that such competition between associates was an eventuality you could not avoid." He looked down again, and Leif noticed that he'd been hiding a book below the level of the counter, and reading it when he wasn't busy.

"Oh, I've read that," he lied, "the main character dies half-way through, and it switches mid-book to a new protagonist."

"What?" Norran demanded, meeting Leif's eyes with intense anger and interest. "Mid-book you say? How could you tell me that? But still… it's brilliant, all the signs are there. It already feels like a short story, I just thought something would pick up…"

"I'll tell you more about it, unless you tell me what Germaine and the others were up to." Leif leaned in threateningly, but the effect was diminished by the glass separating them.

The bell fixed to the top of the door chimed as Fryn entered, walking in distracted with a blank face and a couple of her now over-long bangs out of place.

"Fine then. They were asking why you suddenly abandoned the chase, and if you had started pursuing a new target." He saw Fryn and then turned back to Leif with a confused bunching of his brow. "Something happened to you."

"Anything?" Fryn asked, resting half her weight against the counter beside him. Her eyes were glazed over, and her shoulders slightly slumped.

"I don't know much about it," he whispered in her ear, frowning when he noticed that she didn't seem to mind, as if her sense of personal space hadn't woken up yet for the day, "but are you sure you're getting enough blood? Is something wrong with your knife?"

"I'm alright," she answered, her pale blue eyes shifting slowly to meet his gaze, "don't worry about me."

He checked the clerk out of the corner of his eye; he was pretending to be distracted by his book, but Leif suspected he was merely trying to eavesdrop. He leaned in closer and lowered his voice. "If you need it, I can lend you some of my blood. Fae tend to recover faster from such losses, well, faster than most fee, I hear."

She smiled and shook her head. "I'm fine. You can keep your blood." Her cryptic expression, a mixture of amusement and looking flattered, did not help him solve her problem. He'd have to do it some other way. Pulling away from the counter, Leif walked a few small circles, arms crossed, reviewed the bounty board, and watched Fryn.

"Not herself," he thought, tapping his fingers on his arm.

A thin film of reddish black washed over his vision, as Havrshyk's voice answered him. "She should have taken advantage of your offer; a Bloodcrafter needs blood to maintain their artifact, and a Lich requires it to live. Her reserves must be quite low, for it to affect her state of mind…"

"Keep it to yourself," Leif mumbled. "If her condition worsens, I could just cut myself with her knife when she's not looking, and let it restore her strength. If she's anemic, or worse, we'll be at risk if the brothers don't believe we've given up on the crown," he continued in his head.

"I'm still not convinced of that yet myself," Havrshyk replied, his tone mocking, and light.

Norran stood and set his book on the counter with an unevenly folded piece of paper as a bookmark. "They insisted that you had not given up the chase, even when I told them about your visit with the Earl. I'm not sure I believe it either."

Leif pushed away Havrshyk's stifling company for the moment and refocused on the clerk. "Well, one look at my companion will have you thinking better. We need some time to rest. We hadn't fully recovered from our last target, and thought it would be easier to defeat and disable a thief; we didn't realize that fighting other Hunters would prove a greater challenge."

"Challenge?" Fryn scoffed tiredly, "just not the best timing."

"They went looking for more information—though I'm honestly not sure what they'll find or where." The clerk pointed toward the southern door with his chin and watched them move toward it with a smile. "If that's the price of my peace of mind, it's well enough spent."

They exited onto Shadowvine Way, into a dreary day, not raining, just misty and damp. The street on either side was partially shrouded by a thin fog, and the amber starlamps glowed dully like orange pools. The sloping hill toward the base of the vine was littered with small estates separated by carefully tended pebble-stone walls and gates, with miniature palaces; each section roughly the size of a medium block. "I wonder who lives in the Shadowvine Quarter," Leif wondered.

Fryn nodded.

"Think there's anyone like Harissa or Jason here?"

"No," she said. "I don't."

He shook his head and led the way toward one of the nearer estates. Crossing the street on a quick wing, he looked back in horror as Fryn was nearly run over by a hare-drawn cab. She stumbled backwards onto the curb just as it swept by, bouncing on its incredible shocks, with a severe fae staring them down through the small porthole in its side, wearing a dark green pince-nez and a matching felt top hat. In that same moment, his cab turned the corner on the Earl's Fiveway, and vanished behind the low-noble's wall.

Leif flew back in a rush, the fog deepening despite the mid-morning sun, and knelt beside her. "What was he thinking? Going about like that, he could've run you down!"

She shook her head, and a little color returned to her cheeks. "I'm afraid he nearly did. He turned on Earl's Way, I believe, could be one of the Shadowvine Quarter's residents."

"Well I shouldn't like to make *his* acquaintance." Leif sniffed. "Now we'd best see what Trel's been up to." Standing again, he wobbled back on his heels and straightened. "She went to visit 'an old friend' down Sanvelt Street."

"Sorry-sounding name for a place," Fryn commented, accepting the hand Leif offered to help her up. "Did you see anything we could go for on the wall?"

They crossed over again to the southern side of the street, and followed it in the direction of the Vineskin—but they had no intention of visiting there. "There's a merchant who's been selling mysterious wares around town and is suspected of being a fence for local burglars. We could try looking out for him, wanted for fifty-mint. Good enough for a bite of lunch or two."

"Good for more than that if you economize for once," she replied, "A decent meal should only cost you twelve-mint at a restaurant. It's only because you insist on buying bottles of wine, or multi-course meals we run into the hundred-mint and more range." Her dimples flashed momentarily on her face as she smiled, and then covered it with a false sneeze. "Excuse me," she said.

"You're thinking of when we followed Mythrim to that restaurant in the Snow District, aren't you? That was different. Or the Vineskin? Information." He stopped for a second and considered, staring at one of the starlamps, letting some of the other pedestrians—flying or otherwise—pass them by. A trio of little boys chased each other around one of the lamps playing at 'Hunters and Thieves' yelling as one of them grabbed one of his friends, punching him softly in the stomach, and then picking up his 'unconscious' form by the collar, and threatened the other one to surrender. Fryn got further away, but Leif was still lost in thought, so eventually, she called to him.

"Are you coming? Or are you going to fly into the lamp?" She glanced over at the boys with a chuckle, tearing him from his thoughts.

"Yes, I'm coming!" he said, starting forward, running his hand through his hair with an embarrassed smile. "I just realized, Fryn," he added quietly, "we've never actually gone to a nice restaurant just to have a nice meal."

She laughed. "What's this? We've known each other a month and already you're concerned about something like that?" Fryn continued walking, speeding up as he tried to match her pace.

"I just mean, it would be nice to have a quiet evening without Trel, or the Earl, or other Hunters getting in the way."

"I'm sure," she said, staying ahead of him, "but I wonder whether it wouldn't be nicer to have an evening by myself."

He caught up with her, but was disappointed that their banter hadn't affected the color of her face. She regarded him with tired eyes, and a blank expression, and continued on again. "Don't be like that," he insisted.

"Like what?"

"That," he repeated. "You want things to settle down as much as I do, I'm sure."

She smiled. "What I want is to sleep in."

Before he could comment, however, they were rudely interrupted by a sneering voice from a side-alley. "You're not the only one," he said, revealing himself in the unwelcome identity of one of the Francis brothers—the youngest, Germaine. "I had to get up well before the sun today," he added bitterly, glaring at Leif for a second, before shifting to a cruel grin toward Fryn.

Leif nearly jumped, but he knew he shouldn't be surprised if they'd been followed. "Well, you can get used to it; I hope you never sleep through the night."

"Sharp words, coming from a forked-tongued wanderer," he retorted with his eyes narrowed to slits. "As they say here: broken you will rise, and broken you shall fall."

Fryn met his eyes for a second with a doubtful twist to her mouth. "I don't think that is an expression."

"It is," he said, "and I warn you; if you think your act will deceive us, then you're more foolish than you look—and you look more foolish than most."

"I feel like I should be offended, Fryn, should I?" Leif asked, tempted to return Germaine's sneer.

"I think you should..." she replied uncertainly, "but one wonders whether they should care when they are insulted by such as him."

"I'm watching you," he warned, "you can't keep that thief hidden forever—and yes... we know you have her."

So he doesn't realize we're not turning her in... that could actually be useful... he probably thinks that we're just going to turn her in when they're not going to try to steal her from us. Leif thought to himself.

"I told you before, that's exactly what most Hunters should do... in the words of your companion, 'one wonders' whether you aren't defective," Havrshyk commented idly, somehow, the sword had gotten loose in his scabbard, and edged up as if to see what was going on.

And I told you to mind your own business. Leif locked the clasp on the scabbard so it wouldn't get out, and refocused on their unwelcome guest. "If you're going to follow us, then you can make yourself useful. Have you seen a strange peddler anywhere in the markets?"

Germaine blinked stupidly and scratched one of his overly-long ears. "What do want to know that for?"

Fryn raised her hand just so, to reply before he could. "Because, as we have already said, we are done with that other chase. The thief has escaped, and is probably in hiding. So we decided it would be better to focus our energies on more productive endeavors."

She seemed awfully proud of that speech, and Leif admitted, she *did* sound educated and as if she knew what she was talking about. "Right," he added unnecessarily.

Their would-be stalker snorted and looked around the street from his place in the alley. "I think we already nabbed that one."

"The peddler?" Fryn confirmed. "Perhaps now it is we who don't believe you. Good day." She walked off, and glanced back at Leif, prompting him to follow with a barely noticeable tilt of her head and a jerk of one of her lower wings.

"I believe we'll have more success if we look in the lower income markets of the Boulderwall District," Leif alluded as he ran to catch up.

"Yes, but first I need something solid to eat," she said with a toothy smile and dimples on her cheeks. "My blade needs its repairs, and meat is the building block of blood."

"I could use something like that myself," he agreed. "Did you pick up one of the guide pamphlets at the Lodge?"

She didn't pause, but her voice betrayed some worry. "I didn't, and I'm guessing neither did you."

He sighed. "I guess we'll have to find something. Not that I minded the sandwiches that Old Vin made for us, but I could use something a bit heartier."

Fryn nodded and in keeping with their statement of searching Boulderwall, they followed Boulderstreet until they spied an alley leading north toward Eastwall with an auspicious title: "Quill-Feather Place," Leif read as they passed.

The sharp turn cut through the back entrances of the main street-facing businesses, most of which had something to do with books, or down. There was a quiltist, a middle-class pen-maker, and a small printing house that supposedly spread the latest important news throughout the entire district. Leif had his doubts, looking at its shabby back entrance door that hung unlocked and crooked on its rusted hinges, and a dried-out patch of peat-ashes nearly cemented to the stones.

Still, it was better than being tail-feathered by the Francis brothers. They continued on another block, the alley getting closer and closer, and the air thicker, as the buildings hemmed them in. Leif wondered if they'd reach a dead end, but just as he thought they were about to hit a wall, it turned out to be a screening wall, with paths angling sharply around it to enter what was inevitably the next district. They slid into the narrow gapped paths, having to separate to meet on the other side, and Leif found Fryn just staring outwards with her mouth and jaw clenched.

Eastwall was not like the other districts. It was worn down, and beaten-in by rain, bowed roofs, missing shingles, and half-hung signboards, stained by soot, with cracked windows and unpainted stones; it seemed the last stop of the post, before the leftover undelivered letters were dropped over the wall for the weasels to read. Leif's wings and shoulders slumped, and he subconsciously matched the posture of the surrounding faeries who went about their so-called business, whether it was carrying nearly empty shopping sacks, or 'cleaning' their porch of the dust—dutifully doing chores they could never really complete.

"Ohh..." he said, craning back his head to look at the sky. The buildings leaned toward each other from either side of the street with bracing beams separating and supporting the upper floors so that only a sliver of the sky remained. There wasn't room to see the sun, let alone to fly. "I don't like this..."

Fryn looked at him with a mixture of amusement and commiseration, and placed her hand on his arm. "Not so friendly if you're used to the desert, huh?"

He blinked. "That was pretty insightful."

"You've been like this before, if you get cooped up too long, you start sighing like a pheasant." She gave him a smirk, and withdrew her hand. "Now let's find what counts as a 'market' here."

He didn't reply, just followed, one eye constantly searching, the other tracking her. *Don't see why she'd want to hide here of all places,* he thought bitterly.

"You don't? Even you could vanish here, if you wanted to, in spite of your sun-kissed skin. Just the sort of place a criminal goes to ground." Havrshyk had somehow unlatched the hilt of the sword from the scabbard, and seemed anxious to be involved.

Leif ducked under an absurdly hung string of undried laundry, which he would've argued was also unwashed. Soot and dirt and grass stains on the white undershirts and tan pairs of trousers, matched, or rather clashed, with the mottled-red color of an incredibly wide jacket, which dripped... red-stained water from its cuffs. Fryn walked right under it with one hand catching the drops, and then casting them off with a frown. He barely heard her whisper, 'not faerie' and lightly shake her head.

I don't like it Havrshyk, besides, why do you talk as if you aren't one of those 'criminal elements' as you put it? Leif asked his sword, shivering as a drop of red something trickled down his wing.

Havrshyk laughed coolly and sighed. Which was surprising—if all that remained was his disembodied voice in a sword, how could he affect those kind of expressions, or sounds? *"Because Leif, I wasn't one. But that's a story for another time. For now, you need to learn to use me... if you feed me, perhaps I'll heal you again. I live on, and so do you: it's a good deal, and my only offer."*

Fryn stopped on what sufficed for a curbside in the middle of a tangle where three streets met, turning and looking around with her eyebrows wrinkled and a frown.

"I thought she'd hide with the Earl," Leif mumbled, stopping beside her, hands on his hips.

She folded her wings and considered him for a few seconds. "Well, she will, just not right when we were there. If the other Hunters get it into their heads to infiltrate his estate, and they find her there... he could be charged with trying to foment rebellion." She smiled, mouthing the word 'foment' a couple more times. "I always wanted to say that."

"I'm surprised they stigmatized the Pine District so much, when poor quarters in other cities are this bad off." He scratched his chin, and crossed his arms.

"The nobles in the Snow District have not seen any other cities, and even if they had, they wouldn't visit a poor quarter to begin with. It would be unseemly. Besides, my people have the Pine-Martin to govern and look after them, even if he, well now she, doesn't spread mint freely among them, they are protected from extortion, and usury." She nodded and reached into her pocket, retrieving a folded piece of double-weight card stock. "She said they were down NE Hasseli Way, and then up Kaena Street. Number 1202Ø."

"What's with the letter?"

She started to the street on the right fork with a chuckle. "It means that 1202 was broken into a number of smaller 'flats.' If I recall, it goes Ā, Ī, Ì, Ø…" She muttered through the alphabetical, and nodded to herself. "Fourth flat then."

"What about Sanvelt?" he asked, dodging a low-hanging bit of rope from one of the slanted windows above.

She looked back a for a second, and expertly avoided stepping into a pile of indescribable muck with a backwards flit of her wings. "That was a distraction, I didn't tell you before because if you spoke about it at the wrong time, one of *them* might have heard it."

He bit his lip and jumped the 'puddle.' "Well, alright, but I don't like it."

Their path through what counted as streets in the downward slant of the city was mired by runoff from the higher districts, which churned or aged, in the one-time serviceable drains along the curb. Moss, lichen, bits of ivy, they all competed in the standing water. Leif wondered if they had to worry about frogs, or mosquitos. He'd heard they were a problem in the south, and this looked a lot like what he'd heard the south was like.

After a roughly fifteen minute descent, where oddly the level of the tops of the buildings didn't change, only their depth to match the incline, they found themselves at an intersection lit by a blackened oil lamp post, with a barely legible sign indicating that they had reached the crossing with Kaena Street. Leif frowned. It was almost noon, but here in the 'bowls' of the city, he felt like he'd gone into a city built by moles. The buildings towered impossibly over him, all leaning toward each other so as to block all but directly vertical sunlight, with the effect being that they stood in a close circle of dim lamp light surrounded by a heavy black fog. It didn't help that all around they heard the odd shuffling or shifting sounds of obscure passersby, or other denizens of the dark; Leif cringed.

"This is not what I had imagined when I decided to go see the world," he said, eyeing the mildewed street sign.

Fryn followed his gaze, as if oblivious to his distaste. "Yes, entirely unpleasant," she allowed. "Just left through here." She stepped forward, just to the edge of the light, and he caught her by the tip of her wing.

"Stop," he said, and stared into the fog. Something tickled at the base of his neck, he found his sparks racing through his nerves, his hair standing on end. "Someone's out there."

"Of course there is," she replied, "it's a city."

His sword unlatched with a soft 'click' and his hand went to it, about to fasten it again, but then he reconsidered.

"You've got good instincts, Leif," Havrshyk praised ironically, "I can see now how you survived our encounters. It is one thing to prepare against strategies and tactics of certain styles, but entirely another to counter the instantaneous movements of your opponent's instinct."

"And what do you sense?" he asked.

"Nothing, but I have some reason not to doubt your senses." His voice slid into a slightly flat note, as if he were moving around inside the sword. "Might have something to do with what this viper left in here."

Left felt almost a tapping sensation in his arm, well below the skin, below his scars, were the viper's fang had broken off and fused with his bones.

"Could be," he said, and focused on the sluggish currents of the fog, which twisted about itself idly... except in one place, where it didn't shift at all. He drew sparks from his center, and the ground, and guided them to his hands. The air shifted and edged away, and as he stepped toward the center of the path, the fog did as well.

The area of unmoving fog resisted him, held together by someone else's element, he could feel the pressure more and more as he got closer. Fryn trailed after him with a concerned expression, well, for her it was really an expressionless expression, but she usually did that to mask her concern; or to mask something else.

Leif walked closer to the thick space of fog, in the now almost pitch-dark alley, and felt the weight of the air change, the degree of resistance to his sparks shift into a heavy arc, slashed through in a diagonal from the ground toward his shoulder. He slipped around the trajectory, and smiled coldly, as a blast of air and focused fog gusted through the thin line and slammed into the crumbling pebble stones of the opposite wall—cutting an inch wide incision into the mortar and stones. The assailant launched upwards, rebounded off one of the cross beams separating the houses near the top, and flew at him with all the speed and force of an arrow.

The edge of a blade flashed across his vision, and he felt faint, and cold, as if he'd forgotten how to breath, and fumbled back just in time to avoid a decapitating blow. Fryn dove over him, face hardened, blood drained completely, as her knife formed into a thin razor with a sort of hexagonal crystalline framework—as if she were trying to improve its durability using less blood. His heart fell as she focused on it, and the determination in her face, as she deflected the slash, and spun in mid-air, kicking the weapon out of their hand with an ice-encrusted boot.

Leif rolled to the side, and braced himself against the wall as he channeled his sparks through his limbs, and settled into a low stance, one hand forward, open, the other on Havrshyk's hilt.

"Yes..." he said, aching to be free, *"pay your dues."*

Shut it. Leif jumped from the wall toward the falling attacker, and drew the sword in a flash across his chest. It split the thick green padding of his uniform, but he avoided a killing blow with a backwards wing-burst, and brought an air-hardened hand down in a chop toward Leif's elbow.

Fryn appeared behind him, little dagger in hand, and she caught him with the edge against his neck. He relaxed, and Leif pulled back. "Who are you, and why did you attack us?" She asked, drained of all color except for the blue of her eyes and mouth.

Their attacker was a youngish fae with a sharp chin and black hair, uncombed, and long enough to reach his ears. He stared at Leif with a tight-lipped and fearless expression.

Leif smiled pleasantly. "Not much for conversation I take it?"

He cracked a smile.

"That's a yes then. Now, correct me if I miss something here, Fryn, but could this fae be an associate of the Francis brothers?" he continued.

She nodded, though since she was behind him, their assailant could not see it.

"Right then, and what do we do to our competitors?"

"We remove them," she said simply.

"Right again," Leif said, applauding her deduction silently. "And how do we do that?"

The edge of her knife just barely cut the skin of his neck as he swallowed.

"How do we *do* that I wonder." He stared him down with what he hoped was an intimidating expression.

"I'm not with the Hunters..." he admitted.

"Not of the Commission then? But if not, then we can afford to just kill you," Fryn reasoned.

"No, I, you can't. I was sent to investigate allegations of treason." He avoided Leif's eyes.

Leif sighed. "I guess your king was pretty upset when he lost his crown. But why come after us?"

"Why indeed," Fryn added.

"Why indeed," Leif repeated.

"Why indeed?" their attacker wondered. "It was said among our informants that you had apprehended the thief, but had not turned her in. Some even suggested that you had been bought out by the thief to help her sell it."

"Well, you're wrong." Leif allowed his sparks to dissipate, and sheathed a seething Havrshyk. "We are on a break from our hunt, because of those parasitic Francis brothers. They've been chasing us ever since we both found the thief. We lost her of course, but they don't believe us; but we're not about to tell them what leads we have. We're already splitting the bounty with Trel and Yarrow."

Fryn slowly let go of the Gaersyn agent, and backed off a few steps. "So," she said, "if you wouldn't mind telling your associates that we are not acting against the interests of the king, or the Commission, we'd be grateful."

He dusted himself off and retrieved his sword from the gutter with a sick-at-heart frown as he wiped it off on his now-ruined coat. "I will investigate the matter more fully, but be advised, if we discover that you are working against the Rosenkraun king, we will remove you, regardless of your reputation in Frorin. When you became Hunters of the Commission you relinquished any citizenship you had in any of the countries in Fhoraena, or Elin, or anywhere else."

"Yes well, so be it," Leif answered. "Now let us continue about our business. Hunters are free to pursue sanctioned targets internationally without the oversight or interference of the local authorities."

He slid his sword into a sheath between his green-lined wings on his back, and gave each of them a perfunctory bow, before flying straight up to the far-off rooftops and disappearing from their view.

"Whew," Leif said, stretching his arms with relief, "Loren was right about the dangers of siding with him."

"Best keep that forked-tongue of yours quiet, Leif," Fryn advised with a wry crossing of her arms. "Never know how many of those Grass-Forest Guards will come after us next time."

"Did you see his sword?" Leif asked. "It looked almost like a blade of grass, green, and leaf-shaped, sort of."

"I believe they have their own techniques to make those weapons, after all, iron is not easy to come by in the middle of the grasslands."

"I suppose that makes sense." He started up the street and let his wings flutter a bit to get the tension out of his shoulders. "Short fight, though that would've gone badly if you weren't here."

She caught up with him and nodded. He had the sense that she almost linked arms, and then realized they didn't need to act. He also wondered whether it would be better if they did. He chewed the inside of his cheek and turned over the possibilities. Finally, he stuffed his Fryn-side hand in his jacket pocket, and angled his elbow out with room enough for her to slip an arm through if she wished.

He swallowed silently, for almost as soon as he'd done so, she'd subconsciously linked arms, and they now walked through the stuffy, mired streets, as if they were pretending to be going out on the town like they had in Frorin. Did she even notice? Was it natural? He didn't mind if she did or not.

"Again the hideous adolescent-fee romance novel, ple-ease leave me out of it," Havrshyk complained. The sword latched itself this time.

Before too long, after a pleasant walk through unpleasant and damp streets, they arrived before what could only be described as a dilapidated apartment complex. It rose some five stories, made of crumbling bricks and chipped pebbles, with mortar that sloughed away into piles of dust, a large and largely unreadable sign alluded to the address: 1202 Kaena Street. They stared at the three steps leading to the entry hall, and shared a frown.

A fae in rags with a braided, brown beard sat on the top step holding up a hanger with clips, from which he displayed his 'wares' such as they were—a pair of clean socks, a parcel of wrapped 'medicinal' herbs, and a few pieces of carved bone jewelry.

They stopped before him with arms still linked and looked up in wonder.

"What are you doing in the open if there's a bounty on your head?" Fryn asked him with a puzzled wrinkle to her nose.

He held the assortment of goods from their display hanger in one hand, and stroked his beard with the other nonchalantly. "I'd hardly think I were 'out in the open' as you put it, Lyr Hunter."

So is it a mostly Waverly slum? Leif wondered to himself, and Havrshyk didn't bother to respond, so he felt a sense of relief at having his own thoughts to himself again; if only temporarily.

"Maybe not," Fryn allowed, "but why are you here before *this* building? Were you waiting for us?"

He gave her a mostly toothless smile. "You're a sharp one, seems your hair's got deep roots, as they say."

Leif shivered. "That is not a comforting expression."

"It means that her mind is good, rich, soil, for cultivating you see," the peddler replied. "Your friends are inside, first floor down the stairs, fourth flat." He jerked a knobby thumb over his shoulder at the door, and as they thanked him and passed, Leif noticed in horror, that his upper wings had been split from the tips to the joints, so he could no longer fly; but not so he'd be cursed as a 'Wingless.'

He opened the vinebark door with a light push and followed Fryn inside, only then disengaging their arms. She marched quickly toward a set of stairs to the left and descended with reddened tips to her ears, and a slight flush of purple to her wings. He tried not to rush after her, and patted his face to refocus. *So she did notice... ugh I'm such a fool.* Leif decided to change the subject as soon as they got to the basement floor.

"Why did they split his wings?" he asked with a short cough to clear his throat.

Fryn avoided looking at him as she replied. "I think they do that to someone who's committed premeditated murder, still giving them a chance to repair their ways; after they get out of prison."

"Seems rather drastic..."

"Well, it's better than the death sentence. In Froreholt, a murderer is executed after a month of repentance and near-isolation. We don't behead them though, ah, the executioner uses a lance and pierces their heart—as if they were the serpent being judged by old Arta."

Leif nodded. There were four halls, each leading to a single door, each door marked by an alphabetical. Their destination was behind the foot of the stairs. "In Aelaete it may depend on each clan's customs, but typically, they are exiled to the deep sands. Most die of thirst, or exhaustion, or are killed by vipers and the like. But some survive, and are considered dead; so if they show themselves among the cities anywhere, they can be killed by anyone without judgement. But we don't maim them, if they live and keep to themselves, they can live under the Wing-Giver's hand. He's the one who judges in the end. That's how Chistleton became a city, a few exiles over hundreds of years gathered at the oasis, and built themselves a clanless town."

Fryn knocked on the door.

Silence.

The door opened, and Fryn backed off as Trel appeared with her fluid blood-bow shifting into drawn action in her hands. "Who's asking?" She demanded with a grin.

"Who else?" Leif asked in return. "Were you expecting us to bring trouble?"

She shook her head and waved them in. "Lia's in the washroom now, Nora fell in one of the drains and needed... what works for a bath. Yarrow's over there somewhere," she added, waving toward a room to the direct right of the entry.

Leif and Fryn stepped inside, both cringing again as they saw the yellowed plaster on the walls, the chipped and fraying pressed-reed pillars, and the surely unsafe placement of the oil lamp on the tiny table in the space behind the open door. Trel put away her bow, which coiled into a fluid line, flowing around her form in a few cyclical loops before slithering into the bottle on her belt at the small of her back between the lower wings. She wore a plain uniform of canvas and green, almost matching the clothing of the Forest Guard they nearly killed on the way. Her belt was covered in an assortment of regular tools as well, including but not limited to, a lock-picking set, a few keys, a long knife, a water-bottle, and a locked coin pouch. Her gear jingled as she moved into the back room and collapsed into a dilapidated couch, wings folded awkwardly beneath her.

"I don't know what the builder of the couch was thinking, but I doubt they had all their wings..." She complained, waving toward the other room she'd alluded to earlier, where she could view the inside of the 'kitchen' through a hole cut into the adjoining wall.

Yarrow stood inside with a dirty, frayed apron and his sleeves rolled back, and flour on his hands. He welcomed them with a smile and wing-twitch, and also a wave. "Good to see the two of you again; it seems as though for the past week we've barely even spoken."

Leif placed a hand on Fryn's shoulder, and went off into the kitchen. "What are you cooking up?" he called in from 'the hall,' "Something tasty I hope."

"Not very likely," Yarrow replied with a resigned wave of his hands. Before him on the counter was a bowl of mashed-together bits of flour, oil, and hare's milk, as if he were trying to make some kind of cake. A good drizzling of honey was over the top of it, and a finch-egg sat unused beside the bowl.

"Ooh, this looks rather good," Leif said, pushing Yarrow lightly on the arm. "You lied to me!"

"I haven't a whisk," he admitted, presenting his messy hands.

"Oh… so that's the problem. What's your affinity again?" Leif leaned over the bowl to inspect it more closely. Slightly hidden by the rim of the bowl he noticed a golden band, carefully placed to avoid getting anything on it. *Hmm, did they run off and get married?*

He felt Havrshyk purposefully tighten the lock on the sword even further. *"I've told you before, I'm not interested in your gossip."*

On closer inspection though, he noticed a few coins as well, as if Yarrow had emptied his pockets before 'getting to it' as the saying goes. The ring then, thin, and decorated with criss-crossing green metal inset in its outer side, was probably meant for Trel.

"I'm a wind elemental, if that's what you mean," Yarrow replied.

"Good, yes, that should work." Leif looked up at him and then back at the bowl. "You could blow it around in there, contained, and mix it up that way, right?"

"Elemental cooking?" Yarrow asked. "A bit unusual, but possible, as you say."

"It's most possible, back at my school, one of my fellow students was an exceptional fire-elemental, and he often entertained us by cooking all sorts of things in or with his hands." Leif closed his eyes and smiled. "I tried to do that once, but the result was horrible." He demonstrated with a slight arc of blue energy that crackled between his thumb and forefinger. "Burnt the whole thing, and had the worst flavor."

"I can imagine," he commented, cracking the smallest smile. "It might be a good idea to step out as I try it."

"I'll take my chances," Leif answered, and he backed off just a step to watch.

Yarrow positioned his hands on either side of the bowl, and closed his eyes. For a second, it felt as if half the air in the room disappeared, and Leif caught his breath at the sudden change in pressure, and a whooshing sound spiraled out of the churning mass in the bowl. It only lasted a few seconds, then the wind blew out from it smelling like almonds, honey, and cinnamon, and Yarrow cracked the egg, the full size of his hand, into it, and repeated the process.

Leif gave a low whistle of appreciation. "Well done, on your first try, even. What now, do you bake it?"

"That's the idea," he answered, pouring it into a rectangular bread pan, and then sticking it inside the rusted iron, peat-fired stove. "But I have no idea how it'll taste cooked in *there*."

The sound of splashing and a ringing laugh like little bells alerted them to the 'bath' taking place in the third and final room of the 'flat.' Interestingly enough, there were no bedrooms, just the one couch and one low table. No chairs, benches, or stools, or even a rug. Just hard broken slate for the floor, softened by years of dust. Fryn and Trel laughed on the couch, and Leif went out to join them. He sat down on the edge of the table and smiled at their joke, whatever it was, and looked up at the soot-stained plaster ceiling. There had to be a way to not only protect Lia, and her daughter, but also to not betray their involvement.

A good excuse.

A place to run.

It was quiet once again. He glanced back at Trel, who watched him deep in thought, and Fryn who seemed intensely interested in some scar on the back of her hand. "When Vinellin found you, Trel, was he the one who set this place up?"

"No," she replied, "he merely advised that we find some place to remain anonymous. But it would not be good for such well-known Hunters to be out of sight for too long. Indeed we may even need to reinforce the idea that we have both of us, given up of the chase and have instead pursued something else, or are doing something else." She blinked once and then met her partner's eyes in the kitchen. "Yarrow said something about going to the Tower, we'll see how that goes. But though we have tried to be discreet, for reasons you do not need to know, I fear it is commonly known that we are involved."

"Then..." Fryn interjected, refocusing on the conversation with an earnest gleam in her eye, "...the only thing left then is..." and she added in a whisper, "engagement?" Even just saying that brought some color to her drained face.

Leif shook his head slightly. "I wondered."

Trel nodded, all business, though she seemed to be suppressing a grin. "So, tomorrow we will need you to take a shift watching them here. If things progress as planned, we may be able to move outside the city, with the obvious intention of returning to the capitol."

"Then you'd bring the thief, and the crown, back to the city of the king?" Fryn confirmed.

Trel shrugged. "We can't think of anything else. After all, if the crown is mysteriously returned, then that lays the entire problem to rest. It's embarrassing, but the hunt for the crown will simply be reduced to a hunt for the thief, for a much reduced reward. And if we are successful, enough time will have passed that most Hunters will give up on her entirely."

"But to take the main roads..." Leif wondered, "several weeks in the open, where anyone could track you..."

"As I said, I don't have any other ideas."

The door to the washroom opened, and a wing-blown and dried child wearing a plain green night gown rushed out on her wings, nearly hitting the opposite wall, before she curled up between Fryn and Trel on the couch.

"Today we had to wear these huge cloaks with hoods," she explained, looking back and forth at each of them in her excitement. "But it was so long that I tripped on it, and fell in the water."

"I nearly did that myself," Leif said, "and I didn't even have a cloak."

She ignored him and continued. "So when we got here, I had to take a bath, but it wasn't really a bath, just buckets and over the head!"

They laughed. "Yes, that must have been difficult," Yarrow added. "The 'cake', such as it is, is in the oven. I am sorry we have no other way to commemorate your birthday, Nora."

She clapped her hands cheerfully. "Thank you, Yarrow!" She beamed, eyes pressed closed, hands together, teeth white. A very fine smile, Leif thought. A shame she'd gotten wrapped up in all of this, but then, in some sense, without her, her mother would never be in this situation. She could've just run away.

But at least she wasn't alone.

"Tomorrow then, we'll keep an eye on things here. Let us know if you hear from the Earl, or Vin, they might have some suggestions," Fryn said, even as Nora talked about something else, some moss clinging down from the tops of the town, as she put it.

But as he considered staying there for the night he frowned. Neither of them had fully recovered from their previous injuries, and Havrshyk continued in his stubborn refusal to help him. Havrshyk had insisted that he'd only provide his 'healing services' at the cost of blood, but Leif did not want to stab another fae with that sword, not when he'd heard the *hunger* in his voice. He shivered.

Before they'd left him, Loren had alluded to some connections he might be able to use to protect the girl and her mother, but he'd been discreet. At the very least, he sent them off with a hundred mint for expenses. He just hoped that he came up with something soon, before the brothers found them, or the Gaersyn guards caught on.

Bark and Stone

Fassen:

Eastwall District

Kaena Street 1202Ø

Fryn

Leif had spent the whole night on watch, out on the rooftop, or the sidewalk, or the corridor, patrolling. She subconsciously traced his movements by the changing position of the blood that she had given him, and whenever he entered the 'flat' she felt a measure of comfort. His head injury had taken a lot of effort to heal, but it now existed mostly as a yellow or purplish bump on the back of his head. With the morning they had switched places, and now Lia and Nora were busy making a scrambled egg, tucking and turning its sections with a spoon, encasing slivers of garlic and pinches of salt. How they'd gotten their hands on it, she had no idea, aside from the white salt of Aelaete, or the pink salt of Stanaedre, or the black, smoked wood salts of Renholt, she hadn't heard of anything else. But the salt they used was coarse and gray, perhaps there was a small source nearby, never mentioned in any of the travel guides she'd read.

As her partner slept on the couch, wrapped in his travel coat, with the black sword leaning against the wall, she stepped out into the hallway. Like the previous night, it was dim, without windows, and cold. The Vine was supposed to retain some of the summer warmth, but the Autumn was the shortest season, at least in the north. Cartographers said that there wasn't much difference in the latitudes of Fassen and Frorin, but that the elevation of the latter made for most of the ice and snow, and that the position of the mountains separating the Forest of Grass from the Aelaete Sea, also contributed to the climate; but of course, local rumors said that the pine forest used to extend much further east, but that had been blown away by the explosion of Mt. Waver.

She shook her head and started up the stairs. Out on the street, the peddler was nowhere to be seen, and the few who moved about eyed her with suspicion. She had rich clothing, her sturdy boots themselves were worth twice the eighty mint she'd paid for them. When she returned their stares however, they returned to minding their own business. "What next?" She asked herself softly. "How can we possibly pull this off?"

It wasn't just the brothers to worry about, though they seemed to be onto the scent, but there were probably fifty-odd Hunters in the city against them. Even that artificer from their table was likely searching things out with her own scholastic approach. They either needed more allies, or fewer. If they could just disappear, that would be ideal.

She continued her pattern of looking down each street, checking the perimeter of the building, and flying to its top to scan the area from above, for an hour, and then went back inside. Half the eggs had been left beside the stove, so she cut herself a third, and scooped the slightly watery item onto a saucer and cut into it with her spoon. Nothing was ideal, she knew, but the spoon just made her sigh. "What are we doing?" she wondered under her breath, and chewed on the 'moist' stirred egg with a frown.

Lia looked up at her from where she and Nora were sitting on the ground before the low table, playing with a pile of small stones. She left her daughter sorting them by type, and walked over. She rested her palms on the kitchen counter and looked out the 'window' at the girl, and then gave a kind sideways glance to Fryn. "I will tell you," she said, averting her eyes for a second, and then staring again with passion, "you are putting our welfare before your own, before your job, or your desire for gain or fame. What you are doing is honorable, and I believe it is why your partner was ready to do so from the start, and why you offered to turn in just the... the crown... you are kind."

Fryn blushed. "I'm not though."

"Sure you are," Lia insisted, "why else would you continue traveling with a fae who's so obviously infatuated with you?"

"That's not kindness..." she mumbled, her wings twitching nervously, pulsing with a rebellious streak of embarrassed purple light.

"I suppose not," Lia admitted with a hint of a smile, "but you should consider what it is you want."

Fryn stared at her, shaping her face into what she hoped was a bland expression, but she couldn't prevent the corners of her mouth curling upward as she thought of Leif, and his daily attentions.

Lia shook her head, watching Nora put a piece of feldspar with granite, then sighed. "She's not completely wrong, there is feldspar in granite, but…"

"It's not so easy, not like I thought," Fryn said, returning to the safer topic, "I thought, somehow, that everyone with a bounty on their head should be turned in, that 'justice' was 'rewarding' not just in mint, but also emotionally… but who decides what is just? Was it just that you were coerced? No, but you take the blame, and now 'justice' says you should be punished."

"A lot of new Hunters start out as idealists," Lia said, "but most are really just mercenaries with fancy licenses and titles." Nora moved a piece of sandstone beside the granite, so Lia called over the counter. "That one doesn't go there, *haset*."

"It doesn't?" she asked, lifting the crumbling piece of rock before her eye. "Oh, it's breaking."

"That's right, stones made of small pieces glued together, naturally, go together," Lia replied. Then sharing a smile with Fryn she continued softly, "So what are you going to do about Leif?"

Fryn scratched her cheek, smiled shyly, and shook her head. "I don't know what you mean exactly…"

Lia chuckled. "You know, he's not going to jump if he can't see the other side. He needs a little encouragement. Give him some opportunities to hold your hand, to steal a kiss; take a chance." She dropped her gaze. "I was married once," she waved a hand toward her daughter, "as you can see. My husband was so oblivious. When we first met, it was just after I'd become a Hunter with my polished plaque and a reputation for my speed. I was quickly recruited by a surveying team."

"And…"

"And he was the one who recruited me, our captain, and he had no idea how to talk to any of us. I wondered whether we'd decided to help him out of pity; but it seems most already knew him. It was my job to get a view of the area we would go map first, and he always insisted that he come with me, like an irritating manager. But still, Edward did what he could to get in my way. So one time I told him to leave me alone, and I had never been so miserable. I flew into a rain-storm and barely managed to comeback without a broken wing, and from then on I made any excuse to get him to come with me again—but it took some real clear talking to get a proposal, three years later."

"What?" Fryn laughed, "You made up excuses? Like what?"

"I once said that I needed someone to divert some of the floating seed-pods so I could get a good view of the land, and then another time, I said that I'd gone out and lost my scarf and needed help finding it; never did though, waste of a good scarf," Lia answered, closing her eyes as she reviewed her memories. "But of course, Nora doesn't remember him, he died when she was only two."

"I still remember my parents," Fryn commented, not sure why she did, as if her personal revelations demanded that she do so too. "I was ten, and I knew how to use my element well enough that I could freeze my tea, or try to make it snow outside my window, but I didn't really know how it worked. I woke up in the night, and it smelled like someone had put in too much coal, and it was warmer than I liked, since I usually wanted my room as close to the outside temperature as possible," she added with a wry laugh, "my father did not approve—said it would make my drapes mildew, or mold grow in my blankets, but I did anyway. I tried to sleep in frost because it sparkled and made that crinkling sound."

Lia watched her with a solemn face, wings still, just one finger moving with the tempo of Fryn's speech, occasionally glancing at her daughter out of the corner of her eyes.

"So when I smelled smoke, I didn't really understand, not until it started pouring into my room from the crack under the door. Pure, black smoke, that filled my room with heat and made me choke." She was about to continue when Lia interrupted her, switching crossed ankles and leaning forward from the edge of the counter.

"So is that how you became a Bloodcrafter?"

"Other stories are for other times," Fryn answered, "I wrapped myself in my blanket and jumped out of the window as I'd been taught, and waited on the street for the Guard to come, for my parents to join me. But they never did. By the time the Guard had arrived, dousing it with water, wind, and ice, it was burned through, and they found my parents lying as if they'd fallen asleep with the candle lit, and ran out of air. I often wonder if one of my father's competitors started the fire, but no proof was found of any foul play—it was deemed an accident, and I was sent to one of the academies as a student."

"Student of what?"

Fryn shrugged. "Orphans are often conscripted into the Guard or allowed to become Hunters or mercenaries, if they are raised by a martial school. I was taken in by the Soft-Point Fist under Master Baesil;

fortunate enough that he had a daughter my age and we could often train or run off to play together. Did you train at all in a martial style?"

"I didn't," Lia said, "I merely use what I have on hand, and use it in the same natural ways I use the wind." She stretched her wings and twisted her torso to crack her lower back. "Nora-sae, we need to find a few things in town, are you ready to go out in the cloak again?"

"Yes, mama!" Nora scattered the rocks across the ground with her wings in her haste, and flew over to the thoughtfully placed coat-hooks beside the door to the kitchen. "I want to climb up the moss someday." Luckily even with her loud voice, Leif slept through it, Fryn was pretty sure, because his heart rate was undisturbed by her movements.

They hurried out, cloaked with hoods and hats, Fryn with the painted cap that Leif had bought her at the Festival, and locked the door behind them. Nora listed the types of rocks on her fingers, confusing the heat-changed rocks with the heat-formed ones, and was wondering why they even counted the grained stones as stones in the first place, as they ascended the stairs and stepped back out onto the street.

It was dim, but some of the morning fog had cleared, and shafts of sunlight cut down through the narrow openings between the buildings overhead and glowed brilliantly on the thin layer of water from the early morning dew, which hadn't evaporated yet. Fryn supposed there was a high possibility that it wouldn't at all. A breeze rushed past and then returned the air to its quiet, almost sorrowful stillness. It was gentle, but she would not have called it peaceful, quite the opposite—it was disquieting.

She took in a deep breath and led them down the three steps to the sidewalk, and purposefully froze the patches of water that she stepped on so that it wouldn't stain her boots. "What is it that we need to find?" she asked over her shoulder, subconsciously stretching one of her wings to catch some of the sun as she passed by one of the golden shafts.

"We need some oat flour," Lia answered, guiding Nora by the hand around the half-frozen puddles left in Fryn's path.

"Cream," Nora added seriously, "lots."

"Right then," Fryn said with a laugh, "we'll wing by the village and see what they have."

"The village?" Lia asked, her voice slanted in high pitch and shock.

"No, but this area of the city does remind me of a village. It seems like each block is a town, isolated, divided, small…" She drew in another breath and nodded to herself, it was sweet air, free of any of the expected rotten smells that seem to gather around pools of standing water. "It's not as bad as I thought last night. It's cool, but not too damp."

A sorry-looking fae in an old gray robe exited the door of a tall, narrow house, and waited for them to pass, ignoring him, before he continued in the opposite direction.

"Is everyone here suspicious?" Fryn asked.

"They are of foreigners, and those who look rich, which you are certainly both. Even with the hat, the festive hat, you show that you have status, and by continuing to wear it, you show you are a foreigner—even if they can't see your remarkably silver hair," Lia replied, "which is very fine too. Is it hard to manage?"

Nora focused on this conversation, as if she'd been wondering the same thing for quite some time herself.

"Not very, no, I simply rinse with frost and then hold it in place with a pin, or a braid." They took a turn off of Kaena Street to the west, closer to the heart of town and the North Gate, where the markets were.

"I recommend that you remain in the shadows Fryn, and let us go do the shopping," Lia suggested, "they will not be suspicious if I speak Waverly, but your presence might alarm them. It may not be entirely just, but many of us are anxious around Hunters, even if we've done no wrong."

As the street rose up the slope to the Eastwall Markets, Fryn hung back and watched the two go traipsing up to the various tarp-covered stalls, where whole grapes, glass bottles of juices, milk, or cream, and various diced goods were on display. They chatted intensely with a fee selling cream, with vigorous gestures of arms and wings, Nora watching and learning, copying all the time. Her stomach felt oddly cold, colder than she liked anyway, and she shook the feeling off. She felt tired, and yawned several times as she waited for the two to move on to the next stall and barter over the next thing. All the while, her heartbeat slowed.

It's not right. She thought to herself. Is it because I gave all that blood to Leif?

She frowned. *Did I forget my Bloodknife?* She checked her hip, but such as it was, it was there, still thin, and barely edged. At the least however, she had parted with the last of the weasel blood, the temporary solution to Leif's injuries, and let it flake off of her blade. Now she just needed to wait.

Out in the market she saw a trio of fae moving from the western side of the market, acting as if they were looking at the various fresh goods, but they were always together, coordinated, moving just so to peek under the edges of the other shoppers' hoods. It was good they didn't know that their target had a daughter, but for them to find that out... that cold feeling in her gut resolved into a pit, and she was about to step out into the light to try to alert them, when she faltered on her feet and leaned against the wall.

Her knees weakened if she moved even just a step forwards, and recovered if she moved back. *Just like when I forgot my knife,* she wondered, *that time, when I... what did I do?* She shivered. *I have to go back, or not go further...* She felt she would have blushed, realizing just what connection she had accidentally made with him, but the blood to do so was now too far away. *So if we separate, for any reason, I have to go in full Lichform and leave all my blood to him, or in my knife.* She smiled. "At least now I have no excuse," she whispered, "and he has no choice, haha..."

As she brooded on the reality of her situation, of the reason she could always feel his heartbeat, of why hers instinctively tuned itself to his rhythm, the three brothers—for they couldn't be anyone else—got closer and closer to Lia. Nora ran off from her mother for a moment to pick up a thick bundle of green cloth, and her mother argued vehemently over its price.

The trio was in the aisle across from them, pretending to be interested in the bottles of mixed juice, when Lia turned around and took her daughter's hand, and guided her back to the alley with a basket of paper-wrapped packages and little glass bottles. Nora clutched the bundle of green fabric, and ran forward as they approached.

Fryn stepped back, afraid the girl would run into her, but she added a wingburst to compensate, and flew into Fryn's arms. They fell back another step into the alley, and Fryn accepted the girl's embrace and the rough folded bunch of cloth that was shoved into her face. "What have you got here, Nora-sae?" she asked playfully, holding her as she waited for Lia to join them.

"I got you a greeen cloak," Nora replied, using one hand to pull down the edge of the bundle to actually get a look at Fryn's face. "You didn't have one like us."

Fryn imagined she'd heard an extra 'e' in the expression, and answered with a small smile, "thank you Nora, I didn't know I needed one when I came here."

Lia met up with them and gave a good-humored 'tut.' "Come on down, Nora, we've got to walk the rest of the way." Then to Fryn she added, "We do not often give green to foreigners, because usually that is done for close friends, or adoptive family… but if she thinks you've earned it, I suppose I can't argue. It's a bit used, but serviceable."

Fryn let the girl drop to the ground with a soft 'tap-tap' as her shoes hit the stones, and she examined the folded cloak with frosted eyes. She unfolded it and threw it around her shoulders, slipping her wings carefully through the slits, and clasped it around her neck with a small steel pin shaped like a snail. She put on the hood so that it shaded her eyes and concealed her bangs, but it felt a bit odd, and probably looked odd, since she still wore her cap underneath.

"Thank you, really, I know what this must mean," she said, and gave a short look back into the market, and relaxed as she saw that the trio were still moving around the market stalls. "We should go back a different way, if they get your description, they may try to follow us."

Lia gave a light snort. "I doubt they'll get anything from the merchants, not if they don't speak fluent Waverly. We look after ourselves, and we watch out for each other. No self-respecting descendant of Waver would give up one of their own, a fee, with a young child, to a stranger."

"They might find out anyway," Fryn insisted, "Let's follow the road further east, and then cut back to Kaena from the south." She didn't know why, but she remembered the look she'd gotten from that old fae on the way to the market, as if he wouldn't mind selling out 'one of his own' if they were cavorting with foreigners. Being too far from Leif also made her nervous; she couldn't summon enough blood to reshape her blade, and Leif hadn't recovered enough that she could reclaim what she had 'lent' him.

"If you say so," Lia allowed, "but I still think we'd be safe."

They followed the alley and turned east onto Dorrael Street, dodging the untended drooping vines of morning glories that covered most of the pebble-stone buildings on either side. It was not time for the flowers apparently, since Fryn could not spy even one of the renowned white, bell-shaped beauties. Then, after reaching the cavernous wall-side path, with occasional doors cut into the boulders themselves, they walked in almost complete darkness. The eaves of the boulders loomed over them, meeting with the sides of the buildings, so that they walked in perfect silence, through a tunnel, each of them wary of even the sound of dripping water. There were no starlamps, nor oil lamps, and even though the air was clean, it was stagnant and smelled like dirt. It was exactly the sort of place that a weasel might like to hunt, or sleep.

Fryn shivered. She did not need to think of that again.

They passed by another block, hoods pulled even lower over their eyes, watching the few who passed, all old, or poor, even by the standards of the district. A window shutter opened with a noticeable 'click' when they passed, shooting out a beam of candle-light, so that it blinded them, and then closed just as quickly, and they heard the sound of a bolt sliding home at the door.

"They're awfully suspicious, aren't they?" Fryn asked, just above a whisper.

Lia didn't reply right away, but it was even quieter than Fryn. "I would not have taken my daughter here, it is dangerous, and desperate... they do not bother us because we are in a group, and because your movements are purposeful and strong. Your wings glow with light."

Fryn frowned, but she supposed they couldn't see it. "No more than a star gives light, and that, only when I'm using frost, or when I'm feeling an emotion I can't suppress..."

"You have an affinity strong enough that you could get stronger... some cannot use their light at all," Lia explained, "when you pass through the dark, and they see the pulse of light from your back to your wingtips, they know that you are strong."

They never taught me that at the academy, she thought to herself, and then stopped in her tracks. Just as they were about to reach the end of this section of tunnel, where a ray of sunlight cycled through the foliage and various beams and lines of drying laundry, she saw the shadow of a faerie against the light, and a pulse of light go through his wings.

They were still a ways back, so Fryn shrugged under the cloak, and hid her wings beneath it, folding them behind her back. Lia and Nora did the same, and they waited to see if the figure would move, but he didn't. Moving slowly along the boulder side, they advanced.

Just enough light filtered around his form that they could see that he wore the same fibrous, green uniform of the Grass Guard, and he had his head bowed slightly, as he stared at his hands resting on the pommel of his drawn grass blade with its tip driven just into the ground. She swallowed. *They shouldn't be onto us! We told them that we...*

The Guard lifted his head and pointed it in their direction, as if he saw them, and immediately, the light filtered into the tunnel, setting it aglow with foreign light, tinted green and gold, as it lit up the copper-colored sand and dirt, and the tired gray stone. They stood perfectly visible in full view, and they saw that the Guard's wings pulse with golden light.

"You cannot hide in the dark, because it is an easy thing to light it up," he said, "Fryn Martin, Hunter, who are these companions of yours, and why do you wear the felt of Waverly?" He lifted up his sword and pointed at her accusingly. "One of my companions warned you last night, that if you were found working against the Crown, you would become an enemy of the State, regardless of your license to operate as a Hunter of the Commission."

She pulled back her hood and stepped toward him with a smile, revealing her Festive hat, and her empty hands, held out akimbo. "I am merely looking to avoid having my informant stolen by other Hunters, and to wear the felt of Waverly, how is that any different than the green that *you* wear?"

He lowered the sword and rested his hands on it again. "The green is the color of Gaersheim, not Waverly, for them it means exile, apostasy, repentance. For you to be given it, even in disguise, means that you share in their sense of guilt."

Fryn laughed. "I have no guilt, or sense of it."

"Indeed," he said, almost a sneer, "it is possible to be guilty without 'feeling' it."

She was tempted to say something witty or condescending, but it was usually at times like this that Leif had something good to say, and nothing good came to mind, so she sighed. "Why have you come here?"

"To reclaim the crown, and to arrest the one who took it," he replied.

Fryn glanced back at Lia, but seeing no reaction, she wondered whether they thought like Loren, that it was the Rosenkrauns who had 'taken' the crown.

"I don't have it," she said, turning back toward him, "and if I did, wouldn't I turn it over for the reward?"

He smiled in response and let the full sunlight bend around himself, and the whole tunnel was turned warmer, almost golden, in response. It was as if his mood had softened, but she knew it was a trick. They were close enough now that she could draw on some of the blood she'd stored in Leif, but if she did, if she had to fight, what would Nora see?

"If there is nothing else, then we'll be on our way." She stepped forward, and felt immediately a change in the air; it was unlike the waves of heat that rolled off Mythrim's sword, it was solid, and incredible, and it moved like a knife from the far wall in an angled slash toward her feet. She jumped, scaled her arms in a series of ice crystals like a secondary skin, and bounced back, her knife springing into one hand, as the other opened in a guard before her.

"Now, now, I haven't finished," the Grass Guard said, eyes glinting with his humor, "who said you could leave? I have more questions."

"I said I could leave," Fryn replied, "there's an answer to your first question, and as you yourself admitted, I have no affiliation to this country—therefore I also have no obligation to answer your questions."

"Indeed?" He shook his head, "I disagree." He lifted the edge of his blade and saluted her with one eye staring down the edge, feet shoulder-width apart, wings down, right foot half a step forward, with his back foot pointing out. "You see, I have the power to *make* you. When my lord desires answers, I must provide them, and you have what I need."

"Fryn, this might not be good," Lia admitted, holding her daughter's hand as she backed further into the tunnel to give them room.

Fryn nodded, but there was nothing for it. She focused on drawing from her reserves, reshaping and sharpening the blade in her hand, and it turned a perfect black with damasked waves of red. Her skin went white, her lips blue as her eyes, and she smiled. *They always say something about getting the blood flowing in a fight... but that's not a problem for me.*

The Grass Guard lunged, dirt flying off from his boots as he flew at her with a wing-accelerated kick, tip of his sword aimed toward her neck. She lowered her weight, as if preparing to jump, and she watched him slowly angle up, and she 'fell' to her left, her frosted open hand matching the flat of his blade, she slid into his advance and rose, freezing the grass-blade as she closed in, and pinched it between her fingers— her Bloodknife flashing toward his eyes.

He released the blade and flipped over her, kicking her between her shoulder blades, flipping the sword she'd frozen around the back of her wrist, he snatched it out of the air. It cut a thin line across the back of her hand, severing the brittle tendons.

Fryn let it happen, and followed the twist caused by the kick, folding her wings, she dove into a roll, lifting ice-shards from her path.

But the Grass Guard didn't fall for it by trying to impale her, instead he spun, and reflected a slash of focused light from along the gloss of his sword.

She flattened herself on the ground and threw herself at a diagonal into the air, and rebounded off the Boulderwall with a soft 'crunch' as she crushed the thin layer of dust and sand, and instead of flying at him like an arrow, she arrested her flight by dropping to the ground in a dive, and charged, three lightning-fast steps until she was almost in his face. He grunted, deflecting her first splitting attack with her open hand, and as he saw her knife cutting in from the side, he called down a flash of light from off the ceiling to separate them, or cut off her arms.

I have you! she thought victoriously

She angled her Bloodknife into the violet-amber compressed light, and watched it pass through, melting some droplets, splattering her in a red mist, which frosted in mid air, and on her face, but the beam of light refracted slightly off course, and landed to the side, burning a black line in the clay. Her knife continued, and cut across his face.

She spun, and knocked him out with a closed back-handed fist across the temple, and let him fall. Hidden from direct view, from the way he fell, she knew that his right eye was gone, and only ice remained. She'd gotten some precious little blood, and lost a lot more... but at least she hadn't killed him in front of the girl.

She let the blood slowly seep into her veins, to her hand, and suppressed a groan as the tendons reconnected—thankfully still somewhat iced and numbed to some of the pain. Turning around, she saw that Lia had been holding Nora and they'd been hidden by their cloaks, barely visible behind a low outcropping of rock.

"He's unconscious," Fryn said, "and will probably remain so long enough for us to make our escape. I just hope we find another place to move to soon, because it seems they know we're in Eastwall."

Lia rose and led Nora toward her protectively. "You didn't kill him?" The girl asked.

"No," she said, coming over and crouching before her, "I didn't have to."

"Because killing is wrong?"

"That's right," Fryn answered, pulling up her hood and adjusting her bangs, "but if it comes to a choice between your life, and that of someone trying to take yours, then you have every right to defend yourself even if it means that they might die."

Nora frowned, and looked at the Grass guard with a regretful head shake. "But why?"

"Because," Fryn said, giving her a genuine smile, with her dimples revealing themselves proudly, "just because."

They walked around the unconscious body of the Grass Guard and hurried to Kaena Street. As they peeked around the corner, Fryn immediately pulled them back into the shadows of the side of the building, and pointed up. A shadow had moved across the tops of the buildings, as if another one of the Grass Guard had been flitting around and checking from above.

"The green cloak should be enough to protect us from questioning," Lia said, "I don't know how they'd know."

"I'm not sure they do," Fryn replied. The Guard disappeared for a moment, so they stepped out with a wingburst, and settled into a casual walk, Nora holding her mother's hand, and Fryn holding the basket of groceries.

If they raised any suspicion, they couldn't tell, and went inside the building without any difficulty, and found their 'flat' unlocked.

Fryn noticed the edge of a black sword from the slightly open crack of the door, and sighed. *What was I thinking?* She edged through and found it would only open a little since Leif lay nearly bloodless and unconscious on the other side. Passing back the groceries to Lia, she dragged him back to the couch and put away the sword, and took out her knife. It was still nearly fully-formed, black, and slightly smaller from the damage from the light-elemental's attack.

"Is Leif-fyja alright?" Nora asked, running over and poking him on his cheek. "He looks so white!"

"Yes, I think he's feeling somewhat sick," she answered, wondering why she'd said 'yes.'

"So, what's he sick with?" she insisted.

Lia raised her eyebrows.

"What does she know about these sorts of things?" Fryn asked her quietly, holding up her black knife surreptitiously.

"Less than I know, which is very little..." she admitted. "I thought they were just made up, fancy tales for children who liked to dream."

It would take too long to explain, and she was only beginning to figure out the implication of the blade. When she'd first become a bloodcrafter, she thought that it was a wonderful consolation, that it gave her all the power she'd ever need, and that she'd never be afraid again. She wiped her forehead, slightly overheated with too much blood... too much of *his* blood in *her* veins—which eagerly rose to her face in a rebellious blush. Fryn was only too eager to return it.

She drained most of the blood from her body and tried to restore only her own to her veins, and to separate hers from his, and give it back to him through the same sort of seldom-used link she'd accidentally created when she'd saved his life. *Saving him may have been more trouble than it was worth. Too late to do anything about it now,* she thought. Color returned to his face, and hers, and her Bloodknife shrank to a sliver of what it once was. At least they'd both be able to move about comfortably, even if she couldn't fight very well.

"I need a good steel knife," she said, taking of her hat and watching Leif open his eyes, his curious, playful, mischievous green eyes.

"Fryn!" he shouted, falling off the couch, reaching for the sword, instead his hand fell on her shoulder, and he focused on her face. "You were, I was, what... I thought..."

She put her hand on top of his and tossed an ironic look to Lia and Nora. "I was getting groceries," she explained, "did you have a good rest?"

"No." He stood stiffly and stretched his wings and splayed his fingers and arms out to the sides. "I had a very bad dream."

"What was it, fyja?" Nora asked, staring up at him in wonder.

He rolled his neck and smiled as it popped five times. "I dreamt that it was morning, or maybe afternoon, and the moon covered up the sun. The stars came out, and I saw that the Lich wasn't there, that the Star had spread from one light into a mass of stars, that masked where the Lich had been. The Mountain and the Forest seemed so far away. Then... I heard a voice... an old enemy, 'you're going to fade away.'" He shivered, and Fryn realized that she'd mixed it up a bit, and they now had equal parts of each other's blood. It wasn't so bad for her, she supposed, to feel the invigorating sparks running through her chest; but he did not really like the cold. Leif had closed his eyes, and he reopened them as he continued after a few moments pause.

"Then as the last of my strength faded away, I fell, and when I woke, I felt like I'd been asleep for years."

She frowned. *Years?* Then, her eyes focused on his Bloodsword suspiciously, but she relaxed, and sat on the couch beside where Leif stood. Dreams were dreams, and dead was dead, and Leif was not and could not be a Lich. "Well, we have other problems now," she said, and looked down between her toes.

Sword and Swayed

Fassen:

Eastwall District

Leif

Even after another two days, they saw no more signs of the Grass Guard, or the brothers. Leif was beginning to hope that they could actually lie low for a little longer, and had taken up practicing swinging Havrshyk around in the narrow confines of what they inaccurately called the 'living room' of the flat. Fryn and the others were outside doing something to enjoy the sun in their green cloaks, and Havrshyk was busy complaining about Leif's form.

"You expect to cut anything with that sort of action?" he demanded, his voice echoing through his arms, as a chill frosty air coalesced around the still, black blade.

Leif breathed deeply, drawing in the stale air through his nostrils, as he slowly blew it out his mouth. It was possible to breath continuously, in and out at the same time, but it was impossible to do so and speak at the same time. "That was a blocking counter, not a cutting slash."

"I know better," the sword replied, "and that is just an excuse. And further, in the Swordhand-Palm, there is no such thing as a 'blocking counter'. There is only a sharper, denser edge. Every movement is an attack, and every attack is defense."

"Now you sound like one of those supposed wisemen who claim to have secrets, when really they just used elemental techniques," Leif answered, and shook his head, preparing to try again. He twisted slightly from his hips and advanced one step forward, slashing upwards and outwards in a diagonal from his sheathed position, scattering the fog that had momentarily collected around the motionless blade, as he stopped it abruptly—the blade perfectly extended from his arm, in line with his shoulder, the open hand cupped beside the sheath, with a glowing passive ball of sparks.

"I sound nothing like that," he complained, "and that was a <u>much</u> better attack."

"Thank you," Leif said, moving forward with his charged palm brushing aside an incoming strike, as he pulled straight back on the sword's hilt, drawing the blade home at a close angle with the tip pointing in the mirror direction of his upper right wing. He followed through with a push from his charged-up hand, fingers braced together like a pick, as he pierced an imaginary limb, and grabbed it, twisting toward the trapped opponent, swiping the blade through their shoulder to the opposite side. Then, releasing the severed arm, he advanced one more step, opening his palm, and pushing on the injured chest, wingbursting toward him with the tip of the black sword aimed like a lance for their heart, he turned into the strike and lunged, extending the blade through them, and exhaled.

Leif pulled back gently, and held the sword in the initial guard position he'd so often seen Fryn take, and then sheathed it at his side. He breathed out once more and sighed.

"That was exemplary. It is a shame I couldn't train you as a student," Havrshyk admitted in a rare bit of praise, "a shame I had to 'die.'"

"You're the one who decided to work with Mythrim in the first place," Leif accused, unbelting the sword, and setting it on the low table as he sat in the couch. "Why did you?"

The sword slid out of the scabbard a crack, and a black-frosted, reddish 'eye' resolved into the surface of the blade, and glinted at him in the dull orange glow of the oil lamp on the kitchen counter. *"Why? You ask? Well, I could certainly tell you, no harm in it now…"*

Leif closed his eyes and put his hands behind his head. "Good, I could use a nap."

"Here I thought you were serious," Havrshyk made a light 'tut' sound and continued, "alright, I'll punish you by keeping you awake."

"You can't do that," Leif said, "I have an uncanny ability to sleep whenever I please."

Havrshyk ignored him. "You asked me, so now you'll listen. Do you know why I was imprisoned, or who I was, before he found me?"

"We'd had some wine at the time," Leif admitted, "so I don't recall it accurately."

"They didn't either," Havrshyk interjected bitterly, "and then they forgot."

Leif opened his eyes and focused on a mottled patch of the plastered ceiling. "I'm listening, Havrshyk, since we're stuck together, I'll give you that at least."

His voice faded back in as if he'd been in a different space, adding some new connotations to the expression 'lost in thought,' Leif supposed. *"I was a Captain of the Royal Guard in the time of your irritating friend Ieffin's grandfather, King Inloth Martell—Mythrim told me he was later known as Inloth the Fair, but I think that is a perfect example of historical revisionism."*

"Revisionism, yes…" Leif said, affecting a yawn.

"Yes, revisionism, my point exactly. You said you didn't remember why I was imprisoned in a grave? I will tell you why, because in my loyal service to the Crown, I became a Bloodcrafter. So far as I can tell, I was the first in hundreds of years, after all, few indeed had my devotion to my duty, my will to fulfill it no matter the personal cost." Havrshyk's voice deepened and chilled Leif to his heart. "When I had defended the King with what many would call life, I rose to save him in death. But you see, it is a rare thing to encounter, and the last Bloodcrafter was a murderer, deranged, so I was mistrusted by my subordinates, and my King. When allegations of my depravity, caused by the 'twisting of my mind' from the 'blood of my enemies,' the King immediately ordered my execution. I had no opportunity to defend myself in the Grand Assembly, I was merely standing guard, when my own turned on me with their swords and their pikes."

"So… you felt betrayed… and wanted revenge on the King, only to find out he had already died?" Leif asked, crossing and then re-crossing his legs.

The visible section of the blade darkened even further. "Now you misjudge me too… I thought that I was helping to undermine the enemies of the Crown, that even the drastic methods of Mythrim would have a positive effect. I made excuses about the sacrifice even of the King's own blood. Anything to damage the Commission!" Havrshyk's response was angry, and then full of remorse, and Leif felt almost as if he could see his guilt warring with his passion on his face—but he didn't have one anymore.

"That is the kind of reasoning you should have known better than to fall for," Leif commented, partially to test him, maybe even a little to make him feel worse. He wasn't completely unsympathetic, but he also felt that he'd gotten what he'd deserved, at least for his modern crimes. "And simply blaming the King who wrongly imprisoned you, who are moderately immortal, it is not as if you can say they ruined your life!" But, it gnawed at him, first Ieffin's mistrust of the Commission, and now Havrshyk's, separated by two generations, they regarded the Commission as an enemy.

"You did, and they did; everyone I have been in contact with since I became a Lich has betrayed or ruined me! I should have let the King die, rather than live under this curse! Do you imagine that Fryn is any less cursed? Or You? It's all very convenient, in the beginning." Havrshyk's yelling voice was softened as if it came across a great distance; like he was shouting through a pillow, or from the next room.

Leif lowered his head and frowned, one hand scratching the scars that itched on his arm. "Were you awake, in the tomb?"

"I was awake, Leif, and I reviewed everything I had learned, and dreamt of those I'd never see again. Fryn is a good enough sort of fee, but I was courting a daughter of the house of Frosthall, Ilira, and she's long gone now. Old or dead, I don't care which, I'll never see her now. I had younger students, and my master was grooming me to be his replacement, but there is no Swordhand-Palm there now. Everything I knew was killed the day they put me in the ground." He covered the blade in thickening sheets of ice, and now his voice was very quiet. "I'm done, go find Fryn, and let me be."

"Fair enough," Leif said, standing and stretching his back. "Give a shout if you need me," he added, and walked out. Havrshyk didn't bother to respond. He turned the key in the lock with a sigh and trudged up the stairs with the once-more comfortable, unburdened feeling of balance that came from leaving the sword behind. Out on Kaena Street, which he had only recently learned meant 'argument' or 'debate,' he saw that Nora was busy having just such an appropriate conversation with another child.

Lia and Fryn sat on the steps, watching her wave one hand authoritatively around, two fingers held up, as her opponent crossed his arms.

"Hyn'i sørø sersaerin fjes'la fassenanalan'sør!" The boy interjected, nearly at a yell, red in the face.

Nora shook her head, her left hand holding the apparent object they were arguing over: a piece of quartz, surprisingly clean, considering the dustiness of the street. Though as he smelled the air, he could tell that it had been cleansed a bit by the morning dew, that still drained from the hanging bits of moss and lichen, onto the cobbled street below, into little puddles. Nora tried to hand over the stone, but the boy would not accept it.

"Ner'me setandae'unae!" she shouted, the white stone glistening in the palm of her hand. "Fassenanalan..." she added softly.

"I'mel fassetan?" he asked, uncrossing his arms, and looking down with drooping wings.

"I'mel'la'rin, aesyja'lan," she replied, also looking away.

Over the past few days, Leif *had* seen her playing with the children on the street, since the Grass Guard had moved on—almost made it seem as though things were returning to a sense of normalcy.

"What's going on?" he asked Fryn, whispering as he settled on the top step beside her. Fryn stiffened as she lost her focus, and held up one hand, watching the two intently once more.

"Un, møn... fasay," the boy said, turning on his heel, and flying off like the wind.

Nora watched him leave, and closed her fingers over the bit of quartz and, face red, pocketed the stone in her cloak. She faced them with an awkward smile and a shrug, and sat down on the step below them, one hand gripping the edge of her dusty floral-printed dress.

Lia shook her head and gave a short laugh, "you might not understand what was just happening, Leif," she explained, "but his offering of the white stone was his request to court her..."

"Don't laugh, mama!" Nora complained, pulling up her hood as streaks of red-colored embarrassment ran out to the tips of her wings.

"Seranalan, Nora, don't worry." Then she yawned. "You should've told him that you weren't old enough to court anyone, but then, I guess that's embarrassing for an eight... nine-year old." She reached forward, putting one hand on her daughter's head, and ruffled her hair through the hood.

"Don't..." she wriggled under the hand and scooted over out of reach.

"You should be glad you aren't in my homeland," Leif advised sagely, "you'd have hopeless romantics giving you white bone-earrings every day."

She turned to look at him, as if trying to determine if he were joking. "Earrings? That doesn't sound bad."

Fryn watched him with a surprisingly interested narrowing of her eyes, or was that curiosity? He went on. "You wouldn't like them, they would all be hand-carved, and probably unpolished, sharp bristly points, mis-cuts and so on," he explained, waving his hand about, demonstrating the carving process and the mis-cuts. "I remember I once made a 'beautiful' set of earrings for a girl at the school on the opposite street, and she did accept them, but when she put them in her ears, she got a bunch of tiny cuts and a serious rash—after that she refused to see me…"

"That's awful," Nora said, pinching her ears underneath her hood. "A stone is much better. It can be made into beads, for a bracelet, or necklace, or just kept in a box." She glanced up at her mother, as if checking to see if she'd gotten it right.

Lia nodded slightly, and looked back at Leif. "So in Aelaete they give earrings?"

"And they have to make them themselves, yes," he answered, "there is a devotion to the carving-lessons during the teen years that soon after fades, so that only the professional jewelers remain… but for those years, the instructors are quite pleased. Normally everyone opts for more useful secondary subjects, like botany, or mosaics, or further investment in a primary subject—like book-making, or scholarship in history and so on." Leif's wings twitched as he remembered so many spring days staring at the sun through soot-darkened eyelids, as the other students ran off to play at rings, or debate, or to go read stories in the libraries, and how the mixed smells coming from the kitchens always made him and the other Strafe-Curling Viper students drool; but they didn't have the option to join in those things.

"What did you choose?" Nora asked, lowering her hood and staring at him with wide amber eyes.

He nodded to himself with a smile. "I couldn't; I was enrolled as an apprentice of the Strafe-Curling Viper school of martial arts, and so as one of their disciples I had to focus on training my body and spirit. The training of the mind was secondary to the honing of the instinct, Master Yarl used to say, since strength was not based on numbers or the names of kings. Still that was no excuse for keeping us from sports."

Fryn gave a light laugh. "The Soft-Point Fist had an entirely different philosophy. Master Baesil believed that one could only master the most complex techniques by having a sophisticated and educated mind, so the focus was on external power, and strategic and advanced thinking. Training one's element was not encouraged, since those who rely on them in combat become powerless as soon as their reserves run dry."

"Interesting," Lia commented, then turning back to Leif, she asked, "why did you become an apprentice, Leif?"

"I was the next in line. In our clans, it is sometimes difficult to know how to accommodate the interests of the children, and the needs of the group, so the firstborn is trained in governance, and history, and the second is given to study agriculture and cooking, and the third is trained in combat. Any other children are free to choose within the 'under-allocated' disciplines, which is where our artisans and thinkers come from. They may also go into the primary schools, but most often, they do not."

"So you're the third then," Fryn confirmed, "what are your older siblings like?"

"The firstborn, Salett, was the type to lord her position over us, she had pride, certainly, but also was obedient to our parents and kept us in line. She's since betrayed us by marrying into another clan, but it was necessary, so calling it betrayal is really just in jest. Halin, then took on the position of leadership, even though she is more knowledgeable about medicinal herbs—even went back to school to learn what she needed, and our parents still basically rule the house through their advisory position. Then there's me, sent out since my younger brother Jean, went into martial training, and they wanted me to attain the rank of Master, which as you know," he added, looking toward Fryn, "required my service in the Commission."

"Well, that is very interesting," Lia said with a smile, and then looked out on the street where the water continued to drip and drop from the hanging moss in a soft pattern. "Yes, it is interesting. Fryn was raised that way, as an orphan," she considered, "and you were also forced into it."

"Orphan?" Leif asked, "What about your uncle, and Harissa?"

Fryn shrugged with her wings. "It was in my father's will, that I be raised by the Master if anything should happen to them. Could be he wanted me to grow into a respectable inner-district fee, or that he wanted me to be able to take care of myself. My father never did like where my mother came from, though he was fond of her in spite of her family..."

"Still seems cruel to separate someone from their family," Leif said, "I couldn't demand that of y... someone."

"Neither could I," Lia added quickly, "Edward was not Waverly, and I barely counted, but I still wondered how I could ask him to adopt our language and customs—which is required when marrying a foreigner. We can't leave our people to join someone else's, if we are to survive, they must be required to fully join ours."

"Hmm... I see," Fryn said, glancing away from Leif with a smirk.

He frowned. She must have caught on to his blunder, but, that wouldn't be so bad, right? "As long as my actions reflect well on my family, I am free to live wherever, and to go wherever, I please."

"I see," Fryn said again, and they let the conversation drop. She rested her elbows on her knees, and her chin in her hands, closing her eyes as the angle of the sun turned just right, and a beam of its golden light rested on her face, nearly sparkling as it refracted off her silver hair and blue-lined wings.

Leif moved closer beside her to share in the light, and lay back with his hands bracing his neck like a pillow, just basking in its warmth. "Pretty soon now it'll be Autumn, with Winter not far behind. Autumn is the shortest season after all."

"That is because of the size of the constellations," Lia objected.

He ignored her and continued. "And the Star used to be considered a part of the Lost, making Winter two months long as well; but ten was a very unlucky number."

"Leif..." Fryn sighed. "Even knowing what I do now of your education... I should not be surprised."

"You're surprised that I know that, right?"

"Yes," she said with a snicker, "but not for the reason *you* think."

"See, I knew it."

She leaned back beside him, shading her eyes with one hand, looking at him with a smile. "You don't fool me," she said, eyes flicking off thoughtfully before flicking back to meet his, "but that reminds me, there was something I wanted to teach you."

He smiled back at her. "Speaking of which..."

"About Bloodcrafting," she added, interrupting his comment with a businesslike wave of her hand, momentarily blinding herself since it was the hand she'd been using to shade her eyes. "Or, more accurately, about how to use that sword."

Leif paused, tempted to nod, but also wondering. She couldn't hear Havrshyk's voice when he spoke to him, and didn't know that he was still alive, did she? Why should he hide it anyway? He couldn't very well tell her, 'Oh, Havrshyk taught me all of that already', or anything equally ridiculous like that. So, he hedged. "Does it have to be today?" he asked, closing his eyes to take in a bit more of the sun.

She sat up, leaning so that she blocked the sun from hitting his face, and replied with a light, almost teasing tone, "Yes, today, because we don't have much time until Trel gets back with news of a way out of this—and we all know that we might have to do so at great risk to ourselves."

"Well summarized," he praised with a yawn, "I agree that we have already put our health at great risk with the current lack of proper beds or sleeping hours."

"Come on then," she pressed, standing and stretching, still blocking the sun.

"Alright then, but let it be known that I do so under great duress." Leif stood beside her, and vigorously fluttered his wings, rolled his neck and shoulders, and then shook out one leg and then the other. "Everything that must be done, must be done as quickly as possible," he explained.

"I see," she allowed, "now, you'll need to get the sword." Fryn nodded with her chin toward the door, and Leif suppressed a sigh. Havrshyk would not be pleased with only half an hour's isolation... or would he? He'd been imprisoned for some seventy years, if he remembered correctly, so maybe he just needed moments at a stretch?

He went off as directed, still pondering the issue, and was not welcomed as he entered the flat and locked it. Havrshyk still sat there on the table, which was now covered in a thick layer of frost, and the scabbard and hilt were almost completely fused to the table top by an amorphous blob of ice. "What is all this, Havi?" he asked in a bright and cheery voice, as if he were talking to a child.

"I said to leave me be," came his ill-humored response, "I am busy."

Leif bent over the sword, trying to look into the ice. It looked almost as if a five-fingered hand were trying to break the surface of a frosted pudding-skin, and Leif swallowed, stepping back as he wondered at it. A chill came over him and he shook it out through his wings. "You aren't going to be able to recreate a body for yourself," he said, "that has got to be impossible."

"It is. I tried. Best I could do was ruin what they call a varnish on this table." His tone was decidedly dejected, but not too depressed. "Not much left now then, but perhaps… if you supplied more blood, I could… but no, it's impossible. I couldn't even create a single fingertip out of blood, much less a hand, or a body. No, it's only good for repairing, sustaining, not creating life."

"You're the brooding type, Havi, I could tell the first time I met you. When you were just a chef, but then I thought the serious philosophical look suited you."

"Don't call me that, Aldyr is not hard to say."

"It's pretty hard for me, but Aldi will do." Leif surrounded his hand with a cloud of sparks, and tried to reach through the ice. "Now I need you to come with me, so lose the ice."

"I'm not in the mood. Wing-giver, why? Why me? Ah, fine, Leif, let's go 'play outside.'"

He released his sparks and picked up the sword as the ice sloughed off like water, well, it *was* water, and went back up to Fryn, belting it at his waist. "Where are we going to do this training?" he asked as he stepped outside.

Fryn had removed her coat, and was standing in the sun, arms crossed, her pale skin shining in its soft glow on her face, nearly the same color as her hair. The collar of her blouse was cleanly tucked under her gray canvas vest, the same color as her trousers, which had a pocket on one side where she could keep her knife belted and out of direct sight, but in spite of their time away from any sort of proper facilities, her clothes were clean and her knee-high boots polished.

As she turned to look at him, Leif thought that for a moment, time had stopped, but that was just the image of her cheeky, dimpled smile in the sun, frozen on his eyes between heartbeats. On the next beat, the image vanished, and she was replying. "You might want to give Lia your coat as well," she suggested, "and we'll practice in the back alley over here."

He shrugged off his coat and passed it over to Lia, who then gave it to Nora to do something useful, and then followed her down the three steps onto the sidewalk. "I don't like the sound of the alley," he commented, "I feel like I'm about to get robbed."

She chuckled, and cut a quick turn around the back of the apartment building, where they saw what had, at one time perhaps, been a respectable aviary with room for two or three birds. Now the conical roof had holes, and the various berths in which the finches could nest inside cavities built into the surrounding buildings, had rotted-out stumps that were probably workable perches at one point. The center of the space was occupied by a slight depression, fed by the overhead umbrella roof, where the birds could bathe. It was mostly empty now of course, except that it was half-full of sprouted-and-wilted grass seeds, and muddy rainwater.

"I'm not stepping in there," Leif said, stopped at the rusted-out iron gate, which only hung by one hinge, doing a poor job of separating the aviary from the street.

Fryn crouched before the standing pool, and breathed dramatically on it, scattering webs of frost and ice across the surface of the water. "You'll be on top of it," she explained, rising to a hover over it, she expanded the cover of ice until it was solid throughout, and ridged with little crystals to decrease its slipperiness. Then, she landed in the center, feet together, and faced him with one arm outstretched in invitation, as she drew her blade and hid it behind her back.

Leif stepped onto the ice, drawing a pensive blade, he met her eyes, and then folded his wings behind his back, raising one hand out and forward, straight and pointing toward the sky; the sword angled out from his right shoulder.

"Come," Fryn commanded softly with eyes taunting, cheerful, teasing, "make me move."

"Easy enough on the ice," Leif said, stepping toward her, feet barely shifting out of place because of the textured she'd created and now maintained. She didn't respond, so he charged with a feint of the splitting-hand, as she so often did, and slashed across a diagonal from her left shoulder toward her right hip.

"Wrong," she muttered, and her empty hand snapped forward, deflecting the bloodsword with a swatting of the back of her hand, as her Bloodknife flashed out in a back-handed grip, and blocked his split with the pommel squarely in his palm. He winced, but couldn't react, as the empty hand pushed forward, closed into a fist, and struck him in the stomach, and her wings flicked back to counter, and he went sliding back—as she remained motionless.

"Hardly fair to correct me..." he said, guiding some sparks to his stomach so loosen the overly tightened muscles from her hardened strike, "when you haven't told me what I should do."

"You're a Master now, aren't you?" she asked with one raised eyebrow and a cheeky presentation of her dimples, even if the smile wasn't very large. "You should be able to use that weapon as it should be used, and to fight an opponent on their own ground." She pointed toward the ice with her knife and then looked back up at him. "So far, you've illustrated that you have the instincts of a mushroom farmer, when it comes to using a sword."

He bristled, but held it in check a little longer. This time, he didn't try to copy *her* style, but to apply some of the techniques he had trained in back in his school days. He lowered his stance, and stood just outside of reach, then, he rushed toward her with a two-handed chop at her legs, stepping out into a sideways lunge, nearly to splits, as he twisted, and pulled back, using his wings to spiral the tip of the blade up toward her face.

She smiled, twisted, and her black knife met his sword—it was only for a moment, but a scattering of tiny black crystals told of the deflection, and Leif thought he *felt* something through the collision. It was almost as if they'd switched places, and then switched back, several times. He was conscious of his slow breathing, a constant cycle, and her chest unmoving, as the blood had no need to flow. Fryn's lips were blue, and her face eager, her teeth shining in a wide smile, as she slid the edge of her knife down the edge of the sword, and her free hand grabbed Leif's wrist. She spun it out of his hands, grabbing the sword, and then spinning perfectly in place, she knocked him aside with the flat of it, and then stabbed it into the ice.

"What are you thinking, Leif?" Havrshyk yelled in his head, "You can't use those kind of tactics against the Swordhand-Palm, or any of its variants!

But anything else... Leif complained, hoping that Havrshyk could still hear his directed thoughts even if Fryn held the sword.

"Do you really think you can kill her? If you injure her, just give her some of your blood. You'll be tired for a while, but you'll win..."

The undead sword had a point. Leif approached her slowly, circling, until he was halfway there, and then wingbursted across the ice to her blind spot, and, rolling under her backwards-extending wings lined with a rim of sharpened ice fragments, he nudged the flat of the blade with his boot so that it started to fall and snatched it out of the air before she could reclaim it. He circled back before her.

She frowned. "You can move quickly if you want to I see," she said, "is it because you don't want to hurt me? I only said to make me move; though it is touching," she added, looking away in a forced, demur way.

"You can keep at it this way if you wish," Havrshyk said, sighing in his hand, "but I am the only one who knows how to make her move."

Leif resigned himself to the explanation he'd soon have to provide, and he slid the sword back into its sheath, facing her with one hand on the hilt and the other held out in an open palm pointing toward the sky. Sparks ran through and around, and between his fingers, and his hair stood up on end, and he smiled as Fryn recognized his posture, but didn't comment on it. It seemed though, that she'd tightened her own stance, as if preparing for anything.

Master Yarl once said that predictability in combat was one's greatest weakness, and Leif had relied on several set patterns in the past; but patterns were of no use against a master, and Fryn was not a novice. He stepped into a wingburst, drawing the blade in a diagonal slash toward her cheek, but she didn't flinch. She mirrored his stance and lightly encased her palm with ice as she deflected the slash upwards, and lunged toward him with her knife snapping forward like the head of a spear.

It wasn't that different from what Havrshyk had taught him, her movement was purely linear however, without the added wingburst or the twisting of the hips to open up for greater reach. Leif pulled back as he had practiced before with his palm falling on top of her frozen hand holding the knife, and he pushed on it to leverage his escape. Then, drawing the blade into its winged alignment, he twisted, and burst forward, extending the tip of the blade like a lance toward the delicate 'v' at the base of her throat where the deep blue stone pendant she'd received from Ieffin was nestled in a thin layer of frost.

Setting aside his fear, he followed through, extending all the way open with his wings splayed back completely from his acceleration, and his open palm thrown out behind. The tip of his sword lodged into a divot in her knife, which she held at an opposing angle in front of her face, so that she lost her root, and was sent sailing back toward one of the old finch-nooks with complete and utter shock warring with pride on her face.

She arrested her flight with a wingburst, and flipped so that she kicked off the rock wall, and flipping forward this time, she landed back where she'd been thrown from, and as color returned to her flushed face, she grinned. "That is precisely the sort of technique you can use to eject someone from their territory!" Then, she frowned, looking down in thought, pursing her lips and closing her eyes. "But, that technique... where did you learn it?"

"Indeed..." The sword teased.

"Well, I was nearly killed by such a technique myself, when I fought with Havrshyk," he explained, "and I've also made a point to study you... your techniques," he added, sheathing the sword before he could muddy the explanation any further.

"Let's do this again," she replied, "and this time, I will see if you can use that blade for defense." She saluted him with the knife, and then charged, ducking under his uncertain slash, as she copied his twist from before, and slammed a frozen hand into his gut. He slid back across the ice and groaned.

"Not fair..." he barely said, slipping under a curved thrust of her knife, catching it on the edge of his sword. "You can just armor yourself as much as you like..."

Fryn nodded. "What will you do about it?"

"Not get hit," he answered, and pushed, sliding her back a little as he circled toward the center of the frozen pool. His sparks tingled in his veins and nerves, fingers twitching as he gripped the sword tighter in his hand.

She accepted the challenge and launched a series of attacks, a kick at his shins, which he avoided by pulling up his foot and pressing back with his wings, followed by a cleaving chop at his shoulder, which he avoided at the last second with his sparks-enhanced reflexes, and nearly fell into the horizontal cut of her knife, with her fist aimed toward his face—he tilted his sword into it as he turned, and feinted a push at her stomach. Her eyes widened a little as his hand pressed on her stomach, about to throw her back, and then widened even further, as he grabbed her by her vest, and fell, twisting around her so that her arms locked themselves, and he held the sword toward her throat, once more pointing at the stone.

Her frost intensified, and he leaned over her, one leg locking her knees together, one hand holding hers together, his eyes fixed on hers. For the first time since they began their exercise, she breathed normally, and she averted her eyes, as the skin of her face went from blue to white, to pink.

Leif's heart pounded in his ears, and they simply stayed in that position for almost half a minute, until he realized just how awkward it was, as, for the entire time, she'd kept looking into his eyes, and then looking away. He fell back and let the coolness of the ice flow in through his wings, and examined what he could of the sky through the tiny hole in the conical roof of the aviary.

Fryn didn't move right away either, they just stared up at the sliver of sky, until the minute was complete. Then, when he'd recovered from their impromptu duel, Leif sat up and laughed. It was probably late afternoon, and the little bit of sunlight that wound its way down through the buildings was turning orange.

"I haven't had to fight like that for many years," he admitted, finally looking in her direction.

Fryn didn't meet his eyes, and even as he looked at her, a bit of purple or red went through her wings. She laid on the ice watching the sky a bit longer, and when it became too uncomfortable to remain silent, the light had turned almost completely orange, shot with red.

She sighed, and still not meeting his eyes, said, "That was well done."

He laid back down beside her and shaded his eyes as a ray ran through the hole in the roof onto their faces. "Was it? That's good to hear."

The sword and knife were discarded, on either side of them, in the shadows, which as they darkened nearly made them seem invisible. Leif could hear Havrshyk seething inside the sword, *"once more, why, why must I be forced to overhear all this?"* And for the first time, Leif wondered if he heard some hints of envy, or loss in his voice; pain perhaps.

Sorry about that Havi, he replied gently, you lost everything, as you said, and then you lost it all again.

The sword glimmered with a slight shift in its deep red currents, and a fog coalesced around it. *"I did not ask for your sympathy, don't give it. You are the last one I need sympathy from!"*

Very well then, Leif looked back at Fryn with a shy smile. "You said earlier, that your parents died in a fire, but that wasn't how you became a Bloodcrafter..."

"I did," she answered, turning her head slightly so she could meet his eyes, and then sharply looking away, as if uncertain how she should behave.

He swallowed, and then looked back up. The astronomers would have a good night for viewing the stars. Even before the sun had fully set, he saw the first branch of the Vine behind the silhouette of the Greater Moon. "I suppose we should go look in on Lia, maybe make something for dinner."

Fryn relaxed, as if her body had been completely frozen and only just thawed, and she sat up beside him. "True enough," she said, putting a hand on his shoulder as she stood and then picked up her knife. "Don't forget the sword," she added over her shoulder with a smirk.

Leif picked up Havrshyk and slid him roughly into the scabbard with a sigh, following Fryn out to the street. As soon as he stepped off the ice, it began to melt, and by the time he reached the curbside, he saw it was once more restored to its original state. He rushed around through the door, and down the stairs, uncertain why he felt such a strange sense of urgency, and entered the flat with an embarrassed smile.

Fryn was over sitting on the couch. Nora was curled up in her cloak beside her, writing with a bit of chalk and a piece of slate, teaching her softly how to write her name in Waverly. She'd taught him the same thing the day before, and Leif paused to watch Fryn copy the letters on the slate with a warmth in his chest, and an odd tightness in his throat. He went into the kitchen and leaned against the counter beside Lia, who'd also been watching them.

The Scissortail, as she was once called, was just a single mother, with a plain green apron tied around her shoulders, and flour on her hands, cooking as she watched her daughter out of one of her cheerful, shining, amber eyes. She paused in her kneading of a bowl of some kind of tough dough to wave him over with a wing-twitch, and whispered, "where have you two been? Fryn just came back, and she's not herself..."

He wondered how she would know whether Fryn was herself or not. Leif scratched his chin. He couldn't figure it out himself, what to do, or what to say. There was a problem, and he had no idea how to resolve it.

She lowered her head over the bowl to better conceal her whispering, "and now you're not yourself either."

"I'm not an imposter," he tried, hoping that it matched his usual kind of non sequiturs, and smelled the dough. "What are you making?"

"Bread," she replied simply, eyeing him intently. He almost felt like when his elder sister would interrogate him to see if he was telling the truth about missing date-jam, or candied coconut.

"I'm... not... sure..." he said, awkwardly latching and unlatching his sword.

"Really?" she asked wryly, giving him a raised eyebrow. "You're lying, Leif, and you know what they say about liars, don't you? That their wings will one day fly away?"

He shivered. "That is not something I had heard before, a bit terrifying, don't you think?"

She shook her head. "To a child, they simply imagine them flying off, leaving them behind, it seems lonesome, not painful."

"Well," he allowed, checking that Fryn was not listening, "there was something I was wondering about."

"Really..?" she asked in an unsurprised, wry tone.

"And I have no idea how to explain it."

"So just tell me what happened."

Leif looked around and found another apron on a peg beside the arch leading to the hall, he took it down and left the sword hanging in its place. He slipped on the apron and moved over to the cutting block beside her. "I'll tell you if you give me something for my hands to do."

She held back a laugh, and pointed to the ice-box in the corner. "Take that cut of hare, and slice it into long, thin strips."

He rolled back his sleeves, and ran his hands through the bucket of water that frankly, it was shocking the building even *had* access to clean water, and cleansed them with a fizzling coat of sparks. Then, he took out the carving knife from the drawer and slapped the cut of meat onto the cutting board. It was barely large enough to satisfy two with steaks, and those thin, so he supposed it made sense she intended to stretch it.

"Well, she wanted to teach me something on how to use the sword," he alluded, slicing through the first bit of the meat and then scraping it across the board to the side.

Lia let him continue, though he noticed that she looked pointedly at the sword.

"I only got it recently," he explained, "the previous owner was a Lich; anyway, I don't know much about fighting effectively with a sword since I normally use my fists. So, Fryn offered to help, and we practiced for a bit, but she would not let me simply practice forms or anything, we had to actually fight, to spar."

She stopped kneading the dough and turned just her head to watch him, with a bit of red altering the normally green tint of her wings.

"So after losing the sword, and failing to make her move a few times, I finally copied her style and made her move; but that was not enough, so we tried again… and I could only win by locking her joints… so she couldn't… move…"

The red in Lia's wings flared for an instant, and then faded. She pulled out the dough and rolled it out on the floured surface beside the finished cuts of meat, and said quietly, "What then?"

This time, he froze, holding the knife above the steak, ready to make the last cut. "I just sort of, did nothing. We just waited. Then I let her go, and we just watched the sky, till the sun started to set."

"You were only gone for an hour," Lia said, grabbing some of the thin slices of meat and rubbing them with chopped up marjoram and thyme. "Did you win that quickly?"

This time it was his turn. Leif blushed. "We only fought for ten minutes… I think."

"Master Aellin, putting his students in such indecent circumstances," she chided, laying the meat on the rolled out bread dough, sprinkling it with more of the strange gray salt. "Giving all the fee, all the wrong ideas."

"No, I'm not that sort of…" he lowered his voice. Fryn was still ignoring them, as Nora guided her hand, holding the piece of chalk together she was now teaching her how to write 'fasay.'

Lia crumbled in some aromatic bluish cheese, and then started to roll the ensemble into a log. "I think you need to decide quickly what sort of fae you are, Master Aellin, and make that clear to her, but you don't need to listen to me—I'm just an exile, and a one-time thief." She spread hare-butter over the rolled-up dough and then nestled it into a slightly-too-small baking dish, and slid it into the cast-iron stove. "But I suggest you figure that out before you eat my food."

Leif washed his hands once more and sighed. Then, looking at his sword, he went over to where Nora had apparently hung up his coat on one of the pegs meant to support a lantern, and went back out to the porch.

The peddler sat on the street corner, holding up an array of carved acornwood spoons and bowls and so on, and he gave Leif a welcoming smile that lacked a few teeth. Leif went over and sat beside him, hood up. As soon as they'd seen the Grass Guard, Lia had procured another one of the iconic cloaks for him, and he'd been keeping it with his coat ever since. The single oil lamp post had not been lit, so Leif pointed a finger at the wick, and shot a light-blue bolt of sparks toward it with a sigh.

"How was your day...?" he asked the peddler as the dull orange light of the lamp glowed in the empty intersection.

"Handy trick that," the old fae replied, rattling his wooden wares from his hanging rack, supported by a single post that he supported with his hand. "I sold a bowl, for two mint."

"I sold my soul," Leif said dramatically, "and I don't know what to do." He spun on the peddler sharply, causing him to rattle his goods once more. "They didn't teach me anything, not what I needed to know."

In spite of the lamp, the stars glowed overhead. Leif thought he saw the lesser two moons lagging behind the greater one, dancing or fighting, in the Feather, but he didn't subscribe to fate. He lowered his head again and sank his chin into one hand, resting his elbow on one knee, he struck out his other leg into the street, and slouched, even with his wings. "I think I knew what I should have done, or what I wanted to do, but though they were the same, they seemed at odds."

The sword unlatched itself and slid out a hair. "I know what it is, but for my own sake, I am not going to help you."

"Sold your soul, eh? What for?"

Thinking he meant, 'Why?' Leif glared at him. "It wasn't on purpose."

The peddler corrected himself with a bit of coughing, and straightened his posture, even his split wings. "For what price?"

"Sold it for my self," he answered glumly, "and got nothing in return."

He didn't hear the door open, nor notice when Fryn sat beside him. The peddler smiled. "What were you hoping to buy?"

He bit his lip, and looked down into his hand. "I wanted to get *her.*"

The peddler nodded as if he understood, so Leif frowned. "It's a good word, 'get', because you can't buy something priceless—the things you can't afford: the things you happen to find. Like I found this pin," he said, retrieving something from the mysterious confines of his cloak. It was a bit of twisted silver meant to look like a blade of grass woven into the shape of wreath with a blue-eyed bird perched in the center. It was a marvelous pin, and Leif stared at it. It looked almost identical to the one he'd seen at the Harvest festival at one of the booths.

"Where did you get this?"

"And there it is again," he answered him, "I found it. But I have a sense you found something far better, didn't you? How can you get that?"

Leif ground his teeth, to Havrshyk's dismay, who shivered in the sword at the sound. "I can't."

"I can show you how," the old fae intimated with a grin, and he pressed the pin into his hand, "it is given to you—like the wings on your back." Then, glancing around, he stood up abruptly and started off down the street. "I may see you again, but don't think you owe me none!"

Then he was gone. Leif laid back on the porch and held up the pin in the light of the stars. "Do you think she'll like it?" He asked Havrshyk absently.

A pale shadow loomed over him, and he realized that Fryn had been sitting beside him, and now she leaned between him and the stars, one hand delicately taking the pin, and fastening it to her cloak, she smiled. "Yes, I think I do," she said, placing her hand in his, she bent down and kissed him.

It was only for a few seconds, maybe even only one, but that moment seemed to him to last so much longer, like the sensation of being just about to fall. Fryn pulled away, but he still held her hand.

Trying to find the right words to express what he wanted was not easy, and in the end, he couldn't find anything better than to softly say, "I'm glad I ran into you and that drunk thief."

She chuckled. "I'm glad I saved your life," she replied.

"I'm glad I saved yours first," he cut in.

"So for now, it seems, neither of us is ahead," she answered, then stood up, and let go of his hand. "I'll let you have the first watch."

He nodded seriously, then, recalling a phrase that Nora had told him to try earlier, he added, "Møn fhor'la hyn'un sersaejalyr."

Fryn stopped by the door, her dimples showing with her smile. "You don't even know what that means."

"What does it mean?"

"Good night, my love." She rushed inside before he could respond, and left him wondering about the strange peddler, and the stars.

"Strange isn't it, Havi?" he asked.

"I'm obligated to ask 'what?' in this scenario, right?" The sword answered glumly.

"Yes, you are. It's strange how we can be so confused and torn over something, and then have it all be taken away, relieved, unburdened." Leif rolled to his feet and dusted off the back of his cloak. "Keep this between ourselves, of course."

"I'll tell everyone I know in here."

"Well, let the blood rejoice, because it boils in my veins… in a good way." Leif took a deep breath, and took off to the opposite side of the street where a few over-long stone bricks had been set in the wall so as to create a small ledge. He perched and dangled his feet over the lip and watched the empty streets in a listless state. Then he whispered, "Good night, Fryn, sersaejalyr."

Fasset and Fassen

Fassen:

Eastwall Markets

Leif

Three more days had passed, since things had undeniably improved, all except for their living arrangements, and the fact that they were harboring a fugitive. The market was especially crowded today, and Leif saw that there were a number of the Grass Guard mixed into the regular shoppers, wearing green cloaks of a finer cloth, cut to match those of the locals, but they stood too tall, and their wings didn't droop, and most noticeably, their 'green' was brighter and a bit pastel. He regretfully let go of Fryn's hand and they parted into the two central aisles of the market, after their week of coming and going, the merchants ignored them like they did anyone else.

He hadn't seen the peddler again, though he wanted to thank him, but still, he risked a look in Fryn's direction, and saw that she was busy inspecting parcels of last-year's flour beside one of the imposters. Nora trailed after him, catching up with a sharply accented "Fyrja, tassøraydae!"

"Hellelsør," he replied, crouching and reaching out a green-gloved hand to her. She took his hand, and he led her through the various faeries busy bargaining in Waverly, or offering obviously exaggerated prices to the imposter guards. "We may have to… fasset." Learning what he could of the language was more difficult than he anticipated, but Lia had been adamant that they learn and use as much of it as possible if they were to evade their pursuers effectively. How Fryn could pick it up so easily, and drawl through its lyrical phrases, he had no idea, but he loved to listen to her speak.

"Kaesayalan," the girl replied, holding one finger over her mouth.

The Grass Guard would not let the matter of the missing crown rest, and at this point, even if they just… threw it away, Lia and her daughter would still not be safe, and the allegations of Leif and Fryn's involvement would only grow worse. As it was, Fryn had taken an eye from one of their officers—well, he'd had no insignia, but from his elemental techniques it was more than likely he had been highly ranked. Fryn slipped past one of the imposters, pocketing a slip of paper in her cloak. The boy who'd given the stone to Nora stood beside a fee selling that ubiquitous gray salt, and he twitched his right wing while making eye-contact with Leif, so Leif moved a little to his right, as one of the oncoming guards tripped in a poorly-placed pothole, and fell on his hands and knees on the muddy stones. His hood fell back and his black hair alerted the surrounding shoppers that he was a foreigner, and they made a show of avoiding him.

Leif led Nora around him, and they continued northwards toward the gate. Ideally, at least according to the last letter they'd received from Trel, who had been reinforcing the idea that they'd split off, and that Leif and Fryn had tired of the search and gone off looking for something new, the Grass Guard had visited the Earl of Fassen at his estate with none other than the King of Gaershcim, President Hans of the Commission, Lord Wellsey, Pyrincel, and of course Princess Savis. They had all enjoyed the wine from the top of the vine, but had overstayed their welcome, excepting the princess, who, in Yarrow's words "had made such an impression on the young lord that he insisted she remain as a guest till at least the end of the month." Savis relented and allowed herself to depart from the company of the other High Nobles, and was currently enjoying a game of tablets with the Earl—who eagerly awaited their return.

It seemed that Savis had even been told that Leif and Fryn might visit, but was asked to keep it quiet. Leif wondered perhaps if that was because of Vinellin's efforts, and how the butler had managed to get the important faeries out of there so quickly. Had he given them some slightly-less-than-regal food and called it 'the finest the city had to offer?' Well, it had worked.

They ducked under a green set of drapes separating the Eastwall Market from the North Forest Gate courtyard, and continued westward through the crowd of hare-drawn cabs, carts loaded with grain, and the streams of pedestrians on their way to various businesses and merchant shops. He barely managed to keep Nora with him, as he guided her through the ever-shifting currents of pedestrians, but at least they were sure to lose the scent of the Grass Guard. He paused behind an obviously overloaded wagon, whose hare was barely able to pull it, straining on her leads, ears back in determination or maybe just as they normally were, in order to pull off his cloak and fold it under his arm. Nora did the same, and they blended in with the grays and browns of the regular Gaersyn folk.

He couldn't find Fryn or Lia in a quick scan, so he decided things were going as planned—them moving to the south, all the way to Boulderwall, to cross through the nobles' estates in the Shadowvine Quarter, and from there to the Earl. How they'd get past the ramparts ascending to the base of the vine, he had no idea, since there were likely to be members of the Grass Guard stationed at each of the military outposts in the city.

They could not effectively reach their destination if they both had to protect both of them, though Leif had not wanted to admit it. He took a deep breath and led Nora out of the crowd onto Foreside Lane, a narrow alley with hole-in-the-wall booths kept by run-down merchants, with tired wares; or was it the other way around? Leif shook his head and they continued.

Havrshyk's sword bounced at his hip, the scabbard tapping against his heel with each step forward, Nora rushing to keep up. The sword unlatched, catching the girl's attention, and she stared as it slid out of its sheath a crack to get a view of the area, and she pursed her lips.

"You were wise to heed my advice," Havrshyk commented in his mind, his tone thoughtful and almost considerate. "I had wondered if your disagreement on the strategy would end your relationship in its infancy, but there it is, still clinging onto life—not unlike me."

My 'relationship' with you is not nearly as important to me as is mine with her, Leif replied mentally. The alleyway led to a 'T' lined with mysterious crates, behind some of them Leif spotted a beggar's nook, which was fortunately empty. He took a left and they continued on at a quick pace, constantly checking over his shoulder to make sure they weren't being followed.

"Nefyrja," Nora asked, "why are we going so fast?" She nearly tripped over a bit of old acornshell planking from a broken crate, but he held her up, and she caught her fall with her wings.

He slowed and knelt beside her, making sure her ankle-high boots were undamaged, or that she hadn't stepped on a nail. She waited patiently, much more patiently than he would have, and just watched him expectantly. "Nora," he said, meeting her eyes, "your mother is in trouble, and so are we. If we don't find a good place to hide, bad things could happen to us; they might even take you away from your mother, and put you in an orphanage, or give you to one of the academies... if they do that here."

She swallowed and nodded.

Such a strong child, he thought, more than a little impressed, her mother did her well.

In a rare expression of compassion, Havrshyk agreed, "she should've grown playing with her friends, not being hunted by the Commission and the Rosenkrauns like a common criminal…"

"But, why are they chasing us?" she asked, her eyes not even blinking as she stared into his, and he found he could not look away. He thought of the story he'd told in her home town, of the young fae who'd been entranced by the serpents' eyes.

Leif put a hand on her shoulder and smiled wanly. "Because, someone made your mother steal something, and we were trying to help her. Whoever planned it found out, see, so we need to hide. If we can draw them to us, then we can turn things back around on them. That you see, is one of the lessons I learned from the sand vipers, they always turn around to attack. You think you're winning, but then it springs back."

"But will it work?"

"Of course it will," Leif replied, "because you have the two greatest Hunters in the world on your side!"

"Yarrow and Trel!?"

"…yes…" he *had* hoped she'd say *them*, but he couldn't argue with her choice. "But if we stay out and get caught, they might get in trouble, too. I don't want to disappoint them." He patted her shoulder and then stood, and taking her hand, started on their southern tack again in the nameless section of the Foreside alley. They moved on in that direction until they met up with Aerin Way, a quick walk that took nearly fifteen minutes, and then turned right to cross through the markets to the north of the Commission Quarter.

As they pulled into the crowd, Leif felt his hands getting colder, and he noticed that the Francis brothers were lurking by some of the stalls—as if they'd predicted their path, or figured it out… or had gotten inside information. Nora pulled on his hand, and he lowered his wings, and walked into the thick crowd, trying to copy the awkward movements of someone not trained in martial arts. It felt clunky, as his heels tapped on the pebble-stone pavement, and he nearly fell over more than once, but by following Nora's leading, he found he was slightly hunched over, as if she were trying to show him something exciting.

Once more, she's showing her cleverness, Leif thought with a smile, almost completely obscured from the view of the three brothers, who stood tall and proud with their hands on their weapons, looking so obviously like Hunters.

"Once more," Havrshyk added, "you prove your intelligence is less than that of a child."

They paused in front of a booth with a few bits of honeyed, grilled grains, and he stopped to buy a pair with a mint—which he worried he'd be unable to replace. They munched on those, and strolled out nonchalantly, and then, as they vanished around the next street corner, they finished their treat, tossed the wooden picks in the drain, and continued on toward the Tower District.

"It was probably only a week and a half ago, that we last came this way," Leif thought, looking up at the spire of carved stones that clawed its way up the side of the boulder wall, towering over the Forest of Grass to get a view of the fields surrounding the city and its vine. A green-uniformed Grass Guard flitted from one of the zig-zagging ramparts and crenelated battlements to the Tower—the spire that was magnificently topped by the telescope that Fryn had so eagerly wanted to look through. Now, he saw it pointed toward the horizon to the north, the pale sunlight glinting off its polished brass tubes. Fryn, of course, was now further south, and probably couldn't see it. He suppressed a shiver and looked down at Nora, who made a light 'yelp' and let go of his hand.

"Why are you so cold?" she asked him, nearly at a whisper, brushing some of her auburn curls out of her eyes.

He looked down in shock as he saw that the skin of his hands had faded from his native olive tan to an almost bleached white like the color of Fryn. Havrshyk hummed to himself, but made no comment, so Leif stepped under the eaves of a manor house opposite a bakery and glanced around the various faeries moving around the streets. Coaches rolled by, driven by smartly-dressed cabbies with felt hats, and Leif saw again a figure that resembled that same noble with the pince-nez who'd nearly run Fryn down in the street the previous week, rolling past slowly with a dour expression which only soured and intensified as his eyes narrowed on the girl. The moment hung in the air as he sneered, his thin, undernourished face twisting, as he pointedly looked away in disgust.

The coach vanished in the crowd, and the bell of the Tower tolled the noon rush hour, and Leif swallowed. He was parched, almost as if he'd eaten cinnamon by itself—as he'd once done on a dare. It was a rare enough spice that he had to endure some difficult extracurricular training activities, but altogether worth the effort at the time.

Why? he asked, pondering the unnatural chill that lingered long after the hideous noble had passed.

Havrshyk sighed, and the sword shifted its weight slightly within the confines of its sheath, breaking and recrystallizing into a slightly different, newer shape. *"Your reserves of blood are running low, what with your injuries, I have had to rebuild the sword several times."*

Leif frowned, he felt as if Havrshyk was only telling him half of it, but before he could ask further, Nora gave a low gasp, and ducked into cover behind one of the limestone pillars supporting the house whose porch they had temporarily invaded, and Leif instinctively did the same. A Grass Guard landed on the street wearing a black-banded visor cap and a matching eyepatch, and a long trailing green coat and vest, thick and ribbed, with the veiny patterns of blades of grass. His knee high boots were curled over at the tops, and at his side, his grassblade shimmered with the Guard's elemental light.

"It's *him*," she explained under her breath.

"The light-elemental?" Leif asked, afraid to enter his direct line-of-sight, from any angle.

She nodded.

Leif considered, wondering how they could know if it was safe to move on. *"Can you see him, Havi?"*

"I'm not going to respond to a nick-name like that," Havi replied.

"That counts as a response..."

"I will see what I can see," he said, and then the sword slid out of its sheath an inch, so that the blade had a 'view' through the lattice of the porch's fence, and he gave a low hum. *"The Grass Guard is leaving."*

Leif muttered his thanks and peeked around the pillar, sure enough, there were no uniformed guards waiting to arrest them. Nora watched him carefully, as if she wanted to ask him something, and then she watched the sword as it sheathed itself and locked the latch.

"Is that a magic sword?" she asked innocently.

Leif gave another look around the street, and then brought her out into the thick traffic. "It is a magic sword," he answered, hoping she didn't have to learn what it really was. She might feel sorry for him.

"I heard that."

Leif made sure to keep his surface thoughts buried a little deeper.

"What do you call it?" she asked.

"I... ah... I call it Havi." He scratched the back of his neck awkwardly, and they turned onto the busiest street in the Tower District, West Tower Street.

"Havi?" she confirmed, reaching out to touch the handle, "is it dangerous?"

He took her hand and nodded seriously. "Even I'm afraid to use it. After all, a sword in your hand may be a powerful tool, but if your enemy takes it from you, then of course you become nearly powerless—and it is a much more dire situation if that is a magic sword."

"I've heard the same said about Hunters themselves; use them against criminals and they are very useful, use them <u>as</u> criminals, and they become worse than before," Havrshyk commented coolly.

He obviously meant to make it sound as though Hunters could be considered tools. Commonfae and scholars alike had argued over whether the 'sword' was complicit in its use as well as its wielder, but that was pointless philosophizing. He and Fryn knew they didn't follow orders or do what was most convenient, they followed their convictions, confusing the so-called boundaries of wielder and weapon. They crossed the street into the opposite alley and turned a bit more toward the southwest to cut across the Tower District in the direction of Westlord's Street. Having made it this far without difficulty, there was a good chance of making it into the Estate.

A minute or two passed by without difficulty as they weaved through the richer inhabitants of the city—arrayed in their red argyle and green linen suits and coats, or their green felt and feathered caps, all of which surprised Nora. She was constantly watching them sweep by, as they tried to match the unhurried and leisurely pace of the district's natives, how the couples walked, side by side, but too proper to even bump into each other. She watched how they looked down their noses at them, with their serviceable travel clothes, colored tan, or brown, their cloaks rolled up and held under the crook of Leif's arm, to hide the hilt of his sword—the scabbard was mostly hidden by his coattails.

Leif frowned and paused at the crossing of Jessera and Weylan, as two Grass Guard wagons rolled in their direction, or rather the direction of the Tower. Each one was carved and molded with acorn-shells, almost as dark as the oaks from which they came, and were trimmed in gold filigree of grass blades and heads of grain. Their drivers wore similar woven-green linen uniforms like the guards they'd seen before, but had tight-fitting felt caps, with goggles around their necks, holding the reins of their hares with determination as they, Leif suspected, tried to convey a sense of importance and dignity to the regular folk.

"A city far-flung from the capitol, huh?" Leif mused under his breath.

Nora looked up at him, and then smiled, looking down. "This is Jessera Way," she said, pointing at the sign, "she was one of the founders of Fasset. She'd run away from home, because her family hated her... and so she lived here underneath a large rock, where she could hide."

"My family liked me well enough, I can be grateful for that," Leif replied, his eyes never leaving their inspection of the speeding Grass Guard coaches. There were roughly six Guards in each one, two had spears, two had crossbows, and two had grass blades. Their leader was on top of the second coach, sitting as silent and menacing as a gargoyle beside the driver, his one eye searching the crowd.

"Step behind someone," Havrshyk advised.

Leif pulled back a step as if to check his laces, and an elderly fae in an ermine-lined fur coat stepped in front of him, to get a better view.

Nora crouched beside him with a frown. "But your boots... aren't they belted?"

Good eye, little one... he thought. "Only at the top, but I still adjust the fit on the inside of the calf, see?" He turned out his ankle and presented the crisscrossing cords of his custom travel boots. *Thanks Havi.*

"*Call me 'Havi' again, and I'll draw the attention of the Guard,*" he threatened.

Good luck doing that, Leif retorted with a smirk, which faded as he considered just a couple of the ways in which the sword could do just that—trip him in the alley, surround him in unnatural fog, anything to make the area he occupied stand out.

The carriages rolled off toward the tower, and Leif stood again, as the other pedestrians murmured in awe or respect for their Grass Guard, or sympathy for the King. Leif could not sympathize with the King himself of course, harmless and naïve though he seemed at the Festival, Leif found his unstable emotional health to be... disconcerting. But then, Ieffin had been more than a little odd himself, though he had enough reason to be—and he still fulfilled his duties even if he pretended he wasn't.

They followed the old fae in the fur coat to the other side of the street, continuing on Jessera Way. "It's almost like he doesn't know where he's going," Leif observed quietly.

Nora met his eyes and gave a small laugh in response, "then why are we following him?"

He laughed, earning himself a couple offended and askance looks. "I don't know, let's go another way." They stepped up the pace with a wingburst, another apparently offensive action, as someone even gasped at the wind that flew in their face, and they turned directly south on Kaensal Road to more quickly reach their destination, but as they turned the corner around the carved-stone wall of Tower's Financial Associates, Leif paled and pulled Nora behind him into the immediately adjacent alleyway. She peeked around him, and then sunk back into hiding as she sucked in her breath. Waiting at the corner of Westlord's Street, the main thoroughfare from the west gate, were the three brothers!

"I thought they'd gone after Fryn and Lyrin," Nora wondered, using the Waverly term for her mother.

"It appears that *we* distracted them instead, hopefully Fryn and Lia can get by alright," he said, trying unsuccessfully to suppress a shiver. He looked down at his hands, almost white, as if he'd been drained of his blood as Fryn had often done. "Still, we have to go around them." They rushed over to the west side, flying behind a passing enameled carriage, and into yet another dark alley, this one situated behind bakeries, a restaurant, an inn, and a few other businesses. Leif pulled on her hand to lead her into the dark, bread-scented passageway, but she froze, her fingers tightening in his hand. He glanced back, and noticed that her wings were shivering.

"Don't," she whispered, "it's not supposed to be that dark…"

Leif almost sighed, but he knew she was right, and that tickle at the nape of his neck warned him not to ignore what she said. They edged over against the wall and stared into the almost pitch black center of the alleyway.

Havrshyk sighed. *"Draw me now."*

Leif shivered again, and this time, he *felt* it; his blood felt as though it were slowly draining, as if he were drying out under a winter sun. *I'm not a Lich.*

"You'll be one soon enough if you don't do something," Havrshyk replied.

"Your hand is as cold as Fryn's…" Nora complained in spite of her anxiety.

"I'm sorry," he said, letting go of her hand. He drew out Havrshyk quietly, and held out the black and red blade toward the shadows. "Who's there?" he demanded in a soft tone, so as not to attract the guards.

The shadows faded into the noonday light, as if the walls were lined in mirrors, it filled the path with a yellow-golden glow, and the one-eyed Guard Captain stood there with his sword held before his face in a duelist's salute. Leif held a hand back to protect Nora, and angled the sword toward him, gritting his teeth.

"I hope you know how to bend light," Havrshyk commented wryly, "because otherwise our partnership might just end here."

It's not an even partnership…

"You're right, you haven't been holding up your end,"

"So now I face the Viper," the Grass Guard with the eye-patch said, "I hope you will prove yourself equal to your associate…"

Leif whispered, "Nora, hide yourself somewhere safe, where he can't find you if I… just hide."

She nodded and vanished from his sight.

"I don't make a habit of killing children," the Captain said, "but traitors are something else."

"You'll lose your other eye before you find her," Leif answered, "and anyone who hurts a child, *I will* remove."

"Very well then," he swept his sword to the side, as if scattering the dew from its edge, and launched himself at Leif with a blinding flash.

***

Shadowvine District:

Vassidel Estate Grounds

Fryn

Fryn slipped between the legs of the fountain statue of a finch opening its mouth to chirp toward the sky where, oddly though, water spewed out instead. She spaced her feet directly before each of the statue's feet, keeping her wings pressed against the bird's bronze, feather-textured chest, heart beating quickly with more than the usual amount of blood. Lia waited, peeking around the corner of a painstakingly cultivated laurel hedge, maintained in a boxlike shape with a uniform height so that it was only one head shorter than the enclosing wall of expertly cut stones.

She took deep breaths and turned her head, focusing one ear on the noble's guard's movements. Dodging through the ramshackle buildings of the Eastwall and Boulderwall Districts had taken some dexterity, especially since the faeries in those areas often left refuse in the alley or streets—broken boxes, fallen laundry, poured-out ashes, anything and everything that could be thrown away. "I can see why they call it 'Fassen'," Fryn had commented irritably, when she'd stepped on a discarded, rotten grape.

Lia had frowned, and looked sadly back the way they'd come. "It is not the reason, but it is from the same stream of causes. They see themselves like this," she said, "as refuse, rubbish, unusable, unwanted, the remains of a people thrown away."

Fryn's stomach had twisted at that, and she had been wrestling with the sense of guilt till now when they found themselves effectively trapped in the noble's estate—even though the noble's private guards had no idea that they were on the grounds. It seemed that just avoiding any notice was a good deal more difficult than merely not stepping in something gross. She smiled at that, and waved at Lia with a sharp wrist motion, so that as Fryn bolted, using all her blood to increase her agility and speed, and rolled under the lip of an amanita fly cap mushroom, Lia took her place.

They advanced from the east to the southwest, across the mossy flowerless flowerbeds of the noble's lower fields. There were various artistically positioned rocks behind which they could wait for the occasional servant or guard to pass by, and eventually they found themselves nearing the southern corner of the rectangular estate. It's wall was perfectly built all the way around with only one entrance, one street, the one that slicked up the slope of the hill from the direction of the Commission Quarter. In addition to the stone wall, built high enough that anyone climbing or flying over it had a good chance of being spotted, especially as they got closer to the Earl's Estate, where the Grass Guard were likely waiting to stop them, at a higher elevation, there was also the hedge, that had grown impossibly, completely around, right in front of the walls, so thick that one could not crawl through it or climb it without being seen.

They made it to the corner of the servant's quarters, which Fryn guessed, doubled as the primary supply storage area for the House. They crouched under the eaves of one of the first story windows, listening to a pair of young maids laughing and cooking what smelled like sweet bread.

"...ut you can't jus *say* that to the master!" One exclaimed, her accent sounding vaguely Waverly, as if she'd pronounced 'master' as 'mah-stør.'

"...I can say what I pleeze," replied the other fee, giggling, as if she'd done a good job impersonating the accent of the nobles they served.

Fryn shared raised eyebrows with Lia and they both looked out toward the main drive where the noble's coach was just pulling up in the circle before the landing. It was pulled by a white hare with a black spot on its nose, and Fryn found herself smiling, wondering how soft it was. The driver flew down from the top of the black-stained vinewood coach and held open the door, extending his other arm toward the main entrance of the estate as the previously alluded to 'master' stepped down to the graveled drive.

He wore a green felt waistcoat, with coattails that reached almost to his heels, had a silver-handled dueling foil at his waist, and wore green leather ankle boots, matching evergreen knee-length trousers, and stockings that were cinched under the trousers by green ribbons. He had a silver chain and pocket watch, green enameled pince-nez, and a matching felt bowler hat.

It was the same noble who'd almost run her down in the street! And seeing him now, she saw that he was remarkably thin, as if he were one of the... she considered for a moment, trying to remember what it was called... one of the Norenan Ascetics, who trained themselves so severely, consuming so little, that their bodies shrank to only what was strong. That was the idea anyway.

Lia lowered herself to the level of the ground, and tugged on Fryn's wing to get her to follow suit. "You do not want to get the attention of *him*. He's a loyalist, and an imperialist. I heard that he tried to advise the King to wipe out the 'rebels' in the Forest of Grass, as well as the undesirables who live there..."

Fryn knelt beside her, shifting the gravel with her knee so that it made the slightest 'scrunch.' She glanced back toward the door, and her heart stopped as she saw the rail-thin noble stop in his tracks, standing on the second step. One of his lower wings twitched, and he held up one white-gloved hand, and snapped his fingers.

Immediately, a fae in the customary black suit and bow-tie of the office of butler whisked out the front door, and leaned in close so that his master could whisper in his ear. The butler's mouth barely moved, and he had a mournful expression as he slightly shook his head.

"Lord Vassidel has, at least as rumor has it," Lia interjected softly, "he has advanced many complaints about the current line of the Earldom, and has *offered* to serve more loyally if the king should desire a change in government." She bit her lip. "In spite of his name, he *hates* Waverly, and thinks we should all be like those who rule us. That we should forget the language and our traditions... or face a more permanent form of 'exile.'"

"The exile of the soul?" Fryn asked. She looked back toward the door and her eyes widened as she noticed that the very topic of their conversation was crossing the gravel soundlessly in their direction, as if he was barely touching the ground—though his wings didn't move.

She felt a strange sense of coldness, and the hairs on her arms, and the back of her neck stood on end. *Forgive me Leif... but I have need of more...* She drew a little more through that far-off link that connected his heart to hers, and she funneled blood, reshaping her blade to a denser crystal with a jagged edge, so that it no longer looked like a frozen shard of blood, but a hand-carved ritual blade of onyx dipped in blood. *I hope you've still got enough... but it's hard to tell from this far away.*

Lord Vassidel drew his foil, and nearly teleported around the corner with an elementally enhanced wingburst, as the tip of his blade passed through air at the height of a normal fae's neck, if he were standing upright. But Fryn and Lia had been kneeling, so she stared at the blade that curved down toward her face, and focused on twisting out of its path.

Her instincts failed, her body was already frozen without enough blood flow to enable her to move with any kind of natural agility. Her mouth fell open as a line of fire pierced through her eye and the back of her head. But as Vassidel was about to pull back, Fryn brought her Bloodknife up and through his folded steel foil, shattering it under the instantaneous freeze so that half the blade remained imbedded in her head.

Words failed.

Her left side refused to cooperate, and she felt the tugging of the Bloodknife, as if it invited her to *hide*. Lia seemed to waver in the periphery of her awareness, as she flew up from the ground, striking the emaciated noble with a fully extending kick in his stomach. Fryn longed to slide into the welcoming comfort of the blade, to wait it out, but if she did... she couldn't remember why that was not a good idea. Her right hand still held the blade, and there was the other piece of the sword still in her head. She raised her hand to her face, and clumsily took hold of the metal shard, and started to pull it out. Blood flowed from her heart, directly to her head, where it coursed, and she gasped.

She still could not speak. Her exclamation was more of an animal's wounded cry, as the sliver of metal fell to the ground with her beautiful blue eye still attached. But what came next? She separated the eye from the sword, and, realizing that her left hand was working again, she pressed the punctured orb into the eye socket and screamed as the blood flowed through her veins and the eyes started to heal.

She could see Lia fending off the duelist with a shimmering of wind and air protecting her limbs from the half-length blade that he nearly stabbed her with several times. She still held one hand over the healing eye, but the other held her diminished Bloodknife, now faded to pink. *It was Leif that I forgot, but now I need that blood. No more surprises...* She drew everything that she had once given or stored in Leif, leaving him with only the blood that he had restored, and she shook off the pain, and the dried blood flakes that fell from her rapidly healing wounds.

Leif had taught her something new.

She flew in under the outstretched half-blade of the noble, pulling Lia back from the attack, as she cut across the back of his arm. It was shallow, barely cutting through his element ally enhanced wind, but she drew a little more blood from it, and sharpened the serrated edges of the knife. She pulled back as he tried to parry her feint, and she angled her knife, mirroring the direction of her wing, and then burst forward, twisting, extending, so that she sank her blade into his shoulder. She let it drink, and freeze, as much as she could.

He still fell back, merely extending his wings like sails, as a great wind caught him and drew him a few feet away. He did not cry out, or show any sign that he had felt the injury, or even that he noticed the loss of blood. The ice would numb the pain, but he would be stiff, and weaker... theoretically. Still, he watched her with a bitter expression, eyebrows narrowed, thin lips pressed into a line, the broken sword held out in an *en garde* position.

She could not use that trick again, and her eye bled as it rebuilt itself, running like tears down her cheek and from between the fingers of the hand she pressed against her eye.

Lia moved around behind her, though she couldn't see it. She felt the brush of her wings, and heard the crunch of moving gravel as private guards landed or ran over to help their Lord against the 'assassins'—at least according to their yelled impressions.

"Fryn, I'll hold these off, you deal with Vassidel!" Lia said, picking up the cold, bloodied shard of metal that Fryn had only just pulled out of her head.

Vassidel spat. "The name is *Thassetel,*" he pronounced, and Fryn felt Lia's wings cringe against hers. "It is an important name, and I'll not have it soiled by such a mispronunciation."

"You shouldn't be proud of that... Wing-Breaker!" Lia snapped.

He smirked. "I wouldn't remove my own wings... but not only is it expedient to disable your opponent physically, but to break their morale as well—it is a practical strategy.

"Forry said, 'those who crush, or steal or break, will be broken in themselves. Those whose joy is in the pain that they can cause, or in seeking out the misfortune of others, are themselves miserable, broken, poor. Even what little they have, they will destroy!'" Lia yelled and rushed one of the four guards on her side, as Fryn burst toward the duelist. She hadn't heard a single word in Waverly start with a 'th' sound, but now, hearing one of the meanings of such a word, she understood why they might be superstitious about it. Wing-Breaker, a taboo surpassing her own.

She rushed into the first lunging attack with her open palm, allowing the broken blade to pierce her hand, and she closed in with a back-handed slash across his wrist—as she twisted from her hips, numbing her hand with ice, she let it slice through her hand, then grabbed him by the collar and stabbed him in the heart.

Everything he thought he was faded with one final beat. His lungs did not twitch, his heart didn't try to turn, and his muscles all went limp. He weighed so little. She threw him off herself, shivering unconsciously, and grabbed Lia by her coat, so that they flew off toward the south, over the hedge, and around four turns—diving under a tarp spread over a nearly empty crate of grain and covering themselves with the wheat. Fryn's heart pounded in her ears, and she bit her lip.

Was I right to kill him?

Isn't that what a Hunter does?

She listened as the Grass Guard and the private guards of the late Lord 'Thassetel' flew or ran about, asking passersby about them, searching in alleys, and corners. Her heart and breath stopped as she heard the tarp above them shift, and a hand start reaching through the grain. After what would normally have been ten heartbeats, she heard the tarp fall, and the call that no one was there inside the grain, and her heart resumed its work.

Beside her, Lia shook, her hand quivering, wings twitching, as she focused on slowing her breathing. "Oh let my daughter please be safe..." she whispered.

"We should wait here till it gets a bit darker and no one is around," Fryn suggested, "and maybe wear our cloaks."

"Right..."

***

Tower District:

Back Alleys

Leif

Leif fell to his knees. All his strength left him, and he was glad that Nora was not close enough to see. It felt as though he'd been bitten by the Viper, but this time, rather than breaking the bones of his arm, its venom was being pumped into his heart. The air smelled like snow, or was that his nose? Could he smell his nose? What *did* a nose smell like.

He smiled wearily. Fryn always had a lingering scent of pine and peppermint, and that added crispness that came with frost. Why did it have to be so bright? He closed his eyes and saw once more, that strange black and red landscape: barren, a desert with mountains made of sand. The sky was close, as if he could part it with his hands, and he stood before the crystalline pedestal that he'd seen when Ieffin had bonded him to the sword. Delicate cracks had formed throughout the quartz from the tip of the black blade, though the area around the broken viper's fang was undamaged. Snow blew in his desert, and frosty patterns clawed through his sky. It didn't feel like *his* place anymore, but as if someone else had moved in, with an eclectic mix of unmatching pieces of furniture—like yellow-plaid upholstered chairs around an ancient, stained oak round table; unfitting like scarves and gloves in the summer.

"Leif, what are you doing? Aren't you going to protect that child?" Havrshyk demanded, standing before him in full Lichform, lips blue, black hair frozen into a stylized position, a disappointed frown on his face. He wore that long black coat, and the snow-flake stenciled bits of armor that he had worn when Leif had killed him—his body—and there was a scar across his neck: a testament to his defeat.

"What child?" Leif asked, turning in a quick circle, "Where am I?"

Havrshyk sighed. "The place where the sword meets the heart. Your bond to the sword is not perfect, and without blood, you cannot continue to use it—and so unless you get blood, you cannot *ever* get blood. Get up, and kill that Grass Guard!"

"Is he still there?"

"He should be, after all, a dream can take you very far in only half an hour. Your mind should be rather quick here, hm?" Aldyr walked over and sat on the red sandstone step of the dais on which the damaged crystal plinth stood. "I'll help you, this time." He looked away, as if he'd just admitted something embarrassing from his past.

"How do I go back?"

"Just open your eyes." He stood again, and suddenly pushed Leif in the chest, and he felt his heart beat furiously with fresh blood. Opening his eyes, he saw the blade shrinking in volume against the stones on which he lay, one cheek pressed flat and frozen on the ground. He broke the layer of frost around his body with a ripple of sparks, that tingled through his fingers, trailing off of the supercooled ground, to trace a viper's path along his wings and around his arms.

The sparks sizzled around his hand, arcing to the hilt of the sword, scattering in a static shock as he grabbed it and rose to his knees, looking up at the one-eyed Grass Guard officer. "You're not going to find her," he repeated, leveraging himself to his feet with the blade wedged between stones.

The light flared in a bloom of colors, deepening so that it glowed, surrounding him in a cloak of white and prismatic hues, as the surrounding walls, sky, and ground, darkened to a gloomy blackish gray. The Grass Guard's sword vibrated with green light, seeming to shiver and bend impossibly with each second, faster than Leif could possibly catch with his eyes... unless he watched more quickly. He rushed at him with the black sword keening in his hand, against the burning light-imbued winds that blew through the alley. He cut through the light as if cutting through a dense fog, sparks splitting away from the edge of his blade, and from his arms, as the 'weight' of the light resisted him.

Leif closed his eyes, and recalled the mental image of the alley as it was before, stepping to the right side, spinning with his wings, so that he ran along the wall, and as he sensed the deepening concentration of light before him, he spun around to rush along the left wall—only for a second, as he sprang off it, opened his eyes, and extended the sword toward the brilliant source of light. He couldn't see through the whiteness, or the scattering colors that sprang away from the hungrily red sword, which had thinned to almost the width and thickness of Yarrow's dueling sword. The tip cut through hardened light, and caught against the raging green blade, and Leif saw his opponent's face.

The Captain's right eye was covered by a black eyepatch, but the frostbitten scars trailing down his cheek toward his ear told of the violence with which Fryn had removed it. His teeth were bared, gritted together. Leif's Bloodsword pressed against the side of the Grassblade, caught on the woven, hardened knot of twisted grass that formed the guard and handle. The shock rippled through the razor-like Grass weapon as the opposing forces each tried to uproot the other.

"Beware that green sheen," Havrshyk advised, "he'll cut in two places at once, not even at the same time, two edges overlaid on top of each other: a Pyrincel style."

Leif nodded, even though the Captain couldn't understand why, and he continued closing in, twisting to extend his 'open-hand' in a fist charged with sparks toward the guard's floating rib. His fist slowed through the waves of light, but he felt enough of an impact to bruise if not break, and he wingbursted around to the right side, to use the wall as a foothold.

The guard deflected Leif's following stab and slash, following him in the circle he'd tried to use to surround him, and parried, then lunged, body sinking low, and then rising again with a wingburst as his flexible blade sang toward Leif's neck, the blade bending with the change in pressures and movements, as the hardened green section of light maintained its stiffness—so that it closed in on his neck and heart at the same time.

Leif flared sparks to his eyes, and his wings, barely dodging to the side, but the Captain twisted his hold on the handle so that it rotated with his movements, in a spiral. Leif's eyes adjusted to the higher speed, focusing on the instant that the light flickered between its phases, and brought his Bloodsword up, charged with sparks, disrupting the light as it sailed through the intermittent position of the light-blade, parrying away the blade of grass.

He shifted into a low stance, grabbing his opponent by the belt, and rolling toward the ground, only managing to destabilize him. The one-eyed guard wingbursted upwards, drawing Leif up with him, who scrambled to twist in the air to deflect the now-spinning slash of the glowing, conical blade. Leif released his hold on the belt, flying downwards as the green cone of light extended toward his head. He hit the ground, falling on his back and stared up at it.

"Focus, the blade is in the center, the light just spins."

Leif closed his eyes, raising the sword and with a flick of his wrist, he nudged the center of the cone aside, and rolled backwards, rising to a stand.

The Captain didn't give him time to relax, but pressed his advantage, drawing in all the light in the alley so that the only visible light was that which shimmered around his body, and intensified into a silvery green, and flew directly at him in a flèche, wings thrown back in one powerful burst.

His sparks were low, and he couldn't see past the glare, nothing but the advance of that brightness, and its searing heat. He frowned. Hadn't Mythrim used heat? But then… Mythrim had bested him in the fight, and Leif was no true duelist… He focused all his sparks in his head and in the arm and hand that held the sword, so that arcs of lightning sprang up from the ground to his black sword, and trailed from his eyes.

There was only one way to beat him, and that was to be faster, even faster than his intense light. He stood his ground, charging his nerves and senses to their fullest potential to see and move, waiting for that moment of parry and repost to appear. The tip of the sword, rippling with the light, closed in within a wingspan of his heart, and still he didn't move. It traced now, a constant line that remained imprinted on his eyes, as it drew slowly, so slowly, closer to his heart, that now seemed as if it had forgotten how to beat.

It singed his jacket, and began its delicate slithering advance through his skin, his muscles, and his ribs. The scent of burnt flesh was only barely noticeable, he was so focused on the look of victory on his opponent's face—that same conviction of completion that first the sand viper, and then Mythrim had displayed.

He was slightly aware of the sound of an iron grate moving, and the voice of a little girl yelling in a panic. "Leif! Don't die!" Nora cried, and his heart twitched with sympathy, right before the blade of grass rippled like a wave through it.

Now, he thought to Havrshyk, and felt the pieces of his heart harden into ice, and his hand snapped into lightning-quick motion. Twisting in an opposite spiral to counter the Captain's attempt to bore a hole through his chest, he slid the Bloodsword, burning off segments of Havrshyk's irreplaceable blood, and cut off the Captain's arms and slashed him through his stomach. Leif leaned further into the Grassblade, cracks forming around the hole in his chest, and impaled his opponent so he couldn't escape its leeching influence.

Nora watched, open-mouthed, silent, in horror. The Captain's face went white, and he fell away, a cold and empty corpse. Leif looked at his chest, and slowly pulled out the sword, and waited for Havrshyk to heal his wounds with the fresh influx of blood.

"Not bad, Leif, you'd make a competent Lich, if only you had the right element," Aldyr said lightly.

Leif glanced over at the girl, cowering, wings gray, shoulders shaking, in her hiding place just a few spans away in the drain,. He put away the sword and sighed bitterly.

I find no joy in this, Havrshyk, he replied. "Nora, come quickly," he said aloud.

She didn't respond, so he unrolled their cloaks and wrapped himself in his, clasping it around his neck, and then draped her cloak over her wings, and eased them through the slits. "Come along, Nora, we will be safe now."

"Why…? Why did you?" she started to ask, and then looked down.

Children understand more than they let on, he mused. "We must hurry," he answered, and picked her up, flying down the alleyway to the west. It was getting toward the end of the afternoon, and they only had a little light left. Nora hid her face in his shoulder, the same one that was now covered with a seal of slowly healing ice, and shook in his arms. Leif grit his teeth.

I never wanted her to see that.

"You never had a choice."

Feast and Fast

Fassen:

Earl's Estate

Fryn

Fryn flew in through the door that Vinellin had brusquely held open, without any way of knowing she was there. Lia followed her, both trailing dew in their dark green cloaks, thoroughly drenched by their crawling passage around the base of the vine.

Her boots clacked on the slate tiles of the servants' entrance at the back of the estate, water dripped from her wings, a gentle almost unnoticeable sound, and she smiled when she saw Leif waiting by the entrance to the hallway. She flitted over and landed in front of him. Then, all of a sudden, she looked away, wrestling with an inexplicable awkwardness. They had only just *admitted* where they stood, what they wanted, but she still felt embarrassed. She stole a glance at his face, and remembered that she hadn't returned enough of her blood to his veins. Then she noticed that his heart was not quickened by her approach as it usually was.

He was pale, still needing more blood, and his eyebrows were knitted and wrinkled, and his lips were twisted with a troubled frown. There was foreign blood in his veins, blood she had felt before.

"What happened?" she whispered, already guessing something of it, but not wanting to reveal the tie her heart had to his. Her wings drooped, and the water coating them and her clothes froze into a thin layer of marbled ice.

Leif's eyes refocused on hers, and he gave her a sad smile; just a slight change to his face at the sound of her voice. "I had to face that Grass Guard you fought before…"

She bit her lip as she looked at his coat, and the burnt and cut hole in his chest. "The sword worked?" she asked with a sideways glance.

Lia stepped up beside them, with Vin waiting discreetly a few steps behind.

He didn't deign to notice them as he continued. "Lia, you will find Nora with Princess Savis in the music room."

She nodded, and Vinellin led her down the hall and out of sight. Leif and Fryn remained in the entryway, which was dimly lit with only two of the starlamp sconces activated and tuned to a faded orange glow.

"You defeated him?" she asked once more, reaching out her hand toward his, then pausing, nearly pulling it back, then pushing through her hesitance, she held his hand, and intertwined her fingers with his. A flush of purple ran through her wings, but she didn't care to hide it from him; after all she knew so much about how *he* felt at any given time.

Leif sighed, giving her slightly-warmed hand a squeeze. "I killed him, Fryn, in front of Nora... with *him*." He looked down at the hilt of the sword that rested at his hip beside their hands.

She swallowed, and took his other hand, drawing his attention to her eyes. "You saved her then, Leif—that is all that matters. Lia says, in one of the Waverly books, they have a saying that 'we all must bear our guilt, or else be justified.'"

"That's not very comforting," he replied, "she hasn't spoken at all since we got here, and that was a few hours ago." Leif swung their hands idly, and looked down the darkened hall. "We should probably go see them."

"I suppose so," she allowed, also looking into the hallway. It was lined by golden-framed paintings and landscapes, invisible from the side, barely outlined against the straight paneling of the walls by the far-off light of the main hallways. "Even the servants' halls are decorated..." she observed.

Leif's wings shifted as he shrugged. "You noticed it too? Maybe they just alternate the Earl's 'noble' areas throughout the year, and the servants just change their routes."

"Or they just go through the whole estate, not hidden, but a visible, presentable part of the House," Fryn suggested, "almost like a rejection of the aesthetics of the other nobles..."

A few delicate footsteps echoed from the hallway, alerting them to the approach of a tall feminine figure in a vaguely bluish long-skirted dress. Encroaching might have been a better description, Fryn supposed, as she put on a smile and reluctantly released Leif's hands. Princess Savis met them in the dim light with a cheeky grin, though her hands were folded primly in front, and her posture was perfectly straight and proper.

"It is good to see you again, Ms Martin," she said, saluting her with a friendly nod, "and you again, Master Aellin—though we met briefly earlier."

Leif's shoulders tensed, as he put on a pleasant face; though she could feel his increased blood pressure. His heart was strained, so she slowly lent him what she could of her own blood, to relieve some of the burden on his nerves. "It is my pleasure, Princess, to see you again. I trust your time here has been enjoyable?"

"That is a good way of describing it," she answered with a wry lifting of one eyebrow toward Fryn. "The 'young master' is more energetic in his endeavor to entertain than even the rumors gave him credit for—though since the other guests have moved on, I suspect he has wearied a little, as he has spent a better portion of his time to himself; likely managing the affairs of his house."

"That... does sound like him," Leif replied with a forced chuckle. "Your brother is similarly devoted to his duties, isn't he?"

She nodded, "Oh very, yes."

Leif unlatched and relocked the seal of his sword and smiled distractedly.

"How long have you been staying at the Estate?" Fryn intervened, drawing the Princess' attention away from Leif's lapse in attentiveness.

She waved them toward the hallway, and they followed her as she replied, "Only five, or is it six days now? We toured the vine, and the estate, even exploring the city in some detail..." They moved into a cozy parlor with a warm red glow emanating from the polished granite fireplace, bathing the two couches on either side in its heat. There was a silver tray with stemless glasses and a crystal carafe of a tannic wine on the vinewood table between the couches, which seemed to drink in the fiery red from the fire and intensify it in the blood-red sea aerating in the carafe. Savis waved a hand delicately toward the far couch and curled up on the one to the left of the fireplace. She dropped her cream-colored house slippers onto the red-and-green embroidered rug underneath the low table, and stared into the fire, closing her eyes.

Leif filled the three stemless glasses, cut with the vine of Fassen, which had a new comical, even ironic meaning now, and passed them out as Fryn sat across from the Princess. They held their glasses without tasting, and silence filled the room, with only the odd crackling of the peat in the hearth, for near on a minute.

"Do we need coasters?" Leif asked practically.

Savis frowned. "I imagine that if we did, then Vinellin would have provided them, and seeing as he did not, then I imagine we do not." She leaned closer toward the table and inspected it under a careful eye. "It seems to be enameled vinebark, possibly unstainable?"

Fryn bit the inside of her cheek, and added to Leif in a whisper, "I don't think that was a proper word…"

He nodded. "But we know what she means by it, so let's overlook it this time."

She smiled, feeling some of the weight of their flight out of the Eastwall slums and their entanglements with the guards… and the lives they had to take… begin to melt away.

"I don't have a blessing or a toast," Savis said, not meeting their eyes, "but I'm glad to see the two of you again." She lifted her glass slightly, in spite of herself, and they followed suit.

It was much better than the name "Fassen" would have anyone expect, rich, and deep, like plums, and rye. Fryn swirled it around her mouth stifling a sigh she could not express, since her mouth was already full, so she smiled, and took a deep breath. "Was that fortified?"

Savis's face was flushed, as she'd taken a much larger sip, and swallowed immediately. "I have no idea… but I will give the Earl my compliments. I think he's been hoarding the best of his wines."

"I would not be surprised," Leif commented, turning the glass around in his hand, examining it critically. Fryn could see better in the firelight now, that the hole in his chest was covered in a thick marbling of black ice, as if the wound had formed a wide circle around his heart.

Savis took a smaller sip and sighed, her eyes wandering over the carved figures of a bronze lancer spearing a rearing serpent, and long, iron, tulip-shaped candelabras, on the mantelpiece. "Did you know, that in the past, Froreholt and Waverly were allies?"

"No," Leif answered almost at once.

Fryn shook her head slightly, and took a small sip of her wine, savoring its sweetness and comfortable warmth.

"Legend has it that Waver and Arta were old friends, that they both wandered to the north, where they explored the Ice Wastes for many years, along with the mountains, and the northern forests. So that even when they separated, to settle in their various lands, they would still visit each other at certain times of year to commemorate their adventures and their friendship." She pointed a finger from the hand holding her glass toward the bronze figures on the mantelpiece. "One of their adventures involved Arta's vengeance on the serpent that turned Yndril into the first lich. Waver helped him track it down, distract it, and kill it, and so there used to be a custom at the end of Spring to get together with one's neighbors and wave banners in the streets, and bake sweet breads and share them with everyone in town."

Fryn narrowed her eyes and frowned. "I've never heard of this holiday."

Leif's eyes flicked momentarily in her direction, in surprise, she thought.

Savis chuckled, her voice light and high, like a child's. "I am not surprised... it was something I only learned since I've been here. The Earl has regaled me with numerous accounts of the past shared history of our lands, and it has been very intriguing. I can't imagine why the practice would be forsaken, but there it is." Her eyes twinkled, reflecting serpentine tongues of the fire in their glacial, crystalline depths.

A ponderous period of silence descended on them, the Princess watching, waiting for some kind of comment, Leif brooding disconsolately, and Fryn's heart beating anxiously as she hoped that someone would say something. She silently tapped her finger on the side of her glass, trying desperately to come up with a suitable response. She drained the rest of her glass and set it down with an unwelcome 'clack' on the polished wood, stirring Leif from his reverie.

He picked up the carafe, rising to his feet, and poured another measure in Savis' and her glasses, and off-handedly observed, "it is because your people were ashamed of them. When they fell, they ostracized and excluded them, and so the traditions associated with Waverly were forgotten."

Fryn smiled and stretched her wings over the back of the couch, unlacing her knee-high boots, she pulled them off and set them under the table, tucking her legs under herself on the couch. She reclined, matching the Princess' posture against the arm of the couch, wishing that she could perhaps curl up next to Leif... but things were not quite so informal as to allow that.

Leif sat down beside her and breathed out a long, tired sigh. "I wonder what sort of plan the Earl and his brilliant butler have to get us out of this."

Savis' eyes widened slightly. "Yes, I am curious; you both had to remove significant faeries in order to get here—Leif, the Grass Guard Captain, and Fryn, the Earl's primary adversary, the Lord Vassidel."

"You killed one of the Nobles?" Leif asked, making an impressed 'o' with his mouth. It did not suit him, and neither did the sparse blonde stubble on his chin—which had grown during their time in Eastwall.

Fryn made a show of being demure, affecting a blush and looking away, even though recalling the event sent chills through her wings. She dropped the act and nodded somberly, leaning her elbow on the arm of the couch, and resting her cheek on her fist, looking sideways at her partner—her *partner*, a fae of such silly character and such unpredictable strength... reliable, charming when he wanted to be, and shy and awkward when he didn't know how. But his normally steady heartbeat was cold and damaged, slowly rebuilding.

"Fryn?" he asked, setting his glass, untouched since he'd refilled it, on the table.

She closed her eyes, slowly opening them, as she replied, "He was the same dreadful character who tried to run me down in his carriage the other day—looked like a much more fitting corpse than any lich." *Though I've only seen myself... in a mirror at that...* she considered, pursing her lips.

"He was a frightening opponent," she admitted bitterly, "moving from one space to another like a ghost, his blade snapping and seeming to curl around corners or change length depending on his desire. How such a thin, frail-looking character could have such reflexes and withstand my Blooodknife, I don't know, but he nearly killed me, Leif, the way you defeated Havrshyk."

He swallowed as his face flushed, a mixture of concern, anger on her behalf, and... shame? She couldn't tell exactly, reading emotions was not perfect, even with access to the timing and pressure of another's heart.

"But you're here all the same," Savis interrupted, leaning forward to set her half-drained second glass of wine on the table. "So, it must have ended well, in fact we know it did..."

Fryn marveled that she'd be drinking like that, like her brother; it wasn't a festival, or even a private party. "Savis, did something happen? You're, if I might say, not as you were when we last met."

Savis pressed one hand on her forehead and sighed, scrunching shut her eyes as she gave a resigned wing-shrug. "You might know that

I was being courted by the young Lord Wellsey, and even been proposed to... but over the week or so that we stayed here at the vine," she threw up a hand with clenched fingers in a loose fist, "he decided that he would not wish to be married to a member of the Martell line as long as we were the friends of rebels and renegades..."

"No moons, no stars..." Leif breathed, apparently having picked up some of Lia's expressions.

Savis still covered her face, but she picked up her glass again. "Well, I told him that anyone who abandoned their friends without trial was a five-winged fool, and I told him to scatter like ash!" Her eyes were damp, but no streaks marred her face as she delicately took another sip. Loren has been kind to let me stay here, and Trel and Yarrow have distracted me with some of the local games... tiles, I think it was."

Fryn hadn't played it, so she examined the paintings on the wall behind the Princess, noticing that one of them was a tall double-portrait of a young couple dressed in rich green finery; the fee with amber eyes and auburn hair, and the fae with nearly black straight hair, and green eyes. He looked a bit like Loren, different of course, his nose was rounder and shorter than his ancestor's almost beaklike nose.

"Have you won at all?" Leif asked, sounding a little more relaxed, as he finally took another sip. Fryn followed suit and waited expectantly for Savis' response.

Savis took a deep breath and laughed once. "No, I have not. It's one of those very unique and complicated games, that keeps turning itself over every time I think I know what is going on, or that I'm winning."

"I would be happy to let you win," Leif admitted, "though since I don't know anything about this game, I think you'd win by yourself."

Fryn nudged him with her foot, "that's not comforting..."

Savis chuckled. "Better a little sarcasm to make a problem seem lighter, than someone who makes them seem worse," she chided. "But I think it would be a good way to pass the time until the Earl joins us." She opened a concealed cupboard in the wood paneling of the wall behind the couch, directly between paintings, and came back with a green velvet bag that rustled with the shifting of its contents. Fryn's eyes widened, and she subconsciously held her breath at the sheer number of the inch square bone tiles that spewed from the bag as the Princess dumped it on the table, some of them even skittering over against their glasses and the silver tray with the nearly-empty carafe. It probably should have been empty by now, Leif was pouring smaller servings than usual.

"The object is to start with seven of these tiles, and... the first game I'll teach you is 'Full Inverses,'" she explained, brightening a bit as she worked to turn all the tiles face down. Leif and Fryn helped, and shuffled the mysterious pool of white tiles around so no one knew what was where, and then they each chose seven tiles at random. "Now, turn them over, and if you can combine three tiles, like Noon-Morning-Dawn, then we all get to draw another tile—no you can't hide what you have, you have to arrange all your tiles in the open in front of you." She leaned over and batted Leif's hand lightly, making him arrange his seven openly in a line on the table.

"I don't think I have any that go together... how do you even know what order they go in?" he asked, switching between grouping his months, and moons—which he had two of.

"It's not very lucky to get two greater moons in a first draw," Savis observed gloatingly.

Fryn arrayed her elements from Wind-Fire-Light, her months from Sparrow-Hare, and had Dusk and Summer left over. "What can I do with these?" she asked.

Savis glanced over and frowned, "Well, you can just about say 'tile' now, because they all fit together."

"I don't see it," she admitted, shuffling them around on the table. "How do you put them together anyway?"

"I wish I had a sheet of paper, then I could show you," she replied, "but I guess you'll just have to pick it up as you go." The Princess hummed cheerfully as she moved Dusk beside Sparrow, deftly slipping Hare below it with a cheeky smile. "Wind and Hare are both '3's so put that next," she explained, linking Wind to Hare on the right, and then queuing up Fire and then Light below in sequence, putting on the finishing touch with Summer linked to Wind. "Now you say 'tile' and we all grab a new one and try to get them all to connect."

"Tile?" Fryn repeated, reaching hesitantly toward the group of face-down tiles in the center of the table.

Savis let out a happy cry as she snagged one from the pile, and Leif followed suit, leaving Fryn wondering what she could do with her Vine tile. Leif had picked up a Fee tile, and now made an inverse arc of the two Greater Moons above and below it, linking Fee to Solid, then Winter to the right of Solid, stacking Autumn, then Harvest above it. He shuffled his Sparks tile around with a frown, and Savis inspected his work carefully. "You can put that in line with Solid. You're moving across between Inverse Trees, and up and down are the branches. So, it should fit the '3' line of the Greater Moon and Autumn, and still be next in the elemental tree."

"But I can go from the outer tile to the inner?" he confirmed, sliding in his Sparks piece and added a hesitant "Tile!"

"Yes," she replied. Then, "Yes!" she added excitedly, suddenly producing an almost perfect arc of Dawn-Morning-Noon-Afternoon, linked to a constellation tree through a series of Star-Lich-Mountain, combined with Light at the Mountain juncture with Frost cross linking with Lich. "Tile!" she cheered.

Fryn bit the inside of her cheek and sighed as she drew a Serpent constellation; it would not help her fit in the Vine tile, but at the least, she could—if she understood the rules of the game correctly—link it back in the constellation column by placing it to the left of the Lancer tile: two tiles away from Hare (because it was the fourth month) but still connected through the elemental tree. But before she could figure out what to do next, Leif said "tile" and then Savis immediately shouted "Inverses!" And presented her completed arc of Dawn-to-Dusk, with the other tiles connected and used appropriately.

Leif groaned, and Fryn shrugged. She could feel his frustration, in the excited uptick in his heart rate and the falling pressure as he managed to make his tile, a Frost, link to Harvest and Sparks, though he did not have a completed Inverse. He resignedly poured the rest of the wine and leaned back on the couch, resting one arm along the back so that she could lean back against it, sipping from her own glass. It was… warm, even a little comforting, after what she'd only just survived. Fryn closed her eyes, though the impression of red light from the fireplace still seeped through her closed eyelids, and she swallowed as she shifted away from the arm of the couch, and leaned more toward Leif.

Leif stiffened momentarily, and his arm made a slight jerk, but he relaxed the next moment, and they simply sat there, as Savis, absorbed in her game, tried flipping over other tiles to make them fit: working on all three sets in play at once, even though the game had ended. "I'm back," Leif said softly, so that only she could hear him.

"So am I," she replied.

Their peace was broken by the soft scraping sound of the empty carafe being replaced by a full one, and another tray of glasses being set on the table—scooting over Savis' tiles, and ruining her game, as Vinellin made himself known with a polite clearing of his throat.

"If I may," he presumed, "the Lord Earl has asked that we convene here within the next few moments in order to determine our next course of action." He was as skilled with his use of plural pronouns as ever, Fryn noticed, as though inclined only to get entangled in their affairs if he could do so indirectly.

"You may," Leif allowed graciously, earning a rebellious laugh that Savis, slightly softened by the wine, could not successfully contain.

Vinellin did not reply, but whisked off bitterly, returning a minute later with another, longer couch with room for three. He brought it in with the help of the servant they'd met during their last visit over a week before, Lodt... she thought, though they hadn't really talked with him much. As Loren entered and sat beside Savis with a swish of his burgundy and amber-trimmed coattails, Fryn straightened and instinctively slid her feet back down to the ground. Trel and Yarrow followed and sat on the larger couch.

Yarrow nodded warmly toward them. She surreptitiously slipped her boots back on, and nearly blushed as Trel shook her head mischievously at her. Trel, of course, shamelessly held Yarrow's hand between them on the couch, and continued to raise her eyebrows at them.

"Now," Loren began, crossing his legs as Vinellin stepped forward to pour a conservative amount of wine for the Earl and the two veteran Hunters. "I have been made aware of your respective actions, and I believe it would be wise to relay the potential consequences thereof..." He whispered under his breath toward Savis, asking if he'd used "thereof" correctly, and she shook her head, but he let it drop.

Fryn shared a look with Leif, who passed it along to Yarrow, who simply gave Trel's hand a light squeeze.

The Earl continued. "Lord Vassidel has always been an irritating problem for me, constantly insulting my personality, and casting aspirations on my ability to govern effectively."

Savis snickered.

"and uh..."

"Aspersions, my Lord," Vinellin provided dutifully.

"Thank you," he said, pausing to recollect his thoughts, "Now as I was saying, I did not much like Lord Vassidel, and he was not so fond of me—which will pose a significant problem. It seems that none of you will be welcome at my estate, and I will have to ask you all to leave before the night is out."

Leif's swallow was audible, but he contained any outburst he might have made. It was Savis who complained on their behalf, "but after all they went through to get here... surely they can at least stay the night! We have to help them. Aren't you going to take care of your own?" She asked incredulously. Not giving him an opportunity to respond, but turning in her seat to face him she added, "if you're not going to take care of them then I'll be broken if I don't take them myself!"

Trel nodded, putting on a face as if she were also really concerned, and the Earl suddenly turned red in the face as everyone stared expectantly at him.

"N...n'no you see, of course I certainly meant without a doubt that I would unequivocally, and without fail—you may rest assured—take action on their behalf to help them!" He wagged a finger toward them, alternating who he was countering with each repeated expression, finally settling on pointing toward Savis.

"You will, will you?" she insisted, first challenging, and then relaxing. "You will? Oh... I am sorry, I suppose I was a bit over excited."

"Perhaps," Fryn interjected with a smile, even more of her discomfort and worry evaporating at the exchange, "it would seem to be for the best that we leave the city of Fassen altogether."

"To 'fasset!'" Leif added with a snap of his fingers.

"Very nice," Loren praised, "Yes, it would be the wisest course of action, to be sure, to 'fly away' as you put it. But... it will not be so simple as that, or so easy as your coming here tonight." He paused again to let the severity of his assessment of their situation sink in. The fire crackled lazily in the hearth, and Fryn held her breath. She partially drained and froze herself inside, letting her blood turn red, and breathed through her blade, while the others held their peace. She took a long drink from her glass, sad that its richness and depth couldn't really be enjoyed in such a tense atmosphere. It was like... standing on the street, looking up at the window from which she'd flown, seeing the angry red flames licking and blackening the stones—like watching the roof cave in, and waiting for her parents to come out. No, perhaps it wasn't the same, but their present circumstances soured an otherwise excellent wine. She finished it, and set the empty glass on the table.

Leif watched her out of the corner of his eye, looking mildly protective or concerned, but he finished his wine as well, and slid his glass over toward hers, and in a second, Savis did the same so that Vinellin was obligated to refill their glasses with the fresh wine. Even then, no one spoke, Fryn held out a hand, as Vin bent over stiffly to angle the carafe 'just so' and poured out equal measures (well less than a standard 'glass') without spilling a drop. He deposited her glass in her hand, and she bent her face over it, drew air into her lungs again, drinking in its fog-like thick scent, inhaling it all the way in. She breathed out and took the first taste, rolling it around her mouth, chewing for a second, and then swallowing, letting it suffuse her palate so that she could taste every direction and every facet of its profile—contemplating its unusual nuttiness and spicy notes of plum and strawberry. It filled her head, and she closed her eyes, letting it put her nerves at ease and drain out the tension in her muscles as easily as she so often drained her veins of blood.

"Lord Earl," she said at last, the first one to break the silence. "You have outdone yourself this time. The first 'Fassen' wine we had was a red blend of the worst quality, but now this final wine, our last glass of your vine, is possibly the most delicious nectar I've ever tasted: a satisfying farewell," she proclaimed, almost feeling eloquent.

Loren gave her an overjoyed grin, gloating even. "Well, I should hope so—that wine is over a hundred years old. Since I cannot entertain you for the proper two weeks that courtesy requires, I decided to distill it all into a richer, shorter experience."

Yarrow opened his mouth with a sort of embarrassed shifting of his wings over the back of the couch. "It is a finer wine than any I have had in Rosenkraun, even in the years I... won in a tourney. It has a... depth to it I cannot say I have tasted before. What is... how did you make such a wine?"

Loren stood and examined his wineglass through the light of the fire and breathed proudly, mumbling something as if in a debate with himself. Then, he sat back down, to Savis' surprise, as she nearly spilled her wine, but caught it with an awkward-yet-adorably-so juggling in her hands, as she used her wings to compensate. Their host did not seem to notice however, and he relaxed, lounged really, in his seat, tapping his fingers on the arm of the couch. "No, I will not tell you my secrets until you can come and visit me out in the open, without prices on heads, or plots in the under-things-and-such!" He raised his glass in his left hand

and then they all followed suit in the impromptu toast, and drank a little. "But I fear we are really not staying on topic."

Trel swirled her glass around and nodded distractedly. "Yes, this is where *we* come in."

"Speak, by all means!" Loren allowed dramatically, sharing an ironic smirk with Leif.

Yarrow coughed, one of the light ones, out of formality, not because he needed to clear his throat. "Trel and I have decided to accompany the Princess to the Froreholt Embassies Estate in Rosenkraun. It may be that you could join us and go into hiding either in the Capitol, or elsewhere."

Fryn shook her head. "They are going to search your carriages, or your birds; we can't go with you."

Leif nodded, absently flicking his wings against hers, so she flicked hers back, and he blushed, but hid it quickly, and made a little more space between them as he adjusted his position on the couch.

"Fryn's right," Trel allowed, setting her glass down and, letting go of Yarrow's hand, crossed her arms. "But, if you were to join us after we pass through the inspection, we could travel in greater security, and might be left alone... at least till we reach the Capitol."

"Could we get a map?" Leif asked, directly addressing the butler, who had faded into the background after pouring the wine.

"Very good, sir," he answered, disappearing within the span of a few seconds, without even a movement in the air. He returned just as silently and quickly, unrolling a waxed map of the surrounding region, detailed enough to trace the paths to Rosenkraun and the other cities within the borders of the map.

"While they detain your carriage, we could slip out somewhere," Leif suggested, then he scratched his head and sighed. "But we're in the Earl's Estate. I don't see where we could fly over the Boulderwall without being noticed."

"I also don't want to imagine the child having to climb over that wall, what if her wings give out? She cannot be used to flying very far or for very long," Trel added quickly, pouring over the map with the same desperation that Fryn could feel in Leif's quickened pulse, which threatened to drag her heart beat along with it like a metronome.

Fryn wiped a hand across her face and looked over at the Princess. "Could you take Nora with you? Maybe as your niece, or something...

or…" she switched her gaze and smiled at Trel and Yarrow, "perhaps the child of your secret marriage?"

"All moons lost," Trel affected with a laugh, then she pursed her lips and frowned, checking with Yarrow. "But perhaps… She does have his narrow features, and almost my hair… Oh, if I had a daughter half so precious…" she turned around and sat back down with a disconsolate crossing of her arms. "…but a Hunter doesn't very often *have* a child and remain a Hunter."

Yarrow snapped his fingers and stood sharply, startling all of them. "Then we will announce our intention to retire from the Commission and serve the Princess directly."

"Agreed!" Savis exclaimed, "but you <u>have</u> to actually do it, not in name only."

Trel nodded slowly, catching Fryn's eye with a knowing and somehow relieved wink, as if she were trying to say 'this is how you end a good career.' "Alright, so we retire of the Commission, move all our money to the Snowring Bank, and claim that Nora is ours."

"But Lia is an unknown, suspicious, so she should meet us on the road with Leif and Fryn," Yarrow suggested, "but that brings us back to the problem of how you should escape the city, and where you should meet us on the road." He held his wine and smelled it, taking only the smallest of sips, as if he were trying not to waste it.

They all lapsed into a moody silence, and the fire glowed dully, red embers on the verge of dying or falling through the grate. Vinellin walked over quietly, holding a brick of fresh peat wrapped up in a piece of cloth, and he positioned it in the coals, breathing on it gently as it caught, and the tongues of flame curled around its edges. He returned to his position behind his master, and addressed them with a bright, almost cheerful reminder, "the window within which our guests may leave is not so very long that we can tarry in determining their most expeditious route of egress."

"Do you have a suggestion?" Leif asked pointedly, "because as it is, it will be difficult for us to get over the boulders unnoticed."

Savis nodded, as if she wholeheartedly agreed with his assessment. Fryn narrowed her eyes and watched the Princess more carefully, relaxing when it was clear she was sitting happily beside the Earl, quite unoffended by Leif's tone.

"Well, to put it so bluntly…" the butler replied dryly, arching one eyebrow, regarding him with same eye critically, he dusted off his hands and took a deep breath, "I suppose you must be nearly desperate. I might offer a suggestion, if you'd be willing to consider a proposal with a high degree of uncertainty."

"You say you 'might' offer one," Leif answered expertly, trying to match the cold severity of the butler's expression, though he still had the smallest twisting at the edge of his mouth from trying to hide a smile. "But I submit that you 'will' offer one."

"The words of a prophet," Trel observed sagely.

"Hmm..." considered Yarrow.

Vinellin's shoulders tensed, and his wings twitched, as he prepared a fitting response; but he didn't get a chance as Loren interrupted him just when he was about to speak.

"Now, now, Leif, I'll not have you troubling my servants, whether they deserve it or not is up to me to decide and to deal out," he chided, somehow both coming to Vin's defense, and betraying him at the same time.

"You are most gracious, my Lord, but I *do* have a response for Master Aellin. My suggestion, which I will now offer, is that those who will be vacating the city this night—which I might reiterate is now nearing midnight—ascend to the top of the vine that overshadows this city, and then fly off the end of one of its eight branches for the Forest of Grass. This will take you high over the estate wall, out of reach of most of the guard and may be easier to traverse unnoticed. I am not as knowledgeable about the local geography as others, but I have heard that there are periodic lamp-posts along the major routes to guide the Finch-Post flyers. That might help you find the main road, and meet up with their carriage."

Leif turned to Fryn and she looked down in thought. Eventually, Leif answered for them. "That seems doable, but we still need to discuss this with Lia, and find a way up the vine in the middle of the night."

"Fly?" Offered Lia from the darkened hallway. "What's this about the vine anyway?" She folded her arms and sat down beside Trel, looking between them expectantly.

"We fly, tonight," Fryn explained, "and Nora will ride with the Princess and her escorts."

"Wait, along the vine? I don't know, even from the end of the East branch, it will be quite a distance of quick flying, we might still be noticed by the Guard..." Lia sighed and brushed her hair out of her face, which she had apparently taken down, and began running her fingers through it to braid it once more. She untied a green ribbon from her wrist and held it in her mouth as she wove her hair, and everyone waited. Having tied off the end, she pressed her lips together, picked up Trel's glass and drank some of the wine. "Alright. We'll meet you in the Forest, but do not follow the road so far that it bends northward, otherwise it will be hard for us to find you. My daughter will be good even though she is frightened. Do not endanger her, or reveal her."

"But what about our funds?" Leif asked, leading Fryn to nod as she recalled Trel's allusion to changing banks.

"Your considerable assists will be unavailable to you as long as the Grass Guard has you marked, and the Commission disavows you," Yarrow supplied, standing and looking down at his partner with a sad smile. "I will begin preparations for travel in the early morning, but be aware that it may take an additional day to reach our rendezvous, if we are delayed."

Leif stood as well, adjusting his scarf and green cloak, almost looking eager to engage in his life as a criminal—wanted on suspicion for conspiracy and murder... but it would say the same on her wanted poster, unless they were printed on the same one. *That would be likely*, she thought, and it was somewhat comforting. But if they could get to the bottom of the mess of who had hired Lia in the first place, and track them down, they could actually clear their names.

Leif held out a hand toward her with his shining white teeth in a set smile, and she felt his heart racing, not just through the connection she'd inadvertently created, but also through the skin of his hand. She accepted it and stood as well, bowing her head politely toward their host and the Princess. "I cannot see any other option, though I do not relish flying so high just on my own wings. I am not as... zealous as some of the faeries here," she said, "but I do hope for the Wing-Giver's protection for you and Nora."

Loren also rose and bowed extravagantly, with his wings flicking backwards, "and may Setfjeø watch over your steps, and hold up your wings in His skies."

"Be careful in the Forest," Savis added, "I have heard it is not altogether safe at night."

"No," Leif laughed, "no... it is not. But I am sure we had best prepare."

Vinellin moved toward the hallway to the servant's entrance with a dull heaviness in his steps, almost as if he sympathized for them. "If you will follow me, I will furnish you with some few necessities of travel."

"Good night," offered Trel.

"Farewell," said Yarrow.

And Lia trailed along with them into the darkness of the hall, which grew dimmer and colder the further they got from the fireplace. They were well into the month of the Vine now, and soon the true coldness of Autumn would descend. She hoped, at least for Leif's sake, that by then they could be comfortably indoors.

Descending and Deflecting

Fassen:

The Earl's Estate

Base of the Vine

Leif

Leif stared up at the blackness of the underside of the great vine's outstretching arms and upward-reaching trunk. It towered protectively over a city encircled by stones, as if sheltering them from unfriendly eyes—which at this point, it *was*. He glanced over at Fryn, visible only as a darker and more complete section of the night, with a feminine slightness, and wing shaped voids. Lia stood behind them, tapping her foot on the stone. "We started this with a flight through the Forest of Grass," he observed ironically.

"Quiet," Fryn whispered, "we should ascend as soon as the next patrol passes." They were standing behind one of the snakelike roots that rose from the base of the vine, and then wound its way, boring back into the earth.

"Devouring the soil, converting it to wine, drinking in and pouring out, the blood that's in the earth," Lia mused.

"Nora will be safe," Leif assured her with a worried frown, his fingers twitched as he walked the two patrolling Grass Guards follow the trail with one holding up their amber-colored lamp, and the other resting his spear on his shoulder. "Trel will keep her safe." It was funny, in a way, that when they'd first been stuck together in a night as dark as this, they'd been enemies, and here they were, roles nearly reversed, as friends.

Fryn nodded, and, as the two guards in their pool of orange light moved behind the shadow of another root, they hopped onto the 'devouring snake' and stared up once more at the nexus of branches that spread out at over twice the height of the boulderwall. "It's not very often that I fly so high up on my own," Fryn admitted, glancing back down as if remembering that time exactly.

"Then we had better get as high as we can before the next patrol comes by," Lia suggested, flitting up a few wingspans and digging her fingers into the bark, bracing herself against the trunk with the toes of her boots also entrenched in the bark.

"Very well then," Leif said, "let's get to it." He rushed into the air, hearing the soft crunch as Fryn pushed off the top of the root to follow, and they sailed upwards, the wind tugging at his scarf—which he'd purposefully pinned—but throwing back his hood. They flew in a slow spiral, trying to stay behind the view of the patrols, but it still took a few minutes for them to ascend to half the height of the Vine. There, they found a nook where a branch had been painstakingly pruned, and the knot had formed a divot in the side of the trunk, so they could rest in it. Fryn and Lia stood inside the depression, leaning back against the sides, and Leif sat on top of it, dangling his legs off the side.

"I could keep flying," Fryn informed him, "We flew much further and at a much greater pace when we chased Lia last time."

He pursed his lips and crossed his legs, then his arms. "We've got to conserve our strength, don't want to suddenly get tired. We're crossing over two districts to reach the eastern side."

Lia agreed, "They may even anticipate our action and be waiting on the eastern branches, forcing us to fly north or south, and then into the wild."

Fryn let it drop, and they looked down at the Earl's Estate, where his mansion was somewhat visible from the lamps that remained on in some of the windows, or along the pathways, to guide and facilitate the guards. The sound of the fountain spraying in the pond on the western side of the estate carried on the wind, and he wondered if it had any fish like Ieffin's did.

"Shall we continue?" Fryn asked.

"Alright," Leif said, "but let's try to make our ascent on the eastern side, so that we can fly under the limb and then wait out of sight if we need to." He dove upwards off the marbled section of bark, and flipped in the air, twisting so that his wings splayed out and sent him curving upwards. They moved quickly, perching underneath the eaves of the offices on the eastern side—breathing heavily as they pressed their ears against the naturally-formed walls to listen.

The shuffling of heavy feet, possibly overweight and overburdened, alerted them to the presence of at least the overseer of the vineworks, so they moved along the outside to find seating on some of the thinner stems and branches where the grapes had been harvested from.

"Well, I suppose we continue," Fryn suggested, and they flew from empty stem to empty stem, seeing that nearly every single grape had been harvested on that side. As they reached the end of the branch, a thin tendril that curled lightly back in on itself, Leif heard the scuffing of a boot on the bark above them, so he put on his hood, and clinging to the bark, he climbed up slowly and peered over the edge.

Two guards waited on that branch, one standing by the lamp, the other holding a half-eaten sandwich without crust, the source of a scent of dill, if he was not mistaken. Leif repressed a sigh, and clawed his way back down underneath the branch to the half-harvested cluster where Lia and Fryn had paused to cut open a grape.

He frowned, and they passed him a slice, so he held it in thought. "There are two guards up there, not Grass Guards, just the Earl's I think. We could disable them and fly off, or just leave them and hope they don't see us," he suggested, barely above a whisper.

Lia made a fist, and struck her opposite palm soundlessly, a gesture he could only just see because of the amber light that filtered through the leaves from above. Fryn nodded.

Leif sighed dramatically at Fryn, and they climbed up opposite sides of the branch, and at nearly the same instant, Leif leapt out, and Fryn flew up, and they struck the guards upside their heads, and lowered them to the ground. The half-eaten sandwich fell off the branch, slowly falling down to the base of the vine.

Lia met them at the tip of the eastern branch vine, and they each drew in a deep breath, and flew out over the city. Leif swallowed and closed his eyes for a moment, letting the cold air flow through his hair as his hood once more fell back. Fryn fell in beside him, and held his hand, so he opened his eyes, and marveled at the smallness of the city. The streets seemed so narrow, and the buildings so short, and the sky seemed great enough to consume him. He avoided looking up at the cloudless night sky, or at the greater moon which stared at them like a beacon.

Behind them a shout broke out from the top of the vine, as they were spotted against the moon's light, and Leif cursed the moon under his breath. "We'd better pick things up before they send a bird after us," he shouted toward Fryn and Lia, who had caught up with them, so they flew in a staggered line, her wind seeming to cut back through the air with a greenish tint from her wings, which pulsed with her enhanced flight.

"I'll take the lead," she said, pointing back toward the vine, "hold onto my ankles, and we'll fly en-migration!"

He shared a confused look with Fryn, who shrugged with her hands, so they let Lia move ahead between them, and held onto her ankles, and each-other's arms, so they formed a twelve-winged triangle, and put all their effort together. Leif gulped as Lia's enhanced wind screamed over their wings, and they shot through the sky like an arrow from a bow, or even like a sparrow.

The city seemed to blur underneath them as they heard the cawing of one of the Guard's night-crows taking flight, and they redoubled their efforts. "The greatest advantage we have over their bird is that they can't work together," Lia explained, "now, faster!"

They sped over the edge of the Boulderwall, and out into the dark sea of waving grass, flying low so that they weaved between the bunches of grain and the blades of grass. Leif was constantly amazed that they were able to avoid colliding, as they made just the adjustments they needed to prevent crashing into the grass at their incredible speed.

"Down again!" Lia shouted, and they dove in formation into a break in the grass, and turned south to follow a game trail, then slowed and flew deeper into wild grass, barely twisting and turning to dodge the entrenched grasses. Above they heard a dismayed cry from the raven, as it flew about, sweeping over the grasslands, unable to find them. "Just be glad they haven't tamed any owls..."

They let go of their formation, and landed roughly in the packed dirt, gasping for breath as they sat down under the eaves of one of the larger bunches of grass. "Well, we made it this far," Leif allowed, "but I don't see how we can join up with Trel and Savis, if they know we're out here."

"We can't go to my town either," Lia added, "we're officially outlaws now."

Even though Fryn had flown in a half-frozen state, her wings drooped and her chest heaved, as she leaned forward, curled up, and rested her chin on her knees. Leif had never flown so far or so fast in his life, and he decided that it normally would have been impossible. If not for their coordination, and Lia's elemental assistance and stamina, they should have hit the ground long before.

"I'll take first watch," Leif said, drawing his sword and slamming it into the dirt in front of them. "Try to rest."

Havrshyk shimmered as the blood within his blade glowed dully from the light-suffused life he'd absorbed from the Grass Guard Captain, and he hummed to himself in Leif's mind. *"I had not heard of such a technique before, flying in formation like migrating birds, most interesting."*

Leif smiled, and looked up at the bowed over blades of grass that shielded them from the harsh light of the moon, and the searching eyes of the raven. *Was this how you felt, Aldyr, when you were on the run?*

He laughed hollowly, his baritone voice echoing in his ears. *"I never ran, Leif, I was betrayed, and I stood my ground. I should have killed them. I thought they'd bring me before the Grand Assembly, but no, as soon as they'd bound my hands, they ran me through and spilled my blood before I could drain it, and threw me in the grave. What blood I could save remained in the sword, and I was left there in the dark, separated from it, trapped, bloodless, awake for seventy years."*

"You should have run," Leif replied, sitting cross legged in front of the sword, looking into its depths, which shifted and cast a dim red light on his face.

"Perhaps, but better my honor than theirs," he answered, *"because at least I am vindicated by my own conduct."*

"Not in killing your own people," Leif shot back, "you killed 'innocents' along with the members of the royal family, and nearly killed us several times."

Havrshyk took a deep breath, and the sword clouded to black. *"Must you condemn me also? Do you not think I am constantly beset by my guilt!? But there's nothing to be done for it now."*

Leif rolled his neck and shoulders, loosening his wing joints and folding them behind his back, as he placed his hands palm upwards on his knees, closing his eye, slowing his breathing, as he focused on drawing out his sparks into a glowing blue orb of sparkling energy the size of his eye in one hand, and then pushing it up and over in an arc to his other hand.As it moved it shot out trailing tendrils of electricity to his other hand which he tuned like a receiving pole, and it drew the orb in gently to a rest in the palm of his left hand. He timed his breathing so that as he inhaled, the orb rose to the peak of the arc, and settled down again when he emptied his lungs.

Breathing and tossing the orb of sparks set his nerves ablaze, and he listened with his ears finely tuned to the myriad sounds that wound their way through the grass. In such a confined space, and in the dark, his eyes would have been of little use anyway, and through the sword, he felt as if Havrshyk was 'staying' up with him to help keep watch. The beating of the raven's wings, the gentle rustling of the grass, the shifting of a boot on dirt, and the slow breathing of Fryn and Lia sleeping, leaning back against the grass—as there was not enough room to spread out under its cover—all these sounds put him at ease. The Forest of Grass was not empty, but it was quiet. It's heady scent of clay and golden seeds, and the faint tinge of wild chanterelles or other mushrooms filled the close space, and he felt no movements through the ground.

For the first time since they had arrived in the region, he truly felt at peace. The orb increased in size and resistance becoming more and more difficult to control as each cycle added more sparks and growth. But he persisted, shuffling the orb as it grew to the size of his head, until he started to draw from it, and leech off of it, inverting the exercise so that the energy, intensified and purified, flowed back through his nerves, trickling through his body to his 'core.' It filled his mind, and electrified his spine, and he could hear and feel so much clearer than before. It washed the tiredness from his eyes, and lightened the burdened muscles in his back, stretching and loosening them, crackling softly as the sparks subconsciously suffused the blood Leif had inside the sword.

"Why is it that your exercises always do that?" Havrshyk complained, *"it's filling the sword with stormy skies... I prefer the cold and quiet."*

Leif breathed out slowly, and drawing in the last of the sparks, he grounded himself in the earth, allowing the excess to flow through his hands and dissipate. His wings stopped their static discharges, and his hair fell back into its almost normal wavy pattern, parted off-center like Mythrim and Ieffin. *That is because, it is my world, and my heart, and you are merely renting out space.*

"Hmm, well, I liked my heart better. I carved a decent living space there, halls of red and crystal ice, stairs I shaped from snow, and towers that climbed almost to the overcast sky. I had seventy years, which I marked by counting every day, until I forgot to count, and then I didn't know how long it had been any more, until I had built bridges and buildings from the very ice that was my heart—but I can't make anything in your desert, Leif. It is as barren as it could possibly be."

You don't need much in the desert, water when you thirst, shelter from the sun, but you don't need great castles or bridges, Leif replied philosophically, although he had no idea why his 'heartworld' was so barren. He meditated, keeping his ears open for movement in the grass for some hours, until Fryn sat down beside him and took hold of his hand.

"I will take the next watch," she whispered, her pale, partially drained face lit up by the moonlight, which had finally gained an angle on their small clearing. She looked into his eyes. Leif sighed, and placing his other hand on top of hers, bent forward and kissed her on the head.

"We should leave before the dawn," he commented, "if we are to start making our way to the curve in the road." He made to leave, but she reached over and held his sleeve.

"Don't go," she said, looking away so that her face was shadowed, "stay here." She patted her knee meaningfully, so Leif scratched his head, removed his scarf, and placed it rolled up on her knee and rested his head on her leg. She brushed a hand through his hair, and looked down at him with a smile, dimples showing on her slightly reddened cheeks.

He closed his eyes, and woke up with the sun.

Apparently, Lia had also taken a turn at watch, as he noticed that Fryn had rested her head against his shoulder, and it was Lia who signaled for them to rise with a light tapping on their heads. "We should check the map, and make our way as best we can through the Forest to the southern point of the first curve," she said, opening her small satchel of essential traveling goods.

They had each received one of the travel belts that Vinellin had provided for them, holding a small water bottle with a built-in sieve in the mouth, a few pieces of dried fruit, and some biscuits, as well as a map, a small tinder set, and a few bits and bobs, bandages, and other things that would be useful, but did not supply them with cooking utensils, pots or pans, or even a tent or two—just the basics. Leif nibbled on a biscuit, and watched Fryn adjust her cloak, which she had wrapped around herself, despite the fact that she preferred being cold.

Lia rolled out the map, holding down the edges with a pocket knife, a compass, and a couple pebbles, against the bare earth, angled toward the morning sunlight that had somehow managed to direct one of its first shafts between the tall grass blades into their glade. "We are roughly... here," she explained, showing a few pencil lines on their map, tracing what she had guessed was their flight pattern. It crossed over the East Road and into the expanse of wild grasslands that encroached southwards, until the road turned north for a bit, and then swept in a winding path toward Wellsey and Rosenkraun. They were about a third of the way into the Forest from the area where the road had just begun to turn southwards.

"If we cut due south," Leif offered, "we could meet them whenever they come along."

Fryn tapped her chin, leaning back so she didn't cast a shadow onto the map. "Or we could go west and watch the road, or even the gate."

Lia bit her lip and nodded. "I vote we watch the gate. It could be that they'll think we went away, and won't come back."

They seemed convinced it was a good idea and Leif didn't have a *reason* to go against their plan, but he didn't like it… it seemed too easy. "They may also send out Hunters in the direction of the nearest cities, or even messengers with authorized bounties," he said, but that didn't seem to be the reason for his discomfort.

"Even if they do," Fryn countered, "we will watch from the edge of the forest, and be careful to not be seen."

Lia agreed, insisting that they set out immediately so she could make sure her daughter got out, and they started at a slow flight back westward, using a compass to keep in the right direction. It took an hour or two before they saw the boulders rising above the grass, and beyond that, the arms of the vine.

It was strange staring up at the walls from the outside. Built to keep out the grassfires and the predators of the forest, it now rose up to keep them out. Leif was almost glad to be free of its walls, to not be locked inside like the finches in their cage. The gate was built into an arch between the boulders, with cut granite stones, tall enough that it would deter a weasel from jumping where it couldn't see, with two towers on either side of the closed barbican gates.

He gave a low whistle. "Last time we came here, we just passed on through without trouble, but look now, the gates are shut, and there are at least fifty guards milling around those towers."

Lia nodded, bending a blade of grass before them so that they could peer over it, wrapped in the green felt Waverly cloaks, nearly invisible. A Captain in the ribbed, leather and felt green uniform of the Grass Guard was busy inspecting the changing guard before the closed gates. He raised his arm, shooting out his wings in salute, and they followed suit just a half second behind. A trumpet sounded a single triplet of brassy notes, and the guards lined up on either side of the gates, filing into the towers, leaving only six on the ground. The Captain with his visored cap, his second with a purple braid on one shoulder, and the rest just regulars.

"They won't be first," Fryn predicted, throwing a raised eyebrow toward him with a cheeky smile.

"Maybe not," Lia said, waiting, watching, until after about fifteen minutes she tired of that and flew over to a nearby amanita, and perched on top of it, curling her legs under her as she sat down and chewed her fingernails.

"That's not a healthy habit," Leif observed with a cheeky smile as she realized what she was doing and stuffed her hands into the pockets of her waistcoat. He continued watching as the sun climbed its way to mid-morning, and dark clouds gathered on the eastern horizon. They didn't see any wagons or carriages until what he guessed was around eleven, and they only spied one nearly-empty cart, with a lone traveling merchant. "I wish it were Spring already," he commented, shading his eyes. "Looks like wandering trader," he guessed. "What do you think he has, Fryn?"

"Not wine, certainly," she answered, forming an ice-crystal lens between her thumb and finger, so she could look through it and see better. "I'd guess he just unloaded most of his goods in town, and now has only food and coverings to take back home."

"Traveling merchants don't have homes, Fryn," Lia interjected, examining her fingernails in the light, almost as if she were doing anything to resist biting them. "They have their goods, their cart, and a way to haul said goods and cart, saving up enough mint to one day buy a house, or even open up a shop in a city." She rolled back and let her legs dangle over the edge of the white-bumped red-capped mushroom and sighed. "I thought I'd try something like that as a Hunter scout, and surveyor. But things took a very different turn."

The cart was pulled by a tired, graying rabbit, and it bounced on its shocks over every rut or pebble, but the merchant was relatively unmoved on his spring-suspended bench. He held the reins loosely, eyes on the road between the fluffy gray, black-splotched ears of the rabbit. Leif frowned. "Seems like a dull, potentially frightening life." He looked back, and saw that Lia was holding up one hand just to block the sun over her eyes, so that her rolled back sleeves, and pulled up trouser legs let her catch some of the last warm light of the year.

"They also have no choice but to run if a weasel chases them, or anything like that," she added, "sometimes they simply let the hare loose and hold onto its ears, so it can escape… but that risks losing everything."

The gates rumbled with the sound of a large carriage, built at almost twice the normal length, with bay-type windows in the sides, a single ornate door carved and enameled in white and blue, emblazoned with the snowflake crown emblem of the Froreholt Royalty. The sound of the first bell of the afternoon sounded from throughout the city. It was drawn by two pure white hares, one had a gray spot on its nose, and they both had the same glacial blue eyes that Fryn had. Yarrow hung on the side of the carriage, one foot braced on the step, as it rolled to a stop, and he went over to the Captain with an opened document, dangling with several ribbons, one green, one a pale blue, and the other a glossy silver—the colors of Gaersheim, Froreholt, and the Commission, respectively.

The Captain tipped his cap respectfully when he saw him approach, and examined the document perfunctorily with twitching wings, as if they moved each time he finished reading a sentence. Then, he waved a hand toward his second, snapping his white-gloved fingers, and waited until the younger officer placed a clean pen in his hand and held out an unstoppered bottle of ink. He signed the document with a flourish, and then took off his cap as the carriage started moving again, bowing low until they'd moved on.

"Looks like they made it through the inspection at the gates," Fryn said, startling Lia from her reverie.

She rushed over and bent her face over the blade of grass they were hiding behind, eagerly searching the carriage windows with shifting eyes and wings that slid about anxiously, even while folded. "Where is she?" She pushed down on the grass, climbing up onto it to see more clearly, and then sat on it, biting her nails once more. "Is she not there? Or maybe not looking out the windows?"

Leif looked back as a crumbling of rocky dust skittered down from the battlements of one of the gate towers, and he caught his breath; a huge raven perched there, its powerful talons scratching the mortar and stone. It had piercing red eyes, and a set of black reins in its razor-like beak, held in the hands of its sickeningly thin rider—or at least the rider seemed small compared to the massiveness of the bird. He reached over and took Fryn's hand, and pointed toward the gate. "Quiet now," he warned, "looks like they didn't totally escape suspicion. We're going to have to follow and catch a ride when that bird leaves."

The raven leapt off the gate tower, and swept its wings in a few gale-like beats, scattering the dust on the road, causing the guards to crouch or cower and hold onto their hats. It sailed upwards into the sky, and then circled the areas around the road.

"Down, below the grass!" Hissed Lia, hopping off the grass blade and slinking into the cover of the mushroom. "Quick, here!" She waved toward them, and they rushed under the slight shelter of the mushroom, the only one of three in a bunch that was tall enough for them to creep under. The raven circled southwards, facing away from them for the moment, so Lia rushed back out and directly east. "We'll fly close and move east, then south, depending on its position," she explained, and they followed.

Each time the bird angled toward them, they flew due south, hoping that they could reach the carriage and the bend of the road, before being seen. They flew, evading, constantly darting east, then south, for an hour or so, until the raven tired and withdrew, and after what felt like ages of wandering, they broke out of the Forest of Grass onto the road, and stood under the sun.

The wind shifted, and blew in from the east, bringing the dark clouds closer and closer, hanging low and heavy in the sky. "Oh, I really don't want it to rain," Leif said, walking to the center of the road, looking back to the northwest where the carriage rolled diligently at an unhurried pace.

As it drew close, they saw Yarrow sitting beside the driver, waving cheerfully, and it slowed to a stop. Lia rushed up to the door, and then, after a moment of hesitating, she opened it and flew in. They could hear the calls of "Lyrin!" and "Lyrun!" from the reunion of mother and daughter, and the sound softened as Trel stepped out and joined them on the street.

"It was pretty difficult," she began with a resigned shrug, "to convince the clerk at the Bounty Office that Yarrow and I were retiring. He continued to refuse to believe us, that is until I showed him this!" She pronounced, grinning as she held up one hand, with a dark green, nearly black metallic band, twirled with lines of gold like smoke, or drop of dye as it swirled through water, encircling her finger.

Fryn let out a gasp, and then coughed to cover it. "You mean, officially?"

Yarrow landed beside them, looking toward the storm clouds with a peaceful expression, not that he usually looked different, just less *stern* than before. "They authorized the transfer of funds to our new bank in Frorin, and we have decided to arrange for a private service at the Embassy in Rosenkraun. We have many friends and connections, and a great deal to plan—hopefully this matter will be resolved and you will able to attend once more with an honorable reputation... but as it is, the rumors within the Commission about you two are quite severe, saying that you were corrupted by your first 'substantial prize' and became criminals out of an insatiable desire for riches—even to arrange for the theft of the crown and to sell it for yourselves."

"What?" Leif demanded, "we'd make far more if we turned Lia and the crown over to the Grass Guard!"

Fryn noticed him again, looking up from where she'd been holding Trel's hand in the light to get a better look at the ring. "Then the rumors are probably started by whoever forced her to steal the crown in the first place."

"Probably," Yarrow conceded, looking back over his shoulder. "But we should get moving all the same. We may have to use a similar strategy to sneak you into the Embassy, but once you are there, as long as Savis does not approve the Commission's bounty on you, you will be safe."

They went to the door, and Fryn held it open for Trel—but she stopped and pointed toward a shadow approaching from the northeast: the direction they had to go. Three figures, walking slowly, one holding a lance, one, a drawn sword, and the third sporting no weapon at all.

Leif threw a meaningful look to Yarrow, took Fryn by the hand, and sped into the Forest of Grass. Lia was right behind them, and they flew due north. He spared one last glance, seeing Yarrow return to the driver's bench, and as Trel directed a pale-faced Nora back inside the carriage, his stomach turned, and he hoped they'd be able to out-maneuver the constantly obstructive Francis brothers.

Gravel and Mud

Gaersheim:

Forest of Grass

North of the East Road

Leif

Lia pulled ahead of them, leading the way through and around the bunches of grass. A rumble of thunder sounded from the east, and the sun was blocked out by the clouds. He tried to give Fryn an encouraging look, but she focused on their path, partially drained, her jaw set, and her lips blue. The raven crowed overhead, and they swerved slightly more to the east, vaguely in the direction where the Francis brothers were likely trying to cut them off.

"They'll cut us off if we keep straight," Fryn cautioned, as a fresh gust of wind blew down across the waves of grass, sending a stray bunch of grain into their path. They flew under it, jumping off it one after the other, as it started to spring back.

Leif shook his head even if they couldn't see it. "Then we'll need to slip past them, like oil on water." He was quite convinced he'd gotten the expression right that time, but no one commented on it. Lia merely veered off a bit more eastward and they heard the beating of the raven's wings. It swooped down toward them, and they shifted back west as its talons closed on bits of grass, scattering the clippings and casting loose the dried-out husks of the grass seeds from their pods.

"I'm not liking that raven," Leif announced, casting a mean look toward its receding form.

Fryn cracked a smile, and he felt at least a little better about their situation. "I didn't even know that there were ravens in Gaersheim."

They slipped between a stray boulder and the trunk of a scrub tree, jumping off the stone to rebound back east again. Lia watched the raven turn, and begin its search. "They're not native, no, mostly in Renholt, or Stanaedre... that one's especially big, good in the mountains. I'd bet fifty mint that it's from Vassidel—someone after revenge."

"Over there!" Fryn shouted, pointing slightly north of their path, they saw the three brothers flying in a tight 'v' to cross in front of them and block their path.

"Back in," Lia directed, "ankles!"

They held on, and together they shot under the weaving blades of grass, separating as soon as they could, so they could fit through the ever-tighter confines between the bunches. They criss-crossed through the Forest, growing more and more anxious, as a streak of lightning cut a swath across the sky, followed soon after by an earth-shaking *boom*.

The raven dove at them, as its red eye flashed against the storm's light, and they barely managed to scatter, twisting out of its path. Leif nearly collided with a blade of grass, but he drew his sword, and slashed through it, flying on as they regrouped. To the left the land rose to a slight mound, stones of various sizes rambled around its feet, and it reflected back the pale light of the storm with its white mushrooms, and a pile of white stones that seemed to fill the center of the mound encircled by the broken stones.

They instinctively made for it, veering into a natural path worn into the clay, and noticed the angling of the raven, and the other Hunters to follow them. "It's too narrow in the stones for the raven to catch us unawares," Lia declared, "we may also be able to lose the brothers in the maze."

The path led through the crumbling remains of a hole between a split boulder, covered with lichen, the dried paths of snails, and a few scattered claw marks of a weasel. The boulders, though split, closed in together like the narrow alleys of the Eastwall District, overhanging with moss, and dripping water, the ground littered with broken snail shells, and fine gravel. It narrowed so much that they slowed, and had to land, hugging the side of the rock, peeking out into a nexus of graveled pathways and broken stones.

"Do you see them?" Fryn asked, checking the north.

"Nothing," Leif answered, looking back the way they'd come. "Not even the raven."

Lia stepped out carefully, checking every path, only signaling when she'd looked twice in each direction. "Let's move back east, there's a chance we could sneak passed the Hunters, but I don't want to run into the raven."

They heard a frustrated cry, and the heavy crunching impact of the raven perching on one of the many nearby stones. "Softly now," Leif added, "we don't want to meet that thing in a dark alley…"

"…if it would even fit…" Fryn said, shaking her head.

They advanced without light, hoods pulled over their heads as the fierce winds were channeled through the cracked boulders like a series of untuned whistles. Rain started to fall in fat globules, scattering their spray as they crashed against the sharp spikes of the maze, but they were protected by the impossible overhangs. In about an hour of shuffling along, the rain intensified, marked by a searing line of purple as the lightning struck the ground not far from them. Fryn frowned at him.

"Not my fault if I'm a sparks elemental," he complained, "it is somewhat drawn to me."

They heard the shifting of the gravel in and around the maze as if all their pursuers had split up to find them, or even as if more had come. Lia hummed a minor tune, mouthing some sad words, her wings despondently drooping like their mood. "It's almost like from the stories," she said, looking around. "But who knows."

Leif and Fryn shared a look, but didn't ask; she answered anyway. "You remember how we were telling stories at my village? The Waverly stories are often discouraging, with bad endings, and one of the frequently mentioned mysteries is what we call 'The Weasel Cairn' to refer to a desolate place that's filled with bones and the dead. This is a bit different though," she stopped and knelt, turning over a few pieces of the white gravel. "I don't see any bones, but this place is far from comforting. I think I've lost my way."

"You've led us astray? I thought you were a scout, or a surveyor," Leif teased, also shifting some of the gravel with his boot. He paused, his heel had turned up what looked like a shard of glass, dull and stained gray. "What is this?" he asked, picking up the shard, nearly the length of his arm, holding it out to what remained of the daylight. "Stained glass?"

Fryn stiffened as she examined it. "Do you see those thin green lines passing through it?"

Leif's eyes widened, and he dropped it immediately, shaking off his hand, and wiping it on his cloak. "Serpents!" he hissed, earning a concerned look from Lia. "That was a wingshard…" He shivered and pressed on. "I knew I didn't like these stones, almost placed in a circle, on a little hill, almost like… like a…"

"A city," Lia supplied, shaking her head. "Well, let's leave it be, and get back to the main road." She turned back toward the east, but the approaching sound of footsteps alerted them of one of the brothers, or another Hunter, if more had joined the pursuit, so they took to the wing, flying in a slow hover toward the north, slipping past one of two searchers, but always finding themselves getting deeper into the maze, closer toward the center of what Leif *knew* was once a city. How long since it had fallen, he had no idea—but it explained a great deal about the defenses built around Fassen. "What could have broken those stones?" he wondered finally.

Fryn shook her head, "only one of the stone elementals, a really powerful one."

"That's usually how they get the boulders together in the first place," Lia added, "just for our village it took a concerted effort from a group of stone elementals to shift even medium boulders to surround our town... but they weren't tall enough to prevent a weasel's getting in."

They flew into the center of the city, where a mangled base of ancient and rotted roots melted into a blackened and burnt-out trunk, of what looked like a tree or shrub. The cracked remnants of a foundation for a long courthouse-like building faced them, with broken steps, and a million bones, large and small, finch, and hare, and fee, and fae, with tufts of brown or white fur sticking in clusters here and there. A deep hole was dug into the base of the old roots, and the lightning streaked by, landing squarely on the burnt roots. It sizzled but did not catch fire, washed away by the thickening rain.

Fryn quickly made an umbrella, and led them into one of the few buildings that remained partially intact: a huge, domed temple or assembly of sorts, with limestone pillars, stalactites, and stalagmites, and water dripping through the holes. It had already flooded to about ankle depth, but Fryn tossed her ice-umbrella onto the surface of the water, and it spread its freezing effect until all of the ground was covered in ice—level in places, marbling and gathering into inverse icicles in others.

Their breath fogged in the air, and they paused to check they hadn't been followed. It was quiet for the moment, and the various pews in their crumbling, uneven placement, were angled toward the east. The eastern wall was broken in, and rain water continued to pour in, only adding to the icy wall. The displaced stones had been cast into the chamber, as if something had broken its way in, and they saw a fluid inscription on a plaque beside the entrance.

Lia narrowed her eyes, examining the script. "It's hard to read, but I think this was once a Waverly city… this being a temple for the Wing-Giver, but I don't remember hearing anything about this city in the past. I thought that it was the mountain that had destroyed us."

"And the plagues," Leif suggested, checking Fryn's reaction. She did not look amused, but crossed her arms and looked away. "But then, I suppose it is only natural when a nation falls."

The wind shifted, blowing straight through the temple, and from the east, they heard the confident steps of the three brothers, and turned to see them, now reunited. Grifton with his sword, Gerard resting his lance over his shoulder, and Germaine grinning like an idiot.

"I thought you'd find your way here," he said, "I'm glad we finally get to finish things between us."

Grifton held back a hand and pointed at Lia. "We'll give you an option, come with us peacefully, and give us the crown, and you will appear before the Rose Court, and be shown leniency toward your daughter, though you will perish for your treason. As for you, Leif and Fryn, you can assist us, or face the same, and worse."

"I'm not going to help you," Leif said, and Fryn nodded with him.

"And I'm not going to submit," Lia answered, and they moved back toward the west entrance.

The three brothers closed in, slight eddies in the air wavering menacingly around Gerard's lance, a few flames curling up from Germaine's closed fists, and flakes of stone peeling away from the surrounding architecture to encase Grifton in a supple layer of cushioned stone defenses, thicker plates forming scaled armor on his arms and chest. "Individually, you might have done better, and with the help of your confederates, you might have won," Grifton gloated, "but now you are entirely within our hands."

They spread out in a concave arc, preventing their escape to the east, and on the west, they saw the raven land in the courtyard, its thin rider shielded from the rain by standing under its wing. The raven's rider held up a thin foil in salute, wearing a padded black dueling uniform, with a wide-brimmed hat and a deep green scarf pinned around her neck.

"Well Fryn," Leif said, drawing Havrshyk with a bitter smile, "it seems we must cut off one of our hands," he alluded.

She sighed. "Not the best analogy," she answered, holding up her Bloodknife as well, then, noticing Lia was unarmed, she crouched, placing one palm on the ground, drawing up ice into an intricately formed staff, and kicking the base at the same time as twisting it from the top, she snapped it off from the ground and tossed it to her. "Hold that duelist, Lia, if you can," she ordered. "Leif, with me." They stepped forward, a third of the way into the room, ice climbing up the walls, freezing wind chilling them to the bone, thunder shaking through the stones.

The Francis brothers partially encircled them, careful not to show their backs to Lia, who blocked the doorway, keeping the duelist and her raven outside. Gerard led the assault, flicking his lance forward like the jaws of a snake, Leif ducked and jabbed under the blade with his fist, twisting to block a hacking slash from Grifton, as Fryn slapped away Germaine's flaming hands with ice encasing her arms.

Leif could only focus on Gerard's lance, stabbing, twisting, and swiping, as Grifton alternated with his own closer attacks. He was able to parry and cut a thin scratch into the stone armor on Grifton's chest, but he couldn't break it, and within moments, the scratch was repaired by more disintegrating limestone dust. Germaine burned through Fryn's armor as well, and Leif barely reached out, to twist her, almost like when they danced, to trade places, so that she parried and blocked the lance and sword, and he caught the flaming fist with his frosted, sparks-infused blade—cutting across the back of Germaine's arm, but it was shallow. Within the first minute, they were being pushed steadily back toward the door, and the flash of light and the roll of instantaneous thunder, leaving them nearly deaf and blind at once, was all that gave them any chance at a break for the door guarded by the raven and the duelist.

They flew back out, with the brothers hard on their heels, as Lia spiraled to the ground, crunching low, sweeping the staff at the duelist's knees. The duelist hopped over it, and landed behind her with her foil snapping toward her back. "Who killed him?" she demanded, but they didn't care to answer.

They made a dash past the raven, who tried to track all three of them at once, and snapped its beak at Germaine.

"I'll burn that black pigeon if you don't keep it in line!" he yelled, punching the bird under its chin, leaving a thin trailed of smoke, as he flew past in his pursuit. "Don't let them escape!" he shouted.

They flew into the safety of the hole.

The darkness was only broken by the infrequent flashes of lightning, and the pulsating glow that ran through their wings, as they followed the winding tunnel deeper into the earth. It opened up into a bowl-shaped cavity, filled with warm air, and the scent of fur.

They dropped to the ground, diving into a roll, and Leif flipped back into the air, flying back the way they'd come, as something moved inside the cave. They rushed back up, increasing their speed as the frenzied clawing of whatever lived down there came after them, and they sailed up toward the entrance, where their four opponents were already making their chase.

"Down," Leif yelled back, seeing Lia and Fryn follow him as he flew as low as possible, the front of his coat dragging in the soft dirt, black sword angled up in his hand. He deflected the downward thrust of Gerard's spear, spinning as he rose, aiming to slide out of the mouth of the cave to the right, and deal a glancing blow to Grifton's arm, ringing his sword as he went. Fryn shouted after him, "I killed him!" to the duelist, and cut through her clumsily-raised guard.

They rolled back out of the mouth of the cave as the raven rushed at them with its beak opening like a metal trap to receive them—but they weaved to both sides, and the thing that had followed them made a high, excited, repeating sound as it leapt out of the hole. "E-e-e-e-e-eh!"

The weasel was massive, half again the size of the beast they'd slain in Lia's home town, and its eyes were wild with the chase, and the rumbling of the thunder, its teeth glistening, and perfectly white, one moment, and then dripping hot crimson in the other, as it collided teeth first with the neck of the raven, which flapped its wings in a panic, and fell backwards; tumbling to a twitching death in the center of the courtyard.

They all stopped to watch in stunned horror, as the weasel continued gnawing on the raven's neck, watching them in return. Then, it started dragging it back toward the hole. The duelist screamed in rage, or fear, or some strange kind of combination, and rushed at Fryn with her foil outstretched.

"For Thassetel!" she declared, but Fryn closed her eyes, and pinching the blade with the fingers of her free hand, she twisted into the ascetic's inexorable approach, and stabbed her in the heart.

Then, veins filled, she flushed with fresh energy and color, and stared down the weasel, who had stopped dragging its prey; watching her with interest and what seemed like wonder. The brothers weren't impressed though, Germaine simply spat in the direction of Fryn and the duelist's body.

"Just a finch compared to her father anyway," he said in passing, "and we all know better than to let arrogance get to us."

"Said the most arrogant fool in the Commission," Leif countered, "now we will give you a choice—tell us who is behind this plot against us, and leave, or... I will let Fryn kill and devour each and every one of you."

"And anything left will be for him," Lia added, jerking a thumb toward the weasel, who continued watching their display with intense interest. The rain slowed to a spattering crawl, and the clouds thinned, revealing the looming shape of the greater moon covering the majority of the Vine.

Gerard saluted them with his lance, and then lowered into a stance with the blade angled toward them with his weight distributed more on his left, as he answered, "then as the weasel is my witness, we will leave you to the Weasel Cairn, isn't that the right expression?"

It almost seemed as if it understood. Leif suppressed a shiver, and clenched his fist, tightening his grip on Havrshyk's sword. *Have you heard of this Weasel Cairn?*

"*You haven't thought to speak to me for a while, and that is what you ask? No, first I'm hearing of it.*" He replied off-handedly, as if he felt left out of things. "*Just kill them and be done with it.*"

Lia pursed her lips, bowing her head slightly toward the weasel. "Has'la fjehelansør?"

Surprisingly, it released its burden, and crouched, partially curling up to recline, as if it really intended to watch. Lia nodded and held out the frost staff Fryn had given her toward the brothers, as they began to circle around them.

Leif held Fryn's free hand with his, giving it a squeeze, as the three of them formed a tight triangle, with the three brothers moving in a continuous cycle around them, shifting closer each time, and reversing directions without hesitation. The clouds broke, and the water soaked into the earth, and the stars glistened in the sunset. The storm was passing over the city, and Leif wondered if they had any provisions for dealing with it if it struck the buildings. He had no time to ponder the subject for very long, as Germaine lunged at him with a flaming fist, which he just barely blocked but failed to see the non-flaming fist that sank into his stomach with all the power of his wings. Leif was held up by Lia and Fryn, but each time they'd block or deflect an attack, they had to be careful not to direct it onto each other, so Leif was struggling between the jabs of the lance, and the angled cuts of Grifton's sword.

Fryn's armor would melt under Germaine's fire, her block would break under Grifton's precise distractions, and then the lance would snap toward her face or neck, or any vulnerability. Leif brushed away Grifton's stone-enhanced sword, which scraped at his Bloodsword, losing him precious resources. He was tiring fast, and the lightning storm, which had at first invigorated him, was moving further west, leaving him behind.

"Lia, switch," Leif announced, and as the lance swept up under her guard, shattering the ice staff Fryn had made, he pulled her into his place, grabbing the end of the spear, and extending outward, firing off a burst of sparks in his direction. Gerard pulled back on the spear, along with a sharpened gust of wind, and Leif was forced to let it go, but he was not about to let *him* off so easily. "Fryn!" He traded with her again, as Gerard was about to stab through her guard, Leif parried his attack and cut a wide slash, spraying scattering tendrils of electricity from the impact. This time, though, Grifton slipped between him and Gerard, taking the brunt of the slash on his hardened arms, as he switched up the order of their sequence.

"'Maine, the girl," he ordered, pointing with his free hand, and then lunging toward Fryn with a sideways jump. Germaine crouched, and then launched himself at Lia with both his fists and wings enveloped in a cloak of purple flames. She shivered, and the air rippled around her hands as she blocked his first strike with the back of her wrist, stepping out of their circle momentarily to also deflect his other fist, and then push him back in the chest. She finished with a powerful gust of wind that snuffed his flames, and he skidded back in the mud.

"Trade," Gerard said, allowing Grifton to spin behind him to keep Lia occupied with a series of serrated slashes, as Gerard swung the tip of his spear at both Leif and Fryn, moving around them.

"Lia," Fryn countered, pulling her through the center of their circle as they traded places, and she hardened her Bloodknife, now a jagged, black shard in her hand. She carved a black line through his armor, trading gash for gash, as his sword glanced off her knife and cut across her eye—the same one she'd only recently been able to repair.

Leif wondered if she'd be able to heal it completely, but he didn't have time to worry about that, as Germaine came roaring back into their triple dance. He charged at Leif, and then traded places and directions with Grifton, so that once more he flew toward Lia, and the serrated sword slashed up from the ground at a diagonal toward Leif's head. Leif blocked it with his sword, hoping Havrshyk could freeze the blades together for just an instant, as he spun on the ball of his foot, and kicked out with blaze of sparks. It cracked the brother's limestone chest plate, and shimmered as the heat from the sparks melted some of the metallic flakes together.

"Leif," Lia said, ducking under his leg, as she followed through on his attack, spinning out, over, and then slamming a cyclone-enhanced kick on the side of his head. Fryn barely deflected Germaine's flaming charge, while letting Gerard's wind-sharpened spear graze the side of her leg. Leif twisted out, placing one hand around Fryn's waist, as he pulled her back, twirling out with his sword, nearly taking off Gerard's forehand—only just breaking the skin.

They spun, traded, twisted, alternating attacks and patterns—practiced teamwork, and intuitive improvisation, in a constant dance, each trying to dominate and compliment the other. The sun slipped down under the edge of the Forest of Grass and the weasel observing them yawned, which wasn't right, since it was nocturnal; Leif bit his lip and was tempted to make some sort of comment about it, but by this point he was too tired for any kind of joke.

All three of them were exhausted, except maybe Fryn, who could keep fighting as long as she had blood, but they were cut and bruised in every limb. The sky darkened, and the stars stood out menacingly in the void, occupied by the greater moon, and the two slowly rotating bodies that arced around its face. Fee and Fae, dancing in the sky, constantly in the greater moon's embrace.

Germaine had a black bruise on his eye, a gift from Lia, and Gerard had several scabbed-over gashes on his arms and chest. Grifton too, had bruises through his hardened skin and Leif was convinced he'd broken one of his ribs. They were all breathing shallowly, on the point of exhaustion, life and spirit draining from their continued attack.

"We've... been at this for over four hours, Leif," Germaine complained, letting a wash of orange flame caress his fingers, massaging his hands from their hard impacts against Fryn's ice-armored limbs. They continued their circle-walking, weapons and hands outstretched, as Leif watched them each in turn, avoiding looking at their eyes, but trusting his instincts, and drawing on the static in the air to supplement his almost entirely drained reserves of sparks.

"Then leave us," Leif countered, "and you can go and rest." He noticed Grifton tightening the circle, flakes of gray and white dust fell from his decaying armor. He too, it seemed, was weakening. Fryn's Bloodknife had shrunk by about a third, from the constant need to heal herself, sacrificing limbs to save him or to protect Lia, but she'd been leaving the small injuries frozen and untended, preserving what she could, even after what she'd taken from the duelist.

"You're about to fall anyway," Grifton said, flicking his eyes between his brothers, and then twitching his wings as he refocused on Leif.

Leif was ready, he'd learned their tells—nothing he hadn't done before. "You were foolish to face us," he taunted, "because not only have I killed a Sand Viper, but together we defeated a weasel!"

"Careful where you say that," Lia said with a forced laugh. The air barely moved around her wings and hands, and she slumped in her tiredness.

"We're not going to get anywhere like this," Leif whispered to her, "if we can open up a way, try to find Trel and Yarrow, get them here, and we will hold them off."

Fryn nodded, and flicked one wing against each of theirs to signal her approval, and as the circle closed in toward them, and Grifton made a feint to trade places with Gerard, they tossed each other their weapons instead, and Leif crouched low, and with one outward wingburst, he and Fryn exploded out of their tiny formation, each parrying and countering the attacks, as Lia used the last of her energy to speed straight into the air. She hovered for a second, as Leif and Fryn pulled back together, facing outwards, they were encircled, with Germaine rushing in with both hands joining together to spew out a cone of fire.

They traded places again, Fryn working to freeze the water in the air, and kill the flames, which scattered against her face, blasting away into fog, and Gerard' lance stabbed through the cloud with a spiraling, weaving course toward Leif's neck—but he blocked it with his sword, throwing off his aim so that the tip of the lance cut high over his head, and Leif was able bring the blade back down against Grifton's stone-enhanced sword with a clash of sparks.

They paused between attacks to make sure that Lia had moved to the east, where she continued to hesitate, watching from the top of one of the broken boulders.

Germaine and Grifton switched sides, and Leif tried to borrow some of Havrhyk's blood. *Just need your help a little bit here*, Leif said, parrying the sword with his fist, and the flames of Germaine's fists with the Bloodsword, which had melted slightly in the course of their fight, and even now black droplets trailed down from the blade onto his hand and arm.

"It's a bit too hot for me to risk losing the last of my blood, Leif," he replied coolly.

Leif twisted out of the spiraling nexus of the three connecting attacks, fist, lance, and sword, as he and Fryn swept side by side and struck out. They stepped back as they were encircled again, Fryn taking a long slash across her shoulder, leaving one arm hanging limp, and Leif gritting his teeth as the limestone-shards of Grifton's sword slid through a shallow cut in his stomach, and he resisted the urge to scream. They continued pressing in, trading, and shifting, but Leif had no more sparks, and Fryn could only use her knife in one hand, and as Germaine's fist struck him in the face, Leif reached out and took hold of Fryn's limp hand, still frozen and cold, and he gave her a smile as he pulled her away from Gerard's piercing lunge.

But he continued, lower, and then wingbursting with a continuing flèche he pierced her through the side, so that it broke through her ribs, and into his back. Leif's eyes were dark, and his knees week, paralyzed, and through one last closing window, he looked back at Fryn's pained face, flushed with a rush of color as she instinctively tried to heal. He could feel her heartbeat through the spear, and as Gerard pulled back sharply, he knew that her heart should not have been beating; his blood pooled and readied to flow out, almost eager to explore, and black tendrils of mist wrapped themselves over his eyes, blocking out almost all his sight, seeming to bind his whole body from the inside out, as he struggled to hear Fryn.

"Leif, I... didn't want to lose you... not..." she said, looking down regretfully, her voice hollow, and weak, from a pierced lung, but he couldn't hear the end, or see her face, as the weight of the sword dragged him down. All his limbs went numb, and he fell through the reddish black, until it parted before him like a curtain, and he stood once more on the sandstone dais in his heartworld, the cracked, and nearly splintered crystal plinth in the center was covered in red frost, and Havrshyk was reaching into its broken side fingers closing on the hilt of the sword that comprised his 'self.'

Havrshyk drew out the sword, and the blood-current skies roiled in confusion, black snow scattering across the sand dunes, lightning streaking and making glass on the ground, and he approached Leif with a sad smile.

"I didn't want it like this," he said, running a hand through his black hair, slicking it into position with a layer of black frost. "And I'm quite sure you didn't either."

"Where are you going?" Leif asked, suddenly sensing the hole and all the cuts on and throughout his body. He groaned, and fell to his knees, looking up at Havrshyk bitterly.

Aldyr shook his head and pointed with one hand toward the raging sky. "The only place I can—this sword can only hold one, Leif, if we delay it will shatter, and both of us will die. I am leaving."

He bowed his head just a little, and vanished in a cloud of blood-black mist. Leif looked up at the sky, knowing it was not the sky, but just the outer shell of where he was. He rested his elbows on his knees, holding his head in his hands. His shoulders shook, his wings trembled, and he closed his eyes as tight as he could, but his tears did not obey.

"Fryn... I can't get out..."

***

Sparks flooded his nerves, and the blood pouring from his wounds froze over. He grinned, tightening his fingers on the sword as he saw Fryn's confused relief showing on her face, lying there beside him in the mud. The clouds were thickening again, and he thought there was a good chance of rain. The Francis brothers were already leaning on their weapons, arguing over who had to carry the bodies, but they went silent as Germaine pointed with a suitably frightened face, fully drained of color, in his direction.

Aldyr laughed, startling the others, as he lunged, almost skating across the icy mud, covering his limbs in flexible shards of ice, he wingbursted—and rather than a frontal attack, he struck Germaine with a frozen fist in his throat, spinning, dancing, and turning around him, he changed sword hands, and leaned back, so that his Bloodsword pierced through the center of his body, severing his spine, and drinking all he had.

"Ahahaha!" he screamed in a foreign voice, pulling out the sword and flicking it back to clean its surface of any oily, congealed remnants of blood or spinal fluid, and flew toward Grifton.

"Germaine!" Gerard yelled in a panic, grabbing his lance and flinging it in a spiral toward Havrshyk's intended path, but he followed with an opposite spiral on the wing, deftly glancing off the tip of the lance with his sword, he slid down its length with the tip of his blade angled toward his throat. He twisted in mid-air, extending outwards as it snapped forward and severed his head from his shoulders.

Grifton hacked at him from the side, his whole body and his sword flaking away pieces of dusty granite or limestone, but Aldyr didn't mind that. The stone elementals had a weakness.

He grabbed a handful of the dirt, throwing it in his face, toward his unprotected eyes, twisting away from his attack, as fresh sparks flowed through his arms, his eyes, he could see everything, every moment. He saw Fryn push herself off the ground, to watch them with horror and confusion on her face, he saw Lia leaving the pillar of stone in the distance to find Trel and Yarrow, and he saw the weakness behind Grifton's granite mask.

"Who are you!?" he demanded, voice shaking as he parried his increasingly heavy blows.

Havrshyk bared his teeth in a savage smile. *The wingless and the winged, stood before his feet, they shouted, and they pointed, each trying to defeat; in the end there no one stood, for all of them were slain. Rising up in blood and flame—all their souls to eat,"* he quoted menacingly, "You're about to learn."

"Leif!?" Fryn asked, struggling to rise, digging her Bloodknife into the blood-muddied ground, as she held one hand over the hole in her back. "What...?" She coughed out a trail of semi-frozen blood.

Havrshyk ignored her, spinning under Grifton's wide swing as he stepped in his circle-walking fashion and then charged; splitting a bone through his armored forearm with a chop, leaning away from the countering slash as he continued behind him, he caught the edge of the sword in a powerful hacking blow, shattering it and sending shards of steel and stone in every direction, as he followed it with a cut through his upper arm, severing the limb.

As Grifton clenched his teeth, trying to bend over to pick up what remained of the sword's hilt and blade, Aldyr side-stepped him and cackling, he cut him savagely in the back, and his left two wings were halved, as Grifton fell into the mud. Then, he looked up to the weasel who had been watching their battle, consciously pouring fresh blood throughout his new body. "It is our victory, we will leave the dead to you," he said, wiping the sword on Grifton's back, and sheathing it. "But Fryn, we are going somewhere different now…"

"…Leif…? But no…" she answered, and Havrshyk felt her cold fingers clawing at his veins, horror and loss breaking plainly on her face, he pale eyes widening, as tears fell unfrozen down her cheeks. "You're not Leif! Where is he? Bring him back!"

"I might just bring him back," he allowed menacingly, bowing to the weasel, and flicking an eye in her direction. "But first, you'll bring me back." He almost nodded to himself, proud of his Leif-like wordplay, but he resisted the temptation. It was not an appropriate time. "Come." He flew off to the west, and the thunder storm resumed.

Fryn remained on the ground, but if he was right about the connection she'd made with that body, she wouldn't have a choice. She'd come, and she'd help him, and that was all there was to it. He grinned. I told you didn't I? That you couldn't kill me?

The End

Epilogue:

The Weasel Cairn:
Grifton

The rumble of the sky was distant, though it shook the ground, and all that he could hear was the shuffling and dragging of some heavy burden through the mud. His bones were broken, his blood was spilt, and as the night deepened, even the light of the moons behind the clouds seemed to fade away.

Tooth-of-the-Mountain, they'd called him, invincible, strong, impenetrable, and resolute—he'd bested all the students at the academy, and even defeated his own Master. But now, he was just another battered corpse with broken wings, waiting for the rain to crush his head. He closed his eyes, too tired to groan. The sound of the object being dragged drew nearer, but he didn't open his eyes, he just sensed the approach of the weasel through the ground. The torn and ruffled carcass of the raven fell with a thump beside him, and the soft and sickly splatter of raindrops alerted him to the return of the storm.

One of the drops fell before his face, splashing dirt and some of his and his brothers' blood on his cheek, and he waited for the end to come, for one final strike from heaven to end his life—but even though the rain fell in full force around him, it did not touch his body. Grifton opened his eye that was still above the mud and saw the looming shape of the gigantic weasel, sheltering, or inspecting him.

It turned him over with a six-clawed paw and sniffed his face, tickling it with his whiskers.

"Why do you die? Mountain Fang?" It wondered in his mind.

"I die," he sputtered, gurgling and choking on his own blood, "because I cannot survive."

It twisted its massive head to regard him with one of its amber eyes. *"You die because you choose to accept death, do you not?"*

He spat blood out of his throat, his hand finding purchase on the hilt of his broken sword. "I do not accept it!" he shouted, and he was filled with warmth and fire, an intense and unimaginable pain, as a dark light enveloped him, suffusing what remained of his wings, and wrapping around his limbs, and the sword—where it seemed to be drawn like the eye of its black-red storm.

Chitinous bone, yellow, then lined with red, and white-enameled bone flowed out from the steel, as his blood, his fallen arm, the bones of his brothers, dissolved, and his wings were repaired with a matte bone-prosthetic, and the sword reformed into a long serrated fang that glistened like saliva on his teeth.

His wounds were filled with a black sand, and slowly, his flesh began to heal. His brothers had vanished, leaving only their clothes, and he still lacked his arm, but the weasel watched him with bared teeth and humor in its eye.

"Then I will allow it," he said, "but only you may go."

The weasel moved on, and took up the raven's body in its teeth, and dragged it back into its cave. The rain splashed off his body, but it was as if every fiber in his body had been strengthened and reforged. Its weight and force were harmless, and he drank it in with a bitter smile. "I don't know what sort of beast that Viper is, but I will sink in him my teeth, and avenge my brothers' deaths. Fryn will die, and so will he." He gripped the strange sword in his left hand, his only hand, and watched the rain fall all around, and broke into strangled laughter.

Appendix

Waverly, its People and its Tongue

The events of The Venomsword took place in the year, according to the Waverly Traditional Calendar, of the 4th Age, 784 WV, in the fifth month of the year: The Feather, or Quill. The Viper's Chase begins in the first week of Autumn in the month of the Vine. According to the traditions of the Waverly People, the 4th Age of their civilization is known as 'The Exile' defined by the time they were destroyed in the eruption of the Mountain under which they had been founded, Mt. Waver, named after their original ancestor—one of the creation-story's first creations.

They highly revere the keeping of their traditions, and the protection of their original language, in spite of their living in the lands of Gaersheim. Some resent their rulers, and others are treated as second-class citizens, with obscure practices, strange, non-conformist culture, and a disinclination to be assimilated. But, they are a tightly-knit minority, even within what used to be their lands.

Until the year 0 WV-4, Fassen, Gaerlin, Waver, and other towns in the north plains of what is now Gaersheim, up to the Ice Wastes, were all a part of the Waverly Empire. At that time, the eruption of the mountain blanketed the lands below in ash and fire, and covered the sky. They were wracked by famine and disease, and those who survived fled the destruction, to Froreholt, Gaersheim, and some even to the east beyond the lands of Stanaedre. Their remaining lands were annexed by their neighbors, and they became a small minority in their own cities when they were inhabited again. And because of the association with their apostasy to the Wing-Giver, the dominant religion on the continent, by adhering to the mutilation and their desire for power, of the Wingless Cult, many still look down on their descendants. They are blamed for the actions of their ancestors, as though their people were continually being judged.

Linguistic Notes:

Waverly is a subject-object-verb language with tenses and conjugations at the end of a sentence, and a heavy reliance on particles. Particles denote the subject, object, indirect object, direction, relationship between words, and nuance, of the various words in the sentence to create a specific and cohesive meaning of an utterance.

With eight vowel sounds, and a specific singular 'n' they needed a holistic writing system. According to the oral accounts of the Waverly scholars, their current symbology was invented by the third king of Waverly, the great-grandson of their original ancestor, to utilize base vowels in conjunction with base consonants, to create specific letters for each sound combination. The vowels and consonants were conjoined in writing, and were therefore simple to write, and appealing to the aesthetic taste of their culture. Waverly has 20 consonants, and excludes the old 21st letter because of its association with the final king of Waverly, named Thenaje, who was blamed for the ultimate fall of their civilization.

See the proceeding chart for a list of their characters.

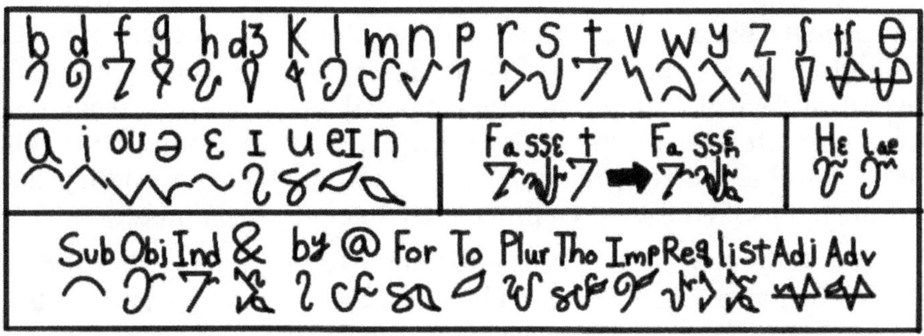

The Commission

The Faerie Hunter Bounty Commission originated in the city of Rosenkraun in the year 412 RK, which coincidentally, is the exact same year as 412 WV-4, since the start of the current Gaersheim calendar is predicated upon the formation of the Forest of Grass as one nation. Prior to that, the region was divided amongst the local lords of Wellsey, Rosenkraun, Pyrincel, and to the north, Waverly. This was done in the thirteenth year of the then Lord of Rosenkraun, but when he became a king, that counter was reset.

The Commission was founded by a banding together of bankers, wanderers, mercenaries, and local guards in order to combat the rise in international crime. One of the most problematic issues was that of independent bands of such criminals who would set up encampments beyond the borders, or in the wilderness of, their neighbors, and steal, or raid, or destroy. The Hunters then, funded by the local governments, were sent after known targets associated with such groups, and their success enabled the organization to expand, and, to begin lending, and storing money in the most well-defended banks in any country.

Since they were not allied to any national entity, they could effectively move money between borders, and pay a Hunter in one city for services done in another. Their couriers were also renowned for their speed and reliability, forcing the smaller Finch-Post to improve their efforts. Eventually, the Commission reserved their messengers for their own use, and allowed the Post their place as the continent's number one delivery service.

At the time of The Venomsword and Viper's Chase, the current President of the Commission had been operating in that position for five years. He was voted in by his fellow managers, a position he had occupied for ten years, after the forced retirement of his predecessor when his health declined with age. He is currently 62, and well regarded by everyone within the organization, and had served as a Hunter for twenty years, renowned for his skills in the Gaersyn style "The Mayfly Sword." His active field duty, and managerial skills earned him the respect of every department, and the Commission has been turning a greater profit in the last five years, by at least twenty percent, than seen for eighty years.

There are rules in the Commission Charter against the slaying of other Hunters, or employees of the Commission, but nothing is said about competition over targets, or the stealing thereof. It is not uncommon for rivalries to form between Hunter factions. There are also no rules against the forming of factions, or teams, in fact, for large operations such as was required to eradicate banditry in the past, it is strongly encouraged; but the division of the reward is always equal shares regardless of the role. It is argued that the one who opens the door is just as vital to the operation as the one who wields the sword.

The Calendar and Constellations

The calendar year of Linaera, the world on which the lands of the continent of Fhoraena reside, is determined according to the eleven months, and the eleven constellations. The number of days in each month is not consistent, since a month is defined by the time period it takes for the Greater Moon to pass through a constellation in its slow orbit around the planet. Some constellations are narrower, or broader, than others, and some are never seen at all during their month. Additionally, there are five seasons, Spring, Summer, Harvest, Autumn, and Winter, but they differ in length depending on the size and number of constellations the greater moon passes through. Harvest, comprising only one month, The Vine, is the shortest 'season' though we would consider it to be the beginning of Autumn or the end of Summer, it is a celebrated and distinctive time for the cultures on Linaera. Summer and Spring are roughly equally long, whereas Winter is slightly shorter, then Autumn, and last of all Harvest.

The year begins on the so-called "first day of Spring" with The Sparrow, and proceeds through to the so-called "last day of winter" at the end of The Lost. Some cultures also ascribe superstitious meanings and readings of the placement of the three moons through the stars, suspecting they might help one know more of the conditions of the world, or themselves, or the future—but serious study of the sky has not given any weight to this theory, even if it is widely pursued by the astronomers of Gaersheim, and the Arcanic Order of the Stanaedre peoples. (Excluding Estenna, which is instead known for its scholarship and dedication to the pursuit of concrete knowledge.)

Indeed, some have used the position of the three moons at the time of one's birth to read into their personality, but again, statistically it has not been seen to be accurate, as everyone changes and grows throughout their lives, and any similarities to one's placement is entirely coincidental. In such records, the Greater Moon is seen as a reflection of one's general Temperament, Fee, for one's External Interaction, and Fae, one's Internal Interaction.

Table 2

Season	Sign	Association
Year Begins: Beginning of Spring	The Sparrow	Wings, Growth, Excitement
Mid-Spring	The Hare	Youth, Industry, Charm
End of Spring	The Lancer	Valor, Nobility, Civilization
Beginning of Summer	The Serpent	Instinct, Danger, Wildness
End of Summer	The Feather	Knowledge, Thought, Art
The Harvest	The Vine	Harvest, Joy of Labor
Beginning of Autumn	The Forest	Hibernation, Preparedness
End of Autumn	The Mountain	Integrity, Resilience
Beginning of Winter	The Lich	Foreignness, Taboo, Power
Mid-Winter	The Star	Hope, Passion, Peace
Year Ends: End of Winter	The Lost	Change, Ambiguity, Longing

But for the record, Leif's placement is:

Serpent/Hare/Vine. Thus he would be expected to rely on intuition, to relate with others with energy and purpose, and to consider himself fortunate and optimistic in his work.

And Fryn's placement is:

Lich/Serpent/Forest. Thus she would be expected to be standoffish, perhaps non-conformist, and to relate to others in an unpredictable manner, and to be focused on cultivating strength within herself for every outcome.

But the caveat for any such combination is that, they may all reflect aspects of oneself, and therefore cannot be relied upon to define one's own identity, or to make predictions.

End Matter and Author Bio

Stephen Hagelin is currently working on his third novel, The Lich's Blade, a continuation from the events of The Viper's Chase, publication of which is expected in the Summer of 2018.

If you enjoyed 'The Viper's Chase' and are looking forward to reading 'The Lich's Blade', tell me what you thought, and I'll discount the next book. Simply share your review of my novel and let us know on the @VaridaBooks Facebook page, or send me a tweet @HagelinStephen. After all, I'd like to know what you thought so I can improve my writing, or so I can be encouraged to write more.

Stephen Hagelin

Author Bio:

Stephen Hagelin is a writer from Woodinville, Washington, who has a keen taste for coffee, wine, and all things pleasant. He writes because he reads, a lot, and he reads because he writes, a lot, and has found that life without words would be dull. Some of his favorite authors include L. E. Modesitte Jr., Brandon Sanderson, Charles Dickens, and P. G. Wodehouse. His recommended novel for you, now that you've finished The Viper's Chase, is "Carry On Jeeves" by P. G. Wodehouse—it is the perfect thing to wash away the bitter taste after the end of this novel...